PENGUIN BOOKS
NO ONIONS NOR GARLIC

Srividya Natarajan, born in Chennai, now lives in Canada and teaches English at King's University College, University of Western Ontario. At the University of Hyderabad she became interested in the caste politics that are central to *No Onions*, parented both her own son and the snakes her husband brought home, and earned a Ph.D. in English. After a year as an editor at Katha Publishers, she began to illustrate children's books for Orient Longman, the Karaditales Company and *Chatterbox*. Her favourite projects were four books in Tulika's *Under the Banyan* series, now translated into six Indian languages, and *Kali and the Rat Snake*. She co-authored *Taking Charge of our Bodies*, on women and health issues, with Veena Shatrughna and Gita Ramaswamy (Penguin India, 2004); and co-directed *Silambakoodam* (2002), a documentary on the hereditary dance teachers of south India. A student of the great dance master Kittappa Pillai, she has taught and performed classical dance for over twenty-two years in India and abroad. Her ambition is to combine writing her second novel with living in a tolerably clean house.

No Onions Nor Garlic

Srividya Natarajan

PENGUIN BOOKS

PENGUIN BOOKS

Published by the Penguin Group

Penguin Books India Pvt. Ltd, 11 Community Centre, Panchsheel Park, New Delhi 110 017, India

Penguin Group (USA) Inc., 375 Hudson Street, New York, New York 10014, USA

Penguin Group (Canada), 90 Eglinton Avenue East, Suite 700, Toronto, Ontario, M4P 2Y3, Canada (a division of Pearson Penguin Canada Inc.)

Penguin Books Ltd, 80 Strand, London WC2R 0RL, England

Penguin Ireland, 25 St Stephen's Green, Dublin 2, Ireland (a division of Penguin Books Ltd)

Penguin Group (Australia), 250 Camberwell Road, Camberwell, Victoria 3124, Australia (a division of Pearson Australia Group Pty Ltd)

Penguin Group (NZ), 67 Apollo Drive, Rosedale, North Shore 0632, New Zealand (a division of Pearson New Zealand Ltd)

Penguin Group (South Africa) (Pty) Ltd, 24 Sturdee Avenue, Rosebank, Johannesburg 2196, South Africa

Penguin Books Ltd, Registered Offices: 80 Strand, London WC2R 0RL, England

First published by Penguin Books India 2006

Copyright © Srividya Natarajan 2006

All rights reserved

10 9 8 7 6 5

ISBN-13: 978-0-14309-961-1   ISBN-10: 0-14309-961-2

Typeset in Minion Regular by SÜRYA, New Delhi
Printed at Saurabh Printers Pvt. Ltd, Noida

This book is for Pati, Richard and Pradyumna

~

Acknowledgements

I am grateful to my friends at the University of Hyderabad, especially K. Satyanarayana, for an uncomfortable, mind-boggling crash-course in how casteism works today; Claire Fanger, Teresa Hubel, Theresa Hyland, Nigel Joseph, Richard Joseph, Jacques McCarthy and Jennifer Vansteenkiste for perceptive comments on earlier drafts of this novel; V.K. Karthika and Prita Maitra at Penguin India for seeing the book into print; my family in Chennai and Hyderabad for acceptance, involvement, love; Nigel and Richard, for being, in my respect, all the world.

Onions do promote a man to veneryous actes.

—Andrew Boorde
Dietary of Helthe

Garlic, leeks, onions, mushrooms, and all plants springing from impure substances are unfit to be eaten by twice-born men.

—Manu
The Laws of Manu

And, most dear actors, eat no onions nor garlic, for we are to utter sweet breath; and do not doubt but to hear them say, it is a sweet comedy. No more words: away! go, away!

—William Shakespeare
A Midsummer Night's Dream

Prologue

~

A LONG TIME ago, each summer, in Chennai city, though the morning sun pressure-cooked the citizens to pish-pash consistency, the sea breeze arrived punctually at 4 p.m. to cool them down. Then one day Mr Seshadri of Seshadri Realties and Construction studied a map, and wheresoever he stabbed the Chennai coastline with a pudgy, gold-ringed forefinger, there his minions put up Sea View Apartments, Ocean Rest Towers, Beach View Palace and all their cousins, in serried ranks along the beach front.

'Oho,' said the sea breeze. 'Is that how you want to play it? You think I am unable to fight my way around corners and creep through the corridors between Seshadri's Perfect Residential Apartments for the Gracious and Discriminating People?'

'Aha,' said Mr Seshadri. 'We shall see.'

And he sent his big shovels along to scoop up the fisherpeople's huts all the way from the Harbour at the northern end to Mamallapuram in the south, and in their place slapped down Coromandel Gem Seaside Homes, Silver Sands Apartments, and many other bijou residences whose names I forget.

'This sewer soup from the pipes in Mr Seshadri's apartments is ruining the neighbourhood,' said the fish, and they headed in large numbers towards Burma for their health. So the fisherfolk were forced to leave anyhow. No more drying of nets or heaping of catch on the beach; no more catamarans lying like burnt bones in the sun; no more black-limbed children rolling like driftwood in the honeycomb surf.

'I am not beaten yet,' gasped the sea breeze. 'See? I am still crawling through a few cracks, chinks and crevices, bloody but unbowed.'

'Hullo-o! So you are still around?' drawled Mr Seshadri. 'Hmm. We are going to fight on the beaches, then.'

Mr Seshadri was among the rupees in a very major way. He had the ear, and sometimes the whole scalp, of the minister for the environment, and of the urban planning minister, and of the secretary for housing development, and of the under-secretaries for this and that. In fact, Mr Seshadri's man, Mr Rami Reddy, knew a conjuring trick that was famous at the Secretariat, which he visited everyday. In less than the time it took to say the word 'dodgy', Mr Rami Reddy could make a sackful of legal tender disappear from Mr Seshadri's capacious pockets and reappear in the Swiss bank accounts of some of the panjandrums who ran Chennai city, without even saying any hard English words like 'abracadabra'. Perhaps he did it with mirrors. What is more, the dosh that Mr Reddy mysteriously teleported was so amazingly dark-complexioned that it was totally invisible to the taxwallahs, who always made their raids on new moon nights.

As for small matters like environmental clearances, Mr Seshadri was the bosom pal and boon companion of some of the highest-ups, and if he mentioned, one evening during gin-rummy at the Gymkhana Club, a little difficulty over such a matter, why, the very next morning the Olive Ridley turtle or other pesky miscellaneous endangered reptile got an extradition notice, Mr Seshadri's earth-movers rolled in, and heigh ho! before you knew it you could buy a flat in Neythal Villa, Thendral Gardens, Temple Trees or Foamy Haven, which had sprouted one behind the other, ever closer to the beached margent of the sea.

By now, if you lived in Sea View Apartments and wanted to view the sea, you had to turn on your television and get *Baywatch*, though if you were the type that liked *Baywatch*, chances are you did not watch the bay very much. But you had no regrets, for you were emparadised in three-bedrooms-and-living room, in an ideal location, with underground carparking, a dish antenna, Spartek tiles, an in-house temple, and the choice between a Stairmaster and a built-in Bharata Natyam dance teacher: all the hospitable conveniences designed by that public servant Mr Seshadri, the World's Greatest Brahmin Benefactor!

'Give up?' said Mr Seshadri, noticing that the sea breeze was still wheezing around in a terminal way. 'Give up?'

Yes, though the sea breeze won a small victory when Ocean Crest fell down because of poor-quality cement, it was all over bar the sweating. Mr Seshadri was given a medal for controlling the population, for now that Chennai city had become a giant autoclave, people died left and right of spontaneous combustion. Meanwhile, Mr Seshadri, who had no more coasts to conquer, turned his attentions inland. Sometimes he sucked slowly and meditatively on his Gold Flake King, and between puffs, he dreamt of new enterprises: 'Sssoap...' he said, puffing; 'Soc¹ ss...' he hissed, exhaling; and yet again, with a third and final puff, 'Chennai Legisslative Asssembly!'

At 4.30 p.m. on that April day in Chennai, although the sea breeze was huffing and puffing, it was a mere mouse-breath, and did not make enough stir to blow so much as a feather off a ledge. In fact, the only time there was a current on Mount Road was when Mr Seshadri or one of his friends whizzed

down towards the Gymkhana Club in an air-conditioned Mercedes-Benz. I know this, because I was taking my first walk down Mount Road in five years, and I was knocked backwards by the sudden draught. By halfway down Mount Road, the sea breeze was nothing more than what Professor Ram, who taught Eng. Lit. at Chennai University, might have described as a pathetic fallacy. On Egmore Road, the temperature was in the early forties and the humidity was about 500 per cent. Housewives who wanted to cook eggs just left them on window-sills and collected them two minutes later. Sometimes, by this time, they were so hardboiled (the eggs, not the housewives) that many senior citizens lost their fillings as they took their first bite.

At the Madurai Muniyandi Vilas Veg./Non-Veg. Hotel (Meals Ready!), the cook called out '*One arm-layte!*' and spattered onions, chillies, and eggs on the dirty griddle, added a generous dollop of bacteria, scraped off the deadly tissue that resulted and tossed it on the customer's plate.

That may or may not be an accurate picture of the Muniyandi Vilas technique, but it was how Caroline Bailey imagined such establishments satisfied their customers. Caroline was from Canada. She was travelling in dingy parts of the world to hustle ethnics, or ethnographs, or whatever one has to hustle to fulfil the purposes of ethnography. She belonged strictly to the e.coli school of international travel. The main teaching of this school was that all comestibles served up south of the Tropic of Cancer were about 95 per cent life-threatening microbes, with a nutrient or two thrown in as an afterthought. As for the water, the H_2 and the O, according to this school, merely functioned as a swimming bath in which the fatal germs frolicked, swallowed seaweed, and beefed themselves up by swimming lengths while they waited to be decanted into the guts of some melanin-deficient traveller. This was why, though Caroline was both hungry and thirsty, she was neither eating nor drinking, but just standing there in a state of miserable dehydration, in a rotten temper, and feeling the first twinges of what was unmistakably cystitis. '*Jeez*,' she was thinking, 'field work is *freakin' broodle*,' which is Canadian for vile and terrible.

The reason Caroline was fidgeting irritably at the corner of Egmore Road and Mount Road was that she was waiting for her native informant. She was worried that he would be late— he usually was—and that they would miss the opening of the play they were going to take in at the Pantheon Theatre later in the evening. All around Caroline the offices were discharging streams of nine-to-fivers, and the cinema theatres were discharging tributaries of matinee-watching loafers. There was considerable traffic on the pavements of Mount Road and Egmore Road. Now Caroline was wearing a Roots tote-bag and not much else besides, and since the sea breeze had left her strictly alone, sweat had turned this not-much very strikingly into nothing-at-all. No doubt this couture was considered perfectly legitimate during the sweaty season in Ontario, Canada. But to the Mount Road riff-raff, Caroline looked uncannily like a Bollywood goddess after she had been marinated in a passing waterfall. Naturally, they wished to get the best all-round survey of this vision of delight in the shortest possible time. The rubbernecks rudely bumped each other about and insulted each other's ancestors, until presently there was not a single party, in either the direct or the distaff line, whose name was not comprehensively mud. Now and then, to Caroline's great annoyance, they spat on the hot pavement, and the spit sizzled in a disgusting fashion.

'*One more arm-layte!*' the waiter shouted to the cook inside Madurai Muniyandi Vilas, even as the germs steamed up from the pavement towards Caroline's fragile immune system. A fine chicken, recently deceased, lived on after death in the toothsome biriyani that a young man sitting at one of the

Formica-top tables was shovelling into his mouth with a strong, regular wrist movement. This chicken left no one to continue its line, for the omelettes that this young man ordered had consumed its posterity completely. While he waited for his next omelette, the young man glanced out the window, for he could see a tall, well-built white woman being harassed by the many-headed, and he wondered in passing if she needed any knights on white chargers. The young man answered to the name Sundar. He was layering the chicken-and-egg delicacies over a basic groundwork of parathas with goat's brain masala and offal curry, and while you and I might consider all this to be a square meal, the proprietor of Muniyandi Vilas was hurt and dismayed when Sundar called out for his glass of tea and his bill.

The proprietor was so surprised that he stopped waving a sandalwood-scented agarbatti round and round the picture of his honoured parent, who was the only begetter of Madurai Muniyandi Vilas. The proprietor took an inordinate pride in the picture, for it was surrounded by red and yellow light bulbs, and when the red bulbs flashed on the yellow bulbs went off, and vice versa, which sometimes caused sensitive customers to run towards the washbasin with their stomachs heaving, only to find the notice 'Do Not Comit Nusance in Sink'. This was a sensible edict to post at Madurai Muniyandi Vilas, because if you stood at its door and spat vigorously, you were bound to hit a rumpot staggering out of one of the four wine shops that surrounded it. Of course, I would never advise you to actually do this, as some of the individuals who got liquored up on the uncontaminated meths sold at these wine shops kept a very sharp eye open for somebody to wallop. From time to time, one of them remembered that alcohol was not a food, and hoofed it over to Muniyandi Vilas looking for a chicken or two to eat, or maybe a piece of goat, or even one of the small boys who wiped the tables. And the various and versatile kinds of nuisance such rumpots could commit in two square feet worth of sink had to be seen to be believed.

'There is something wrong with the food today?' the proprietor asked Sundar in a touchy voice as Sundar finished his tea and came over to the desk to pay his bill.

'The food is very good,' said Sundar. 'But this is a frightful evening for me. I have no appetite.'

'Why? Perhaps you have a big examination tomorrow?'

'No,' said Sundar, morosely. 'I am acting in a play.' He glanced at the clock beside the paternal picture. 'In about two hours and twenty minutes. I am on my way to the Pantheon Theatre. I greatly fear that the crowd is going to hurt itself laughing at me.'

'Oho,' said the proprietor, impaling Sundar's bill on his steel spike with one hand and scratching his groin with the other. 'That will be twenty-two-fifty.'

At 4.40, somewhere in the middle of Mount Road, lodged in the bumper-to-bumper like a Jezail bullet in an Anglo-Indian colonel's bottom, was the Pallavan Transport Corporation No. 27A bus that contained Akilan. Well, maybe it did not exactly *contain* him. He hung from the door rail by the tips of two fingers, and bore a poetic resemblance to an oversize jackfruit hanging from the tree by its slender stalk. Only one of his toes was actually resting on the footboard, and a good part of his considerable bulk was travelling outside the bus proper. His dark face, with its plump, lugubrious lower lip, was the face of a dromedary that had recently suffered some nameless disappointment. Akilan was the native informant Caroline was waiting for. Since he did not enjoy being a native informant, an ineffable odour, as of 16-per-cent-proof, emanated from his breath.

The bus pullulated with bodies. Every now and then it stopped and heaved for a long moment like a Discovery Channel dinosaur about to lay eggs, as the people who wished to get off struggled against the people who wished to get in. Some people who had wished to get off four stops earlier were still on the bus, fighting their way towards one of the doors. Since the conductor could not tell which limbs belonged to which faces, the change from the ticket money passed into the wrong hands, or more often did not pass at all. The passengers suspected that the conductor was using the confusion to appropriate funds that did not belong to him. This did not worry them too much. They did become fractious when he tried to grope some of the lady passengers, but whenever any of the passengers made bold to express discontent, the conductor waxed sarcastic. Like this:

'So *I* am putting a hand on her? Can you see, sir, how this lady is standing on my foot? I am only a humble servant of the public transport, and the *gowermant*, to be sure, is paying me to entertain the public when it stands on my foot. Move on, there, move on! Also, if any passengers wish to deposit any bags on my head, they may feel free. It seems some people think of this bus as their grandfather's personal *Toyyotta* with *powwerr steering*—'

A party humbly asked him when the bus would reach Anna Square.

'Anna Square?' the conductor choked, glad of the diversion from his misdemeanours. 'You want to get off at Anna Square and you jump on a 27A with your eyes shut? What is the use of these soda-bottle-caps?' He flicked a finger at the man's bifocals. 'When some people's parents send them to school,' he sneered to the other passengers, 'what do they learn? Fly-swatting, that's what! Do you think they learn how to read a bus sign? This One-and-a-Half-Eyes is ten miles away from Anna Square, and getting further every second. *Ten miles!*' A smile of great satisfaction flickered across his lips as he turned back to the distressed party. 'How should I know how you can get there? Do I appear to you as if I have a brother-in-law who runs a helicopter service? This country—' he began, but the bus creaked to a stop at the Egmore Road corner, and as the party wished to get off without losing his clothes, he did not wait to hear how the country was going to the bow-wows.

The bus began to move again.

'Stop the bus!' cried a party who had been bereaved, in the crush, of a slipper. 'Stop the bus!'

'Stop the bus!' cried the party's support-base. 'His slipper has fallen off!'

'Here is a man—a *considerate soul*—who wants me to stop the bus,' said the conductor, slowly swivelling his head to help his whole audience participate in his aggravation, 'In—this— traffic. For—a—slipper. All I can say is, brother, throw out the *other* slipper.'

'Yes, yes, throw out the *other* slipper!' the chorus chimed in.

'If you throw it out quickly,' the conductor went on, 'at least some barefoot bastard will get a pair, and that way, there will be a few blisters less to go around in this benighted city, which, if you ask me—*hoi!*'

Here was another aborted speech, for at this point the party made an attempt to bowl the other slipper out the door, right arm over the wicket, and the slipper hit Akilan smack- kersplat over the sinuses. Tears came into Akilan's eyes. His fingertips slipped off the rail, and he lost his toehold.

He fell off the bus.

'*Hoi!*' cried the conductor to Akilan. 'You never bought your ticket!'

'Ohh!' the women shrieked, craning their necks to get a good view of the remains. 'Aiyyayyoooww! He is dead, poor lad!'

The passengers banged on the walls of the bus to alert the driver, and with a great screech of brakes, the bus came to a halt.

'Which pubic-hair plucker hit me with a slipper? Come out and show your face, you son of a bazaar whore!' Akilan squawked as he came round to the door. Since the traffic had been moving no faster than a slug, it appeared Akilan had lived to propagate his family name after all.

'Which sisterfucker is telling on my mother's name?' the slipper party shouted as he battered his way through the crowd at the door, doubling up his lungi to give himself kicking room. The passengers came spilling out of the bus, and out of all the other stopped buses and cars and autorickshaws, to help arbitrate this dispute. The conductor took his hands away from a schoolgirl's bottom and placed his head in them. He could feel a migraine coming on.

Akilan offered to break the slipper party's knees. The slipper party offered to break Akilan's jaw. Akilan's sympathizers held him back. The slipper party's seconds held him back. An impasse was reached.

'Oi! Look over there!'

Suddenly, all the sympathizers on both sides abandoned the arena and began to crane their necks in a certain direction. Akilan craned his neck too, and what did he see but Caroline's head, which stuck out about a foot above all the noggins of the ungodly, as she walked in beauty among the two-storey buildings. And Caroline was calling:

'*Ack-eelan*! Gemme *oudda here*!'

'I am coming!' Akilan roared. He shook himself loose and started towards her, kicking the forlorn slipper into the traffic as a final gesture of contempt for his enemy. He looked very menacing indeed, with a streak of blood running from one nostril.

While Sundar, Caroline and Akilan were moving towards their common destination—the Pantheon Theatre—Professor Pattabhiraman (or Professor Ram, to give him the elegant diminutive he preferred) had already reached it. In fact, at a quarter to five, he was doing a close reading of a poster that was pasted unevenly over the terracotta eczema and graffiti of the lobby wall. The poster made it known to the public that the Chennai Cultural Club was presenting A NEW VERSION of *A Midsummer Night's Dream*. Underneath, in bold glaring letters, was the part Professor Ram liked best: DIRECTED BY PROFESSOR RAM! The next line was satisfactory too: STARRING PROFESSOR RAM AS OBERON! And, in much smaller letters, *With the students of the Chennai University Drama Association*. Up to this point, the professor felt, no scholar could take exception to this poster; no, not Gibbon, not Macaulay, not even the good Doctor, whose works the professor tanked up on every single night before he pulled into Morpheus' garage.

But below this unexceptionable prose came a message on which the professor took a very critical position indeed.

Proffesor Ram(bo) is a BIG WANCKER

it said, in red permanent marker. Professor Ram could substantiate (or prove) that the marker was permanent because he spat surreptitiously on his finger and tried to rub this line off, and it didn't work. Professor Ram awarded this particular effort a cipher, to be shared by the sentiment and the orthography alike. He was only grateful that Mrs Ram, who stood beside him admiring the poster, was not acquainted with the new dirty words that swelled the otherwise limited vocabulary of the misbegotten, yankee-doodling, late-night TV-guzzling generation X.

Professor Ram and Mrs Ram, seen side by side like this, made a most edifying spectacle, rather like Yin and Yang. Whereas Mrs Ram was shrivelled like a sun-dried salt-fish, Professor Ram was gibbous, like a custard-pudding. While the professor's frame bulged with gratuitous convexities, Mrs Ram was alarmingly concave all over. And while the professor's eyebrows were a thick bushy streak across his forehead, Mrs Ram's eyebrows were thin gothic arches yearning towards her hairline.

'Is it not marvellous, Ram?' said Mrs Ram. 'The big evening! What *is* that red stuff on your mouth?'

'Nothinngg, nothinngg. I must have bitten my lip, it's oka-yy,' said Professor Ram, in a scrumptious professional baritone. Professor Ram tended to let his vowels linger in the air for the smallest fraction of a second longer than was necessary, for the especial delectation of Chennai's cultured circles. He could not help being aware that his baritone was God's gift to the inner ear. Was it not the celebrated baritone that persuaded a million All-India Radio customers to buy Laryngeez Throat Drops, reminding them, unforgettably, that it was 'Available in three flavours! *Lemon*! (Poing!) *Ginger-Lemon*! (Poing!) *Regular*! (Poing!)'? Was it not also the voice, anguished yet plummy, that asked 'Why does the boss give *him* all the promotions and bypass me?' and then revealed that the trouble was caused by *Bee Oh*, easily banished by Appadurai's Armpit Allure?

''D evening sir,' said a voice beside the professor.

'Oh, Sundar!' said the professor. He noted without enthusiasm that there was another poster on this wall announcing that the Chennai Cultural Club was presenting P. Jiva in *Ekalavya* the same evening, and that Sundar was studying it with unnecessary curiosity. 'All set for your bit of glory?'

'Yessir. Isn't this one of your students, sir?' Sundar asked, pointing to the picture of Jiva on the poster. 'I've seen her around the university quite a few times.'

'Hmph!' snorted Professor Ram. He had the great artiste's natural dislike of going halves on the limelight. 'Ten to five!' he exclaimed suddenly, glancing at his Rolex. 'I mustn't stay here chatting! I've got to make sure the costumes and sets are ready!'

Professor Ram and Mrs Ram bustled into the theatre by the green-room entrance. Sundar followed at a more leisurely pace, a thoughtful look on his face.

In which Chennai cherishes Culture at the Pantheon Theatre ·

~

WHEN THE AUDITIONS for Professor Ram's alternative version of *A Midsummer Night's Dream* were announced, a month before the events described in the Prologue, Sundar decided to enlist, because Professor Ram had the final say-so on his academic life. Professor Ram liked many people to audition for his plays so that he could turn most of them away. The afternoon before the audition, Sundar tried to borrow *A Midsummer Night's Dream* from the Chennai University library.

'This is the first time anyone has tried to borrow it since 1956,' the librarian said. 'Funny. At this very moment, three other students are looking through the indexes for that same play.'

Sundar jogged down to the stacks. There he found that indeed Amandeep, Murugesh and Rufus were running their greasy, semi-literate fingers all along the shelf on which the Swan of Avon displayed his wares, and that they were pulling out and discarding, one after the other, *Measure for Measure* and *The Merchant of Venice*.

Now Sundar knew that Rufus, Amandeep and Murugesh were interested in the old Swan the way they were interested in crocheting antimacassars for the Rotary Club fund-raising. He divined that they had a particular reason for wishing to study

A Midsummer Night's Dream. He could guess what this reason
was. In fact, if he was honest with himself, it was a much better
reason than pleasing Professor Ram.

While the other three peered over his shoulder, Rufus
licked his finger and skimmed rapidly through the Introduction
to English Drama and the Shakespeare Chronology and the
portentous remarks of one S. Ramaswamy who had edited this
volume.

'Stop, machaan!' Sundar said. 'Here's the Cast of
Characters!'

'Helena! Hernia! At least two chicks, da-dai!' Rufus gloated,
for he remembered how after last year's play two minor
characters named Tito Cherian and Anitha Narayan went
missing—together—for weeks.

Sundar winced. 'Her*mi*a,' he suggested mildly.

'Yeah, Her*ni*a,' said Rufus.

'Ti-Ti-Tit-*Ti*tania, man!' Murugesh stuttered, as he usually
did when in the throes of excitement. '*Ti*tania is duff-duff-
duffnitly a babe, no? She has a ti-ti-ti-*tit* in her name!'

'Hippolyta! Lysandra! Two more, yaar!' sang Amandeep,
seeing the end of privation.

'Lysan*der*, you dyslexic bastard,' Sundar said. He was
somewhat older than Amandeep, Murugesh and Rufus, and
more familiar with the printed word. Though he had recently
washed up on the shores of academe after connecting with a
UGC fellowship, he had spent the last three years drifting
around a sprawling basement bookshop, wearing a bunny-
rabbit lapel-ornament that said Your Friendly Assistant, and
pacifying customers who got in a snit because they never found
any dirty pictures in *The History of Sexuality* or any good
recipes in *The Raw and the Cooked.* 'Lysander is a guy, for sure.
But the play has got four *fairies* in it, machaan. Look! Pease
Blossom, Moth, Mustard Seed and Cobweb.' He shut the book
with a joyous smack that annihilated the entire population of
silverfish that had lived in it undisturbed for five decades.
'Machaan, you realize what that means? Four more dames!'

'Thank you, you Bastard up there!' Rufus carolled.

Amandeep, Murugesh, Rufus and Sundar spoke like this for the same reason that they removed the mufflers from their motorbike exhausts. It made them feel like men. Like sophisticates. Like libertines. Every day, in front of their mirrors, they practised how they would say 'Fuck, machaan!' without blushing, and how they would smirk when they mentioned the 'chicks' or 'babes' or 'sarakku' who were worth pursuing, and how they would snarl when they cursed the 'cunts' and 'bitches' who turned them down flat, or giggled at them, or slapped them when they tried to get fresh. What they never mentioned was how they were willing to sell their immortal souls on e-Bay in return for some clear-cut opportunities to get fresh. For the truth is, though Amandeep, Murugesh, Rufus and Sundar talked the patois of hoochie-coochie-boys-about-town who cruised Parry's Corner for pussy every night, actually they only went as far as the local Mummy-Daddy store, to buy Haldiram's Potato Bhujia, which they consumed stick by stick while they watched *The Matrix Reloaded* or *Popeye the Sailor Man*. For the truth is, Amandeep, Murugesh, Rufus and Sundar had so far been unable to infiltrate the protective gaggles in which the campus female was to be found at all times. Yes, the simple truth is that Amandeep, Murugesh, Rufus and Sundar were full of unspoken hormonal despair. They waited impatiently for Love to enter their lives, and while they waited, they watched English and Hindi and Tamil movies, and then they went home to lonely beds and the midsummer night's wet dream.

No wonder this quartet appreciated the casting arithmetic of *A Midsummer Night's Dream*. The more job opportunities a play had for members of the opposite sex, the better their chances of speaking tête-à-tête with one of them. Oh, the possibilities of intimacy boggled the minds of Amandeep, Murugesh, Rufus and Sundar. If the little god of libido would deign to speed their courtship, who knew what may or may not happen? Maybe one of the fair ones would come to the canteen for a cup of coffee. Maybe she would agree to walk along the beach, hand in hand with the lucky one. Maybe she would even bid the chosen one to live, and he would definitely live, her Protestant to be, even though Rufus was a Catholic, and Sundar was an agnostic, and Amandeep was a Sikh, and Murugesh had been born again just two weeks ago.

But you know what happened this year, of all years? This year Professor Ram fell under the spell of The Completely Different Theatre Festival. He saw a *Murder in the Cathedral* in which the four Knights wore nothing but saucepans and walked freely around the audience space. He saw a *Waiting for Godot* in which sixteen Vladimirs and an equal number of Estragons in white face-paint took the main roles, each Vladimir or Estragon bouncing the previous one off the stage before occupying his place. Dazzled, Professor Ram felt the itch to snatch up a traditional play and make it speak in tongues. So instead of putting the Swan on as per usual in the soup and fish, this year he took a blue pencil to the *Dream*, and put in his own plot and his own dialogue, and generally took such obscene liberties with the Swan's intellectual property rights that Sundar and his friends wished with all their hearts to speak to the Swan's lawyer.

As a consequence of these liberties, only two women joined the cast this year.

The new literary criticism lecturer collared the part of Titania. She was fresh out of the University of California at Berkeley, where she had acquired the habit of saying that things were 'always already'. While they did not have anything against it, especially because she was as curvaceous as a Coca-Cola bottle, and quite pleasant withal, the students never understood why things were always already, and so naturally they called her Always Already. To the rehearsals, which were very strenuous, and involved breathing in and out in three different ways, pretending to be a tree, saying 'huh, huh, huh, huh' or 'MMMMMM' both loud and soft, Always Already wore an extraordinarily shapeless garment that made her look like an old, lumpy, Anglo-Indian lady on her way to church. But even if it had made her look like Disco Shanti rising from the waves, she was no good to Amandeep, Murugesh, Rufus and Sundar, for she was a lecturer, and a lecturer was strictly out of bounds. Besides, Professor Ram regularly told them in a blistering voice, within her hearing, they were as expressive as cucumbers, or bolsters, or Hollywood action heroes, among other inanimate things, and the resultant trauma prevented them from reaching their inner libertines.

Did I mention another female cast member? Her name was Sasi. She was cast as Bottom, because Titania had some love-business with Bottom, and while Professor Ram by no means gave his blessing to heterosexual hanky-panky on the stage or off it, he had never heard of homo-eroticism. Anyway, what you really need to know is that Sasi was already married.

If Amandeep, Murugesh, Rufus and Sundar were scandalized to find that Ram had excised Hippolyta, Helena and Hermia from *A Midsummer Night's Dream*, it was nothing to how scandalized they were when they found out how they themselves were cast in this play. They tried to resign from the cast, but were informed that they couldn't do such a thing. Ever since, they wore the look of those who were about to die as cattle, especially when they thought how, after play night, they would be marked men, and how, in the university corridors, in the library, in the canteen, in the bus stop and in the toilets, it would follow them, the cry:

'*Dai*, FAIRIES!'

~

Well, when we last saw Professor Ram, at the end of the Prologue, if you remember, he was hurrying backstage expecting to see the sets for his play going up. But when he got to the green rooms, he found nothing there: no boxes, no suitcases, no Lucas Dorairaj who had promised on his mother's name, just two days ago, to help with the make-up.

Professor Ram trotted out onto the stage, and there was still the same aporia and absence. Where was the superbly artistic and breathtakingly unique set (for Professor Ram sometimes slipped into the lingo of the rupee-a-line grubs who reviewed these plays) that Lucas was supposed to be putting up at this very moment? Where was everybody?

As Professor Ram stood stage right with knitted brow, one of his students came scurrying down the central aisle. This student's name was Shastri, and he was the assistant director of the play. Since Shastri had been working towards his Ph.D. at Chennai University for over fourteen years, under Professor Ram's supervision, he had naturally become the professor's full-time chamcha and right-hand man. Some unkind persons suggested that Professor Ram's own right hand had atrophied completely. They even insinuated that he would not let Shastri finish his thesis, because if Shastri finished and left the university, Professor Ram would have to start eating with his left hand, which, as everyone is aware, is against the scriptures as well as being most unhygienic and intolerable. If you had hung around the university at the time I am speaking of, you too would have seen Shastri buying Professor Ram's groceries and frying Professor Ram's bajjis, typing Professor Ram's notes and wiping Professor Ram's god-pictures, filling Professor Ram's prescriptions and milling Professor Ram's coffee. Sometimes you would have seen him right beside Professor Ram, thinking Professor Ram's thoughts; and at other times you would have seen him just behind Professor Ram, inhaling Professor Ram's farts.

'Professor!' Shastri bleated. He looked scruffy and

emaciated. His hair adhered to his forehead with sweat, and his eyes popped out behind his glasses. 'Professor! The sets have not arrived! I have just been to the booth to phone you, but your son said you had already left!'

'Some traffic delay-y, not to worry-y. The traffic is so-o heavy todayy!' intoned the professor.

'No, no, sir, it is not a traffic problem I am speaking about—it is far worse than that!' Shastri groaned. 'Mr Dorairaj has—has been—'. Unable to go on, he handed over a folded copy of that morning's *The Bindhu* to Ram and began to bite his nails. Professor Ram usually pored over India's Principal Newspaper after breakfast, but today the press of dramatic affairs had left him no time for such pleasures, causing him to miss this item:

WELL-KNOWN CHENNAI ARTIST NABBED
Chennai, April 12.

T. Nagar police today apprehended one Lucas Dorairaj for allegedly torching a number of cars parked in front of his residence, resulting in extensive damage to property. T. Nagar precinct S.I. Muthukrishnan stated: 'At first we suspected that it was the modus operandi of the dreaded criminal Auto Ravi aka Anthony Selvamani. Along with his accomplices, Maruti Manohar and Youssuf, he has been terrorizing the householders by setting fire to the automobiles which have been parked in the backside of their residences, while the victims are watching TV.' But when the culprit was observed making a getaway in a red Maruti van, the police gave chase, and he was apprehended at the corner of Pondy Bazaar and Thanikachalam Road. Upon arrest he disclosed that he was an artist.

On being questioned as to his reasons for committing this heinous act, Mr Dorairaj remained mum. An unidentified source close to the culprit disclosed to the press that he had been suffering from depression as a result of his financial status. 'This has made him feel that he has been forcing his art to seek employment as a commercial sex worker instead of pursuing art for art's sake, especially since he has started a set design business.'

It has been ascertained that Mr Dorairaj initially torched a huge heap of costumes and properties designed for a performance of *A Midsummer Night's Dream* which is slated for this evening at the Pantheon Theatre. His original intention seems to have been to sabotage the performance, but the blaze got out of control. It was put out in about forty minutes by fire-engines from the T. Nagar as well as Adyar Fire Depots.

S.I. Muthukrishnan assured the public that there is no terrorist connection in this case. But Mr M. Siva, President of the Hindu International Association, has made a statement alleging that this is a communal attack, perpetrated against caste Hindus by...

At this point Professor Ram fainted and could read no more.

'Ey, Shastri, run to the road and buy a tender coconut!' said Mrs Ram to the assistant director. She attended to Professor Ram's own coconut tenderly with a handkerchief soaked in eau de cologne.

'How strange,' thought Professor Ram, as he revived. 'How strange—wormwood and gall—marker ink—so remarkably similar-tasting!'

'We must pass up the chance of staging this year's play, Charu,' he said to Mrs Ram, in a sepulchral shadow of his former voice.

Now this is exactly what Mrs Ram was determined not to do. Mrs Ram held the opinion that if you lay down with the stage you would wake up with glamour, and she was partial to her annual injection of glamour. Leaving the professor sucking tender coconut water through a straw and pressing his reflexology points to calm himself, she went away to phone some doyens of the Cultural Club for advice. She also alerted the professor's colleagues from Chennai University. All their friends commiserated with the afflicted couple. In one voice they submitted that they would perish incontinently if they couldn't see something from Professor Ram's hand this year, as they depended on him so much for cultural gratification.

'Why don't you try Navrang?' one of the professor's colleagues suggested after they did some back-and-forth on the telephone. It emerged that Navrang had been doing props for Chennai troupes since Professor Ram was knee-high to a full wig. Mrs Ram wrote down the address carefully on the back page of *The Bindhu*, and Professor Ram, Mrs Ram and Shastri climbed into the Maruti van.

'Let's go,' said Mrs Ram, beginning to look more and more like Liberty Leading the People. She was displaying a firmness of resolve the professor had never, all these years, given her credit for. 'Sundar, get in!' she cried, for she could see Sundar shambling about backstage in an aimless way, trying to lasso a bust of Lord Curzon with the end of the curtain rope. Sundar got in, and they took off with smoking tires for Kodambakkam, where Mr R. Kannan of Navrang Sceneries and Properties Palace rented out false beards by the kilo.

The Navrang office was a table set in the middle of a large and cluttered room, covered with properties from floor to ceiling. A weedy old man sat languidly behind this table on a five-hooded metallized-plastic serpent. He was cleaning his ears with a safety pin. Since each ear accommodated masses of silvery hair, his task required ferocious concentration.

'Be seated, be seated!' said the weedy old man, waving a hospitable but vague safety-pin around the room before renewing his excavations with his eyes closed, the very picture of a man searching for the meaning of Meaning. Mrs Ram looked around helplessly and then lowered her bottom onto a

papier-mâché throne which had one leg missing. Shastri and
Sundar clattered around the room, knocking over unstable
cardboard battlements. Professor Ram entrusted his person to
some rolls of backcloth which subsided under him. Looking up
at the weedy old man from somewhere just above the floor—
a very disadvantageous position indeed—he coughed and began:

'Mr Kannan?'

'Yuss,' said the old man. 'I yam Kannan. Myself. See there!'
He gestured towards the cupboards that lined the walls of his
properties palace. 'All top firstu-class famous actors are giving
the sutti-ficate, taking photo with myself and my sceneries. All
photos and sutti-ficates of Manorama, Selvaraj, Sivaji, Sowcar
Janaki etcetera, backside of the cupboards.'

'I am Professor Ram, from Chennai University—'.

Professor Ram crisply outlined his troubles and stated his
requirements in the matter of costumes and sets for his
production of *A Midsummer Night's Dream*. 'Urgent, Mr
Kannan,' he concluded. 'All the costumes and props must be
ready in...' Here he looked at his Rolex, '... *fifteen minutes*. It
is now 5.20. The curtain goes up at seven. Of course I realize
I am asking for the impossible.'

'Tch tch tch tch...*whaa-at*, sar,' said Mr Kannan, with
many reproachful clicks and sighs. 'Never yanybody in my
whole life is asking me to prepare full sets for yay play in
twenty minutes, sar. And-a how many years I yam doing
sceneries business, sar?' he demanded, his head on one side. He
opened the safety-pin and scratched a '60' on the table. '*Six*-ty
years I yam doing sceneries business, sar.'

This was quite revolting to Professor Ram, as he himself
had been on the stage only a matter of forty-eight years, not
counting his debut appearance as the hindquarters of the
Emperor Shivaji's horse in the non-stop hit *Sons of Mother
India* in 1955.

'But for your sake, I will do special effort, sar. Because you
are having yay ass-picious face. *Just* you tell what type is the

play, and I will supply all the sceneries and costumes. Yeverything.' Mr Kannan paused for a second, giving Professor Ram a shrewd look. 'Just Rs 500 advance, cash *vonly*, no credit card, sar. Credit Cuts the Love,' he explained piously.

'Yes, yes, cash is fine,' said Professor Ram, drumming his fingers impatiently on a collapsible PVC elephant. 'Hurry up, Mr Kannan, we are wasting precious seconds talking.'

With a sudden burst of energy Mr Kannan jabbed his safety-pin into the many-headed snake and leapt off its coils. He flew around the office and flung open the doors of the many cupboards that lined its walls.

'Hist-arical?' he enquired, as moth-eaten beards, discoloured crowns, gold-painted papier-mâché daggers, epaulettes, cloaks and tacky bits and pieces of armour came tumbling out of the first cupboard.

'Mythol-agical?' he demanded, scattering five-hooded serpents, rubber Ganesha faces, spare arms and extra heads, brocaded skirts, breastplates, papier-mâché musical instruments, plastic lotuses, brass OMs and other divine attributes in all directions. 'Shocial? Famly pra-blems? Yinglish?' He noted the expression on Professor Ram's face. 'Of course, sar, if you are telling before only, I yam able to supply more *firstu-class* items from my priwate godown.'

Professor Ram surveyed the impedimenta that had come out of Mr Kannan's cupboards in a stricken way. 'Is there anyone else who supplies costumes in Chennai?' he asked.

'Not only no one in Chennai, yeven no one in yentire India. We are also having yay make-up man. Cheapest cost! Don't need for yany heshitay-shun!'

Ram pursed his lips. 'We need five pairs of tights,' he said.

'Tights? You want the *tights*? Just you have to clap your hands, sar, and tights are arriving. How many colours you need?' Mr Kannan pulled out multicoloured tights from a trunk and smacked them against the serpent, making Mrs Ram flinch. 'Quality tights, full stretchu, *just* like ly-cra!'

'We need a donkey's head,' the Professor hissed through clenched teeth.

'No pra-blem,' said Mr Kannan. His torso disappeared into another trunk and he hauled out a mangy horse mask. 'Horse, donkey, all same thing.'

Professor Ram felt it was no use arguing about this. He threw down his final gauntlet. 'We need a Tree of Life!'

'I know this Tree,' said Mr Kannan, 'but what is Life?' He took up his pin and savaged his ear-canal while he pondered this, saying frantically, 'Tree...Tree...'

He hurled some bows, swords, fly-whisks and spears out of the way, and a polyurethane tree stood revealed. It was about four feet tall. It was afflicted with a little known Asiatic tree fungus that covered its bole with scabs, and it had no leaves at all.

'Tree,' Mr Kannan panted.

'It has no leaves at all,' Professor Ram argued.

'Yuss,' Mr Kannan conceded, 'but ten minutes time, *just*, my boys are putting the paper leaves with Sellotape. So, all good?' he said briskly. 'Now we are ready. You are giving complete list of items, *now* vonly I am packing for taking.'

The costumes were chosen and packed at a quite astonishing speed. Shastri and Sundar carried the cases to Professor Ram's van. Mr Kannan supplied a couple of nephews to help backstage, and with much dignity admitted that he, yes, he himself, was the make-up man. Now that the van held two costume trunks, the make-up boxes, a roll of backcloth, a large carton ('That is Sellotape,' explained Mr Kannan) and the Tree of Life, the humans had to travel to the Pantheon Theatre in autorickshaws.

Well, now, Mr Kannan forgot to tell Professor Ram that some of the properties, such as the backdrop that he had chosen, were over fifty years old. In fact, this vintage backdrop, which was intended to represent the Indian jungle, had not been cleaned since 1947. It had been painted for an amateur production of *The Man-Eaters of Kumaon*—just weeks before the sahibs decided to go back to Blighty, having turned the last tigers in India into rugs. When it was unfurled at the Pantheon Theatre, this backdrop exuded dust like the Thar desert, and all the actors started having coughing fits. As Mr Kannan's nephews shook it out, they ripped open a hole through which you could have passed a couple of man-eaters and a cow, along with all the horses in the Emperor Shivaji's stables.

'The backdrop has a hole in it!' cried Professor Ram, who was galloping from one end of the stage to the other and spurring his various assistants into a state of preternatural efficiency.

'Aiyyo!' said Mr Kannan, slapping his forehead. 'No prablem,' he said, as he slapped one of the nephews. 'Dai, Thambi!' he said, as he slapped the other nephew. He felt obliged to copy Professor Ram in the matter of frenzied activity. 'Dai, Thambi, stick this hole up with Sellotape!'

'The backdrop is too dark,' wittered Shastri. They all stepped back and looked at it. Mr Kannan had to admit that the oil paint, which had darkened over the decades, gave this stage a murky, brooding quality.

'Machaan, it will be good in a movie called *A Midsummer Night's Nightmare*,' Sundar whispered to Amandeep.

'Script by Stephen King, yaar,' Amandeep whispered back.

'Don't need for worry,' Mr Kannan said with hysterical briskness. 'We will stick something-and-all on it.'

'Some fairies, Ram,' Mrs Ram chipped in brightly. 'Remember that book little Ranga was reading?'

Mrs Ram sneaked a picture-book from the younges member of the cast and haphazardly cut pictures out of it, and Mr Kannan's nephews stuck the fairy figures on the backdrop with Sellotape. Now, this book was called *I Believe in Fairies: A Testimony of Personal Encounters with Peter the Pixie and Elvira the Elf.* It was illustrated by the slapdash hand of its author, an ex-theosophist, and the sinister look of the fairies may or may not have something to do with the fact that the author was six or seven times arrested for interfering with minors.

Anyhow, the fairies on Kannan's backdrop bore a very loose resemblance indeed to the figures of Amandeep (Pease Blossom), Murugesh (Cobweb), Rufus (Moth) and Sundar (Mustard Seed) who, while being by no means unhandsome, were definitely lubberly and uncouth fellows, and between you and me, A-1 lemons in the roles of fairies. This became painfully obvious when they got suited up in their fairy outfits and stumbled out bashfully to be examined by Mrs Ram. Since Professor Ram kept calling out, 'Are you finished yet, Mr Kannan?' Mr Kannan had gone off his stroke and slapped the rouge over their stubble with a plasterer's hand, and now their faces had the synthetic pink-and-white complexion of gods in calendar pictures, or of Ronald McDonald, which comes to the same thing.

And the faces were nothing to what came below the waist.

'Ram, where are their *costumes*?' cried Mrs Ram. She was deeply distressed to observe that the so-called tights worn by Amandeep, Murugesh, Rufus, and Sundar were drawing a regrettable amount of attention to their family jewels.

'*These* are their costumes!' Professor Ram answered in a tone of frigid despair.

'But Ram, don't you think they are...ummm...*baggy-baggy*?' asked Mrs Ram. Indeed she was right, for the garments had been stretched by the goolies of many bulbous thespians of yesteryear, and had a grievously postnatal look.

'We can tie a clath round the...*ahem,*' Kannan said. He wrapped four identical pieces of candy-pink brocaded fabric over the tights like loin-cloths, and held them in place with Sellotape. After these adjustments the four fairies looked like Third World superheroes, except that I cannot remember having seen any superheroes looking as embarrassed or as despondent as this quartet.

The four young bucks were thinking bitter thoughts, and cursing the hopes that had trapped them in this predicament. They were wondering why they never realized before that Love was a grossly over-rated emotion, and indeed, as Always Already often said, nothing but an Ideological State Apparatus that sustained the late-capitalist order. Their toes were curling with stage fright. They were tripping themselves up flip-flop at every step. Someone had emptied a jorum of molten lava into their insides.

Suddenly, Amandeep decided to bolt. As he turned to flee, he tripped over one of Mr Kannan's nephews, who was sticking green crêpe-paper leaves on the Tree of Life. The Tree came down with a horrendous, nerve-rending crash. Amandeep lay among the ruins, breathless and paralysed, and all his will drained away from him.

'Ad-da-da-da!' said Mr Kannan sadly. 'Now see what you are doing! The tree is com-pletely broken, com-pletely. Thambi,' he continued, distributing a few quick slaps between his nephews, 'stick it with that Sellotape'.

Professor Ram looked at his watch. 'Oh, by golly!' he said. 'It is fifteen minutes to curtain-up and I am not yet dressed! Hurry up, hurry up, everybody! Hurry up with that tree! Mr Kannan, where is my costume?'

At forty minutes past opening time, the audience was still waiting for the Chief Guest to arrive. The Chief Guest was the man who had coughed up the Rs 25,000 that had made this play feasible, and the play could not start without him. This Chief Guest was Mr Seshadri, and he was late because he was fortifying himself at the Gymkhana Club with many full pegs of Johnny Walker. The notables were growing restless in the front rows. In the back rows and in the balcony, the thugs and hooligans from the university were working with vegetables, with the brochures they had collected at the door, and with a wisdom beyond their years about the principles of aerodynamics, to create missiles that accurately expressed their unrest at this delay. One conclave of oafs was unwrapping the packages on which the government advised couples like this: 'We Two, Ours One.' They were inflating the contents of these packages as much as they could without flattening the little nipple at the end that distinguished the prophylactic from a mere balloon. Another section of the mob was polishing up the groans, howls and flatulence which it had developed especially for this occasion.

When the Chief Guest finally arrived, the glamorous socialite lady from the Chennai Cultural Club made her welcome speech, causing the microphone to emit demented yips and squeals.

'We are happy to present to you two alternative plays this evening,' she chirped. Her diamonds sparkled and flashed under the single spot that lit her, and her silk sari unravelled like toilet paper over one arm. 'The first and foremost play,' she cooed, 'is directed by *none other than* a great doyen of the limelight who *needs no introduction* to the audiences of Chennai. He has done *yeoman service* behind the footlights, for which the government has conferred many titles on him. Today we will see him *expanding his horizons*, for he has *taken pen in hand* to improve upon the work of the *great William Shakespeare himself*. Ladies and Gentlemen, please bring your hands together and give a hearty welcome to: *Pro-fe-ssor Ram*! And helping him make this evening's play a *grand success* is our wonderful Child Prodigy, little Ranga, none other than the one and only grandson of Chennai University's own respected vice-chancellor, *Doc-tor Mohan*!'

There were ripples of applause from the notables and heavy groans and howls from the dickey area of the theatre. Then the glamorous lady went off, and music began playing, and a saffron light came on. Professor Ram had asked for such a light to symbolize the hidden Hindu message of the play, even though it made the actors look like a hepatitis epidemic. It was clear that the play was beginning at last, for Professor Ram's voice oozed out of the speakers like this:

'Over hill over dale, thorough bush, thorough brier...'

A long gibbering cry, not part of the script, issued from halfway between the balcony and the back benches downstairs.

'Sh-sh-*shit*, machaan,' the voice wailed, 'my rope is tut-tut-too *short!*'

This was the voice of Murugesh, who as Cobweb was to astonish the audience by bungee-jumping from the balcony railings like Lord Greystoke travelling among the apes. Murugesh was sobbing thus because the ungodly had taken his jungle trapeze and looped it around the chairs, and now the end of it was too short to let him reach the downstairs aisle. Murugesh was corkscrewing (this-way—that-way, this-way—that-way, as he himself put it later), about eight feet above the spot where his presence was required before the curtain went up. Small pieces of Chennai's colonial heritage, chafed by the rope, crumbled slowly and fell like dandruff upon the citizens below.

'Look, machaan, Murugesh is doing a circus up on the balcony!'

'Jump, da, jump!' the ungodly chortled heartlessly. 'We will inform your family!' They pelted him with paper rockets and the odd tomato. Some helpful parties leapt up to catch him, but as they caught his tights instead, they merely left him in a more embarrassing plight than before.

'Sundar! Get me d-d-down, machaan!'

Sundar, in the character of Mustard Seed, was tripping along the downstairs aisle, while Ram resumed the voice-over: 'O'er park o'er pale, thorough flood thorough fire, I do wander everywhere.' Shakespeare did not mention it, but Sundar was also wandering thorough the audience, and this was what caused his troubles.

'Look machaan, it's Sundar! Oi! Catch him! Sit down with us, Sundar!'

'Ey, I'm telling you, let me go. I have to get on the stage, man. Ey, you cheap wankers, come on, man, please.'

'Sssshhhh!' said a big noise in the front row, trying to glare the offenders down. But as anyone could have told you, this was very hard to do in a darkened theatre.

'Okay, Sundar, if you're in the play, you should be on the stage, no? So what are you doing here, man?'

'See, machaan,' Sundar said, 'we are using alternative spaces and destroying the convention of the fourth wall'.

This explanation was greeted with catcalls and whistles.

'Which wall is it, man? Oi! Oi! Thro-ow him over the fo-ourth wall!'

Now the hoi polloi stopped sitting on Sundar. They hoisted him up in the air and began to swing him about.

'Sssh, sit down, you mayiru, I can't see anything!'

'Doesn't matter, man, nothing's *happening*!'

'Let me go da, *bastards*, the curtains are opening! I'm supposed to be on stage!'

As the curtains opened, Moth and Pease Blossom were discovered stage left on either side of the Tree of Life looking like a brace of bright pink popsicles melting in the footlights. They were aware that they had to break into choreographed moves with the other two fairies. The other two fairies had not shown up, and Moth and Pease Blossom were in a state of radical indecision. Should they come out of their freeze or not? Now and then one of them thought the other was starting to move and twitched spasmodically.

Behind the curtains, Professor Ram sensed that something had gone wrong among the fairies. His fruity voice wobbled as he set off again:

'And I serve the Fairy Queen,
Dew her orbs upon the green...'

Now his voice stopped altogether. Then it floated up into the hall in a tense whisper.

'Fairies? Fairies? Please get set! Fairies? FAI-RIES!'

The rabble in the rump area, who never paid much attention to the dialogue, were all along under the impression that Murugesh, Sundar and the other riff-raff were just stage properties of one sort or another, or some low-grade comic turn. Now they were suddenly filled with wild surmise. 'Fairies?' they sang out in several different keys. 'Fairi-fairi-fairi-ries! Fa-a-a-a-iries!' they ululated. '*Dai*, FAIRIES!'

They got up and began to dance in the aisle, making up a song to the tune of *Ennuyir Thozhiyay* which was a great hit of the moment. 'Ennuyir Fairy-yay!' they yodelled, flatter than a tyre outside a vulcanizing shop.

Under normal circumstances, Professor Ram would have saved his own person for an electrifying entry some minutes into the play. But this was an emergency. He felt that nothing would quell this anarchy but a personal appearance.

'I must go on now!' he said to Mr Kannan, who was still fixing his accoutrements. 'Oo-argh!'

Professor Ram exclaimed like this because Mr Kannan, who was trying to snap the clasp of his saffron cloak, had just skewered his jowls for the sixth time. The professor was a small-sized but portly man with a face like a star of the silver screen. Like all these stars after their expiry date, he had run plentifully to jowl, and Mr Kannan was having trouble locating the crease of his neck.

'Maybe you should leave the cloak, sar!' Mr Kannan said desperately, groping among his dewlaps.

'No—arghurgh!' Professor Ram hissed. 'I must have it, for it symbolizes the traditional Hindu order!'

You probably want to know how the Hindu order came

into *The Midsummer Night's Dream*. The brochure that went with Professor Ram's version explained it like this: it seems Oberon (Professor Ram) quarrelled with his wife Titania (played by Kalpana Kamath, Always Already to you and me) over a changeling (the Prodigy) that Titania had imported from India. Oberon did not specify why he wished to have the changeling, but perhaps he wished it for the same reasons the author of *I Believe in Fairies* wished to explicate the ways of Peter the Pixie to little boys. The quarrel resulted in a terrible disintegration of public facilities all over the universe, including the facilities that kept the lower orders in their place, and as a result, Titania fell in love with a working-class bozo called Bottom who was hanging around the forest. I have read the Bard's version of the play, and I can say that from here onwards, the Ram interpolations came thickly, one upon the back of another, especially when Oberon began to say acid things about the role of woman in Hindu society.

Back on the stage at the Pantheon Theatre, Bottom asked for a side order of dried pease. As Amandeep bumbled into the wings to fetch it, he stepped on the end of Professor Ram's cloak. Professor Ram heard the dull roar of tearing fabric.

'Adda-da-da!' Mr Kannan sobbed. 'The cloak! It is completely broken!'

'Mend it!' Professor Ram snapped. 'Quick!'

It took Mr Kannan less than a second to fix the cloak up with Sellotape. Professor Ram came forth from the wings like a politician greeting his constituency, arms up, palms outwards, at once demanding peace and conferring a blessing.

Well, you know how it is with Sellotape. About ten minutes after his entrance, as Professor Ram strode about saying nasty things about the role of woman and swinging his cloak, the Sellotape that had mended the rip at its end found itself irresistibly attracted to the Sellotape that had healed the hole in the backdrop. There was a moment of adhesion. Suddenly, with a dismal ripping, the backdrop gaped open. At last the actors could account for the funny smell all around the stage. Mr Kannan's two chokra nephews were revealed just behind the curtain, wreathed in clouds of cannabis.

Professor Ram soldiered on. About four yards of Sellotape, along with one or two cut-outs of Elvira the Elf, were now trailing from the end of his saffron cloak.

'Psst, Ram!' Mrs Ram hissed from the wings, 'look behind you!'

'The Four *Vedas* are covered with mud!' roared Professor Ram, swishing his cloak around the stage some more. His Sellotape tail gathered all sorts of odds and ends, here a few leaves from the Tree of Life, there a scarf that had fallen off one of the fairies, and here again an ear that had fallen off the so-called donkey mask. He was in high gear, declaiming about the sanctity of traditional marriage, and he did not hear Mrs Ram's sibilant warnings. The philistines in the balcony were bouncing off their chairs and rolling down the aisles. As the tail became more conspicuous, the mirth of the mob infected the stern front rows.

At last Professor Ram realized that he had unintentionally become a comet. Since the Hindu-order-cloak was a cloak that Ram did not wish to desecrate in any way, and since he wanted the show to go on without further interruptions, he tried to get the Sellotape off with many sly jerks and twitches.

'Ram!' hollered a wit from the balcony section. 'Ei Rambo! Okay, man, you can scrape the dog-dung off your foot now. Everyone can see you stepped in it!'

But no matter what Professor Ram did, he could not dislodge the Sellotape. Not, that is, until he hit upon the idea of attaching it to a fellow thespian. He passed it adroitly to Bottom. Ten minutes later, Bottom pressed it emotionally against Always Already. Towards the end of the play, as Always Already clung defiantly to the changeling, she attached the tail to the Prodigy's elbow.

And now the Prodigy's big scene began. In the Swan's

version, the changeling child went about minding his own juvenile business. In Ram's version, he was a very significant character, and I hope you don't think this had anything to do with the fact that he was played by the vice-chancellor's grandson. What Professor Ram called the dee-nooma of the play occurred when the Prodigy stood under the Tree of Life and lectured the quarrelsome fairy couple for a full ten minutes about Maya, Dharma, Yoga, Karma, Right Living, Harmony, and other cosmic matters. At the end of the speech, there was a tableau, for all the characters, including the four fairies, seemed to be irresistibly drawn towards the Prodigy. They gathered around to hear him pontificate. The Prodigy, lifting his right arm in blessing, spoke thus:

> As and when I do perceive perversion
> Of the Natural Order of Dharma
> And a proliferation of egregious Adharma,
> To offer protection to the righteous
> And to eliminate the unrighteous
> From time to time I descend myself...

When the Prodigy finished speaking the lines, the notables in the first ten rows rose to their feet and roared their approval, realizing that the child stood revealed as Lord Krishna himself, no less, and they were pleased with themselves for recognizing this. It was a very powerful and moving moment. Many people in the audience were weeping buckets, even those who came to scoff. Some people said that was because they laughed themselves into stitches when the Sellotape from the Prodigy's outflung arm gripped the Sellotape that held the Tree of Life together, and this caused the Tree to fall apart neatly as if cloven by lightning.

But those people were not to be trusted, because most of them were busy releasing the huge flotillas of inflated condoms that had been saved for the end of the play. As these objects writhed downwards with high-pitched howls, the theatre reverberated with the thunder of prolonged and insane flatulence. All the actors stood hand-in-hand just behind the debris of the Tree of Life and bowed unevenly. Professor Ram went to the microphone and offered abject thanks to this and that dignitary and, of course, to Mr Seshadri. Then he said that he could not have achieved anything without his better half. This was the moment Mrs Ram had been waiting for since the curtain came down on last year's play. She joined the cast and looked around complacently, daring anyone in the audience to take her glory away from her.

Then Professor Ram invited the Chief Guest to say a few words. Mr Seshadri wove up onto the stage. He had tears in his eyes, or at least in the one eye which he devoted to the present moment—for if there was one thing that marred Mr Seshadri's beauty, it was the fact that his eyes did not look in the same direction, one of them being fixed at all times on the main chance. He rocked gently from side to side as he hiccupped:

'I am sohic. Mooved byhic this evening's message! I wish— I wish to—' here he lost his place in the sweaty piece of paper typed by Mr Rami Reddy, which he had palmed all evening. He searched for it with his forehead creased, the prongs of his Brahmin caste-mark rippling with concentration. 'To prevent— to present the revhic—reveeered Professor Ram with this humble hicgrain of rice. On which an artish has enhic— engraved Chapter Six Vershes. Fourhic and five of the *Bhada— Bhava—Habhagad Vita.*'

Mr Seshadri put his hand into his pocket and whipped out the enamelled box in which the grain rested. He held it out and Professor Ram took it, but instead of letting it go, Mr Seshadri leaned on Professor Ram slightly and carried on talking.

'Profeshor Ram openedhic my eyes to religion!' he said. 'Glories of hic-hic-Hinduism! Relijush men like myself—hic— should partishipate in Legislative Ashembly elections!'

Professor Ram looked very silly indeed, hanging on to the box. After a very long time Mr Seshadri let go of it, released

Professor Ram, and tumbled down the steps. He took with him, on his shoe, six yards of Sellotape, several pictures of Elvira the Elf, a loincloth, some scraps of backdrop and half the Tree of Life.

～

On the stage the socialite lady stood in the glow of the single spot once more and mumbled that they would now watch a one-woman play, called *Ekalavya*, in the folk tradition. Sundar, trying to depart in obscurity by the green-room exit before the great unwashed in the balcony caught up with him, did not care to see the play. He was wiping the rouge off his face with his loincloth dipped in coconut oil.

But as he crawled out into the night air, he heard a voice raised in song. It was such a voice as he had never heard before in his whole life. It was a voice that seemed to erupt out of all the warm, dark, velvety spaces of the earth and the sky and the ocean, and it caused his hairs to stand up, his heart to thump, his juices to flow, and his scrotum to tighten like a knot in a wet shoelace. He crawled back into the theatre to find out who owned such a voice as this. As he could not go towards the back rows, he slid into an empty seat in the second row, where he sat for the next forty minutes, his mouth open very wide indeed.

The owner of the voice was Jiva, Professor Ram's student, the young woman Sundar had noticed maybe a dozen times at the university, and admired from a distance. She was telling the story of how a tribal archer worked out with a Brahmin coach, though the coach was only a likeness he had fashioned out of clay, and how the original of this statue turned up after the archer had graduated with a top rank and asked for his fee. And the fee was nothing but the archer's right thumb. This seemed to Sundar a singularly nasty and underhand demand. The *Man-Eaters* background was cleared away, and there were no props on the stage except a clay bust. The bust had a certain familiar look, especially around the gizzard, but Sundar did not pay much attention to it. Sundar felt he did not care if the story this performer was singing and dancing was the story of the Three Little Pigs, for she was a very, very beautiful young woman, with skin the colour of old bronze, and a long heavy black plait, and huge, intelligent, flashing eyes, and a body that showed plenty of burnished muscle.

When the actress went off the stage at last, the world looked completely different to Sundar from how it had looked when he had sat down on that seat. Even the seat looked bright and shiny, not at all like the squeaking, clattering, arthritic heap of joints it had been when he had first descended into it. The theatre had stopped looking and smelling like a mangy pi-dog, and had begun to look like a—Sundar could not say what it looked like, but it looked very tolerable indeed. And the voice of the fat man who was sitting on Sundar's left and who had been chattering away to a vaguely familiar-looking tall white girl on Sundar's right, across Sundar's body, right through the performance: why, even this man's tones sounded fairly dulcet.

'I mean, clearly,' the man was saying now, in his fairly dulcet voice, 'the Ekalavya myth is about emasculation, and the thumb is a kind of penis substitute'.

'Yeah,' said the tall white girl. 'I so *todally* get it. The archery teacher is a Brahmin, eh, so that makes this play, like, a comment on how the Brahmins oppressed all these other guys, the tribals and the daylights and that.' She stretched her cramped legs and got up to leave.

The fat man shook his head. 'Caroline, that's such a predictable interpretation. In fact it's just the kind of boring reading I'd advise you to avoid, if you ever want to get *Social Text* to notice you. Anyway, all that caste-oppression stuff is history. The tables are pretty much turned now.'

'Come on, Chunky, you know that's crap. Why do you write on daylight self-expression then?'

The fat man looked wise and enigmatic. 'It happens to be the topic of the moment, Caroline,' he said. 'Maybe for me, it's just a way of returning the gaze of the West,' he said. 'By-the-by, the locally accepted pronunciation for the once untouchable castes of India is da-lit, not day-light. Excuse me,' he said to Sundar, because Sundar was still sitting there in a rapture, watching the spot where the actress had exited, and his long legs were blocking the passage. Who is this Jiva, he was thinking, and whereof is she made, and how can I get her phone number, and does she already have a boyfriend?

'*Excuse me!*' the fat man snarled, much louder. Sundar drew in his legs, and the fat man pushed past him. Sundar noticed his fingers were heavily bandaged.

A man with a face like a camel brought up the rear.

'I'll see ya tomorrow, Ack-eelan,' the tall white girl called back over her shoulder to this man. 'Tell Jiva she was fabulous.'

'Excuse *me*,' said Sundar starting up, 'do you know the lady who did this play?'

'I didn't get her name,' said the fat man, before the white girl could answer. 'But I can tell you who the director of the other play was. The earlier one. Professor Ram—he happens to be my Daddy, so you might be justified in saying I'm kind of acquainted with him.' He chuckled at his own wit.

Sundar looked upon him with a new disfavour and wondered how he had ever thought his voice dulcet.

'I already know your *Daddy*,' he said. 'I am asking about the lady who did the second play.'

'Jiva?' said Camel-Face.

'Yes, man, do you know her?'

'Yes,' said Camel-Face, 'very well'.

'Er, ah—I would like to meet her,' Sundar said, blushing. 'I'm Sundar, by the way.'

'I'm Akilan,' said Camel-Face, studying the streaks of pink make-up on Sundar's face. 'You are at the university too?'

'Yes,' said Sundar.

'Then you can see her on Monday,' said Akilan. 'She is going there at ten o'clock, for the statue ceremony.'

'Glglglgl,' said Sundar, for his heart was full.

'See you,' said Akilan.

They left, and Sundar followed them out in a reverie. In the lobby he noticed the poster with Jiva's face. He looked around for a moment, but there was only Shastri by the door, and so he prised the poster away from the wall. He did this with such regard to the poster's health that he took several irregular flakes of Pantheon Theatre with him.

As he came out of the theatre, Sundar saw that the pudgy son of Ram and the white girl had stopped an autorickshaw outside the theatre. The son of Ram was haggling over the fare.

'But I don't *mind* paying extra!' the girl exclaimed.

'You must never allow these assholes to make a fool of you,' said the son of Ram. 'As soon as you agree to pay one-and-a-half times the fare they will ask for double. They're a bunch of—of scoundrels.'

'*Iruvathanju rupai,*' he said to the auto-driver in a green-card accent. 'Twenty-five rupees.'

The auto-driver offered some unprintable suggestions about what the son of Ram could do with his twenty-five rupees. He moved his vehicle forward towards Sundar.

'Jiva,' Sundar sighed.

'What?' said the driver.

'Take me to Pallavakkam,' said Sundar.

'One-and-a-half,' said the auto-driver.

'Anything,' said Sundar, who wanted to return to his delicious dream of running around a tree with Jiva. 'Whatever you say.'

The auto-driver cheered up. 'For you, I will just charge the fare,' he said. 'Now *tha-at,*' he jabbed a finger towards the son of Ram, 'is the kind of pubic-hair-plucker I would like to turn out of the country. Ada *thhooo!*' He spat. 'That fat pumpkin cheapskate, thinking I cannot understand what he says in Engilish. And the white-crow, who spends more money one night in her five-star hotel than I earn in a month. Yesterday a po-liss caught me for not having a black spot on my headlight. Can you believe this? Fifty rupees fine, or forty rupees mamool. I am going to start a revolutionary party. I am going to teach these high-caste loafers and America-tourists to respect poor people's rights. Look out for me one of these days,' he said, as he bumped the auto in and out of the pot-holes on Taramani Road. 'My name is Thiru.'

$\sim$

It was nearly half-past-ten in Chennai. The sea breeze skulked around Marina Beach in a tired way. In his bedroom at No. 16, First Main Street, Mylapore, Professor Ram took off his greasepaint, exhaled strongly, let his waistline sag, and spent five minutes improving his muscles with his trusty Bullworker. He creamed and polished his face, oiled his hair and eyebrows, and riffled through his jowls, chin by chin, putting antiseptic on the wounds made by Mr Kannan's pin. Then, in the privacy of his study, he switched on his computer. The blue light soothed his senses, and the sensation of being half-naked and lacerated by the gaze of many eyes (it was the tights, he knew he should not have gone in for tights) slowly wore off. First, he plugged into *e-prarthana.com*, the prayer website, called up the virtual pujai for Lord Krishna and devoutly clicked the cursor on the incense and the flower basket. Then he typed busily for half an hour.

'The symbolic force of the contemporary interpolations, worthy of juxtaposition with the brilliant verse, both blank and rhymed, that flowed from Shakespeare's own pen, cannot be denied. Hinduism can revive not only India, but the whole world,' typed Professor Ram. He went back and added '(by Professor Ram, the applause, the delight, the wonder of our stage)' after 'contemporary interpolations'. 'Furthermore, a new approach to the role of Brahmins in the revival of Hinduism is the crying need of the hour,' he typed. '... As Professor Ram's play proves beyond any question,' he was adding, when Mrs Ram called from the dining room.

'Ram? Aren't you having your milk?'

'I'm coming in a minute,' said Professor Ram. 'I had best get the review over with when everything's still fresh in my mind. It is almost done.'

'In short,' he concluded, 'Professor Ram's startlingly original and thought-provoking *Midsummer Night's Dream* is, in the opinion of this connoisseur, a flawless masterpiece.' He saved the file, stretching luxuriously in his paisley-print office chair, and decided he would send it by e-mail the next day to his cousin, who was the editor of the *Arts and Culture Review* supplement of *The Bindhu*. The review would be published under Shastri's name.

Professor Ram joined his wife at the dining table. Mrs Ram was mixing, with a loving hand, three heaped spoons of Evacu-eeze in a glass of sour buttermilk. In a thousand thousand households across Chennai, similar nightly charms and philtres against stopped bowels were being spooned into milk or curds or water. The enema bag is as much a sign of true Brahminhood as the sacred thread. Indeed, in many poonal or sacred thread ceremonies, the responsible parent draws his son aside and hands over, along with the esoteric *Gayatri* mantram, a copy of the *Bhagavad Gita*, the life insurance, and other such signs of being twice-born, his own personal secret prophylactic against constipation. 'Fleaseed husk, O best beloved,' he says, in a hushed voice; or 'Castor oil, my first-born son...' ; or 'Evacu-eeze, O child of my loins: three heaped tablespoons in a glass of sour buttermilk morning and night.'

'Chunky should stop taking that artificial stuff,' said Professor Ram, whose own personal panacea had been rejected by his son.

'Poor boy,' said Mrs Ram. 'You know how he suffers. It is

especially bad now, with the jet-lag. He tells me he has not moved his bowels since he left Toronto.'

'He should do it the yogic way,' said Professor Ram. 'It is the traditional way.'

'Do what, Daddy?' said the son of Ram, wandering in.

'Elimination, Chunky. It is greatly assisted by yogic postures, especially Mayurasana and Matsyakurmasana. I have advised you about this many times.'

'How will it do him any good? He's just full of shit,' said Jayanthi, breezing through the dining room. Jayanthi was the other child the Rams had produced. 'Gruesome. Look at him, does he look like he can even bend over and touch his knees? No wonder the shit is backed up all the way to his brain,' she said, getting a bottle of water out of the refrigerator.

'*Jay*! I will not have you speaking of your brother in that shameless way!' said Mrs Ram, who was appalled by her daughter's vocabulary. 'Send these girls abroad to study and they come back not knowing how to respect their elders!'

'So you want him to get married or not? Who's going to marry him if he looks like a Before ad for diet pills? You've asked the whole clan, haven't you? Has anyone come up with a bride yet?'

'Shut up, Jay,' said Chunky.

The Rams looked at each other.

'We have already placed an advertisement in *The Bindhu*,' said Mrs Ram complacently. 'Your father and I drafted it with the help of Chennai's best e-astrologer. He says it will produce a result within a week. And what is more,' here she paused significantly, 'it is mutual'.

At No. 5, Varadan Street, Pallavakkam, Sundar lay in bed in a state of some puzzlement. He was conscious of having unfamiliar urges that had never come over him before. For instance, every time he thought of Jiva, he wished to depart at once for a hill station with her and to chase her through coniferous forests, or to save her from a tiger, or at least to waggle his hips at her under a waterfall. He could not understand these desires any more than he could make sense of the feeling that once came over him when he leaned against a scaffold and a bucket of cement fell down on him from the top of a building. He considered the possibility that it was a kind of sickness or a cramp, and waited for it to go away. But it did not go away. In fact it came back stronger, especially when he looked at Jiva's poster, which he had placed under his pillow. This time he wished to go with Jiva to Paris and do some indifferently choreographed break-dancing on one side of the Champs Elysees accompanied by sixteen well-muscled young men while she did some frankly impossible extreme bhangra on the other side with sixteen nubile and negligibly-clothed young women.

Just as his eyelids began to droop, he realized, aghast, that the moment had come to him, Sundar, as it had come to Leonardo di Caprio, Hrithik Roshan, Shah Rukh Khan, Prabhudeva, etcetera, etcetera. Now he knew what these signs meant.

He was in love.

In which the Vaidyanathans discuss Matrimony at No. 5, Varadan Street

~

IT HAS JUST occurred to me that all the bona fide novels I have ever read have Heroes. I say to myself, here I am, in Chapter 2 already, and here you are, in danger of cutting my Hero dead if you bump into him on Mount Road, all because I have not introduced him to you properly. If you are anything like Sundar's uncles and aunts you will want to know which village his family comes from, their genealogy, their status, how much they earn, and so on, and I hope some of your questions will be answered as you read on.

To cut a long story short, as the editor once said when he shaved a couple of pages from *Clarissa*, my hero's name, according to his birth certificate, was Kalyanasundaram, and though his father sometimes called him Karl when he wished to be provoking, everyone else called him Sundar. He had a very engaging face, slightly sunburnt at the moment, with big eager eyes and a nose that was a tad off-centre, all of this topped by a shock of wavy hair that looked like an upside-down tropical fern. The proprietor of an Unlimited Meals hotel was rumoured to have said politely to Sundar one day that he needed to know if Sundar meant to ask for any more helpings of anything. Because if he did, the proprietor said, he (the proprietor) would like to start packing straightaway, as he had heard of several more profitable jobs than keeping an Unlimited Meals hotel. Such as being a door-to-door salesman of feminine hygiene products, said the proprietor bitterly, ladling more rice onto Sundar's empty plate. But Sundar's body was tall and lean, so perhaps my source was exaggerating. Or perhaps it was a tapeworm.

On Sunday morning, the dawn had barely broken over No. 5, Varadan Street, where our hero lived, when the sun poked a hot inquisitive claw into our hero's side like a cat that wished to have its breakfast served right speedily. Our hero tossed about for a while, basted in sweat. When he was well done on all sides, like an early Christian martyr, he decided to get up. He tumbled out of bed and went sleepily towards one of the two functional bathrooms in the house, but he found that all was locked and barred. His father Vaithy was leaning brokenly against the large plastic water-drum outside this bathroom with *The Bindhu* in his hands. Once in about ten seconds Vaithy looked up and groaned:

'When is the boy coming out of there?'

Sundar's mother Saraswati—known to the family as Sachu—called out from the bedroom: 'Do not harry him, he will become constipated. Pah! I can never understand why men are so impatient.'

From this exchange Sundar understood that his older brother Kicha had occupied the bathroom, and that his father was next in line of succession. In short, Sundar had no hope of using the loo on that floor for another hour at least. Kicha's matutinal ablutions were complex.

'You'd be impatient too if you had smoked two cigarettes and drunk two tumblers of coffee and couldn't get to a bathroom,' Vaithy growled. Sundar's father was a tall, thin man with a sallow, intellectual face and the same unruly hair that Sundar had. He began to bang on the bathroom door: da-boom, da-da-boom, da-boom. 'Ei, Kicha,' he hollered, 'when are you going to come out of there?'

Kicha did not reply. On the other side of the locked door he began to make a sound like a few million cubic feet of sewage being sucked down a plug-hole, which went on for about ten minutes. Guglglguglglglglgl!

'Gargling,' Sundar remarked conversationally, leaning against the wall across from his father.

Then for five minutes Kicha made another sound which went like this: Grrrrhgrrmm! Grrrrhgrrmm!

Sundar tipped his head on one side, considering. 'Clearing his throat.'

'What, I say, Kicha,' Vaithy bellowed again, jitterbugging with frustration. 'Are you planning to bring down this toilet too?'

Kicha replied with long trumpet-blasts. Sundar listened with keen interest, for he had heard such a blast only once before, and that was when he had gone walking along the Adyar river and come across a washerman's donkey in labour. Paarrrmmp! Prraaaarrrmmprraap!

'Cleaning his nose.'

And now all the passages in the upper half of Kicha's body were clear and open in both lanes, but there was still congestion in the nether regions, for Kicha, Beethoven of the thunderbox, always saved the bowel arpeggios for the end.

'Now,' said Sundar, 'for the *Fifth Symphony*'.

Sachu emerged from the bedroom, sniffing. She disapproved of Sundar's facetiousness. 'Appa,' she said (this was how she addressed her husband Vaithy, for it was unlucky to speak your husband's name), 'I want that paper when you have finished with it, and you will have to lean on something else, since I need that water-drum. Sundar, you have to help with the buckets. Uma will be coming up in a minute.'

Sundar's mother was transferring water from buckets to drum, from drum to buckets, in a complex and esoteric ritual which was meant to free up the largest containers in the house against the arrival of the municipal water lorry. Her voluminous housecoat slapped wetly against her legs.

Sundar's older sister Uma came up presently, looking bright-eyed and bushy-tailed though she was still in her ancient smocked nightie. Sundar helped her carry the buckets down the stairs to the kitchen and to the bathroom used by their grandparents. Through the window they saw a little scrawny man with a straggly tuft shimmying towards the house on his bicycle.

'Amma!' Uma yelled up the stairs to her mother. 'I forgot, the paatu-master said he was coming today!'

'*What*?' Sachu shrieked. 'But he was supposed to come tomorrow!'

'Yes, but he can't because he has an All-India Radio concert tomorrow. He is here already,' Uma said, as the doorbell rang. She heaved a sad hissing sigh like a firecracker falling into a puddle. If there was one thing in the world that Uma would give her whole collection of second-hand Dorothy Sayers to miss, it was her singing lesson.

Sachu bustled down the stairs.

'Come in, come in, Master,' she said. 'The silly girl forgot to tell me you were coming today. It is the water-lorry day, it will be a bad time for singing.'

At this the singing master felt he had received a gift, a windfall, a refund from a government department.

'Oh, in that case, I should go back and come another day,' he said, with a nervous chuckle, whipping his bicycle around smartly.

'No, no, she must have the lesson,' said Sachu firmly. 'Uma, go and put on your pottu.' Uma's red dot had rubbed off in her sleep and she had not dressed yet. 'The lazy younger generation,' Sachu said to the singing master. 'Wake up whenever they like, don't even wash their faces, just loll about the house.'

Uma came back in five minutes, her long curly hair freshly braided, her small neat body encased in a salwar suit, and a red dot lighting up her forehead. She brought a grass mat with her and unrolled it on the floor for the singing master to sit on.

'How is your Thatha?' asked the singing master, nodding towards Sundar's grandfather's room.

'Thatha is fine,' Uma said. 'He is cleaning his teeth. Some in his mouth and some in a cup.'

Pati, Sundar's and Uma's grandmother, waddled out of the kitchen.

'Welcome, welcome, Master!' she chirruped. Sundar's grandmother was only about four-and-a-half feet high, and the general consensus on her shape was that if you threw her at a hard surface she would bounce. No one cared to test this hypothesis, as Pati had the sweetest disposition in the world. She wished at all times to heal the spirit and delight the flesh by means of food and drink, for she considered food and drink to be the alpha and the omega, the eros and the thanatos, the first cause and the final cause, and, in brief, the complete encyclopaedic what-not of existence.

'I have brought you a nice steaming tumbler of coffee,' Pati said. The singing master was a nervous man, and his doctor had told him recently that he must cut out coffee to save the lining of his stomach. There was a brief battle for the singing master's soul between the doctor and Leo Company's fragrant mixture of 20 per cent dark roast and 80 per cent pea berry. Leo won. The singing master accepted the coffee, and cooled it by pouring it back and forth between the tumbler and the bowl that came with it.

'We will begin the lesson as soon as I finish the coffee,' the singing master said to Uma. She was sitting on the mat facing him, her music-book open before her, the harmonium whining steadily in her left hand. He was praying for the arrival of that water lorry. He could hear Vaithy upstairs, rattling the bathroom door.

'If you are not out of there in two seconds, I will break down the door!' Vaithy was roaring.

But Kicha did not reply.

∾

Sundar's brother Kicha was the ever-dutiful, Brahmin, first-born son who tirelessly applied himself to the upkeep of the Vaidyanathan family image. Vaidyanathan was Vaithy's proper handle, and Kicha had an official moniker too, which was Krishnamurthi. Kicha had the kind of regular handsomeness that made maamis with eligible daughters sit up and take notice. His hair glistened with Brylcreem, his economy-size chin exuded Old Spice, he had curd-rice in his dental cavities and lime pickle under his fingernails, and he always wore a half-sleeve Hanuman vest under his polyester shirt to protect his armpits. The maamis sighed to themselves, 'Here is a face that has a nine-to-five job, and knows exactly how much its next increment will add up to. Here is a face that has life insurance, and at least one credit card, and mutual funds, and a Bajaj scooter bought on an instalment basis, and a company housing loan, and cumulative education deposits, and a retirement savings plan.' And they got it right on every count. Such a man was universally valued, especially by maamis. Naturally, they set no store by the opinion of Kicha's siblings, which was that Kicha was a fatuous ass, and ought to be banned by the government.

However that may be, it was no use those maamis making a play for Kicha. At the age of twenty-five, after he had got a science degree from Chennai University and settled down to a job in the research and development branch of the Jagadambal Pappadum and Condiments International, he had married a most presentable Brahmin girl called Chitra. Sachu had chosen Chitra out of all the applicants for Kicha's hand because Chitra was doing her MA, and seemed to be crouching, just before the wedding, for that great spring across the ocean to the shores of the You Essay, which as good as made her a green-card bride. But after the wedding, to Sachu's great disappointment, Chitra lost all her ambition and started to make a baby. Instead of her MA thesis, she was brought to bed in due course of a magnum opus whose real name was Vaidyanathan II, but who was called

Raja. He was called Raja because he was the real despot of No. 5 Varadan Street, being as fair as a musk-melon, and as pink as a rose-apple, and as plump as a rasgullah drowned in sugar syrup.

'Shall we begin?' quavered the singing master, for he could hear the fair, plump Raja toddling down the stairs, and Raja did not agree with the lining of his stomach.

It was too late.

'Goo!' said Raja, staggering onto the mat (for he could not walk too steadily yet) and putting a fist into the harmonium. Uma offered him a truck and a teddy bear. This gave Raja a bright idea, and he began to belt the harmonium with the truck, putting plenty of wrist into it, until Chitra came down the stairs and tore the truck from his little fingers.

'Thooothi!' Raja shrieked, reaching for the battered instrument. 'Thooothi!'

As this clamour continued, Thatha came in, thumping his cane on the floor.

'Who is making the precious light of my eye cry? Huh?' he asked.

'Saaaaa,' sang Uma, holding the low sa in a shaky but passable way.

'Besh, besh, excellent,' the singing master said, trying to take the music book away from the precious apple, who now commenced to rip pieces out of it.

Uma moved to the middle of the scale.

'Paaaa,' she bawled. There was very little difference between the sa and the pa, and the singing master looked a little desolate. This was a thankless job, he thought, feeling the ulcers germinating in the lining of his stomach.

'Waaaah!' Raja yelled.

'*Saaaa*,' Uma yowled, blasting her way towards the upper sa. But though Uma's eyes rolled up to the ceiling, and though Uma's chin tilted at a dangerous angle, and though Uma gained a clear inch or two in height in the effort to soar

towards the note, she alighted about two-thirds of an octave
below where she wished to be. Her voice was working like a car
stuck in loose sand. The more she churned the wheels, trying
to dig herself out, the deeper she sank into the rut in the
gamut.

The singing master began to look deranged. 'Good,' he
giggled. '*Very* good. A leetle higher,' he coaxed, crushing the
music book in his hands. He planted his fingertips on the mat
beside him and raised his whole body clean off the floor, in an
agony of supplication and encouragement.

'Try it. You need to push it a *leetle* higher. Saaa!' he
begged, levitating, his whole will, urging Uma up, up, up.

Uma tensed her spine and arched it like a bow, as if she
was finally going to fit the note to it and shoot it off towards
the exact pitch. She took a deep breath.

'Saaa...' she caterwauled, flatter than Jane Fonda's belly.

The singing master's topknot came undone and stuck out
in all directions like spun sugar. His muscles quivered with the
strain. He could smell the idlis steaming in the kitchen. If it
were not for the idlis and the coffee, he would not come here
any more, for he considered Uma's singing a health hazard.

A faraway rumble reached No. 5, Varadan Street.

'The water lorry!' Sachu called, flapping down the stairs in
her housecoat, fa-plap-fa-plap-fa-plap. 'Sundar! *Sun*-dar! Look
at this now! That boy disappears into the bathroom just when
the water lorry arrives!'

'Loy-yi! Loy-yi!' shrieked Raja, taking Uma's chin in his
hand and trying to direct her attention to his own precious
little self.

'Oh, we cannot concentrate any more,' the singing master
gasped, wiping his eyes. 'We will sing just two geethams and we
will stop for today.'

'A little refreshment before you go, Master?' said Pati,
rolling out of the kitchen with a plateful of idlis and chutney.

'Why not?' said the singing master, clearing away the

remains of the music book and the harmonium rapidly. 'An idli served by your hand is like the ambrosia of the gods,' he said, tucking in. Those geethams had a temporary reprieve.

~

The reason people up and down Varadan Street were waiting for the water lorry was that there was no municipal water supply to this boulevard. Varadan Street was in Pallavakkam, which was basically marshland, and for centuries no one wished to live there except the egrets which rode about on the backs of the buffaloes, and the red-wattled lapwings which made their nests in the rushes and dashed about shrieking *Will-you-do-it? Will-you-do-it?* One day, Mr Seshadri heard their clarion call, and he said, 'Why not? Most definitely I will do it.'

The land was very cheap. There were no overheads such as payments to the casual labour Mr Seshadri sometimes employed to break people's kneecaps if they refused to vacate their hovels, or to incendiary professionals, who charged a lot for slum-sanitization programmes. Besides, the best-planned accidents went wrong sometimes. Once or twice it turned out that some of the ordnance Mr Seshadri's arson-engineers used became incontinent, and some children and infirm women became collateral damage. The gendarmerie came along, clinking the old bangles and asking if Mr Seshadri would accompany them to his mother-in-law's house, by which they meant jail, and Mr Seshadri had to develop chest pain in order to satisfy the law. This was when the riff-raff from the slums circulated the patently false rumour that Mr Seshadri ate up poor people and drank babies' blood for his beverage. In fact he was a strict vegetarian, and so queasy that he apologized to soybean nutri-nuggets before he consumed them, and as a rule, in any case, you must never believe anything the slum people say. Mr Seshadri's very expensive American heart specialist, who did his last triple bypass, told me that his heart was as soft as a rotten mango, and in fact closely resembled such an object, pickled, except that the bath it floated in was not brine but Johnny Walker Black Label.

Mr Seshadri considered the whole Pallavakkam proposition to be money in the bank, or at any rate, money in the seams of Mrs Seshadri's mattress, and under Mr Seshadri's garage floor, and in sundry other places where Mr Seshadri chose to secrete the hard-earned moolah that he did not like to share with the government. So Mr Seshadri planted the flag of his Realties and Construction (Budget Developments Section: Highest Quality at Lowest Prices) upon this drowned bog, and before this flag could actually be sucked out of sight by the mud, he put up forty identical buildings, each building consisting of three identical apartments, one on top of the other. Mr Seshadri argued that this was for the especial convenience of those of his prospective buyers who desired to make careers as slum landlords.

'See, sar,' he said to them, steepling his pulpy fingers, 'if you are wanting to do rentals bizness, just you have to cut off the electricity, take out the lightbulbs, and ask the corner cigarette-shop man to tout the tenants for you. Each unit is complete as per family requirements,' here he showed them the plans, 'and it is having living-cum-dining, bedroom, bathroom, kitchen'.

Well, about three years ago, Sundar's mother Sachu got into a mood where nothing would do for her but her family must invest its little all in a pleasant suburban mansion. She had worked ever since she had finished college in the PR department of Seshadri Realties and Construction, and when Mr Seshadri announced the completion of Numbers One to Forty, Varadan Street, instinct told her that she should put in an early bid. But her husband Vaithy thought otherwise.

'There is no municipal water supply,' he pointed out to Mr Seshadri, who kindly gave them a personal tour of No. 5. He happened to be there that morning, schmoozing up business.

You see, while there was no water in the municipal pipes, there was more than a drop or two in the soil, and Mr Seshadri naturally wished to unload all forty buildings before the monsoon set in and the residents started having a sinking feeling when they found out how they would have to buy catamarans or fibreglass rowboats to get from their front doors to the street, and down the street to Taramani Road three-and-a-half kilometres away, where they were sure to find land transport.

In response to Vaithy, Mr Seshadri opened a tap, thrust a cup under it and quaffed the contents. 'Firrst class water,' he said, smacking his lips and slurping his tongue. 'From your own purrsonal well in the backside.'

Vaithy and Sachu believed him, and neglected to drink from the cup themselves. The house had many advantages, after all, as Sachu pointed out. It was quite affordable, and it had three floors. Kicha and his new bride could occupy the second-floor bedroom; Vaithy and Sachu could occupy the first-floor bedroom; and Thatha and Pati, who were finding stairs difficult these days, could take the ground-floor bedroom. All the cooking could be done on the ground floor, and the kitchens on the first and second floors could be used for storage. The upstairs living rooms could be slightly modified to serve as bedrooms for Uma and Sundar.

Having made these careful calculations, Sachu bought the house after all.

The amount of family that could be packed into this house was not seen as an unmixed blessing by all the parties concerned. To be candid, it gave Uma and Sundar a pain in the neck. Kicha alone was responsible for a considerable amount of spondilitis among his siblings, and when you added to him and little Raja the three hundred and thirty-five uncles and aunts and cousins who began to use this house as a motel every time there was a wedding or a funeral in any branch of the clan (for the house did, after all, have three storeys), you can see why

Sundar asked the gods if they would be so kind as to send him to this world, in his next incarnation, in a reed basket which could be discovered floating among the bulrushes; and why Uma dreamt of being cast away on a desert island surrounded by dangerous waters full of man-eating piranha, and keeping company mainly with skunks or even snapping turtles.

Anyway, Sachu invited all the uncles and cousins and aunts to Varadan Street for the housewarming. It was wonderful how freely they offered their criticism of the size of the rooms, the situation of the house, the view from the windows, the distance from the market and the absence of proper facilities. But nothing they said remotely matched the scale, pitch and sharpness of Sachu's own remarks when, after she let the milk boil over ceremonially, she opened the tap to wet her cleaning rag, and found that what Mr Seshadri had drunk with such a show of relish was a vicious brew of bog-mud and salt. It turned out that the water from the purrsonal well would not do to cook in. It would not do to wash clothes in. It would not do to wash the floor with, since it rapidly changed the complexion of the mottled mosaic tiles Sachu was so proud of. Even the basil plant, when it was given this toxin, mutated into something resembling Professor Ram's Tree of Life.

Mr Seshadri's other Budget Development customers were also opening their taps around this time, and the hue and cry they raised was loud enough to bring down the walls of a dozen Jerichos, especially if they were walls Mr Seshadri had put up. They called Mr Seshadri a bloodsucker, which any of his dentists would have told you was a lie, for he had no visible fangs or sucking mechanisms at all. In the end, Mr Rami Reddy, Mr Seshadri's all-round troubleshooter-man, oiled his way across a wing of the Secretariat and greased a few well-chosen palms. As a result, the Municipality agreed to supply water to Varadan Street in water lorries, which were colossal tankers with thick rubber pipes running out of them.

The queue for the water lorry was already complete, three

doors away from Sundar's house, by about 7 o'clock that Sunday morning. Only, at 7 o'clock the queue lacked the human element, for at that point it consisted only of the buckets, brass pitchers, jerry-cans and other utensils of those who planned to collect water from the lorry. As soon as the water lorry's rumble was heard, the human owners of the utensils rushed out to claim their places. Sachu had woken up at 5 o'clock to put in her two big drums, which were almost at the top of the queue. There were only about thirty plastic buckets and three brass pots ahead of her drums. Most of them belonged to Bucket Maami. Nobody knew her real name any more. She was called Bucket Maami because of a combination of wealth, insomnia and lack of scruples. She was able to buy more buckets than anyone else on the street, she was able to line those buckets up at 3.30 a.m., when other hardworking citizens were catching their eight hours, and she had the gall to actually do this every single time the lorry was due.

'Ayyo, ye gods! That Bucket Maami's hundred-and-eight pots and pans are here already!' moaned an irascible neighbour. A coarse young woman at the end of the queue mentioned something about what a dog did among Bucket Maami's mother's genitals. Some of the low people who rented the houses on Varadan Street used some very shameless language when speaking about Bucket Maami, general sentiment in these parts being strong against her, as the neighbours feared that the water would run out before they got their turn at the pipe. Some of them even went so far as to call her Bucket Mayiru to her face, instead of Bucket Maami, and if you do not know what mayiru is, I am not going to tell you. Indeed, people unjustly exaggerated the number of her buckets, for she represented her claim through a mere twenty-three vessels, and very shamefaced these vessels looked too, huddling together like sheep in a storm.

The water lorry-driver deliberately drew up twenty yards away from where everyone was standing. The queue was forced to move, and this caused noisy dispute, because some operators sought to worm their way towards the head of the queue while regrouping. Bucket Maami and Sachu, however, serenely held their places, despite efforts by the vulgar-minded to distract them.

'So, your daughter's singing lesson is going on today?' said Bucket Maami as she filled her sixth bucket. The whole street could hear Uma's barbaric yawps.

'Yes, it is necessary, as you know so well,' said Sachu, referring to the fact that Bucket Maami's daughter had learnt eight geethams from the very same singing master. 'When we were young, the bridegrooms only wanted girls who could cook and keep house. Nowadays, even an ordinary government clerk is demanding talented girls, knowing either singing or Bharata Natyam dance. For an NRI boy or an IAS, the girl has to give at least one concert, and have the photographs ready.' I need hardly tell *you*, dear reader, that an NRI boy is nothing but a Non-Resident Indian and an IAS boy is in the Indian Administrative Service, and that such boys are considered priceless catches by discerning maamis.

'These are difficult times,' said Bucket Maami, with undisguised complacency. Just last month her daughter had snagged an NRI computer engineer worth about half a million ('*Dollars*, Sachu, not rupees,' Bucket Maami had smirked). The fingers with which this boy tied the marriage-knot had that sleek manicured look which never came but to fingers embedded in many profitable Silicon Valley pies. Now this Silicon Valley engineer's fingers had also kept time, on the day he visited Bucket Maami, while her daughter sang those selfsame geethams, eight in number. The very next day Sachu had engaged the singing-master's services and allowed herself to dream.

'What about that alliance your brother-in-law brought

from Bombay, is that working out?' Bucket Maami asked. 'Ayye! Mind what you are doing, you idiot!' This last was addressed to Bucket Maami's emaciated servant-girl, who took away each filled bucket and came running back for the next one, because this servant-girl had slipped in the slush and splashed Bucket Maami's sari.

'No, the boy is having Saturn in the Seventh House. The other horoscope my brother brought is for a boy who failed his dentistry entrance exam three times and is going for veterinary. I cannot give my daughter to a man who is all the time up to his elbow inside a cow's anus,' said Sachu.

'Quite right,' Bucket Maami said.

'So, every Sunday these days, I am looking in the Matrimonial column of *The Bindhu*.'

'Uma is a very clever girl, but somewhat—*wheatish* in complexion,' said Bucket Maami, putting her finger on the nub, not without malice, for her own daughter was whiter than a lab coat. 'Are you trying Fair & Lovely?'

Sachu winced. She herself was fair and had rounded limbs, and what is more, she had a Bosom—not like the apologetic mosquito-bites you saw these days on girls like Uma, but a magnificent escarpment, a continental shelf that made her look as if she wore a double-thickness Kevlar vest, the kind of bosom, in short, in which all the most beauteous actresses of the Seventies rejoiced.

'It is no use, I am buying ten tubes on the discount offer, but my Uma will not take so much as an iota to her skin. You should talk to her. She is *such* a difficult girl,' Sachu sighed. 'You will not believe how troublesome she is, saying she will not do this, she will not do that. Even her singing lessons she hates, and says she has no talent. Imagine that, Maami! If only she was a little pliant...'

'She is not like your Kicha. Kicha is such a fine boy,' said Bucket Maami. 'How is he by the way? Are his injuries healed?'

Two weeks earlier, the second-floor toilet at 5, Varadan

Street had developed a crack right across its floor and, without any warning, had fallen into the first floor toilet. Kicha was sitting upon the second-floor pot, reading *One Hundred Party Jokes* to stimulate his bowels when this happened, and he abruptly found himself one floor below where he expected to be, his trousers still down among his ankles.

'Yes, yes. The doctors say it is a miracle that he is not more severely hurt, because when the bathroom fell down it brought down so many huge bricks, and also pieces of the commode.'

'It is such a disgraceful incident,' said Bucket Maami. 'I told that Seshadri fellow that he should have put more jelly into the earth before he started the foundation of these houses, but you know what he tells me?'

'What?' Sachu asked.

'He says to me, if you put all the garbage and waste from your house into the plot, the soft parts will be filled up in two years. Preposterous! If it had happened to *me*, I would have made my husband file a case. Why shouldn't your husband file a case?'

The way Mr Seshadri had marvelled over it, you would think that the collapse of Kicha's toilet was one of the more baffling mysteries of the world, like the Bermuda Triangle or what happened to the sailors on the *Marie Celeste*. But actually, this was routine behaviour for Seshadri's Budget Developments for the Rupee-Savers. There was a similar subtle subsidence going on under many houses in Varadan Street, and Bucket Maami was quite right to think that Sachu and Vaithy had a legal case. Yet Vaithy did not make a fuss about this incident. This was because investing in this Budget Development was Sachu's idea. Ever since the toilet had collapsed, Vaithy was able to say frequently, 'See what you made me invest our nest-egg in?' which he had never had a chance to do before, for Sachu's decisions were generally unimpeachable.

'Oh *him*!' Sachu snorted. 'My husband is no good at that kind of thing. But make him a union leader and he can fight any boss and ruin his own prospects. Anyhow, Mr Seshadri is *my* boss, and it would be too unwise to fight him.' She shrugged. 'Now we have a daily problem, of course, because there are only two toilets in the house, and you know how it is with the men, they spend all their time sitting in there.'

People failed to realize that the most tragic fallout of this event was not the reduction of No. 5's mod cons by one toilet, or even the multiple abrasions Kicha sustained on his buttocks, but the psychic damage Kicha suffered. He was found wandering among the ruins in a post-traumatic condition, interfering with the workers who were helping to clear away the debris.

'Have you found my book yet?' he asked, again and again. But *One Hundred Party Jokes* was pulverized forever, and Kicha, who never learnt why the chicken crossed the road, was inconsolable.

'I will go and come,' said Bucket Maami at last, filling her final bucket and ignoring the people behind her who were muttering that they were so glad the lauda-ka-bal had collected enough water to keep her unprintable bottom clean, and other maledictions. Bucket Maami looked at the hem of her sari with great distaste, for it was trailing in the grey-green putrefaction created by the overflow from her buckets. It reminded her of the waterlogging Varadan Street would face again, once the rains began.

'I told that Seshadri fellow to put more rubble into the earth,' Bucket Maami grumbled as she receded squelchily with the last bucket. Sachu stepped into the quagmire with her drums. Sundar came out of the house to help. Through the corner of her eye, Sachu watched the singing master climb onto his bicycle and leave.

'Is your father out of the toilet?' Sachu asked.

'Yes,' said Sundar.

'Good, bring the drums in. I must have a look at *The Bindhu.*'

∼

'I have brought you some coffee,' Pati said to Sachu, who had changed out of her wet housecoat and settled down to a close scrutiny of *The Bindhu*'s Sunday supplements.

She skimmed through the news quickly. The Bharatiya Janata Party was coming back to power in Madhya Pradesh; a Hamas activist had been killed by Israeli assassins; a cut-out of the chief minister had fallen down and crushed three sanitation workers. Devi Theatre was showing a new movie called *Raajiyam*. A father from Tirunelveli had placed a big advertisement to contact his missing son. 'Mother Serious, Sculpture OK, All Is Forgiven,' the copy said, and offered a reward for information about this prodigal. A blurred picture was included, and Sachu could not see why any sensible mother would wish to have such a ruffianly specimen back. Sachu glanced at the Next Week's Engagements column to see if Mr Seshadri had been called out to be chief guest at anything. The only thing she saw there was an announcement about Sundar's university, where a statue of Dr Ambedkar was to be unveiled by the vice-chancellor the next day.

Sachu liked to keep up her spiritual evolution by reading the 'Tidbits of Vedic Wisdom' column everyday, because it was written by a famous Chennai thinker called Mr Swaminathan. She often found in it advice relevant to whatever problem occupied her mind at that moment. Today Mr Swaminathan had written thus:

Tidbits of Vedic Wisdom
Follow the divine example

The sanctity attached to the Hindu samskara (or duty) of marriage is nowhere better exemplified than in the relationship between Sri Rama and his consort Sita, who embodied duty, self-control and promo-tion of universal harmony. It should be a matter of great concern that instead of following the ancient and lofty ideals of this divine couple which for thousands of years have helped us to prevent family break-ups, we Hindus are just blindly following in the footsteps of Western culture and misdirecting our energies towards promoting sense-enjoyment, lustful propensities and self-interest, leading to divorces and disintegration of society. As one to whom Manu the Lawgiver has given charge of the household, it is the wife who should stand like a rock, impervious to changing fashions. In my opinion it is still not too late for womanhood to rise up proactively to protect the sanctity of Hindu marriage.

Sachu turned the page. The Sunday 'Matrimonial' column stretched out before her, hundreds of lines of fine print: brides, grooms, mutuals, Jains, Christians, Muslims, Hindus, Tamilians, Marathis, Malayalis, Telugus, a confusing blur of castes, subcastes, sub-subcastes, persons with horoscopes, persons who were willing to send photographs, citizens with five-figure salaries, citizens with six-figure salaries, non-resident Indians, all volunteering to uphold the sanctity of marriage. She took up her fluorescent green marker—her red marker, which produced more auspicious outlines, had gone missing a couple of days earlier—and started to make her shortlist. She became so involved that when little Raja came to her and tried to tear the paper into little shreds, she actually smacked him sharply with her marker, which shocked him so much that he forgot to bawl. Searching was hard labour, until Sachu saw an advertisement that made her throw down the green marker with the finality of one who had found the answer to all her prayers.

Extremely cultured parents of Tamilian Iyer, Vadamal, Rohini boy (the advertisement went), issueless innocent divorcee due to unavoidable circumstances, 32/160, looks younger, studying for a PhD abroad, expecting six-figure salary shortly, teetotaller, strict vegetarian (no onions or garlic), seek non-Koundinyasa, convent-educated, domestically trained, graduate, musically talented, unencumbered, innocent Brahmin girl from decent, cultured family, no specs, widows and divorcees please excuse; and for his sister, Bharani, 23/158, studying abroad, a strict vegetarian (no onions or garlic), broadminded, highly educated, Brahmin boy from decent family, clean habits, good prospects. Early marriage as both children returning abroad shortly. **Mutual preferred**. Decent, highly culture-conscious families of same subsect please respond with biodatas, family details, photos and horoscopes, to Box No. 12978/4, *The Bindhu*. Advertisement for selection only. Serious parties only may contact Phone No. 8692233.

Sachu marvelled at the length of the advertisement, for each word was worth its weight in gold in the Sunday edition of *The Bindhu*. She was especially struck that the advertisers had thrown away coin of the realm on so much repetition of the words 'decent' and 'cultured'. It suggested an admirable squeamishness. For a second Sachu wondered if five geethams, which made up Uma's repertoire as of now, could legitimately be construed as 'culture'. But this thought was driven out by the thought that the advertisers had plenty of money to splash around, which was certainly going to be very advantageous for the family that made an alliance with them. It was also most convenient that it was a mutual offer: for after Uma was married Sachu would have to start worrying about Sundar, unless they were married at the same time. Besides, when two siblings married two other siblings, it allowed quite a bit of negotiation. What you lost on the swings—on your daughter's dowry and wedding expenses, that is—you gained on the roundabouts—that is, when you collected the same for your son. Thus Sachu reasoned, but in truth she had a deeper reason for being attracted to this advertisement.

Deep in her heart Sachu felt that the most delicious thing about this offer was that the bride and groom were already studying abroad. Sachu's nephews were all slogging away at engineering or dentistry, with one eye fixed steadily on their

favourite uncle, who was none other than Uncle Sam. Then
one day the cry would go out, 'Ramki (or Pattu or Ambi) is off
to Chicago!' And there were the mothers—Sachu's sisters-in-
law and cousins—buying thermal underwear at Punjab Hosiery
Depot and pressure-cookers and idli-plates from Saravana Steel
and Appliances, and there was Ramki (or Pattu or Ambi)
broiling in the serpentine queue outside the American consulate,
saying to the emerald-green fluttering dollar, 'Wait for me, I
am coming!' and two months later, there was Ramki (or Ambi
or Pattu) at the airport clutching his visa and the six bottles of
pickle that his Gomathi Maami had thrust into his hands at the
last minute, and then he really was off! And there was the news,
five years later, that Ramki had wangled his green card, and
there was the NRI bride, and the wedding at the Chicago
temple to which the three hundred and thirty-five could not
go, and there were the pictures, which came thick and fast, of
Ramki's car, and Ramki's cawndo, and Ramki's dawg, and
Ramki's bride's Bharata Natyam factory in Chicago, proudly
displayed on the international Family Website, and then... and
then... (this was where Sachu's eyes glowed with covetousness)
and then there was the Pregnancy, at which point Ramki's
mother got on that gravy plane and flew over the oceans for a
long stay that was sometimes parlayed into another green card.
Oh perfection! Sachu had no access to good fortune of this
kind yet, but if this alliance worked out, she thought, if this
alliance just worked out...

Sachu called a family conference immediately.

One and all politely expressed their regrets, on the grounds
that other pressing matters such as unavoidable circumstances
prevented them from attending this conference. But once
Sachu had made up her mind about something, it was almost
impossible to deflect her. Slowly, resentfully, mutinously,
regretfully, Sundar put down the latest Harry Potter novel,
Uma switched off the stove on which she was making pulao,
Thatha spat out his betel leaf, Pati turned off the TV which was

showing a rerun of the *Ramayana*, Vaithy stubbed out his cigarette, Chitra put Raja, who was asleep, into his crib, and Kicha tore himself away from *More Party Jokes for All Occasions*. They straggled into the hall on reluctant feet.

~

Sachu addressed them as follows:

'All of us are aware that Uma is twenty-seven, and it is my deepest desire to see her married.'

'But I do not *want* to be married,' Uma said, scowling.

'Uma, you are not a sprout that came out of the sod just yesterday,' Sachu retorted. 'The longer you wait, the less chance you will have of marrying a decent boy with good prospects. It is not as if you are the Beauty of the Three Worlds, you know.'

'Yes, I know that, but twenty-seven is not ancient or anything, and I feel that I might meet someone who will like me, and whom I will like—'

'That kind of thing happens only in the cinema, and it is not going to happen in this family.'

'Why not?'

'Because I will not have you bringing home some dubious boy that you pick up from the gutter! We are respectable people, we are Brahmins, we have a tradition, and we have to maintain it! Now listen to this,' said Sachu.

She read them the advertisement.

'The best thing is that it is mutual,' said Sachu. 'And think, you will both be able to go abroad.'

'*Me?*' Sundar yelped. Until this moment he was not aware that he was in any way directly concerned in this conference.

'Yes, you, Sundar. Oh, I know boys your age, and the urges you have. Believe me, you will be very happy once you settle down. Look at Kicha.'

Sundar felt he would much rather not look at Kicha, especially at a moment as fraught as this one.

'But I can't marry now!' he gasped. 'I have—' He nearly said, 'I have fallen in love with a beautiful woman,' but he stopped himself, because it occurred to him that he barely knew her name, and that she certainly did not even know he existed. So he said instead, 'I have just started work on my Ph.D!'

'I can't marry now either,' said Uma. 'I'm happy with my job.'

'Oh, what will I do with such a pair of quarrelsome whelps—why can't you be like Kicha here?'

'Now, let me give you some advice,' Kicha began, for he was ever ready to do his bit for the good of the family. 'As the eldest son of this family it is my duty to see that you are both decently—'

'Oh *cork up*, Kicha,' Sundar muttered in an undertone.

'*Shut up*, Kicha,' Uma snapped, quite audibly.

Kicha looked very hurt.

'You see how they have gone wild?' Sachu said to no one in particular. 'You see how they swear in front of their elders? If you have the slightest respect for age, you will listen—don't listen to me, at least listen to your Thatha,' Sachu said. Her bosom was heaving like an ocean liner in a storm.

'Thatha?' Sachu prompted Thatha, who seemed to have missed his cue.

'What? Oh. Ahem. You two—um—you two must listen to your mother,' Thatha said vaguely to Sundar and Uma. 'Now, Sachu, you don't get um—upset,' he said.

Sachu's sigh of weary reasonableness was so gusty it knocked over Bucket Maami's ornamental jasmine bush two doors away. '*Upset*? Why should anyone care if I am upset? No, I'm not upset. Don't worry about *me*.'

'Er, I must go now.' Thatha edged away, for even an indifferent meteorologist such as himself could see the cumulonimbus gathering on Sachu's brow. 'Call of nature,' he said, diving for cover. Vaithy, Sundar and Uma watched his exit with narrowed eyes.

'Shall I make some more idlis?' Pati asked, for she believed that food would fill any breach. But Sachu did not want distractions. The end of her sari had come into her hands, which was a sign that condensation point had been reached. Soon after her marriage to Vaithy, Sachu had modified her physiology so that all her excretory functions were performed, like Niobe's, by her tear glands. As a consequence she was generally able to weep copiously whenever she wished, and when she was not weeping she went about wreathed in thick and contagious fogs.

'Your crying now is self-contradictory,' her husband, the ruthless logician, put in. 'You just said you were not upset.'

'*Not* upset? How can I *not* be upset? After all the years and years I have spent slaving for you all, and denying myself, cooking and cleaning, giving up my time, never—'

'Yes, we are very grateful, Ma—' Uma cut in.

'—taking the smallest step without thinking, how is this going to benefit my family? My children? Praying in every temple I see, breaking a dozen coconuts a week, trying to inculcate some values into these children who all admire their father too much to know the meaning of their own religion! A father who encourages the boys to refuse even the sacred thread ceremony—what will my relations think?'

'But *I* did not listen to him, did I, Ma?' Kicha piped up. One of the reasons he caused cervical anguish was that he liked reminding people how he was keeping up the family honour.

'No, Kicha, you did not, but that boy Sundar—! If these people ask me, does he have a poonal, is he a properly initiated Brahmin boy, what will I tell them?'

'You can tell them no, he does not need it, because all a sacred thread is good for is to scratch the gutter of your bum, and that is very unhygienic,' Vaithy observed.

'Listen to him!' Sachu cried, turning to Pati.

'He is just tired and hungry,' Pati said. 'Vaithy, the pressure-cooker is cooling, and the idlis are soft and fluffy. Let's all eat first and continue this discussion afterwards.'

Sachu ground her teeth. If these were her supporters, what need had she of opponents? 'Do what you like, children, I don't want any say in your lives, I will just go away somewhere, I don't know where, where I will find one soul who can appreciate me—'

'Oh calm down, Sachu,' said Vaithy, injudiciously lighting a cigarette to keep his own nerves steady.

'Calm down? *Calm down*! You are a fine one to talk. Running away when you were his age to join the Naxalites, instead of fulfilling your obligations to your family. If your uncle had not gone after you and brought you back you'd be an encounter-death statistic by now!'

'Look, we have a packet of murukkus. They need to be eaten up before they go stale—'

Sundar gaped in astonishment. He knew that Vaithy had toyed with the idea of becoming a barefoot doctor in the early Seventies, but had to give it up because he had failed the medical entrance examination, and Thatha had said if he did not get a job or at any rate a wife, and settle down, he was going to knock him flatter than a paper-roast. Besides, after practising going barefoot for a while, Vaithy had developed corns, spurs and carbuncles in his feet and had begun to feel he was not cut out for this vocation. This was how Vaithy had become a cog in the wheel of Jagadambal Pappadum and Condiments International. But Sundar did not remember hearing about this enterprising desire to join the Naxalite rebels before.

'Did you really join the Naxalites, Appa?' Sundar asked.

'No,' said Vaithy simply. 'I went looking for them in the forest, but I could not find them. The Naxalites were not hanging about waiting for people to join them, Karl.'

'Karl!' Sachu exploded. 'What is this Karl-Karl? His name is Kalyanasundaram, and I do not like to hear my father's name sullied!' Sundar was named for Sachu's father, according to tradition. 'And he is not any communist fellow with lice in his unwashed beard, to be called Karl-Karl. At least I hope he will not be like his father, ruining his career by sticking his nose into every dharna and picket of the Pappadum Employees Union!'

It must be put on record that Kicha had collared the Jagadambal job not through nepotism, but purely through personal merit and solid virtues. True, his father was already an employee of this august organization, but this was no advantage to Kicha, because Vaithy was a leading light in every ruckus that the labour kicked up against the management.

'I am merely doing what I think is right,' said Vaithy, warmly.

'What is right about it, tell me? All your age-mates are climbing the ladder and you are stuck on the bottom rung! It is a miracle you are not sacked yet!'

'But I may soon be,' said Vaithy. 'Now that Jagadambal Pappadum has signed the contract with Nestlé, it is becoming too multinational for me. All my bloody ladder-climbing colleagues are getting brand-new tax-defeating perks. I may go in for the golden handshake.'

'Yes,' Sachu shouted, very excited by now. 'Go ahead! Ruin us! All you will have to show for years of service will be a Pillayar medallion mounted on Formica and a broken-down HMT watch!'

'They will also put our pictures in *Jagadambal's Journal*, the in-house magazine,' said Vaithy. 'Right next to the picture of Mrs Sadasivam handing out the tiffin-boxes to the winners of the Potato-and-Spoon race!'

Sundar felt an insane desire to laugh.

'And now,' Sachu raged. She stretched out a forefinger and tapped it down hard on the table with every word she spoke. '*Now* you must be difficult, just when we need the money most to get these children married! I have consulted the computer astrologer, and he says if we do not seize this chance, there will not be another auspicious time for a marriage in this family for five years!'

'I cannot understand this new craze for money-grabbing charlatans who bring together superstition and artificial intelligence.' Vaithy blew out a most provocative smoke-ring.

'This astrologer is very good. He practically fixed up Bucket Maami's daughter not more than two months ago! Oh, what is the good of your sitting here, being cynical about everything? I don't know why you make the pretence of contributing to this conversation, you may as well just go right up to your room and watch those wrestlers you are so fond of—'

Vaithy remembered that there was a World Wrestling Entertainment show on TV, and he got up to go upstairs and catch it, for there was nothing he liked to watch so much as the women mud-wrestlers on WWE.

'Sit down right there!' Sachu cried. 'And in Heaven's name, don't light up another cigarette! You sit there like a zamindar, smoking, smoking, smoking, while I am here, slaving away trying to din a little sense into your wayward children! You might use your breath to better effect than to cloud up the room with that noxious fug—you might consider that what I am saying is for their good, give them some advice—'

'Excuse me. It is not logical to say they can do what they like and then to say they must take your advice,' said Vaithy.

'Logical-illogical, what do I know about it?' Sachu cried. 'I leave all the coldness and cleverness to you men. Women know only love and devotion.' She began to sigh like the monsoon tearing up the rain forest over the Western Ghats. 'And yet you don't seem to feel that all my devotion to your interests deserves anything in return! My feelings don't count, nothing counts, all the things I have done all these years to keep this family going, the sacrifices I have made, the—'

'Come on, Ma—'

'We never said—'

'I know what you need, you need some buttermilk, shall I make—'

'—illnesses I have nursed you through, the career I have

given up to do all this—others, others, others, never a thought for myself, no, not even enough time, some days, to mend the holes in my petticoats, the things I have done to keep you happy—and yet all of you hate me! You have always joined forces against me! You think I am only fit for drudgery and that you are all clever people who can despise everything I stand for, tradition, God, family—oh, I don't know why I stay alive at all—' and with this Sachu began to climb the stairs in the particular way that was familiar to her audience. For she climbed with the tread of one who was about to Do Away With Herself.

Two or three times a week Sachu went to the roof-terrace and stood by the wall, sometimes merely to see if it was true that Mrs Murali next door was carrying on with the iron-box man, or to see if the Hameed family, whose menfolk were in the Gulf, had actually installed its new dish antenna yet. At other times it was to throw herself off the roof because of annoyances caused by some member of her family. But always, so far, she had desisted at the last minute and given her family a chance to redeem itself, especially when she reflected that there was simply no dignity in falling, even to one's death, into gloopy muck that looked like engine grease and smelt like throw-up.

'Let her go,' Vaithy muttered. 'She will just stick in the bog-mud anyway.' But he did not mutter this loud enough for her to hear.

Uma and Sundar gave each other resigned looks and followed their mother up the stairs. They were feeling very worn out, and it was fortunate that Sachu's desire for extinction was not so acute that she hurried up the stairs.

By the time they reached the first-floor landing, Uma had made some calculations: 'I don't want to get stuck with a frightful bore. Or worse still, a man who will tell me, when I join him abroad, that he already has a white girlfriend. I don't like housework much, and the people who placed this ad sound like people who want a cook-and-bottle-washer. No, it just isn't possible.'

By the second-floor landing, she was saying in her head, 'But I am going to have to get married some time. You must either join the Naxalites and disappear into the jungles forever or marry and live like ordinary people. You must not do one thing and hanker for the other, and take your frustration out on everybody around you. That is what I think, anyway, though I love Appa. Then again, each time a proposal comes, it will be an action-replay of this same horrible scene. Amma crying, Appa saying mean things, me not knowing what to do. And Amma does work very hard, both in the office and at home, while Appa reads the newspaper and explains wrestling holds to the WWE women. I really ought to make her happy. Say yes, then? If I don't like the man, I can always cry off later.'

And by the time they reached the third landing, Uma was saying to herself, 'Besides, it may be pleasant to go abroad. At least, I won't have to live near Kicha any more. And yes, if I say yes, and this match is fixed, the poor singing master can stop coming here, and much suffering will be alleviated.'

Maybe the last was what really clinched it, for the day which dismissed the music master would be the happiest day of Uma's life.

Sachu drew the terrace door-latch and passed out onto the roof, cursing herself for not having the forethought to put on her slippers. She hoped the scene would not have to be drawn out, for the terrace floor felt like lighted matchsticks under her toes. She went purposefully towards the low parapet wall. Just as she prepared to take the fatal plunge, Uma said, 'Okay, Ma, I'll agree to see him and let him see me. But I won't wear a silk sari and I won't keep serving him murukkus and coffee, mind. I mean it. And I won't, won't, *won't* sing.'

Sachu turned around with a martyred smile. 'I knew that without their father's influence my children would come to a sensible decision.' She trotted across the hot terrace. 'Now

Sundar, you just need to agree so that your sister can be made happy.'

All the way up the stairs Sundar had been composing a speech in his head. It was meant to quell his mother completely, and it went like this: 'Do you know that in my Eng. Lit. courses I read about adventuring heroes who choose their own destinies? Do you know I have just finished reading *Jane Eyre*? Do you know that all over the world there are people who think choosing for themselves is perfectly normal, especially in the matter of a wife or husband? Do you know how absurd it seems to me that you should be arranging my life for me in this way?'

But now he merely said, 'Huh?' For he was flummoxed and flabbergasted, not to mention staggered and knocked end-over-heels, by Uma's capitulation.

'That's settled, then,' said Sachu briskly, turning to go downstairs again. Their ears were beginning to smoke in the noonday heat. Uma followed her down. Sundar followed Uma. Uma did not meet his eyes this time, and Sundar did not get a chance to ask her cuttingly, as he meant to: 'So is this the Uma who has read every Modesty Blaise novel forwards and backwards fourteen times, tried to fashion a kongo out of old door-knobs and vowed death to all unequal gender practices? Pshaw!' He had always yearned to use this ejaculation, encountered so far only in books. 'Pshaw. Not to mention pthoo and pcheee.'

'I will phone this number given in the paper right away.' Sachu took the stairs down two at a time.

Ten minutes later, Sachu poked Vaithy in the shoulder as he watched a blonde female mud-wrestler sitting on a brunette female mud-wrestler's bosom and banging her (the brunette's) head into the muck. He was not exactly the best witness to her triumph, especially in this mood. In this mood, when he wished to block out the world, he put on his scooter helmet and kept his eyes glued to the screen with special concentration, since the helmet restricted his hearing. But Thatha had gone to sleep, and Kicha had gone over to see a friend. So Vaithy, Sachu decided, would have to be the first recipient of her momentous news.

'It is all fixed up,' Sachu said, gloating.

'Hmm, what?' said Vaithy, lifting the helmet free of his ears.

'The meeting is fixed up. The bride-seeing. The family is coming here tomorrow itself to see Uma and Sundar. In the evening. You should come home early.' She giggled a little. 'They seemed very impressed with the way I presented our case.'

Her triumphant smile was as big as a banana.

In which Various People pursue Learning at Chennai University

ON MONDAY MORNING, Sundar popped out of the bus at Anna Square like a bean from a pod and sucked in a long, shuddering, snoutful of air. He had been obliged to travel nose-by-armpit with several stale citizens who had dangled from the straps, and who had not invested in Appadurai's Armpit Allure. Sundar needed air badly because he was feeling very dull-witted this morning, what with tossing about in bed all Sunday night, mulling over what a strange thing Love was, and worrying about the matrimonial fix his mother had put him in, and agonizing about what he would say to Jiva when Akilan introduced him to her this morning. The last problem nagged him so much that he had studied an article in *Debonair* called 'Fantastic Opening Lines that the Stars Use to Fascinate Women', and he had by heart many gambits such as 'Excuse me, you have a very interesting energy', or 'Excuse me, I couldn't help noticing your tattoo', or even 'I'm not very familiar with Mexican cuisine, can you recommend something?' though he was not entirely clear how he was going to pilot Jiva into a place where there was Mexican cuisine.

'What an idiot I am,' Sundar thought as he walked through the huge double doors of Chennai University's main lobby. 'I should have found out from Akilan where I could find Jiva. If that bugger doesn't show up, I may not find her today. Maybe I won't find her ever. I will never, never see her again—' He was interrupted in these morbid thoughts by the babbling of many voices. The lobby, normally a quiet spot, was crawling with bodies. There were photographers from *The Bindhu* ordering people to say cheese, and a video man making a video film, and people falling over left-right-and-centre, for they tended to forget that the video man's cable was snaking around between their feet.

'Yesterday was a very special day,' Dr Mohan, the vice-chancellor, was saying into a microphone, 'because it was 14 April, the birthday of the Father of the Indian Constitution'.

In the wall behind the V-C was a niche which had once housed a statue of Victoria Regina, Empress of India. In the early decades of the twentieth century, Chennai's best and brightest, including Professor Ram's own grandfather, had made their bones in the freedom movement by adding moustaches to the royal upper lip and muttonchop whiskers to the royal jowl. By 1940, though Tiptop Bandbox had a standing contract to clean the Empress's soapstone phiz with detergent and caustic, she never lost that five-o'-clock shadow. When the sun finally set on the British empire, the Empress was auctioned, and a half-blind, old dressmaker in Armenian Street bought her for a mannequin, though he had to close down his establishment soon afterwards. Although, from time to time, someone had proposed putting another statue in the niche, nothing had been done, and it had stood empty for many decades.

Today, this niche appeared to have an occupant, for Sundar could see in it a shape covered by a silk cloth. Around the V-C stood half a dozen drummers, young men and women, holding their drumsticks poised over their cow-skin thappus.

'We at Chennai University are celebrating this special day,' the V-C continued, 'by unveiling this image of a great thinker and son of India. It stands very appropriately in the lobby, facing the stairs which all our students take to go to their classrooms.' There was a big round of clapping. The cameras flashed, and a professor tripped over the video cable, and the professor's handbag flew open and sprayed its contents all around.

'There goes Laurentia's handbag again,' Always Already whispered, for she was among those present, looking exceedingly photogenic. Indeed, the video man could not decide whether to focus on her or on the large and handsome white girl who was drifting around with a micro-cassette recorder, asking the thappu drummers questions. Some students helped to pick up a duster, an apple core, half-a-dozen broken ballpoint pens, a chocolate wrapper, a novel by Toni Morrison, a number of bills, some marker pens, a small paperweight and a handful of coins.

'Thank you,' said the professor, when these paraphernalia were restored to her. She spoke wearily, as if her bag misbehaved two or three times a day. 'There is something wrong with the clasp.'

The V-C waited a few seconds for the disturbance to die down.

'I wish,' he resumed, 'to thank many people for contributing to this cause: Dr Laurentia Wesley Arul, who personally paid a large proportion of the cost of sculpting and transporting this statue; S. Akilan for creating this very expressive sculpture; the members of the Thappu Artists Association for performing appropiate music; and the Campus Beautification Committee, in which you all know I have a great interest, for making this a part of the campus improvement scheme.'

With this he turned to the silk cloth and whipped it smartly off the statue, and there was Dr Ambedkar cast in bronze, sitting quietly on a rough granite pedestal, and reading from a bronze book in his hand. The title of the book was *Annihilation of Caste* and the book had fallen open on a page with the following text:

You cannot build anything on the foundation of caste.
You cannot build up a nation, you cannot build up a
morality. Anything that you build on the foundation
of caste will crack and will never be whole.

The photographers took pictures of the V-C shaking
Akilan's hand, and of Professor Arul standing beside the statue
clutching her handbag as if it was a weapon of mass destruction,
and of the thappu players with their drums. The video man
missed all this action because a professor who had just come in
tripped over the cable and knocked the video man right out of
his loafers, and all the parties had to go through all their
movements again. Then the thappu players began to strike
their drums, moving their legs in a light dance as they tapped
out the patterns, sometimes slow and sometimes fast, and
many citizens were so stirred by this music that they nodded
and stamped and explored the concept of syncopation.

Now, the professor who had just come in and got tangled
up in the cable was Professor Ram, and he really ought not to
have been so astonished by the commotion. He had received
the circular, saying that this statue was to be unveiled, which
the V-C had sent around the university. But Professor Ram's
memory had refused to retain this information. This was
because Professor Ram disapproved strongly of Dr Ambedkar.
He had campaigned for many years to consecrate the niche to
some worthier image. He felt that Dr Ambedkar could not
hold a candle to Sri Rama, who was his own favourite all-
purpose divinity, or to Saraswati, who was the education
goddess.

Professor Ram toddled towards the stairs, barely nodding
to the V-C, and taking great care not to brush against any of
the other people in the lobby. Now Professor Ram was as broad
in the mind as he was in the beam, and discriminated against
no one, especially when they knew their place, and in fact was
so opposed to invidious social distinctions that he thought
casteists were people who worked in plaster-of-paris, and *racists*

were people who studied equestrian form. It was merely that he was a martyr to ticklishness. Whenever he was in danger of rubbing up against people from certain social backgrounds, this condition was exacerbated. Moreover, many of these people were supporters of the Reservations Policy, which Professor Ram hated and deplored, and rubbing up against such people felt no different to Professor Ram from rubbing up against a jellyfish on one side and an electric eel on the other.

As Professor Ram reached the foot of the stairs, he was very disturbed to see Sundar hanging vacantly over the banisters, scanning the crowd, and apparently enjoying what Professor Ram considered nothing but savage rites and devil worship.

'Meet me at 12.20 sharp, Sundar,' Professor Ram roared into Sundar's left ear.

'Yes, sir,' Sundar said absently, for he had just spotted Jiva in a corner talking to Dr Arul and the tall white girl, and his heart was making striking experiments in percussion. He shouldered his way through the masses to reach that spot, but when he got there, Jiva had vanished.

'You'll probably find her in the canteen, Sundar,' said Dr Arul. So Sundar made his way to the canteen.

Now, dear reader, no doubt you wish to follow Sundar to see if he made any progress on the Jiva angle. But if you will bear with me for a moment, we will track Professor Ram's movements as he takes the two flights of stairs at a terrific clip and rushes down the corridor to the English department. He was rushing thus because the sound of the drums was putting him on the rack. Outside his office he overtook his colleague, Professor Nagarajan, who was shuffling along with his palms pressed over his ears, for *his* suffering was, if anything, even more acute than Professsor Ram's.

'Can you believe what this university has come to?' Professor Nagarajan cried hoarsely.

'It is an abomination! Just another instance of that studied low-caste insolence,' Professor Ram replied, and the sound you could hear over the drumming, like a pair of hedgehogs making love in a tin trunk, was the sound of Professor Ram's upper molars grinding against Professor Ram's lower ones. All the annoyance Professor Ram had endured from the lower orders of society over the years had resulted in his gnashing his own pappadum-crunchers to a powder, and so at this date he had nothing in his mouth but pottery, though it was pottery that cost 3,000 rupees per unit.

'They were tightening the drums over a fire outside the library, Ram, when I came in this morning! Siva-Siva!' He pinched his nose between thumb and forefinger. 'We are breathing the pollution of smoked cow-skin!'

'What can you expect, Nagarajan? It is the low-caste mentality! The pariah aggressiveness! Everyone is writing about the atrocities committed on Harijans, but do you ever hear in the press about an event like this, when the whole university is filled with the inauspicious sound of funeral drums?' Professor Ram lowered his voice. 'How can Dr Mohan even allow it, thappu drums in the halls of academe?'

'I asked him about it, and he said that this group uses the thappu for protest music. As if that is an excuse!' bleated Professor Nagarajan, screwing up his weaselly face and shaking his head mournfully.

'It is all the fault of that Arul woman, for starting this Ambedkar statue business. It is going to become a cult, mark my words, Nagarajan. What right have these people to bring their private icons and idols into the university's premises? If you had held the fort when I was gone... no, it is too late. Laurentia has single-handedly lowered all the standards we set up, and now that she has developed a following of all these third-rate people who are squeezed into the university by the Reservations Policy, we can do nothing to dislodge her.'

'Oh Ram, now that you mention the Reservations Policy, I remember, I need to talk to you urgently, as it were. Could you, in a manner of speaking, spare me five minutes?'

'Come into my office, my dear Nagarajan, and take a seat. I just need a minute to do my early morning pujai, and then I am at your disposal. Shut the door quickly, and let us try to drown out these polluting sound waves.'

All the branches of the Hindu pantheon had sent their representatives to beam diverse blessings at Professor Ram from the walls of his office. Professor Ram certainly deserved these blessings, for he not only made sure that Shastri wiped all these gilt-framed pictures of Sri Rama and Saraswati and Lakshmi and Krishna, but he personally, with his own hands, decorated them with garlands of sandal-paste pellets, and calmed them down with aromatic essences every morning, so that his office was always full of the pleasant odour of sanctity.

While Professor Ram lit up his incense-stick, Professor Nagarajan let his eyes wander around the office. They passed over the plaques and framed certificates on the walls that said 'Professor Ram Pulls It Off Again', and 'Professor Ram: The Greatest President of the TamBrahmAss', and came to rest on the press cutting that was captioned 'The Inimitable Professor Ram', which showed him shaking hands with the chief minister. Taped to the glass over this press cutting was a sheet of paper, and Professor Nagarajan slipped on his reading glasses and went over to take a closer look. He read a message on it which went:

Proffesor Rams peenis is like a saltfish. It stinks becoz of too much masstubation. I bet you are thinking who wrote this? Ha Ha.

'What is it, Nagarajan?' Professor Ram asked, coming up behind his colleague.

'Oh, nothing. Some ignorant fool's idea of a joke, no doubt,' said Professor Nagarajan, whipping off his glasses and polishing them vigorously.

Professor Ram read the message. Hot blood boiled up into his face so fast he nearly lost his eyebrows. He tore the sheet from the glass and crumpled it fiercely in his hands.

'For another 4,27,000 years, it will be Kaliyuga, my friend,' said Professor Ram, and his voice was full of woe. 'The Age of Darkness and Iniquity. The Reservations Policy is merely one more sign of the times.'

~

Perhaps you do not know how the Reservations Policy is rocking the foundations of civilization in hotbeds of educational intrigue like Chennai University. Well, if you were in any of Professor Ram's classes, you would have noticed the special teaching methods he used for students like Rufus and Thamarai Selvi, such as throwing their papers out of the classroom window, calling them names like dolt and nincompoop, which were not in the attendance register, failing them in every examination, giving them his sincere blessing when they dropped out of the course, and treating them at all times as if they stood no higher than vermin in the evolutionary order. Some critics had quite a beef about this, and they alleged that Professor Ram treated these students in this manner because they came from backwater towns like Dindigul or Palayankottai, and had Christian names and non-Brahmin surnames, and were the same colour as soya-sauce. But you, being fair-minded, would not, I am sure, have made any judgements on this issue before you heard from Professor Ram.

Professor Ram always pointed out how students like Rufus and Thamarai Selvi came to the university without fully brushing the straw out of their hair. Naturally—Professor Ram said— they had no understanding of the finer nuances of English grammar. Nor did they show an aptitude for Sanskrit poetics. They had an incorrigible attitude to diphthongs, and could by no means be given speaking parts in the annual play. And yet (Professor Ram often complained) these students got into the university in spite of having lower marks than many Brahmin students. What was it that allowed them to do this? Dear reader, in a word: *the Reservations Policy*, which set apart a certain number of seats for students who belonged to certain castes. It was clear as anything to Professor Ram that the pendulum of political reaction, as he called it, had swung too far in the pro-low-caste direction. It was heart-rending, Professor Ram said, how the Reservations Policy was just snatching the curd-rice and mango pickle from the mouths of twice-born boys, especially Brahmins.

Now the government described the Reservations Policy as a kind of positive discrimination that favoured hitherto *downtrodden* minorities and castes. A great many misguided people, such as the Subaltern Historians, thought that being *downtrodden* was the experience of many of the sons and daughters of Mother India, and that this happened when the heel of some powerful and vicious party on top of the pile came down heavily on the neck of a helpless party at the bottom of the pile. But it was patent to Professor Ram, and to all the top-notch, top-caste historians like Drs Iyer, Iyengar, Chaturvedi, Namboodiri, Trivedi, Shastri and Pandit, that at least since the 1960s, the boot was on the other foot. These eminent thinkers pointed out that a certain reverse troddenness—or '*trodditude*', as Dr Chaturvedi preferred to put it—had come into being, whereby those people, such as the parayar, at the very bottom of the caste hierachy, had manoeuvred their persons into a position from which they were able to apply the foot-leather to those people, such as the Brahmins, at the summit of the pile. As Iyer et al (1991) have observed, the 'so-called scheduled castes *stomp with an upward motion* and grind the upper castes into the stratosphere *with an unprecedented gravity-defying aggression*, a phenomenon to which we may apply the term "*uptroddenness*". The lower orders in general being uncontrolled breeders, the numbers of feet all pressing upwards against *the depleted Brahmin ranks* are, literally, legion, and the consequences of this, when one factors in toe-jam, and the nearly solid pall of atmospheric pollution over every major metropolis which offers an increasingly effective surface to stomp the victims *against*, are, as may easily be imagined, *devastating*' (emphasis mine). Some of the individuals at the very apex of the pile, like Sachu's nephew Ramki, felt very suffocated and *up-pressed* indeed (to use a term that Dr Chaturvedi has recently coined), so much so that they retreated to realms ever more rarefied and cultural, or sought the blessings of the greenbacks goddess in the land where the silicon chip lived cheek-by-jowl with the potato chip, or in any other place where the dollar was considered legal tender, for the dollar was one of the few poultices that effectively stopped the pain of uptroddenness. This was forcing, as Shastri, Shastri and Rao (1995) put it, 'the Westward flight of *genuine talent and intellect* that is so characteristic a feature of our times'.

If you are still with me, dear reader, you will grant that Professor Ram's wrath was righteous. But you probably wish to know if it was based purely on abstract and theoretical considerations.

Not at all.

Professor Ram's decision to clean up the mean corridors of academe was really the fruit of many harrowing practical experiences. Take the case of Dr Ariyanayagam, a backward-caste professor who had been at the university almost since the Dark Ages and was still a force on these premises right through the Eighties. It came about that a young and idealistic Ram was walking around the campus with Dr Ariyanayagam one summer morning in 1986, after explicating to his class a poem whose name I must look up, though I think it was something like *Intimidations of Immortality*. Dr Ariyanayagam was swinging his cane jauntily, despite being longer in the tooth than Peking Man, and a mere professor emeritus at that. Suddenly, Professor Ram saw a flower beside the path that he had never before seen on the Chennai University campus. He was passionately interested in plants of all kinds, especially since he had done his

Ph.D. on Herbaceous Borders as a Metaphor in Romantic Poetry, which made him one of the first eco-critics in the universe.

'*Gloriosa Superba!*' cried Professor Ram, pointing to this flower, in a transport, his heart completely clogged up with thoughts that lay too deep for tears. 'To me the meanest flower that blows—'

'Ha! Got it!' Dr Ariyanayagam exclaimed, as, before Professor Ram's horror-stricken eyes, he lashed out gratuitously with his cane and decapitated the bloom. That was the last time anyone saw this plant flower, for it sank into a despondency, or a consumption, or maybe a quinsy, and by gradual degrees passed clean away.

Professor Ram told Dr Ariyanayagam what he had done, but Dr Ariyanayagam was unrepentant. As for apologizing to the flower or expiating his crime by giving away a cow or feeding seven deserving Brahmins, he would not even hear of it. So naturally Professor Ram was confirmed in his poor opinion of backward-caste professors like Dr Ariyanayagam. In fact, after this, he developed a dislike for Dr Ariyanayagam that hardened into an immune reaction, and by and by he became so severely allergic to all backward-caste professors, and to all low-caste people, and to all their non-vegetarian sympathizers, and to everyone except Brahmins, and more specifically, Brahmins who were his family and friends, that he could not spend a minute in the same room as any of these allergens without coming out in hives and rashes and psoriasis and what-else, and his family and friends had to start a trust fund to keep him in antihistamines. And when the Mandal Commission pronounced, in the 1990s, that there should be more reservations in certain jobs for the backward castes, Professor Ram went to the hardware store and bought a blue plastic broom so that he could join his Brahmin students as they swept the streets in protest, to show how the educated and up-pressed upper castes could not get any decent jobs in this benighted land.

When Dr Ariyanayagam finally got very frail, and the university put him out to pasture, Professor Ram was able to stop popping Avils like jignuts, and there was great rejoicing among his friends. They developed an unspoken pact to keep Dr Ariyanayagam's potential successors at bay. Whenever the posts that were reserved for scheduled or backward-caste lecturers came up, Professor Ram and all his friends at the university scrutinized the applications sent in by the candidates, and they were always shattered and disappointed to find that no candidate was worthy of initiation into the august priesthood that performed the rites of higher education in Chennai. This gentle vigilantism saved many a tender Chennai student's sensitive mind from odious and vulgar non-Brahmin teachers like Dr Ariyanayagam, and the public-spiritedness of Professor Ram and his friends was commended by one and all. Professor Ram was recognized as the godfather of this benevolent consortium which, under his generalship, made sure that all the Reserved Category positions at the university went a-begging for a long, long time, right down to the turn of the century.

But at last in 1999, when the cat was away on a year's sabbatical at the University of Western Ontario, the mice struck back in their usual underhand way. They chose a moment when Professor Ram's side was weakened by the absence of its leader, and by an ingrown toenail epidemic that caused three Brahmin members of the panel to miss the interview. The backward castes fielded a candidate who was so widely read, and had such high percentages, and such a brilliant teaching record, that only a fine soldier like Professor Ram, who was given a silk shawl by Acharyas Incorporated for his Dedication to Excellence, could have blighted this candidate's chances at the interview. The demoralized rump of the panel that Professor Ram originally put together was definitely not equal to this task. The candidate just chomped up the feeble questions these interviewers posed, and went on to take large bites out of the interviewers themselves, and corrected their errors, and challenged their expertise. To tell you the truth, the only thing more ghastly than the mangled remains of the interview panel was the fact that this candidate was a woman. A woman, moreover, with such a face that Professor Ram frequently remarked: 'You know Laurentia's face? I have met fire-extinguishers with more sex appeal.' When Professor Ram said this, all his colleagues, including Professor Sambasivan and Professor Venkataraman and Professor Nagarajan, held their sides and laughed. They laughed even harder when Professor Ram, intrigued by the fact that Dr Arul was not related to anyone who was anything whatsoever, did some research into her background, and found that she was raised by missionaries at a Bethel Mount orphanage. Sometimes they forgot to stop laughing when Dr Arul walked past, and after three months of this, Dr Arul ate her lunch all by herself and never went down to the canteen with anyone for a cup of coffee.

Never will Professor Ram forget or forgive the events of that fateful summer. For this backward-caste field-mushroom not only accepted the job but, with infinite presumption, also rejected Professor Ram's advice about how to do it, with terrible results all around. She promoted Marx and Fanon when he requested that she promote the good Doctor and Abhinavagupta. She did not seem to notice that the whole department blackballed her for this. The next year she compounded her sins by proposing a Feminist Criticism and Theory course and, as Professor Ram frequently pointed out, such things as Marx and Fanon and feminist criticism in the hands of the untutored provincial roughnecks that the government admitted into the university courses were like loaded missile-launchers in the hands of babes and sucklings. In no time at all, Professor Ram's work on Sanskrit poetics was unravelled, and the curl came out of his students' diphthongs, and these were only two examples of all the decay and ruin that came about with the advent of Dr Laurentia Wesley Arul.

It was only after Dr Arul got into the English department that Professor Ram really took up cudgels, and prodded his somnolent upper-caste students into a state of spiritual awakening. He launched debating societies like the Committee for the Renewal, Acceptance and Promotion of the Poonal, cultural troupes like Stagecraft for Intense Consciousness of Karma, study groups such as the Society for Hindu Ideology and Thought, and Protectors of India's Sanskrit Scholarship, sports organizations like the Project for Universal Kabbadi Expertise, a newsmagazine called *The Brahmassthra*, and even a website called culturewins.com. Himself the Founder and Lifetime President of the Chennai Chapter of the TamBrahmAss, the famous association of Tamil Brahmins, he took all these small organizations under his wing and orchestrated their activities in the service of culture.

In Professor Ram's opinion, Dr Arul was not the most pernicious of the beasts that slouched towards Chennai University to be born. No, it was the Reservations Policy itself. To address this evil, he organized prayer meetings for the success of Brahmin examinees, and gave away free pens at examination time to all poor Brahmin students, even girls, and sponsored the Poor and Deserving Brahmin Boys Vedic Education Fund. Yes, all in all, Professor Ram threw both auricles and ventricles into this cause. If he had a few setbacks now and then, as he had this morning when the thappu-players rapped out the tattoos of unrighteousness in the very citadel of higher learning, he was undaunted, for he adopted the motto of the Nineteenth Tufted Lancers: 'Bash on Regardless!'

On this fateful day, dear reader, another battle was being fought in this epic war of attrition between culture and anarchy, excellence and upstartism. For Professor Ram had advised his son Sankaranarayanan (or Chunky, as he was affectionately interpellated) to apply for the Open Category post of Lecturer in Drama and Folklore at Chennai University. Of course I need not remind you, who have no doubt suffered from this distinction, that an Open Category post is different from a Reserved Category post, since anyone, Brahmins included, can apply. And though Chunky had the best prospects in the world all over North America, he had agreed to take on this job because he wished to stand by his father in his hour of need.

~

'What I needed to see you about, Ram,' Professor Nagarajan was saying when we went off the narrative rails and began the theoretical digression above, 'is the job interview this afternoon'.

'Drama and Folklore,' said Professor Ram, with a keen glance at his colleague.

'Hmmm. Ram, this interview is definitely going to be a little—tricky,' Professor Nagarajan went on in a slightly quavery voice. 'You see, Laurentia has been put on the committee. *You* can't sit on it because your son is going to be interviewed. Of course, this is foolish, because we know you are the soul of rectitude, as such, and anyway your son is a most deserving, most deserving boy, most suitable—'

Professor Nagarajan looked like an old cabbage and smelt like an old cabbage and in short he was nothing but an old cabbage on pins. He had a trick of flashing his hand to his nose and then, in a smooth, practised movement, to his crotch, not lingering in either station, but flickering on to the next. It came from fears, when he started his career as a teacher, that something was hanging from his nose and that his fly was open. He did this unconsciously all the time, but with great frequency when he was anxious. Right now, he was quite feverish with anxiety, for he did not wish to offend Professor Ram in any way.

'Your son is clearly the most meritorious candidate, there should be no question, that is, no question at all—'

Professor Ram wished to tell him to stop drivelling, but kindly refrained.

'What about the UGC representative? Can we expect him to be on our side?'

'It is another *woman*, as it were.'

'Which woman?'

'Erm—the *Kurien* woman.'

Professor Ram expelled an exasperated breath. 'These women don't seem to have anything to do but hang around and be put on committees,' he said irritably. 'They will form a fascist non-Brahmin caucus and try to push one of their people in, especially as they hate everything I stand for. They have no understanding of culture, you see, and they hate the idea of anyone else having such mastery. It will all become a matter of favouritism and caste-politics. Let me see, now—you are going to be the only one on the committee on our side. Bad timing, in*credibly* bad timing. I wish Professor Subbu had not found it necessary to make his pilgrimage to Benaras just now.'

'And our dear Venkat missed his connecting flight at Frankfurt,' said Professor Nagarajan. He plucked at his trousers.

'It is a tragedy,' said Professor Ram emotionally. 'It is always our people who get invited to go to conferences abroad.'

Professor Nagarajan nodded. 'Yes, and poor Sambasivan—in hospital—'

'If Sambasivan had taken good care of his digestion,' Professor Ram said severely, 'he would not have let us all down like this. Appendicitis! At his age! I have taught him the correct yogic care of the alimentary canal a hundred times if I have taught him once.'

'Merit will win in the end, Ram. As the poet said, all is not lost, the unconquerable will. We have God on our side, as it were. I am writing an article about all this for the TamBrahmAss magazine. Still, in the short run, we are in a desperate situation, Ram,' Professor Nagarajan said with trepidation (nose, OK, crotch, OK), for it had occurred to him that Professor Ram might want him to work a miracle and somehow charm his son into the job. 'The girl—your student—what is her name? The dark one—the Hottentot Venus, as it were? Hmm, ah yes, Jiva. It is appalling, she is actually a scheduled-caste student, Ram, and there is no reason why she can't wait for a Reserved Category post to come around. Still, she has submitted her thesis, after all, and it was on drama and myth, wasn't it, Ram, which gives her quite an advantage. How far did you say Sankaranarayan had got with his thesis, as it were?'

'He has begun work on it,' said Professor Ram. It was irksome to him that he had to sound so defensive. 'But remember, my dear Nagarajan, that Chunky is North-America-returned.'

'Erm—Canada, my friend. Not as much clout with the V-C as, say, Berkeley, California. You know, there *is* something... have you considered the expedient of asking the girl to absent herself from the interview? It would be a graceful way of resolving erm—the issue.'

'Do you really think — ? Of course she will do it for me,' said Professor Ram. 'After all, I am her teacher!'

'*Guru saakshaath parabrahma*,' said Professor Nagarajan piously. 'The teacher is equal to the ah—Over-Soul ...' (nose, OK, by gum! crotch, all right, by golly!).

'Exactly,' said Professor Ram, who looked very deep and broad and transcendent, and was indeed a dead ringer for the Over-Soul.

'In fact,' said Professor Nagarajan, 'I saw her in the lobby—erm—cohabiting, as it were, with the enemy. I could send her up to see you right now, if you like, if you like, that is.'

'Yes, capital, do that, Nagarajan,' said Professor Ram.

Professor Nagarajan took the hint and toddled off, establishing a mystic connection between schlong and schnozzle at regular intervals.

~

Left alone, Professor Ram had a few seconds of uncharacteristic doubt about inviting Jiva to step aside for his son's sake. It was

not as if Chunky did not deserve it, of course: it was not that
at all. It was just that he did not wish to put himself even
temporarily at the mercy of one of these low-caste Ambedkarites
who was probably a closet anarchist and an anti-Brahmin
insurgent to boot. In the first place, Professor Ram had agreed
to supervise Jiva's thesis with great reluctance. In fact, he had
only agreed when the V-C himself mused that it was exceedingly
strange, and required explaining, that in a career of nearly
three decades, Professor Ram had never supervised a single
Ph.D. by a student who wasn't a Brahmin.

But Professor Ram looked around at all the framed
accolades on his walls and took courage. Was he not the
precious vial full of Culture, he asked himself—studying his
face in the glass of the Sri Rama picture that hung above his
desk at the right height, for Professor Ram loved to see himself
thus palimpsestically reflected against his divine namesake—
and did he not convey this ambrosial essence to the lips of the
undeserving, who did not know the difference between the
lyrical ballads of Wordsworth and the boat-songs of the prawn
fishermen? Yes, he said to himself, there was none like him,
none.

'Come in, Jiva, come right in,' he said when Jiva knocked
at his door a few minutes later. He wafted her in with an
elegant movement, like a magician extracting an egg from a
customer's ear.

Jiva came in, and the door creaked shut behind her.

Professor Ram jumped out of his chair so abruptly that she
thought he had sat on a board-pin, but it was only to open the
door again, and to prop it open with the sandalwood lotus
doorstopper that he had got for winning the Noblest Chennaiite
contest.

'You never know who may be passing by,' said Professor
Ram. 'We don't want to set any tongues wagging, do we?'

Though Jiva was not uneasy earlier, she became so now,
which just shows you how perverse human beings are.

'Now tell me. What can I do for you-ou?' said Professor Ram, and his tone was so saponaceous that Professor Nagarajan, passing through the corridor outside, remembered that his wife had asked him to buy some Lux Supreme on his way back from work.

'*You* sent word to *me*, to come and see you before my interview, Dr Ram,' said Jiva.

'Ahhh yess, now what was it—yes, now I remember, I just wanted to check that your preparation for your viva voce examination was going well.'

'I think it is going quite well, Dr Ram.'

'Good, good. Make sure you read your whole thesis through several times.'

'Yes, Dr Ram.'

'That will be all. Oh, by the way, there was something else, now I come to think about it. I wonder if you could do me a little favour,' Professor Ram said. 'A little token of your esteem for your supervisor, heh heh.'

'I will try,' said Jiva.

'I wonder if you could refrain from attending the interview for the Open Category Drama and Folklore post. It is this afternoon, I believe.'

Now, though Professor Ram's tone was as sweet as a honeycomb caught in a mangle, and bell-like too, for some reason Jiva just looked at him blankly, with no particular expression on her face.

'I am sure you will see the logic of it. I have your best interests at heart, you know. The reason I am saying this is that the Reserved Category seat will be falling vacant six months from now. It will be advertised quite soon. It will be easier for me to guarantee you that job if you don't antagonize the department by competing for an Open Category post. In fact, I will give you my *personal* assurance that you will get that position, unless,' and here Professor Ram looked up at the god-pictures, 'unless the gods see fit to claim my life before then'.

But the gods were smiling above Professor Ram's head, and they seemed more than willing to let him complete his allotted lifespan. Indeed, the translucent plastic Ganesha that was lit from within by a bulb shed a particularly benign effulgence on Professor Ram's face at this moment.

'Are you saying you want me to miss this interview, sir?' said Jiva, at last. Her voice was unsteady. 'But why?'

'Well, Jiva, as head of this department, I would like to make sure that there is a good balance of talents in the pool, and—no offence meant—it would not do for backward and scheduled-caste candidates to start competing with the talents that Open Category candidates bring. Besides, you will get an equally secure job in the future.'

'Oh. But I am sorry, Dr Ram, I cannot—'

'Before you refuse, Jiva,' said Professor Ram, and his voice was no longer like a sucking dove's, 'consider how you are placed in relation to your viva voce examination. I think a wise acceptance of the truth is better than an argument. You are going to need my recommendation letters, you know.'

'I don't think it is fair, Dr Ram. I am sorry, but I don't think I can miss this interview, especially because I have worked on drama and folklore in my thesis.'

'That will be all,' snarled Professor Ram, and it was remarkable how the room abruptly stopped smelling like a soap factory.

Sundar followed Jiva's trail up and down, up and down, all over the campus. When he got to the library, someone told him that she had just left for the hostel; when he got to the hostel, they told him she had just left for lunch; and when he searched in the canteen, someone told him she had gone to the English department to meet her supervisor, Professor Ram. So he tried the English department, and his heart leapt up when he ambled past Professor Ram's office, because the door was half-open, and the gap framed Jiva's firm back and Jiva's long plait, and he could see that Jiva was talking to Professor Ram.

'Excuse me,' said Sundar, launching one of the fantastic opening lines when she came out two minutes later. 'I couldn't help thinking—'

But Jiva stumbled past him with averted eyes, and indeed, she hardly noticed he was there, for she was focusing all her energies on not crying. This was a situation Sundar had not planned for. Bafflement made him pause at the wrong place. Professor Ram looked up from his desk and spotted him.

'Sundar! You are very late! I told you to show up at 12.20!'

'Yes, sir,' said Sundar miserably, watching Jiva's back disappear down the stairs. He was feeling like a man who had held out his cup for a refill and was told by the barmaid that she was all out of the milk of Paradise. 'Sorry sir, I got held up.'

'Come in. I have something to discuss with you.'

Sundar shambled into Professor Ram's office, slackly.

'I just wanted to ask you how you were getting along with your paper.'

'Sir?'

'Your *paper*. For the ACS *conference*. You do realize you have less than a week left to finish it?'

'I've started work on it, sir.'

'Yes, I'm taking that for granted, but what I want to know is, how *far* you've got. Do you have a draft written?'

'Uh, like—not a complete one, sir.'

'Well, pass it to me when you finish,' said Professor Ram. 'I had better make sure you are on the right track. I hope you are using the secondary reading I recommended to you—two articles of mine, if I remember right, and one by Sankaranarayanan. So you are going to be representing *me* in a sense. Make sure you use the correct citation format— Chicago, not MLA. The proceedings are to be published, you know. I've turned down a number of papers to squeeze yours in, so don't take this too lightly. It is not every student who gets a chance to be published at your age. Can you show me what you have written?'

This paper that Professor Ram had shanghaied Sundar into writing was for the conference of the Association of Commonwealth Studies (the ACS) which was to come off that very weekend at the university. Professor Ram was masterminding it, and as a result, Shastri had been doing a great deal of legwork for the last few months. The conference was called 'CONFLUENCE 2002' and, according to the Call for Papers, it was all about bringing together traditional Indian aesthetics and postcolonial theory. I myself hoped to attend, if I could raise the registration fee, which was quite hefty. As Professor Ram told Professor Nagarajan, it was necessary to filter out the undesirable elements, such as students, and especially those undereducated mofussil buffoons who asked peculiar questions and brought the tone of such conferences down so badly that it was like being in a Palayankottai bus-shelter.

Sundar was sticking strictly to the facts when he said his paper was not complete yet. He had started writing it three days earlier, and he had put down the title which Professor Ram had recommended at the top of a clean sheet of foolscap like this: 'The Tay Poems of William McGonagall and Abhinavagupta's *Abhinavabharati*: An Intertextual Exploration.' Under this title there were some lines like this:

'When one considers the Tay poems of William McGonagall—'
'William McGonagall was born in 1830 in Dundee, Scotland, and is one of the'

'A genuinely unprejudiced reader of William McGonagall's œuvre will find—'

Yes? Will find what ? Wha-aat? Sundar had studied the Tay poems closely, chewing his pencil until it became mush, but he had not found a thing worth mentioning, and he had read somewhere that whereof you don't have anything intelligent to say, thereof you should draw a veil over your half-baked ideas. So that is where the paper stood at the moment, and Sundar entertained grave doubts about showing it to Professor Ram.

'The paper—I—like—'

There was a knock at the door.

'Come in,' barked Professor Ram, annoyed at the interruption. 'Yes, Shastri?' It was indeed Professor Ram's nodder and right-hand man, and he held two diskettes in his right hand and several rolls of chart paper clamped in his armpit.

'I have finished the article, sir,' said Shastri, panting. Professor Ram had expressed a wish, a couple of months ago, for an article about his own achievements for *Reader's Digest*, under the heading, 'The Most Unforgettable Character I Have Ever Met'. Shastri was hoping that the completion of this task would raise his stock with Professor Ram.

'Good, good, leave the disk here, and I will rewrite it,' said Professor Ram, with a faraway look in his eyes. He was thinking of how Jiva had slighted his recent offer.

'This other diskette, sir,' Shastri wheezed. 'It is having the eighth draft of my thesis.'

'Well, print it out, print it out!' Professor Ram said abruptly. 'You know my views about electronic submissions. Get it to me by the end of the week. But now, my young friends, to more pressing matters. I have been thinking—this whole glorification of Ambedkar—coming on top of the quota system that allows all these unprepared Reserved Category students and lecturers into the university—this whole glorification of Ambedkar really ought to be stopped. Someone ought to protest. We have many smaller organizations, but some charismatic young person has to provide true spiritual and moral leadership.'

'I have already started making some posters about this

matter, sir,' said Shastri. He unrolled the chart-paper and Professor Ram saw the legends:

Propiciate Saraswati Devi! Stop worshiping false gods!
Gandhiji, not Bhimji, is the Real Father of Our Nation
Down with fony Buddhists! Long live ancient Hindu
glory!

Shastri looked at his supervisor with a tiny hopeful smile on his thin, bloodless lips. Being the student editor of *The Brahmassthra*, and the unanimously elected president of the Anti-Reservation Society of Egmore, he naturally felt that he was the crown prince. Indeed, he had made these posters partly to remind Professor Ram of this fact.

But Professor Ram ignored Shastri and his posters except to point out that propitiate was spelt p-r-o-p-i-t-i-a-t-e. He studied Sundar's face.

'A leader with strength, charisma and credibility,' he said, again, in a dreamy voice, and Shastri felt he was doomed.

'What about it, Sundar?' said Professor Ram. 'What do you think?'

'Sir?' Sundar said vacuously, for he had not followed Professor Ram's train of thought.

'Sundar, I appoint you the leader of the Brahmin cause. I hope you will fulfil my expectations,' said Professor Ram in a ringing voice.

'Sir?'

'Now I want you to go out and mobilize people against the statue of Ambedkar. Shastri will help. Never mind if they call you names—Brahmin fundamentalist, bigot, mafioso—these are just the slings and arrows. Remember that it is our job to do our duty by Culture.'

Sundar heard Shastri draw in his breath sharply. He himself drew in his breath sharply. Professor Ram made a sharp exhalation that expressed great decidedness. It all sounded like an early morning pranayama class full of Californian screwballs.

Sundar was about to protest when he reflected that a moment when Professor Ram had forgotten about his McGonagall paper was not a moment to cross Professor Ram in any way.

'I will see you later, Shastri,' Professor Ram said dismissively, and Shastri melted away, rolling up his posters resentfully as he left. 'By the way, Sundar, I was just wondering what you plan to do about the job you applied for.'

Sundar suddenly remembered that some weeks ago he had sent in an application for a job as a lecturer in Drama and Folklore. The interview was to take place this afternoon, he recalled.

'I just wanted to let you know that my son Sankaranarayanan has applied for the same job. You'll probably meet him at the interview—if you still want to attend it, that is. Do introduce yourself—*if* you attend,' said Professor Ram casually. 'That will be all. Good luck.'

At once Sundar decided not to take this interview seriously. There was as much percentage for him in competing with Professor Ram's son as there was for Sisyphus in trying to get the toothpaste back in the tube.

It was almost three in the afternoon when Sundar gave up looking for Jiva and repaired to the canteen, hoping to mend his broken heart with brinji-kurma.

'Oi!' a voice called through the window. Sundar peered through the bars and made out Akilan's face. He was with the tall white girl again, clearly enjoying being the object of burning envy among the university's male population.

'I'm going to have some lunch!' Sundar shouted above the din of all the citizens clamouring for food.

'Get me a plate of brinji-kurma also!' Akilan shouted back.

'What about—uh—the lady?'

'Nothing for her!'

Sundar bought two plates and took them out. Akilan was lounging in one of the many nooks that punctuated the walls of the old Indo-Saracenic building.

'Hi!' said Caroline, glancing up. She was sitting beside Akilan, listening to her little cassette recorder through earphones and transcribing her morning's interviews. 'I'm Caroline!' She went back to her work, frowning with concentration.

'Hi! I'm Sundar.'

'Sundar, I want some help with something,' said Akilan. 'I have a letter here, which I want you to write in proper paappaan English.'

'What is paappaan English?' Sundar asked, for he was always eager to extend his education.

'English like your Professor Ram is writing, man. Have you never heard the word paappaan? It means Brahmin. Here, catch the paper properly, don't let it fly away. Caroline is already correcting the spelling.'

Sundar read the letter between belts at his brinji-kurma. It was from one Kadiresan who was writing on behalf of the Melmaruvathur Muthumariamman Temple Festival Chariot-Pullers Development Trust Fund, and asking for help to support the indigent families of those who had pulled the temple chariot in Melmaruvathur for decades.

'This is quite neat, machaan,' Sundar said, putting the letter in his lap. 'I don't know why this Kadiresan has asked for your help.'

'If you say it is good, that is enough. I will tell Kadiresan,' Akilan said. 'He is my colleague.'

'You mean you are a chariot-puller?' Sundar was impressed.

'Actually I am not,' said Akilan. 'I am an artist. I am the student of Lucas Dorairaj. You know him? Sometimes he comes to the university. He teaches me how to do the sculptures. Stone and bronze.'

'Ey man, that sculpture of Dr Ambedkar—it's really far out! I like that book he's reading.'

'That was a book *he* only wrote.'

'Your statue looks different from the usual statue with the hand stretched out. Do you sell many statues?'

'I only got one chance to sell my sculpture before. That was a clay statue which Jiva used in her play.'

'That was a great statue, too.' Sundar paused in the act of bringing a spoonful of brinji-kurma to his mouth. 'It even reminded me of someone. Who?'

'Your own Professor Ram, man.' Akilan sighed and shook his head. 'What's the use, man. Sculpture is not providing enough income. These days I am unemployed, though I was having a regular job before.'

'Where were you working in?'

'In a cut-out company,' Akilan said. 'I was painting the cut-outs. That time it was a nice job. But afterwards I got promoted to sales agent. That time I have to go from door to door and tell the customers if they are not paying for a new cut-out of a big film star like Rajni or Arjun, or even our chief minister, I am uhh—not responsible for what happens to them. Then I am taking the money to my boss. He is doing the rotation to create a new cut-out. He is giving my commission and he is putting the remaining in his profit column.'

Sundar was dazzled. 'Machaan, it is fascinating. I have never met an out-of-work cut-out extortionist before.'

'But the pay is no good.' Akilan yawned and twisted his neck this way and that to get the cricks out. 'And the job is a shit job. Some people are getting so angry they are calling police, and so I am also having mamool expenses. I am wasting too much money to keep the police quiet. That's why I left it.'

'So how are you making enough money to pay for your rent and food?'

'I am having one-two small side-business, so I am getting little-little cash here and there. But last week the police have taken my teacher, Lucas, to jail. I am spending all my money to give the bail amount. I have not had a bath for one week because my financial condition is very dangerous. If I can get fifteen rupees, I can buy a Mysore Sandal Soap. I cannot stand any other smell.'

Sundar felt in his pockets and pulled out two twenties.

'Thanks, machaan.' Akilan collared the notes smoothly. 'I will keep the change. Then I can treat you for a lunch tomorrow.'

There was a moment of silence and the peaceful champing of the last few mouthfuls of brinji-kurma. They put the plates away.

'Jiva is also helping me,' said Akilan, pianissimo, flipping a cigarette out of his pack and into his mouth just the way Rajni did it in all his films. Such was Sundar's feeling at the sound of Jiva's name that the heat surged into his face and his breath became short. 'Whenever someone is coming to the university and asking for a native informant, Jiva is giving my name.'

'Oho,' Sundar whispered, glancing over at the white girl. 'So this Caroline, she is only with you because you are informing her about natives?'

'Ada *chee*, you were jealous?' Akilan chuckled richly. 'Ho ho! By the way, man, you wanted to meet her, no?'

'Who?' said Sundar, confused. 'Caroline?'

'No, man. Jiva. You wanted to meet Jiva, no? She was here before, but now she is in the interview, in the seminar room.'

'What? Which interview? Why didn't you tell me before?'

'You didn't ask me, man. Drama or something else, I think. Hey, man! Don't take my letter with you!' cried Akilan, for Sundar shot off so fast towards the seminar room that he forgot all about the Melmaruvathur Chariot-Pullers and their needs.

Caroline looked up. 'Hey, where'd he go?'

'Gone with the wind,' Akilan kissed the letter, folded it and tucked it away in his shirt. His fingers encountered the twenties in his pocket. 'I think I need another plate of brinji-kurma. You want some cool drinks, Caroline?'

∾

Through the glass doors of the seminar room, Sundar could see Dr Arul and Dr Kurien and Dr Nagarajan and the V-C, who made up the interview panel, pouring out coffee for themselves. They did not have any candidates with them yet. Jiva was sitting in a corner of the outer room with her file on her lap, staring blankly at the wall, and when Sundar sat down as close to her as he dared, she did not say anything. A ten-tonne truck seemed to be parked on Sundar's chest, and as Sundar was unable to breathe, he did not say anything either, but just watched Jiva whenever he thought she was not looking in his direction.

The son of Ram came in with a large Samsonite briefcase and started to take many folders out if it. His hands were still bandaged.

'Hello, hello,' Chunky said affably. 'You must be my fellow candidates. I am Sankaranarayanan. I can't shake hands, as I have an injury, but best of luck to you, and may the best man win.'

'Or the best woman,' said Sundar, and he was not at all sure why he said this.

'Of course. The ladies do have an advantage over us, don't they! You must be Sundar. My dad told me about you. Have I seen you somewhere?'

'No,' said Sundar, quickly. 'Er, Sankaranarayanan, this is—Jiva.' Jiva looked up in surprise and nodded to Chunky.

'Congratulations on your fine performance in the *Ekalavya* play,' said Chunky, and Sundar kicked himself. Why couldn't he have thought of such a simple opening?

'Thank you,' Jiva replied.

'You had quite an interesting message in that play, about power relations in the pedagogic context. I wonder if you intended it to be a comment on the micropolitics of caste?'

'I am from the Dalit community,' Jiva said quietly. 'Many Dalit artists are protesting against inequality and injustice in this country. I belong to a group on campus called Students for Democracy.'

'That's extremely interesting—I mean the democracy part—though not entirely news to me. I notice that many Dalits are talking the language of modernity and democracy.' Chunky set a clutch of folders on a side table and pushed the rest back into the briefcase. 'Isn't that teleological-progressive, humanist-Hegelian metanarrative a problematic anachronism? It makes us forever a part of the dialectic of a type of progress that was imposed on us by colonialism—you know, a model of progress that is not our own.'

Jiva could tell from the way his lips were moving, and from the way his grinders were wearing down, and from the way he did not need to breathe between sentences, that Chunky was suffering from acute codswallopitis.

'I don't think Dalits so far have had a real part in this famous democratic narrative,' she said, shrugging. 'Just when we start demanding real democracy, you say that we should think of something else.'

Chunky thrust the accusation away with fluttering hands. 'Oh, I'm not suggesting that we *vacate* the discursive space of democracy altogether,' he said. 'I would merely advocate that Dalit ideologues *situate* the debate more carefully in the aporetic embrace of global capitalism before foreclosing on future strategies of political dissent. To put it slightly differently,' he said, 'you need to *map* the practices of codification, representation and discursive control under the sign of Western universalism before you re-mobilize the moribund, discredited, and perhaps always-already impossible liberal-democratic discourse of human rights. Having said which,' said Chunky, 'I must confess that I'm totally guilty of being a radical myself. I have written *quite* a lot on the Dalit question, so the literature you refer to is familiar to me.'

'I was not referring to any literature, actually,' Jiva said.

'The trouble with Dalit theory is that it does not really take into account all the really significant developments in North America. It's embarrassing, I mean, I know the Indian academy is always about fifteen years behind, but people really ought to read at least Derrida and Foucault if not Homi Bhabha and Judith Butler. In fact, I'm a little worried that my paper will go over people's heads.'

'Your paper?' Jiva asked politely.

'I'm presenting something on a radical Toronto-based Tamilian artist who works with farm materials. At the ACS conference this weekend. Are you presenting too?'

'Nobody asked me,' said Jiva.

'I would appreciate your comments on my paper, then,' said Chunky, ever gracious.

At this moment the glass door opened and the department secretary smiled at Chunky and asked him if he was ready to meet the interview panel. Chunky passed through the doors, staggering under the weight of his CV and references. When you are at the cutting edge of every bandwagon, as Chunky was, you accumulate plenty of autobiography to hump around.

There was a long heavy silence.

'I would like to join Students for Democracy,' Sundar said suddenly, sounding like an old goat that had fallen into a deep well.

'You can go to a meeting, if you like,' said Jiva with a non-committal look at him. She was feeling more composed now, but that interview with Professor Ram had made her feel particularly thin-skinned. She felt wary of anyone who had any connection with him. 'I am not sure you will like it.'

'Will you be there?'

'Maybe. It seems the Brahmin groups—the TamBrahmAsses—are organizing a protest against the Ambedkar statue. Students for Democracy will want to do something about that.'

'I'll come,' said Sundar, forgetting completely about having been appointed leader of the Brahmin groups. 'Just tell me which day.'

'I will probably put up some posters tomorrow, to say which day.'

That truck on Sundar's chest seemed to have driven away. His heart did a quick dance under his ribs. He moved infinitesimally closer to Jiva.

'Tell me about your thesis,' he said.

In another ten minutes, Chunky came out through the glass door, smiling with satisfaction, for the V-C and Professor Nagarajan had been wonderfully cordial. The two women on the interview panel were mere feminists, and Chunky felt he had flattened them with postcolonial theory, which was a much cominger thing than feminism.

It was Jiva's turn. She thought of Professor Ram's words, and her hands started trembling so violently that she dropped her file. Sundar picked up her papers for her.

'Best of luck!' he whispered. 'I hope you get the job! Really!'

She smiled and went through the glass doors.

Now that Jiva had gone, Sundar had no intention of staying on to be interviewed. He mentioned something to the department secretary about an acute stomach ache and legged it out of there. His mother wished him to be home earlier than usual today.

The university was very quiet, for it was now nearly 5 p.m. The corridors and stairways were deserted, and there were no lights in any of the offices. As Sundar went past Professor Ram's darkened door, with its saffron sign that let you know whether the Professor was In or Out, the fat scrawl of a marker pen caught his eye, and he grinned to himself. For someone had taped a message to this sign, and the message was as follows:

Proffesor Ram is a syfilitic sore. If you have him, you will need antiboitics. Come to me for getting them!!

In which a Battle ends in a Draw at No. 5, Varadan Street

MONDAY WAS THE day of the engagement that Sachu hoped would lead to an engagement, or maybe even two. She woke up early in the morning to strengthen her fortifications and prepare her armaments, for when a family met a family with a view to a matrimonial alliance, it was nothing but a day in the trenches for both parties.

'I want you to tell Mr Seshadri that I have sunstroke,' she said to the switchboard lady at Seshadri Towers. 'I have to take the day off.'

'I want you both to *behave yourselves*,' she briefed the troops before they left for work and for the university in the morning, 'I want everything to be *perfect*.'

'I hope that Sundar remembers to come back from the university in time to make himself decent. He won't even bother to wash his face or change into a good shirt until I remind him,' she said to Vaithy, hoping that he would take the hint and present himself like a sensible Brahmin paterfamilias, and not like a failed seditionist.

Sachu instinctively adopted Bucket Maami as her Emily Post-maami and agony-maami, and the whole morning the communication lines buzzed between No. 5 and No. 7, Varadan Street.

'Maami, what is the best food to offer people whose children are foreign-returned? They are coming at six o clock, so we cannot ask them to eat a full meal.'

'Buy some cake from Hotbreads, and keep many cool drinks ready in the fridge.'

'Our fridge is not working properly. Can you send your servant-girl over so that I can store the drinks in your fridge?'

Sachu's Pepsi had not rested more than twenty minutes in Bucket Maami's fridge when Bucket Maami's phone rang again.

'My God, Maami! Suppose the parents are orthodox Brahmins? What will they say about the eggs? Everyone knows that cakes are made with eggs!'

'Do you think anyone can live abroad nowadays without eating a few eggs? Never mind that, if you want to be safe, you should make some pakodas or murukkus. But you must serve them with coffee, definitely not cold drinks.'

'But that is so traditional! Suppose they think we are too old-fashioned for their taste?'

'All right, then, have the cake ready in the kitchen, but out of sight, behind the gas cylinder. If they seem too modern for pakodas you can whip out the cake and cut it in no time at all.'

Sachu tried to fry some pakodas, but she was so nervous that she splashed hot oil here and there, and by the time she had held her hand under the tap, and put Burnol on it, the pakodas were completely incinerated.

The phone screeched in Bucket Maami's house.

'O-ọ-oh Maami, the pakodas are burnt, and I don't have time to start over again! Can you send your servant-girl to the Jagadambal Pappadum store to buy half-a-kilo pakodas and half-a-kilo murukkus for me? My servant-woman is cleaning the house!'

'Very well. You should have some sweets also, since it is a happy occasion. I will tell her to get some Mysore-paaku. Jagadambal makes it so well.'

Sachu spent half an hour pushing all the odds and ends around the house into Sundar's bedroom. Bucket Maami's phone went off again.

'O-oh, Maami! So many questions! I was pushing all the rubbish into Sundar's room upstairs, but now I wonder, will the family want to see the house?'

'Yes, my daughter's alliance wanted to see the house. You should clean up *all* the rooms, Sachu.'

'*Chitraaa!*' Sachu yelled up the stairs even before she hung up. 'You have to help me clean up the house, I can't manage everything by myself, and they will be here by six o'clock!'

Chitra came down the stairs placidly with Raja in her arms.

'Raja has not done his potty yet,' she said.

'Let him do it later,' Sachu snapped. 'Here, give him that new Mickey Mouse gun Sundar bought, it will keep him quiet. Now put all these things into the big drawer in that cabinet. I have no time to sort the rubbish and throw it away. My God, your father-in-law's cigarettes and communist books! Who bought this dirty book? Remember not to open the drawer for *anything* when the alliance people come. Ayyo, I need two weeks and sixteen hands to clean this house properly.'

Sachu's phone rang.

'Sachu,' Bucket Maami said, 'when you are clearing the house, if you find the *Cook and See* cookbook that I lent you, which you lost, give it back to me.'

'Certainly. Maami, I have just found the picture of Kicha which came out in *Jagadambal's Journal* when he made his new invention. Shall I show it to them?'

'Leave it on the table. Then, when they come, you can seem to find it suddenly and talk to them about it, and show them the picture also.'

Sachu turned her attention to outfitting the troops. Bucket Maami's phone made demented yelps.

'What should Sundar wear, Maami? Suit or jibba-veshti?'

'Does he have a proper suit?'

'No—though there is Kicha's marriage suit.'

'Ayyoyyo, talk sense, Sachu. Sundar is much taller than Kicha. It will look shabby if the pant is too short. Let him wear a jibba-veshti. These days all the NRI boys are going for ethnic fashions. And your girl should wear a grand silk sari.'

'O-oh Maami, I have begged and pleaded, but Uma says she will not wear a silk sari!'

'Then I will send you my blue cotton Venkatagiri with the gold border and buttas. That should definitely be grand enough. And if she gives any trouble—call *me*.'

'You are *such* a good friend, Maami!'

By three o'clock, the food had arrived from Jagadambal's store, the house had been sanitized till it hurt the eye to look at any of the surfaces, Sachu was as knackered as a runner after the cross-country, and as for Bucket Maami's little servant-girl, who had worn a deep groove in the pavement between the two houses, she had gone to sleep standing up against a street-lamp.

'You should eat something,' Pati said to Sachu. Pati had stayed aloof from all this preparation. 'That way you won't have the jitters.'

'Just make some coffee,' Sachu said. 'Can you make a decoction in the big filter, so that we can have about twelve cups of coffee when they come? Then change into a good sari. And your teeth—'

Pati's teeth were like the shelves of the District Central Library, whose patrons generally helped themselves to many books and never bothered to return them. Whenever a tooth passed beyond the veil, Pati mourned it by sucking violently on the void it left in her gums, and this made a noise like a steam-engine fussing on a metre-gauge siding.

'What about my teeth?'

'These people may not like that shoop-shoop sound you are making. These people who have been abroad are so particular about the sounds people make.'

'Chee-chee!' Pati clicked her tongue contemptuously and

then transferred it to the hiatus and slurped more than ever. 'Not liking sounds! I never heard of anything so ridiculous in my life! Maybe you think the boy divorced his wife for making sounds?'

Bucket Maami's phone rang hysterically.

'Maami, I have just remembered, the boy has divorced his wife! I must know why he got divorced, is there a way of asking?'

'Ada-da-da! Divorce! Are you sure you want to give your daughter to this family? Suppose the boy is a total waste? Many NRI boys are already living with white girls! Or even with boys! Do you know that two men can soon get married with each other in Canada?'

'What?'

'This is true, I have read about it in the paper. Have you never heard the word Homa-seshwal? Such boys cannot do their nuptial duties with women. And also in Canada two women can get married with each other. They are called Lebanese.'

'Muruga, what a world this is! But I am sure it is nothing like that with this boy. He seems—the whole *family* seems to be very respectable. They seem to be such *spiritual* people. If you see the way they have written the advertisement, and hear the boy's father speak—he says his son is very particular about all our traditions, and I don't think these Homa-whatever people worry about things like that.'

'Be careful, the family may be one thing and the boy may be another. But if they are religious-minded, then you should show that your family is also the same. Why don't you get your father-in-law to start his pujai just before six o'clock?'

'Good idea, Maami. I will ask him this minute.'

At five o'clock, Sachu's squadron reported to headquarters, and many mutinies had to be put down. The way Sundar struggled against the jibba-veshti, you would think it was a straitjacket. It was only when Bucket Maami made a personal visit and practically went into orbit with high dudgeon that Uma agreed to wear her blue cotton sari with the big gold border. At five minutes to six, however, there was a brief moment of calm. Uma was looking exceedingly pert and pretty, with her long curly hair softly braided and looped about with fresh jasmine, and Sundar was got up like a heart-throb in the ethnic bridegroom centrespread of *Femina*. They were stashed away in Sundar's bedroom, and Sundar was passing the time by laying out to Uma, at great length, what an idiotic scheme he thought this marriage scheme was, while Uma was reading *The Xanadu Talisman* for the twentieth time to keep her courage up.

'So, can we call it off then?' said Sundar. 'Shall we tell these people to bugger off?'

Uma read on enigmatically, saying neither yea nor nay.

A smell of incense and flowers and the tinkling of the brass bell filled the air downstairs. Thatha had agreed reluctantly to do his pujai instead of doing what he usually did at this hour, which was commune with his bowels.

The only awkward note was struck by Vaithy, who refused point-blank to take off his helmet, and it may have been his way of being battle-ready for all I know. Also, little Raja was watching *Popeye the Sailor Man* in a way that boded trouble.

The doorbell sang *Happy Birthday to You*.

'They have come!' Kicha gasped. But it was only Bucket Maami's servant-girl wanting Bucket Maami's umbrella which she had left behind. Sachu thrust the umbrella at her. 'Go, go!' she shouted, for the little girl was showing a tendency to fall asleep against the door-jamb.

Five minutes later, the doorbell sang *Twinkle Twinkle Little Star*.

'They are here!' shrieked Kicha.

'Turn off the TV!' Sachu yelled to Chitra.

'He just keeps turning it on again!' Chitra wailed, for Raja was a twenty-first century techno-baby and knew all the right buttons.

Little Raja began to squall, and he also turned the volume up to maximum.

The doorbell sang *Jingle Bells*, and used up its repertoire.

'At least turn the volume down!'

'What? I can't hear—wait, I'll turn the volume down!'

'TURN THE VOL—' Abruptly Raja tired of the game and switched off the TV. Sachu's bay echoed in the silence. She took a deep breath and opened the door with studied casualness. A stout gentleman and a minimal lady stood on the doorstep, exuding intimidating waves of refinement.

'Welcome, come in, come in,' Sachu said in her most cultured voice.

'I am Professor Pattabhiraman,' said the gentleman, putting his palms together as he came in. 'Please do feel free to call me Ram. This is Mrs Ram.'

The next generation drifted in.

'This is Sankaranarayanan, my son, and this is Jayanthi, my daughter.'

Sachu's throat fairly clogged up when she saw that Mrs Ram was upholstered in a Kanchipuram silk which had a file of peacocks in gold thread marching stiffly from right to left, and a herd of unsociable elephants in silver thread marching from left to right, and that these two species together occupied so many square feet of the sari that it was hard to tell what colour the silk was. This sari gave Sachu plenty of heartburn, for she herself was wearing a mere ikkat, and though it was a very expensive ikkat, it had no gold thread at all. How sad it was that Varadan Street was opening the hostilities at a disadvantage simply because Uma was so stubborn! For Sachu's own choice of napery was dictated by the rule that the mother must not out-dress the daughter. Still, Sachu said to herself, the way Mrs Ram is wearing it, her Kanchipuram silk looks like an old crêpe-bandage.

Now Mrs Ram was one of the Brahmin ladies who lunch, especially on other ladies. All ladies who lunch can price a sari at a hundred paces, and even tell you which tailor stitched the fall. Where Mrs Ram had intended to deliver a stunning left hook by being practically armour-plated in precious metals, she actually found her jawbone stopping Sachu's swift uppercut of fine taste. The ikkat that Sachu wore seemed to reproach Mrs Ram's Kanchipuram silk the way antique jewellery reproaches rolled-gold from Burma Bazaar, and it gave Mrs Ram sciatica at once, for she thought Sachu had planned this. But the ikkat, Mrs Ram consoled herself, was excessively starched; and she despised the way Sachu was crackling like a pappadum whenever she moved.

'This is my husband,' Sachu simpered, addressing Professor Ram, but giving the young Rams the once over. 'He has just *this second* got back from work, on his scooter,' she added hastily, for Mrs Ram's eyebrows practically disappeared into her hairline, as if to say, 'Mark this, the husband is wearing a helmet, which means they have no car.' Some people have suggested that Mrs Ram had a facelift the last time she visited Canada, but I happened to be present with her the day Sachin Tendulkar lofted a ball to the fence ten feet above deep square leg, and I know she was following this ball with her eyes when the wind changed. As for Vaithy, it was a good thing for one and all that his helmet's visor cast his face into deep shadow, for the fiendish rictus he wore made him look like one of those hollow pumpkin gargoyles people put on the tops of new buildings to stave off the evil eye.

'And this is my husband's mother. My husband's father is just finishing his pujai. This is my older son, Kicha, and this is my daughter-in-law, Chitra.'

There was much taking off of slippers and fussing with baskets of fruit. All the while, in the offing, Thatha was chanting the Thousand Names of Lalita, offering flowers to the gods from a silver casket, speeding it up a little towards the end, so that he could lift one buttock and produce a long stuttering fart like Rufus's motorbike from which Rufus had removed the mufflers. Sachu blushed. But the Rams were too polite to notice. Or maybe they were deeply gratified to think how their prospective relations by marriage spent their days in acts of unselfconscious piety, consecrating even their wind, so that it became as incense in the nose of the Paramaatman or Over-Soul.

Jayanthi, who was standing awkwardly behind her mother as if she did not know what to do with her hands, scooped Raja up and kissed him.

'Hmm. The girl is very nice-looking,' Sachu said to herself, 'but clearly a difficult case for her mother. The hussy—she hasn't bothered to wear a sari. The boy is a little tubbier than I might have wished, and beginning to be—Muruga!—*bald.*'

Mrs Ram greeted Thatha as he rose from his prayers, and at the same time arranged to greater advantage the many diamonds that were judiciously distributed all over her person. When she saw the shabbiness of the furniture in the living room, her left eyebrow climbed a millimetre higher than its partner. One of Professor Ram's supernumerary chins wobbled infinitesimally in acknowledgement.

'Now I will call my children down,' said Sachu. 'Sundar! Uma!'

They waited. 'This is my second son, Kalyanasundaram, and this is Uma, my daughter,' Sachu said, primping herself.

Sundar saw Professor Ram before Professor Ram saw him. The sight made him produce a sharp, indescribable yelp, which was an aborted version of one of those skirling, bubbling, surround-sound screams that you always hear in the lonely house just before the transvestite axe-murderer starts in to dismember the heroine's second-best friend with the meat-cleaver, and the screen goes black.

'Oh, do you know each other already?' Sachu asked, mystified by the look that passed between Sundar and Professor Ram.

'He is my student. My—well, I can confess it in this context without violating any rules—my favourite student.' Professor Ram smiled brilliantly at Sundar.

'What a small world it is!' Mrs Ram exclaimed. 'Whew-whew-whew-whew!'

Years earlier, Professor Sambasivan, driven nearly insane by sexual privation during his wife's difficult pregnancy, had told Mrs Ram out of the blue that her laugh was like the divine tinkling of the baby Lord Krishna's silver anklets. It had got him nowhere, but ever since, Mrs Ram had taken to whiffling like a pair of squeaky windscreen wipers. Though she was chief satellite to the Jupiter among Chennai's cultural planets, and though in general she was such a personage as could curdle milk at six paces, she could be gracious when occasion demanded it. She laughed this silvery laugh as often as she could this evening, to set her hosts at ease. Every time Mrs Ram laughed, Pati asked her if she needed a glass of water or ginger pastilles for her throat, and Mrs Ram said no, no, she was in the pink, and whiffled some more. At which Pati turned to Sachu with a despairing look, as if to say, and you object to my noises.

Sachu went up to Uma and guided her by the shoulders towards her destiny.

'Uma, this is Sankaranarayanan,' she said, and Uma folded her palms in greeting. Her eyes were demurely lowered. Her lips twitched, because she could not help noticing that she was to be mated with what was far and away the most singular case of callipygea in the southern hemisphere. This evening, Chunky had packed his hindquarters into a tight pair of trousers, which Mrs Ram had chosen for him because they were slimming, and these trousers lovingly defined the contour of each of Chunky's buttocks. Anyone could see that Chunky's buttocks were as substantial as prehistoric megaliths. Indeed, some people who knew Chunky's buttocks well would never allow that Jennifer Lopez's were in any way outstanding. They even called the Venus of Willendorf 'concave-butt'. They professed themselves willing to wager their mothers against a hundred rupees that Chunky had beaten the Venus of Willendorf in respect of rump fat, though since I have never personally met this lady, I am unable to tell you if these are fair odds.

Yes, all in all, nature had lavished much care and craftsmanship on this part of Chunky. In fact, it seemed she had looked upon her work, and seen that it was good, and felt that you could not have too much of a good thing, for she had repeated the gestalt in most details when she made Chunky's kisser, so that Uma's would-be looked the same both advancing and receding. This thought passed fleetingly through Uma's mind, anyhow, when her eyes flickered upwards and took in two fat cheeks, and a puckered mouth around which there was a beard coming—not systematically, but in disheartened tussocks.

'Sundar, meet Jayanthi,' said Mrs Ram in her turn, bringing her daughter over to meet the prospective lord of her life.

Jayanthi was a ravishing young woman, and she looked a lot like one of the ethereal nymphs that the Bengal School loved to paint, though her hair was cut short like a boy's and the angles of her face somehow expressed impudence. The neck of her salwar suit was cut alarmingly low at the back. On the score card, the last two items neutralized the effect of Vaithy's helmet, which he showed no sign of doffing.

'Hi, Sundar,' Jayanthi said in bell-like tones, startling everyone. So far, the two families had functioned on the understanding that the young women were meant to be seen but not heard, except when they were asked to sing. Sachu made a mental note that they seemed more than modern enough for the cake, eggs or no eggs.

'Nice to meet you,' Jayanthi went on. 'Call me Jay.'

She put out her hand instead of putting her palms together. Sundar shook it in a daze, for he could not help thinking of Jiva at this moment, and he was completely gobsmacked by this sudden plethora of beautiful women in his life.

'I must go in now,' Thatha said suddenly. 'Call of nature.'

'Let the children do their namaskaarams to you, Maama,' said Mrs Ram.

'Ah,' Vaithy said, sotto voce, 'here come the bloody push-ups'.

Thatha and Pati stood together and the girl did a full prostration first, with a mulish expression on her face. When Chunky stretched his length at Thatha's feet, face down and succulent haunches topside, Vaithy's foot twitched in a most significant manner and Sachu was obliged to sidle up and stick an elbow sharply into his ribs.

'Shall we all sit down?' Professor Ram fluttered an elegant wrist towards the moth-eaten sofa.

The two young couples sat clumsily beside each other, and for a long time they did nothing but fidget with their clothes and listen to their elders.

'It seems Sankaranarayanan has hurt his hands,' Sachu said, for she had noticed that Chunky's fingers were bandaged up.

'Oh, it is a temporary condition,' Chunky snickered lightly. He did not wish Uma to think that he was in any sense a cripple.

'Your boys,' said Mrs Ram, looking at Kicha and Sundar with her lips pursed, 'are quite fair'.

'Yes.' Sachu glowed with satisfaction, not realizing that Mrs Ram had said this because she wished to make it clear that she disapproved of Uma's complexion.

'No horoscope encumbrances for either of your children, I hope?'

'No, nothing to worry about on that score,' said Sachu. 'We just had the horoscopes recast by Arundathi Matrimonial Services. They are offering a fantastic e-astrologer service, A to Z in all matters. In fact, Arundathi is providing astrologer services to our top industrialists.'

'Yes, we have heard they have amazing predictions. But we have our own family e-astrologer, who is the personal astrologer to the chief minister and also to our home minister,' Mrs Ram whiffled. 'He works for a very big concern called Pa-Mistry.com. They have actually developed their own horoscope and nadi jothidam software, and they use software like 'Predicta' and 'Sunsines' to do Western astrology as well.' She brought out a tiny silk handkerchief and patted her upper lip. 'They also have a huge stock of international brides and grooms for Brahmins. Even the prediction which our astrologer Sri Sri Sri Panchapakesa Sastrigal made, that we would get a result within a week for our advertisement, has come true. So astute and precise! You won't mind if we get a second opinion about your children's horoscopes?'

'Not at all!'

Kicha had planted himself on the other side of Chunky from Uma, despite Sachu's semaphoric efforts to head him off.

'So, Mr Sankaranarayanan,' he began, 'you are from Canada? How is Canada?'

'It's fine, nawd a bad place to live,' Chunky replied. 'I have a prudy nice cawndo out there.' Chunky spoke like this whenever he felt that the natives needed to have something to look up to, though he was seldom able to keep it up for any length of time, having been educated for most of his life in Pazhavinaiyur, and then in Chennai.

'It must be having many Canadians!' Kicha said, marvelling secretly at his own conversational skills. 'Have some buttermilk. Have it, don't be shy. So, you are doing a Ph.D?'

'Yes, on Diasporic Fictions of—'

'Good! Good!' Kicha came back, clapping Chunky familiarly on the shoulder. 'Brilliant!'

'Uma is domestically trained, I take it?' Mrs Ram asked Sachu. Her eyes did not stay in one place as she spoke, but wandered around the room. Mrs Ram was making the calculations which would establish how much the Vaidyanathans were worth. (The fans were terribly decrepit!)

'Very well, indeed. From the age of twelve she is able to take care of our entire household. And her cooking—! Terrific! In fact, all these items that you see on the table, they have been made by her own two hands!'

'You see, it is so hard to get servants in countries like Canada and the USA, whew-whew!' (The TV was not a flat-screen!)

You know how in the old epics they had these Games before they started walloping each other into scrap metal? Well, dear reader, it was the same in Varadan Street. The chief combatants perked up no end when Mrs Ram mentioned servants, because it was the cue for a game that Brahmins love to play whenever two or three gather together, and this game is called My Servant is More Atrocious Than Your Servant.

'Why, it is becoming almost *more* impossible here,' Sachu exclaimed. 'It is *shocking* the demands they make! Do you know my servant-woman's mother fell down and fractured her arm and she wanted me to pay the doctor's fee? She did not want to go to a government hospital!'

'That's *nothing*!' Mrs Ram cut in. 'The other day we saw one of our old servants, wearing a sari that I had given up as lost, walking back from Pondy Bazaar, cool as cucumber, swinging her arms, and do you know what she had bought?' (The mosaic floor was so old-fashioned!)

'No, what?'

'A *colour* TV!'

'Unbelievable! But my last servant was *worse*—she got a flat from the government, which she rented out, and she still lived in her old cheri hut—'

And it was one each on the scoreboard, patient reader, and

they were well away, with plenty of empathy and camaraderie building up between the Varadan Street Wannabes and the Mylapore Manglers.

~

'The boy has his poonal?' Professor Ram asked, by and by.

'The sacred thread,' began Vaithy, 'is only for scratchi—'

'Yes,' Sachu forestalled him desperately. 'Of course he has his poonal.'

'There are those in today's world who are born Brahmin and don't wear the sacred thread. Others cannot recite the *Gayatri mantram*,' Professor Ram said, his face darkening.

Sachu piously hoped that this would never be said of *her* sons.

'The *Gayatri mantram* has acquired a whole new meaning since the valorization of Spivak,' Chunky chuckled. The others looked at him blankly.

'Our whole family is uncommonly blessed in the matter of spiritual evolution. Take my older boy—Kicha—' Sachu said. 'Very devout, always helping his Thatha with his pujai and reading the "Tidbits of Vedic Wisdom" column of Mr Swaminathan in *The Bindhu* each and every day.'

'Mr Swaminathan is my own uncle,' said Professor Ram. 'He is my mother's brother.'

'My God, really? How lucky your family is!'

Professor Ram bowed gravely in acknowledgement and held his palms up to the ceiling, meaning: it is all the Lord Rama's doing.

'Yes,' said Mrs Ram, 'we value culture and our Hindu heritage so much. In fact, Mr Swaminathan was the one who reviewed the Professor's first book on Hindu dharma. Whew-whew!'

'Oh!' mewled Sachu, in an ecstasy. 'Who would have thought it! Professor Ram has written on Hindu dharma! It is our favourite subject!'

'Just a modest volume,' said Professor Ram, using thumb and forefinger to show how small it was. His Rolex gleamed.

'Wait! I have the book right here.' Mrs Ram fished a spiral-bound volume out of her handbag.

'*Daddy What is the Significance of the Poonal and One Hundred Other Questions About Hinduism,*' Sachu read. 'A book that shows the eternal relevance of the golden values of Hinduism,' said the blurb at the back.

Kicha was saying 'So, Sankaranarayanan, how is the weather in Canada?' when he looked up and saw the part of the title of this book which was not covered by Sachu's fingers.

'*One Hundred*—you have found it!' he exclaimed, feeling as if he had found the lost sheep. 'You have found my book! Can I look at page 113—'

Sachu ignored him, and flipped through the pages. Professor Ram's imaginary son was a pestilential seeker after truths, full of satiable curtiosity. No sooner had his father answered the question 'Daddy what is Untouchability?' ('Son, it is an unfortunate practice that crept into Hinduism under foreign occupation. People outside the Four-Caste system used to be kept at a distance from people of the higher castes for hygienic reasons. This practice does not exist in free India, where we take our cue from Mahatma Gandhi, and practise tolerance towards all. In fact, Gandhiji called the untouchables 'Harijans' which means 'children of God' and we should try to bring them into the Hindu fold by calling them this name') than the brat asked, 'Daddy, what is the Four-Caste System?'

Sachu read the reply admiringly:

'"Son, the *Rig Veda* says that the Original Purusha or Cosmic Man was broken up into the people of the four Varnas or main castes who made up our society. His mouth or head was made into the Brahmin or priestly caste, His arms into the Kshatriya or warrior caste, His thighs into the Vaishya or trading caste and His feet into the Shudras or farming caste. The guiding principle was purely division of labour, and as such there is no room for conflict between the castes. How can there be conflict between the parts of a single body?" Aaha, aaha, Professor Ram! How beautifully you have expressed it!'

'Daddy really is indefatigable,' Chunky said. 'You should see some of the prayer meetings he organizes.'

'Have you ever attended any of the prayer meetings, Sundar?' asked Professor Ram. 'Of course, you shouldn't be scared off by the word "prayer", you know. They are gatherings where the students are encouraged to focus their yogic energy for the good of the world. We also discuss the noble texts of Hinduism. Right now we are discussing the *Sundarakaandam*.'

'Daddy, what is the *Sundarakaandam*?' Jay asked in an odd voice. For a moment Sachu thought she was mocking her father.

'Whew-whew!' Mrs Ram cackled. 'These children love to pretend that they know nothing about our ancient heritage! Jay, you know very well that the *Sundarakaandam* is the most sacred section of the sacred epic *Ramaayanam*!'

Vaithy made a sound like sandpaper on old dealwood. Pati slurped at her gums with delicious abandon. And the way Uma was sitting there, Sachu felt she had seen some Beanie Babies that looked more animated.

'Shall we have some refreshments?' Sachu said, with a significant look at Uma.

'Whew-whew-whew-whew!' said Mrs Ram, signifying assent.

Sachu looked many different kinds of daggers at Uma, because it was the duty of a would-be bride to serve her in-laws. But Uma stared blandly at the floor and did not pick up either the pakodas or the murukkus. Sachu was forced to hand them around herself.

'Give the children some first,' Mrs Ram said.

'Oh, my children never eat at all,' Sachu sighed. 'Perhaps I am one of the few mothers in the world who has never heard her children say: Give us another helping, Amma!' She felt that refinement required a certain decent depreciation of gross appetites.

Mrs Ram took one pakoda, out of politeness, and nibbled at it delicately. But before the plate could move on to Professor Ram, she leaned towards Sachu and said in an urgent stage whisper, 'Not for him! He won't have any! My hubby is so particular about what he eats, especially now that he is reading the *Sundarakaandam*! This pakoda contains onions!'

'Oh!' Sachu bit her lip helplessly.

'Purity, purity, purity!' Professor Ram declared, rolling his eyes up so that he could see his own eyebrows. 'My whole existence is governed by an everlasting search for purity! You must think me such a traditionalist, Mrs Vaidyanathan, but it has been an obsession with me from the time I was a babe-in-arms. A pure heart and a pure mind are supported by a pure body!'

Sachu was mortified. What a mercy that she had not taken out the cake from Hotbreads! Muruga! If onions caused such shock waves, what effects might eggs have had!

'We never cook onions in our home,' Professor Ram clasped his hands together and shuddered. 'We feel onions should not be a part of the Brahmin diet. "Garlic, leeks, onions, mushrooms, and all plants springing from impure substances," Manu the Lawgiver wrote, "are unfit to be eaten by twice-born men"'.

'Yes,' Sachu agreed abjectly. 'Yes, I am with you completely. We only started having onions here when the children started to ask for them.'

The words were already out of her mouth before she remembered how the Rams had asked for a bride and groom who were completely onion-and-garlic-free. How could she have forgotten that line in the advertisement, the same advertisement which she knew by heart, backwards and forwards, as well as she knew her own name? That line which said in parentheses, '(no onions or garlic)'?

'As a matter of fact,' she improvised despairingly, 'even the children have gone off onions completely, and we have practically given them up. Yes, we all *hate* onions so.'

'*Who* says we do?' Vaithy roared suddenly. Professor Ram, who was sitting by him, jumped a clear six inches into the air, because he had begun to feel that Vaithy was a prop, and he did not expect props to suddenly start taking speaking parts in medias res, like the helmet in *The Castle of Otranto*.

'Onions,' Vaithy spat, 'are very good for the sex life. They heat up the blood and function as an aphrodisiac.'

Having delivered himself of this, he sank into a torpor like the dormouse at the tea party, and Professor Ram was unable to get a single word out of him for the rest of the evening.

Sachu's fair face had turned purple. Out of the corner of one eye she could see Sundar helping himself to a generous handful of onion-filled pakodas. Out of the corner of the other eye she could see Kicha opening his mouth to tell Chunky a joke. She felt that the only way to stave off complete ruin was to throw herself into every conversational nook and cranny.

'Being fastidious about food is so sound,' she said. 'Research supports the scriptures in this matter.'

'The Professor is so particular,' Mrs Ram took up where she left off. 'You might say he is almost finicky. You know, we had a cook last month—oh, she was definitely Brahmin, we checked, but she never told us that she had worked for a Chettiar family for six years. Imagine that! A hand that cooked Chettinad food, all those meats and eggs and spices, taking up the ladle in our house!'

'No! Not eggs!' Sachu threw up her hands in horror.

'I sent her away as soon as I heard,' Professor Ram said. 'As it is, the spiritual damage was great, and on top of everything she was trying to make an argument over it, and whining about having mouths to feed back in Madurai.'

'The Professor is very compassionate, but he is also very firm when he has to draw the line.' Mrs Ram shook her head and the diamonds winked in her ears. 'Servants!'

'Well, of course, one has to be careful even with people who are not servants,' said Professor Ram. 'One of my Harijan students came home to leave a chapter of her thesis, on a hot and sunny day. What could I do? I am not the sort of man who'd send her away without a glass of water.' He paused, his face stern, his eyes on the pakodas. '*But! But* we gave away the glass to charity afterwards.'

'Tch, tch,' Sachu clicked her tongue sycophantically. 'He is a crusader, that is what your Professor is, Sundar. You are so blessed. Even I am not so particular about purity.'

'Ah, but the times are changing,' Mrs Ram said, as she helped herself delicately to several pakodas. 'It has become so dangerous to talk about these preferences, except among ourselves. Why, Chunky is even doing a paper on Harijans at the conference this week. Aren't you, Chunky? Not that he will do anything against his father's tradition—it is only because the Professor himself gave him his blessing that he is presenting it!'

'The next generation must find its own solutions,' declared Professor Ram. His hand hovered over the table. 'We can only hope to guide them in the right direction.' He picked up a murukku and examined it. 'My problem is not with Harijans as such, but with the consequences of encouraging them too much. All these Reservations!'

'The year my older son applied for medical and engineering,' Sachu said, pleased that the murukku had passed the test, 'the cut-off mark was 92 per cent for Open Category students. And the IIT cut-off was even higher.'

'It is a national disgrace,' Professor Ram said, crunching.

'For one year during his Plus Two, my poor Kicha woke up at 6 o'clock every morning to go to Brilliant Tutorials. We spent money like water, too!'

'And, no doubt, that year some Reserved Category nincompoop got the place which already had your son's name written on it. It is a great loss to the country, a great loss… tragic, tragic.' Professor Ram bit into another murukku gravely.

'But even if he did not go to IIT, the Brilliant tuition was not wasted,' Sachu said. 'He got such a valuable science degree that he is practically the backbone of the Research and Development at Jagadambal Pappadum.'

This biographical sketch of Kicha bored Professor Ram inordinately, and once, in fact, he nodded off, only to feel a sharp crack when the side of his head connected with Vaithy's helmet. Vaithy seemed to be fast asleep now. Professor Ram tried to keep himself alert by thinking hard about posterity. 'People will be hungry for details about my life,' he thought to himself. 'Such as what I said on important occasions like this one. I really must start a journal.'

His thoughts were interrupted by a strange yammering noise.

Now Kicha never listened to anything people were saying to him because, as he once pointed out, if he spent all his time listening, how would he generate his own thoughts? It was not often that he had a thought. But when he did, it always annoyed him if the other people were still talking, for he yearned to give utterance before he lost the precious nugget. It was always a disconcerting experience to be near Kicha when he was having a thought, for his brain began to rattle in its box loud enough to be heard all the way down on Taramani Road. It was also Kicha's custom to make it known that something was forming inside his head by yammering like a cat watching a sparrow on the other side of the window.

'Kicha led the team which took out a patent on a new product,' Sachu pushed on, over the sound of Kicha's thought. 'Oh!' She pretended to notice for the first time the copy of *Jagadambal's Journal* with Kicha's picture, which she had left on the table earlier. 'Why, his picture was in the paper! Would you like to look?'

In truth, Professor Ram was not interested in any pictures in the paper except his own, but he looked politely at the back page of *Jagadambal's Journal*. The picture showed five men and women, all in lab coats. It was impossible to tell which face was Kicha's, for the photo was the size of an old ten-paisa stamp.

'Tell them about it, Kicha,' Sachu implored.

The yammering stopped. It was a great relief all round when Kicha's thought burst out into the open.

'Our Jagadambal research team,' Kicha said, 'has patented an idli which is flat and stackable, and puffs up instantly when hot water is added to it. A travel-friendly idli.'

'A brilliant invention!' Mrs Ram made a little clapping movement. 'Professor Ram's picture was in—'

'Paw-ti,' little Raja interrupted, going up to his father, and slapping his leg with his new Mickey Mouse gun. Kicha felt the germ of another thought forming in his head, still on the subject of the instant idli.

'The idli is precooked to a temperature of 156 degrees Celsius,' said Kicha, taking the gun from Raja, 'and is completely germ-free'. Absently, to help his thought grow, he pressed the trigger. At once the gun opened up on top; a jet of water spurted out of it and fell on the murukkus; a plastic Mickey Mouse sprang out with an accordion and began to play *Fur Elise* while spinning round and round in such a way as to bring all conversation to a halt.

'Ting da ding da ding da ding da ding!' Mickey played.

'Paw-ti?' said Raja to Sachu.

But Sachu was trying to wrestle the gun away from Kicha before he did any more damage with it.

'Da ding da ding? Da deeng da deeee-eek?' went Mickey, running out of steam.

'Paw-ti,' sobbed little Raja, going up to Mrs Ram.

Mrs Ram liked to think that babes and sucklings just came naturally into her arms. She felt that she made a very good Auntie.

'Oh the iddle *chellum* thing!' she shrieked. 'Oh, ook at iddle Raja, chuch a cute *ching*, he knows, he simply *knows* I am part of the family! Cho *chweet*! He knows I'm going to be his Pati! Say it again, chweetie—Pa-ti?'

Sachu's heart gave a little bump of gladness. Oh, it said, what a good omen this is! But little Raja screwed up his face in dismay, and began to wail.

'PAW-TEEE!' he yowled, doubling over and banging his palms on the ground.

'*Chitraaa!*' Sachu cried, for something about little Raja's body language expressed the meaning of his word better than his tongue could.

Little Raja's mother ran up with a plastic doo-doo box, and scooped the infant onto it just in the nick of time. He stopped wailing. Though the smell of Raja's product made Mrs Ram's nose crumple up quite a bit, Raja gurgled happily, and his mother beamed at him.

'Isn't he just so clever? He has learned to ask for his potty! Krishna—Rama—Govinda!' Chitra crooned, while she tweaked Raja's toes.

Sachu marched across to her. 'Take him out!'

'What? I can't hear you—Rama—Krishna—Govinda!'

'*Take him out!*'

Raja left in state, still on his cacca-box. His mother looked a trifle miffed.

Chunky was overcome by envy at the fluency with which Raja expressed himself on the potty. He leaned over and asked Kicha, 'What *does* he eat?'

'Idlis, Jagadambal idlis,' Kicha said, adroitly wedging himself into the conversation again. 'Take the company I work for, Mr Sankaranarayanan—'

Sachu rolled her eyeballs at him from behind Chunky. She wished him to make room for Uma, who was still sitting beside Chunky like a plastic doll. Kicha paid no attention.

'Take Jagadambal Pappadum and Condiments. All

completely Brahmin. The management is Brahmin. The owners are Brahmins. Every member of the administration is Brahmin. Even today every single appalam and pappadum is handmade, according to the traditional method, by credentialled Brahmin factory-workers. *Pure* Brahmins. That is company policy, company policy. We just have our sources and investigate all our employees.'

'This is why your company is so popular,' said Mrs Ram. 'We all feel a hundred-per-cent safe that our food has been handled by pure hands.'

Sachu felt she would have to get a new cornea, or new eyeballs, because the old ones were dwindling away due to friction, what with all the occasions on which she was obliged to roll them at various members of her family this evening. It seemed to be Pati's turn now. She had held her peace all this while, except for that shoop-shoop, but now she began to do the thing Sachu dreaded. She began to take an interest in Chunky's welfare.

Pati leaned over and spoke to Mrs Ram, her eyes twinkling. 'I could tell right away that your son spends many hours reading.'

'Why, yes,' Mrs Ram said, pleased that her son bore the marks of scholarship upon his brow.

'On his stomach,' said Pati, nodding wisely. 'I always tell my children that if they keep lying on their stomachs, naturally their bottoms will become bigger and bigger. When you lie on your stomach, all the food that you eat gets pushed out of your belly, and then it has to go somewhere, doesn't it? Have some more murukku,' she said, holding up the plate. 'Jagadambal murukkus. Very crisp and crunchy. We get them at a discount because of Kicha. Jagadambal uses very good oil.'

Sachu's worst nightmare had come true.

'Speaking of oil,' Pati continued blithely, paying no heed to Sachu's grimaces.

'Uma,' Sachu shouted. 'Bring the coffee!'

Uma stared at her hands fixedly.

'I will bring the coffee,' Kicha offered, leaping to his feet.

'Speaking of oil,' Pati went on, 'your son ought to try the new herbal hair oil which they are making in Kerala. They say it cures baldness completely. That Rajiv Gandhi used to buy it, poor fellow, but he got killed before his hair grew back.'

Mrs Ram laid down the arms of courtesy and took up the rapier with the edge. So, she thought, I'll show them. I can give as good as I get.

'Have you ever tried to use Fair & Lovely on Uma?' she said.

'She feels that it is much better for girls to be natural these days,' Sachu parried.

Pati said kindly, 'It is the sun in our country, it makes people quite brown. I suppose you feel that it is better to get a bride from India rather than one from Canada itself. Is it because of your poor boy's divorce?'

'It has nothing to do with that. It's just that there is too much of this feminism and all these other ugly trends in the West these days. All the Brahmin girls in Canada have been corrupted. No sense of the importance of purity, you know. Many of them are not even interested in marriage. We don't want that kind of girl in our family.'

'Of *course* not! Why would you!'

'It's so hot,' Jay said suddenly. 'Could you show me the washroom?'

Sachu jumped up to take her to the downstairs toilet which she had cleaned so nicely with Sanifresh. To her consternation, it was now full of Thatha.

'I'll take her upstairs,' Uma said.

The two girls disappeared up the stairs.

'They are making friends already,' Sachu said, with a

foolish snicker, waving the white flag. When the girls came back ten minutes later, Jay looked subtly different in a way they did not understand, and she was limping a bit.

'You've got some brick-pieces in the bathroom,' she said, rubbing her foot. 'Ow!'

Pati left off sucking her missing tooth. 'Last week,' she explained in ringing tones, '—no, it was two weeks ago—our top floor bathroom collapsed, and all the rubble fell into the bathroom below it.'

'Yes,' Kicha said, coming back with the coffee. 'That's right. Ma, why didn't you serve this cake to the guests? You must have forgotten it—it was behind the gas cylinder. Heaven knows why things keep falling down there. I hope the cockroaches didn't get into the cake.'

'Coffee for you, Professor? Coffee for you, Mrs Ram? Sundar, pass the Mysore-paaku to your Professor!' Sachu chattered hysterically.

'I was actually *inside* the toilet when it fell down,' Kicha said chattily. 'I was actually on the—'

'It is the bog,' said Pati. 'The foundations of this house are definitely sinking.'

'Why, is this true?' Mrs Ram said, looking up nervously. Her eyebrows travelled nearly all the way to the back of her neck.

'Oh, it is a tiny problem, it is going to be fixed this very week,' Sachu said in a weak voice.

'No support,' Pati said. She leaned towards Jay, who had sat down beside her. 'No support,' she said again, pointing to Jay's chest.

'What?' Jay looked up, startled.

'I was reading *One Hundred Party Jokes*, when the whole toilet—you won't believe this—the *entire toilet*—'

'If you don't wear a boddy,' Pati said to Jay, '*those* will be hanging down to here'. She delicately prodded Jay in the belly. 'Dingle-dangling before you are thirty. No support.'

Now Pati said this in a clear voice like the TV anchor on *The Children's Hour*. It became obvious to one and all that what Jay had done in the toilet was take off her bra. Mrs Ram looked as if she had swallowed a pretzel, whatever that is. She altogether lost interest in the subject of what was wrong with the Varadan Street architecture.

For a little while after Pati scored Varadan Street's equalizer, there was silence among the married couples, and in this silence the unmarried couples found their tongues. Professor Ram waggled his eyebrows at Sachu and said to her conspiratorially: 'Mrs Vaidyanathan, isn't it amazing how the children appear so involved with each other already? This generation doesn't know the meaning of shyness! Even our Jayanthi, who's normally quite reticent, and hardly ever speaks to us—even Jay is nattering away, did you notice?'

This is what Jay was saying to Sundar, in a very soft voice. 'Chunky's been foraging in chatrooms for female companions. Under the title Hellraiser.'

'Oh?'

'I kid you not.' She smiled at him sweetly. 'He subscribes to every single agency in Canada that offers to expand his penis size. If all their claims were true he would have to carry his equipment around rolled up like a hose, and lend it to the fire department whenever needed.'

'Yes,' said Sachu who, at the other end of the room, could see but not hear the couples. She glowed with the same parental gratification that she detected in the Rams' eyes. 'Heads close together too! Such a handsome couple! And look, my Uma is so interested in what Sankaranarayanan is saying to her!'

Chunky was saying many things to Uma, most of them beginning with 'Back home in Cya-nada'. If Uma did not respond with great enthusiasm, Chunky knew it was because Indian women were naturally modest.

'Have you done any computer courses?' Chunky said.

'Yes, I work for Price Waterhouse, and I use accounting software.'

'Good, you godda be computer-liderate to come out West where I live. Back home in Cya-nada, kids start on computers before they are out of elementary school. I hope you have done some cookery classes? I just can't get used to Canadian food. And back home in Cya-nada, you really have to have wheels. Have you done any driving courses?'

Suddenly Kicha leapt up. 'Oh, my God! I just remembered—I have some samples of the idlis right here! Jagadambal's Jump-Start Your Day Instant Idlis! Let me bring them for you!' He cantered across the room before Sachu could stop him, and gripped the cabinet drawer's handle.

How Kicha pulled and tugged at that drawer, which would not yield! How Sachu threw herself on it and tried to wrench the handle away from him! How there was a crack like a country bone-setter making a miscalculation! And how Kicha flew backwards like the Angel of History, and fetched up at Professor Ram's feet with the drawer in his hands! How some of the books jammed into that drawer earlier did the Fosbury flop over Kicha's head and landed in Professor Ram's lap!

'Ah—' said Kicha, with a grunt of quiet satisfaction such as was sometimes heard from a travel-weary knight of old when he spring-cleaned his attic and found that the Holy Grail was stashed there all along. He fished four packages out of the debris.

'The idlis.'

He poured them into Mrs Ram's expensively draped lap.

'Keep them,' he said to Mrs Ram. 'They are for you only.'

Professor Ram glanced at the books that lay on his knees. One was called *Why I Am Not a Hindu* and the other was called *The Communist Manifesto*.

'I think we will take our leave now,' said Professor Ram.

As he went over to put on his shoes, Professor Ram picked his way grimly through an obstacle course. This obstacle course was made up of two overflowing ashtrays, a copy of a book called *Women Writing in India*, six packets of Charms Mini filter-tips, a paperback with a picture of a blonde floozy who considerately got herself murdered in a nightie that was more see-through than a vodka bottle, a poster of a very dark-skinned girl acting in a play, which Sachu had confiscated from Sundar's room, and finally, a box of cake from Hotbreads, abandoned near the mangy sofa.

'How could you let him do his potty here?' Sachu cried to Chitra as they washed up together in the kitchen. Uma and Sundar were in their rooms, shedding their finery. The Rams had gone away without offering any clear indication of what they proposed to do, and Sachu was on pins, for she did not know how the score-card stood.

'But he was asking for his potty,' Chitra said calmly, 'and none of you noticed, what was I to do?' She carved the Hotbreads cake into pieces and packed them into a storage box. 'Potty-training is a very sensitive period. Raja may be traumatized forever if he is rejected. Babies think of bowel movements as gifts, you know.'

Vaithy came into the kitchen looking for a matchbox to light his cigarette.

'I never heard such rubbish in my life!—Appa, pass me that towel—gifts! Muruga! You are getting all these newfangled ideas from these stupid American books!' Sachu said.

'If you don't understand American books, why do you think you will understand American culture?' Vaithy growled. 'Why do our children have to get married to—to—' and here he remembered Professor Ram's justification of the Four-Caste System and words failed him. 'Ha!' he bellowed, smacking his helmet, which he had taken off at last, against the wall. 'Cosmic Man's body! Division of labour! Ha! I notice your Professor

Ram did not mention what happened to the cosmic fellow's arse, but I can tell you! It became the—the *cloaca* you want Uma to take for a husband!'

Sachu looked at him reproachfully.

'She will be quite happy to marry him. He is a most eligible boy, and if you had not been sleeping, you yourself would have seen them talking together like a couple of lovebirds from the cinema. In fact, she will probably come down now and tell you off, you and her grandmother, acting as if you deliberately wanted to spoil the match!'

'But, adee, he has not enough hair on his head to keep his brain warm!' Pati wailed. 'Surely you do not want the child to marry, at her age, a fellow who will be a bald man in another two years?'

Kicha came in to mix his Evacu-eeze.

'A lot of very great people are bald,' said Sachu impatiently. 'In fact, all over the world people shave their heads.'

'Mahatma Gandhi was bald,' Kicha said.

'Be quiet, you! Opening that drawer and disgracing your mother, instead of sitting still! What they must have thought about the cigarettes—the dirty book! The *cake*!' Sachu moaned.

'There is bald and there is bald,' Pati said resolutely. 'Now if he looked like that Bucket, it would not matter if he was bald or if his hair stood straight up on his head.'

'What Bucket?'

'David Bucket. That football boy who can bend the ball when he kicks it. He is a very nice-looking boy.'

'He is probably just a Homa-whatsit, already married to another man. And anyway we cannot get him for our daughter. All my cousins will burn up with envy if we conclude this alliance with Professor Ram. A man who has published spiritual books! An evolved and superior person! With oh—such a fine style!'

'He is not so evolved that he has stopped eating, that's for sure,' Vaithy muttered, breathing out smoke like a dragon. 'He looks like a bullfrog in the mating season!'

'No one in this family can be self-righteous about eating!' Sachu exclaimed. She lowered her voice so Pati would not hear. 'Look at your father! Sneaking pakodas at his age, and making us a laughing-stock by breaking wind in front of all these people!'

'What do you expect? Eating is one of the few pleasures he has left. And the pujai nonsense was not his idea—you made him do it!'

'And your mother, saying that the snacks were from Jagadambal! After I had just said they were made by Uma! I felt like such a fool! Oh, I cannot bear it if they turn us down for some silly reason like this!'

'Here,' said Pati kindly, 'just drink some buttermilk and go to bed. Everything will be fine in the morning.'

'She's really cute, isn't she?' Chunky said for the tenth time, as he and his sister went up to their bedrooms, back at No.16, First Main Street, Mylapore. 'What did she say to you when you went upstairs? Did she say anything about me?'

'Said she found you fascinating, Chunks,' Jay drawled, 'but a bit too much cellulite on you for her taste. If I were you, I'd start thinking of getting a rope right away, to hang myself when she turns me down. Or maybe you can use the rope for some exercise. I think you should start skipping—as in jumping rope. Two hundred times before breakfast.'

Chunky's face was thoughtful.

'Good idea. I'll get a rope from Mylapore Sports tomorrow,' he said. 'Do you know a website where I can look up herbal hair oils?'

Professor Ram and Mrs Ram had gone up to their bedroom too. Now, we do not know the sleeping arrangements of Professor Ram's divine namesake and his consort, but presumably if they lead by example, as Mr Swaminathan suggests, their bedchamber reflects the Hindu ideal of sexual self-restraint. Anyway, in Professor Ram's case, what had happened was that when Mrs Ram hit her mid-thirties, about sixteen years ago, Professor Ram reached over one night in bed and, with a twist of his wrist, plucked from her head a perfectly silver hair that she never knew she possessed. Mrs Ram resented the fact that Professor Ram had noticed this silver hair when he never noticed how she started backcombing her tresses in the Sixties, or how she finally gave up the beehive in the Seventies.

Professor Ram explained it in his deepest, most solemn voice: 'Charu, we must acknowledge the fact that we are entering sannyaasam, which is the third stage in the life of the Brahmin person.'

Tonight, Professor Ram and Mrs Ram were too tired to conduct the Ram side of the post-mortem. So they just moulted their special clothes without looking at each other and fell into their separate beds. Separate? Yes. When Professor Ram sold the double bed and velvet mattress that had served them since their nuptial night, and bought Formica single cots with two bedside tables between them, Mrs Ram finally realized that the entry into sannyaasam would be marked by the complete cessation of the old rumpy-pumpy. She truly understood, then, that the Hindu wife's duty was to curb lustful propensities and promote universal harmony.

In which you will find Reading, 'riting, 'rithmetic, and some Fainting in Coils

———————————— ⁓ ————————————

THE THAPPU-PLAYERS WERE drumming up a storm all around Professor Ram. The macabre thunder they made masked Mrs Ram's footsteps, for the professor did not hear her come up to him. But he did see the wicked flash of her Malacca cane as she raised it over his willy—*Chop*! It was gone! Mrs Ram took the organ to the beach outside the university, and left it to dry there like saltfish. When it became pathetically detumescent and flat, who should come along and pick it up but Laurentia Arul. She gave it to Jiva, who took it away to her office in the English department—wait! Stop! *How did Jiva have an office in the English department?*—and began to use it as a bookmark in her copy of *Annihilation of Caste*. Professor Ram looked down at himself. In the place of his lost danda, a gigantic onion had sprouted, full of onion juice.

'Aaaarrgh!' shrieked Professor Ram, waking himself up. 'Haaaaarraaagh!'

He tottered to the bathroom to piss. When he had finished, he put down the toilet lid and climbed onto it shakily, getting his hips in line with the bathroom mirror. He needed the reassurance of his eyes. Siva-Siva. Oh, Lord of the Phallus. He turned sideways and checked again. It was all still there, his gear and tackle and trim.

'Wake up, Charu!' he said when he came back to bed.

'But it is only four o'clock in the morning!' Mrs Ram groaned.

'Wake up! I have had a nightmare. Wake up!'

When Professor Ram had nightmares, the first duty of the Hindu wife was to roll out of her single bed and bring him a tumbler of warm soothing milk, and the second was to massage his legs until he dropped off again. So while Mrs Ram was pressing Professor Ram's calves, not lustfully but impersonally, she brought up something that was worrying her: 'Ram, I was a little surprised this evening. You didn't even ask if Uma could sing!'

'It went out of my head completely,' Professor Ram exclaimed. His voice came out slightly muffled by the pillow. 'What an evening! Onions! A poster of my student Jiva—I wonder where *that* came from. *Why I Am Not a Hindu*! Siva-Siva! Marxist literature!'

'Cigarettes! Hotbreads cakes! A house that is collapsing!' added Mrs Ram. 'And I thought there was something strange about the father. Imagine wearing your helmet the whole evening, inside the house! And did you notice how, when our Chunky was doing his namaskaaram, his wife banged him in the ribs with her elbow?'

'They are probably concealing insanity or something. Let us drop them, Charu.'

'Only, Ram...' Mrs Ram hesitated. 'Ram, isn't it odd that Jay has not said anything?'

'That child has a diabolical streak. I don't know what she will come up with next,' said Professor Ram.

Mrs Ram blurted out, 'Ram, she hasn't bought *any* sanitary napkins since she came down for the vacation, and she is looking fuller than she was when she left for Canada! What does that suggest to you?'

'It is the Canadian food, my dear Charu—surely you remember how I myself put on a pound or two during my sabbatical there!'

'No—put it together, Ram! Ram, *a mother always knows!* And it is so easy for a girl to be with a man in Canada! Oh, it is terrifying to think what everyone will say about us! We will never be able to show our faces in this city again! You will never be able to do another play! The shame and scandal—an illegitimate grandchild—I am *sure of it!*'

Professor Ram shuddered strongly all over his person.

'Can't you talk to her, ask her—'

'Haven't I asked her a dozen times? Haven't I asked her in oblique ways and then directly? Will she open her mouth and answer me? Not she! She gets that *look* on her face—that stubborn look that frightens me. I never thought I would see my own child as an enemy!'

For a moment Mrs Ram felt so bad that she thought of asking Professor Ram to put his arms around her. Then she remembered the whole duty of the Hindu wife. She wrung the polyester pillowcase and cracked her knuckle-joints; she choked back a sob.

'Sssh, Charu, don't get hysterical now, she will hear you. It seems there is only one safe thing to do. The sooner we push this alliance through, the better it will be for all concerned. Even if they find out, the boy is completely under my thumb, and the father doesn't seem to be very intelligent.'

'Push it through *quickly*,' said Mrs Ram. 'Before it—she— starts *showing*. And there is something else to worry about too.'

'What's that?'

'Lakshmi. She was very bitter, even though she was the one who filed for divorce, not Chunky.'

'Oh, Lakshmi's abroad somewhere. I wouldn't worry about her too much.'

'Remember how she said that she would come back from the ends of the earth to make sure Chunky didn't ruin any other woman's life? Such cheek, considering she was the one who damaged *him*. Push this alliance through before she appears from God-knows-where and destroys our poor boy's chances.'

'You have a point,' said Professor Ram, plumping his pillow thoughtfully. 'We don't know what destructive thing she might be capable of.'

'And Chunky said in the car that he liked this girl Uma, though she is on the dark side,' said Mrs Ram. 'And it is true that the family is not at all well off. But we don't have any other offers for him.'

'Uma is quite good-looking, in a wholesome kind of way,' said Professor Ram.

'Is she? I didn't notice,' said Mrs Ram.

'Hmmm. As a matter of fact, the boy could be an asset to me. At the university, you know. Things seem to be coming to a head there.' Professor Ram tested his pillow. 'Complete loyalty is hard to find.'

'Then it is decided. Phone them first thing in the morning, and we will fix up a meeting to discuss the financial side of things,' said Mrs Ram. Again she felt a twinge of yearning. 'Ram—'

'And now, Charu,' said Professor Ram, nestling his head into the pillow and turning on his side away from her. 'Compose yourself and stop nagging me. Let me get some sleep.'

At a quarter to nine on Tuesday morning, over an hour before she was due at Seshadri Towers, Sachu jangled her bangles at a passing autorickshaw on Taramani Road. The driver saw her only after he passed her. While he was looping the loop to come back to her, the scooters and pi-dogs on both flanks caught it. The expletives which hit him from all sides just bounced off him, as he was a very macho auto-driver indeed.

'I have to go to Kottivakkam and come back to Seshadri Towers within fifty minutes,' Sachu said.

'Waiting charge,' said the auto-driver laconically, fiddling with his radio knob. 'Five rupees over the meter.'

'The Supreme Court has issued notice to the Central Government and to Mr Narendra Modi, chief minister of Gujarat, on a petition seeking impartial inquiry into the communal violence in Gujarat,' said the radio.

To a woman who had just organized a double NRI alliance single-handed, even very macho auto-drivers were child's play. (Alas, Bucket Maami's assistance was forgotten almost as soon as the battle was won; indeed Sachu had forgotten that Bucket Maami was going to book the wedding hall that morning.)

'Waiting charge,' Sachu agreed, and there was iron in her tones. 'No extra.'

The auto-driver studied her face for a second, and then, without any argument, plucked at his starting lever and turned on his meter.

'Three Dalit members of Keeripatti panchayat, in Madurai district, were hacked to death last evening as they travelled to Madurai by bus, allegedly in retaliation for contesting the elections in this constituency reserved by statute for Dalits.'

'Switch off the radio,' said Sachu irritably. She did not want inauspicious reports of death and misery to spoil her pleasure, for she was meditating deliciously on the conversation she had had with Professor Ram that very morning at around 6 a.m.

'Mrs Vaidyanathan? Oh, good morninng, good morninnng. I hope I am not calling too early for you-u,' Professor Ram had said in his chummiest, plummiest voice.

'No, no, Professor Ram, I am happy to hear your voice, and anyway, I am awake because of the water lorry—' Sachu answered.

'I have come to a decisionnn, and our son—our children— are happy with my choice.'

'Oh! What is it?' gasped Sachu, gripping the receiver in a fist that was suddenly slippery with perspiration.

'Mrs Ram and I feel that it is a special omen that Sundar has come into our life at a time when I am reading the

Sundarakaandam. In fact, we believe that Sri Rama himself has spoken, and that he is directing us to conclude this alliance with your family.'

In her heart, Sachu blessed the hotline that was always open between Professor Ram and his heavenly namesake. She managed to say something appropriate before she became incoherent with thankfulness.

'We must discuss the financial details,' Professor Ram continued, 'and set a date for the wedding. Let us do this right away, because you will want to get the invitations printed quickly. It has to be very soon, because Sankaranarayanan has a tight schedule. He has to leave for Australia, where he is due to present papers at three separate conferences. Shall I meet you at your home about an hour from now, on my way to work? My family will be with me.'

How simple it all seemed then! How nervous she had been before this, and how her family had very nearly ruined everything—Kicha by obtuseness, Raja by incontinence, Pati by talking too much, and Vaithy by not talking at all! All in all, Sachu felt as if affliction had come for her head and gone away with nothing more than her hairdo.

'Everything is settled,' Sachu told Sundar and Uma. 'Your marriages will take place in less than a fortnight.'

Their faces were longer than the last hour before the weekend.

'But you didn't even ask us if we liked them!' Sundar groaned, clapping his hand to his forehead.

'What rubbish is this? Do you have any objection to the girl?' Sachu demanded.

'No—yes! I don't want to marry her!'

'Why not?'

'I don't know—I just don't, that's all.'

'That is not a good enough reason. She is very pretty and she is from an excellent family. The boy has such good prospects. Oh!'

'What is it now?'

'I am getting chest pain, listening to your foolish arguments! Besides, I have to go to work now.'

It is just astounding how the wedding season in Chennai brought on enough angina to keep an army of cardiologists in the style to which they were accustomed, and a perfect rash of near heart attacks. Most respectable citizens with children of marrying age took night classes in clawing at their ribs and gasping in agony, so that when the moment came, and they were obliged to untangle the recalcitrant beautiful from winsome Wild-Oats with the cowlick and the motorcycle, and splice her to Buck-Tooth with the bank balance and the Ford Ikon, they were able to deliver the emotional shakedown with hundred-per-cent professionalism. But Sachu's angina was genuine. You will know the reason soon, dear reader; in the next chapter it will become clear.

Still, when Sachu entered the sanctum of Mr Varadarajan of V.R.V. Printing Press, clutching a sheet of paper on which she had typed the double wedding invitation, her step was buoyant and her eyes were bright, and there was no indication that she had had a brush with chest pain that very morning.

'I want this paper,' she said, riffling through Mr Varadarajan's samples. 'This pink one.'

'Magenta-woolly-finish-handmade-Number 263!' Mr Varadarajan barked. His assistant was taking notes.

'The gold picture of Ganesha on one side through a hole, like that, and lamps all around.'

'Die-cut-golden-casted-Ganesha!' Mr Varadarajan translated. 'Self-embossed-lamp-motif-border! Pearl-print-base-overleaf! Right! Are you bringing the matter, madam?'

'Yes,' said Sachu. 'Here it is.' She handed over the paper and sat down to discuss prices and discounts with Mr Varadarajan. While she haggled, the assistant typed her matter into his computer. Like this:

By the divine grace of His Holiness Sri Sri Sri Jayendra
Saraswati, Sankaracharya of Kanchi

*We request your kind presence and august blessing on the
doubly auspicious occasion of the weddings of*

Sow. V. Uma
(d/o Sri K. Vaidyanathan and Smt. Saraswati
Vaidyanathan, Chennai)

with

Chi. P. Sankaranarayanan (MA, London, Ontario)
(s/o Sri (Prof.) S. Pattabhiraman and Smt. Charumati
Pattabhiraman, Chennai)

and of

Chi. V. Kalyanasundaram
(s/o Sri K. Vaidyanathan and Smt. Saraswati
Vaidyanathan, Chennai)

with

Sow. P. Jayanthi
(d/o Sri (Prof.) S. Pattabhiraman and Smt. Charumati
Pattabhiraman, Chennai)....

'I'll telephone you with the venue, date and time by this
afternoon,' Sachu said. 'They are not fixed yet.'

Mr Varadarajan appreciated the precipitateness of NRI
weddings. His own son had arrived in India from San Francisco
one Friday at daybreak last year on a very short vacation, and
Mr Varadarajan had found a bride, fixed up the hall, engaged
a priest, conducted the wedding and bundled the couple off on
a honeymoon before his son could say jet-lag. And it was still
Thursday evening in California at that.

'If you give me the venue and date and time before 3 p.m., madam, the proofs will be ready tomorrow itself,' said Mr Varadarajan.

Sachu agreed to do the needful. She got into the autorickshaw and left for Seshadri Towers, well pleased with her morning's work.

Mrs Ram, on the other hand, had woken up this morning feeling seedier than an old pomegranate. It was the second night in succession that her husband had kept her up during the still watches, and the whole duty of the Hindu wife had not spared Mrs Ram time to catch above twenty-five winks per night on her own account. Then there was the meeting with Sachu early in the morning. Worse still, Mrs Ram's new cook had failed to show up today, and Mrs Ram had used up all her resources making breakfast. At eleven o' clock therefore, she felt too ill to make the proper four-course meal that Professor Ram liked, hot-hot, at lunchtime. This was when she bethought her of the packages of Jagadambal Jump-Start Your Day instant idlis that still lay in her handbag.

'The answer to a housewife's prayer!' the package enthused. 'Spread dehydrated idli chips on a plate. Just boil a pan of water and pour on chips, 3.5 cc per idli. Let stand for 5 minutes. Watch the idlis turn as fluffy as those your granny used to make! Serve hot with chutney and sambhar, and Jump-Start your Day!'

Mrs Ram followed the instructions, except that she was too tired to make chutney and sambhar. She coated the idlis with oil and chilli-powder. This was how, when Mrs Ram's servant-woman Thaayi headed for the university on the No. 27 noon bus, the woven plastic lunchbag she was carrying held a tiffin-box full of Kicha's astounding brain-children.

After Thaayi had left, Mrs Ram phoned Sri Sri Sri

Panchapakesa Sastrigal at Pa-Mistry Matrimonials and told
him she wanted to hand over Uma's and Sundar's horoscopes
for cross-checking. Now, Mrs Ram's marriage to Professor
Ram had survived the seven-year itch, when the heart said,
'Oh-oh. I have gone and married the wrong man.' It had
survived the fourteen-year itch when the brain said, 'Fourteen
years and it still hasn't worked. If I don't leave now, I will
become an old flour-bag and never have a chance with anyone
else.' It had survived the twenty-one-year itch, when both heart
and brain were pretty much out of it, but the bowels said,
'Twenty-one years of my life wasted, that is more of my life
with him than without him, and I should get out before I start
throwing up.' It had gotten over the twenty-eight-year itch, the
menopausal itch, when the dry vagina said, 'Enough is enough,
what do I need a man for? I don't even know if I want to bed
anyone. Thank God for the whole duty of the Hindu wife.' It
was coasting towards the thirty-five-year itch, the really fatal
one when the third eye opens and says, 'Are these breakfasts
and clean collars all that I shall see of the Spirit before I die?'

This was the best time and the worst time to have dealings
with godmen such as Sri Sri Sri Sastrigal. Mrs Ram was playing
with precisely this vaguely extra-marital fire. She was growing
to love the special way Sri Sri Sri Sastrigal looked deep into her
eyes whenever he put her in touch with the Over-Soul. She
shivered deliciously all over when he placed a reassuring hand
over hers, as he promised that the blessings of the goddess were
always with her. There was no denying it: she was becoming
addicted to the way his voice rumbled low and deep in her ear,
and the way his breath tickled her cheek, as he explained some
intricacy in the planetary chart. It was all so comforting, and
yet—and yet—it took her out of her body and made her spirit
soar into the empyrean. The big tilakam on his forehead, a
splash of bloody red from nose to hairline, mesmerized her like
anything. Sometimes, she felt that he knew every detail of her
life, and that he saw into her *heart*, and that he *understood* her

better than anyone else in the whole soulless world.

When Sri Sri Sri Sastrigal told her he could make time for her immediately, Mrs Ram's heart went pit-a-pat. Sri-Sri-Sri, went Mrs Ram's heart. Threefold auspiciousness and spirituality! At once she felt more energetic than she had felt in months. She changed her sari three times before she was satisfied. She powdered her face, tried to pencil a few hairs into her skimpy eyebrows, added three bangles to each of her wrists and put on a dash of lipstick. Sri-Sri-Sri. She stopped an auto outside No. 16, First Main Street. As the auto slalomed up Mount Road towards Santhome, where the living saint lived, she noticed a tall white girl going into an Internet café with a dark lugubrious-looking man. She thought the girl looked like Caroline, who had been introduced to her on the night of the play as Chunky's colleague from Canada. She was unable to place the man.

'Jeez, this is shiddy!' Caroline puffed, as she tried to bring her seat down to the right level in front of a small shabby monitor. 'Darn. This seat's stuck. I hope they get my laptop repaired real quick. Why don't they have air-conditioning in these crummy places?'

'Because they can't afford it,' said Akilan, swatting away flies from his face. He was in front of another computer.

Caroline mopped her brow frequently and took several large swigs from a Bisleri water bottle before she finished her letter.

Hi Mom,

It's already loads hotter here in Chennai than in midsummer London ON, and they say it's going to get a lot worse before it gets better. I'm doing pretty good, though, and I've started drinking lots of water like you told me to. My work's coming along nicely. I've seen a couple of really interesting shows already which are right bang on the spot as far as my topic goes. Did I tell you what it was? Folk theatre as protest in Tamil Nadu, though I guess that's a bunch of Greek to you. Trouble is, I don't get to see too many shows, but sometimes I just hang with these theatre guys and girls, and they're really cool. There's an actress here called Jiva, about my age, who's just finished her Ph.D. She's awesome. I'm getting to like her. Tomorrow we go on the road to see a show at a village about 80 km away from Chennai—where I am staying now. The hotel's fine, honest, and I like everything here except these really weird dudes who keep staring at me like they've never seen a female before. I'll write again soon. Love to Julie and Dad, and I hope this SARS scare isn't getting to you.

Caroline

Akilan put a big OM on top of his letter, just like Brahmins always did, and under it he typed like this:

Respected Sir,

I am having neither mother or father in this world, as they have attained the Lotus Feet of Lord Muruga when I was at very young age. Some relatives are taking care of me, but of late they have also attained Moksha. As a result I am leading a hand to mouth existense, and I am not able to have any education.

My friends are telling that you are a grate guru and you are teaching many boys like me. You are aware of the valeue of the education. But it is impossible to get this blessing if I am not able to pay the fees. As an orfan Brahmin boy who is struggling to make both ends meet in the middle I am forced to apply to benifactors such as your good self for your sucker. You are my Mother, my Father, my Guru and my God.

Lord Muruga will bless you for your genarous heart and your divine soul.

Please send your donations, in cash or kind, c/o K. Sundar, No. 5, Varadan Street, Pallavakkam, Chennai - 600 172. As I am without a roof over my head, I am collecting my mail from my friend's house.

May the choicest blessings of Godess Bhagavati of Chotanikarai always be showered upon you and your family.

Yours truely,
Anantharama Iyer

Now and then Akilan consulted his *Pocket Oxford Dictionary*. When he finished, he carefully made a copy of his letter on disk, paid the Internet café man a rupee and had his page printed out.

'Will you edit this letter before I xerox it?' he said to Caroline.

'Sure. Let's get oudda here and gedda drink. We took fifteen minutes each.'

'I am—ah—not having any funds,' Akilan confessed.

Caroline gave him a wry look, but she paid for both of them. While she was paying, Akilan sat down at a table, pulled out some envelopes from his satchel and inscribed them with the names and addresses of Professors Ram and Nagarajan and Subramaniam and Venkataraman, and many others who he knew subscribed to the Poor and Deserving Brahmin Boys Vedic Education Project. He was planning to go to the university that very afternoon and drop these letters off by hand, thus saving several rupees on stamps.

∼

When Sachu phoned Kicha at the Jagadambal office to ask him if he had booked Jagadambal Caterers for the weddings, he was taking a tea break and improving his mind. Any lip-reader who knew his job would have told you that he was reading Mr Swaminathan's 'Tidbits of Vedic Wisdom' in *The Bindhu.*

'Yes,' said Kicha. 'Don't worry, Ma, everything is under control.'

'Have you got the dates right?' Sachu persisted.

'Of course. Saturday, the 28th of April.' Bucket Maami had found a wedding hall free on that day and had put it on hold for Sachu.

'Wedding in the morning, reception in the evening?'

'Yes. I read it out from your paper, Ma. Eight hundred people for the wedding, six hundred and fifty for the reception.'

'Have you given the cheque for the advance?'

'Yes.'

'Good. Before the offices close this evening, I want you to go and pay the full amount on the hall—they won't hold it otherwise.'

'Umm.'

Sachu hung up, and Kicha was free to go back to *The Bindhu.*

Tidbits of Vedic Wisdom: Decline of Morality Everywhere

Though God's inexhaustible compassion towards all His children was to be the theme of this humble column today, an incident has arisen which has compelled the present writer to abandon his usual spiritual regimen and offer for his readers' consideration, instead, a shocking piece of intelligence about the corruption and degeneracy of our present-day civilization.

As readers may be aware, a group of godless miscreants known as 'the biscuit bandits' are travelling on the evening trains between Chennai and Hyderabad and offering their companions biscuits which are contaminated with soporific substances. As soon as the sedatives are taking effect, the biscuit bandits are making away with the goods and valuables belonging to the unwary passengers. As the present writer was travelling from Hyderabad to Chennai last week, he was offered a Tirupati laddoo, which he was unable to refuse, as it is a devotional offering made to the Lord Venkateswara of the Seven Hills.

Though the Southern Railways has issued a warning to passengers against accepting the biscuits, they have refrained from mentioning the Tirupati laddoos, and as a result I became the unfortunate victim of a heinous crime. After I consumed the laddoo, I lost consciousness, and when I woke up in Chennai the next morning, all my goods and valuables had been purloined by the miscreants. The Tirupati laddoo is having religious significance, and it is a very sacrilegious act to use it as a criminal weapon, but gone are the halcyon days when all self-respecting Hindus would have banded together to protest against such a desecration of their devotional offerings.

Everyday when I am walking on the Marina Beach in front of Chennai University, on the hallowed ground where monuments have been erected in order to memorialize our best and brightest, there are thugs and goondas who are moving freely and snatching the gold chains of respectable married ladies. Not only that, but the standards of public decency have reached their nadir. Notwithstanding the noisome particles of an excretory nature, young unmarried couples are effecting in broad daylight on the public beach certain exchanges of intimacies that are better reserved for the privacy of the bedchamber where Lord Surya the Sun-God himself may not blush to observe them. Indeed, an upright and law abiding citizen like myself is overcome by vicarious modesty—nay, shame—and as a result of averting my head from these blatant evils I have developed severe spondilosis. What is the world coming to? Have we reached the deepest troughs of iniquity that Kaliyuga can offer?

Kicha clicked his tongue vigorously. He was in complete sympathy with Mr Swaminathan. He took a sip of his tea, which tasted strongly of office boy. That youth always held the tea-glasses with his fingers dunked up to the second joint in the lukewarm contents, and it was a good thing he was a certified Brahmin, or there would have been mutiny among the senior staff.

'Ah—you're looking at *The Bindhu*,' said a voice behind Kicha. Vaithy was lounging against a desk with a tea-glass in his hand. 'There's a letter to the editor about your new invention,' he said vaguely and wandered away.

Kicha pawed through the pages until he found the Edit Page which carried the 'Letters to the Editor'. 'Another Dismal Performance by Our Cricket Team,' no, not that one, 'Chennai Going to Dogs,' no, can't be that, 'Size of Tirupati Laddoo,' no-oo, 'Idli fiasco—'

Idli fiasco! The letter went as follows:

Idli fiasco
   Sir,—Apropos Mr Swaminathan's article on Food for the Gods (Tidbits of Vedic Wisdom, April 12) the trend of instant foods is completely contradictory to our Hindu culture. Traditionally the ladies were conferred the honour of cooking and feeding their families. Because of degeneration of moral and familial standards, including going out to work, etc., the fair sex has neglected these duties. Many are forced to eat instant foods, and some are having them without even knowing that many preservatives are used and it is a great health hazard. Even in my family, we are using instant foods when the ladies are 'out of house', i.e., having their menses. Instant foods are completely unable to have a home-cooked taste. Jagadambal's Jump-Start Your Day instant idlis which has just come on the market is the worst, and I feel it is a public service if you warn your readers that after the idlis are

inflated, they have a rubber feeling in the mouth, as well as a taste like therma-coal.

S.K. Iyer, Tambaram

As he read that last lacerating paragraph, Kicha's tea slowly turned to slop in his mouth. Tears leaked out of his eyes and dripped unheeded onto the newspaper. They dripped all over an article about Chennai University's celebration of Dr Ambedkar's birthday. They obliterated a big picture of Akilan standing beside the statue he had cast. They dripped onto Kicha's shirt as well. There was a cheque in Kicha's pocket, and the tears turned this cheque into pulp. All in all, Kicha made a very soggy and sorrowful spectacle. He may be forgiven completely for forgetting that he had not actually booked Jagadambal Caterers yet. He had told Sachu a little white lie about doing so, because he wished, like a dutiful son, to keep his mother's blood pressure down at all times. She would have been worried if he had merely told her the truth, which was that he meant to use his tea-break to do this very thing. He meant to, that is, until the pain of social rejection drove it out of his head completely, together with all the thoughts that he had painstakingly had over the course of the day.

In the research scholars' common room at the university, Shastri picked up a piece of paper marked ERRATA from a stack of papers on a table, took a paper marked CONFLUENCE 2002: SCHEDULE from another stack, and united these two papers by means of office glue. He was sweating profusely. He had already performed this task with a hundred and twenty-eight papers, and would have to perform it with a hundred and seventy-two more, before he was done.

When the ACS conference was planned, Professor Ram bid at once for the role of convenor. He longed to hold office as president of the Association for Commonwealth Studies, and being convenor of a conference was definitely a stepping-stone. As soon as he heard that his bid had been successful, he summoned Shastri to his office.

'Shastri,' he said, 'I am organizing the ACS conference this year. You may take care of all the details.' And so Shastri immediately bought a notepad and a pencil and reported for work.

'Who are we inviting, sir?' Shastri asked.

'Oh you can ask some of the top Theory people,' said Professor Ram. 'Like Derrida, for instance, or Spivak. And put it down in the brochure and the Call for Papers that they are coming.'

'But it will take time to invite them and get their replies, sir,' said Shastri, his glasses misting up with bewilderment. 'How can we say that they have accepted?'

'Oh, let's not split hairs, Shastri. The names will be helpful, don't you understand—how else will we get all these tight-fisted Indian academics to pay their registration fees? They'll only come if they think some really famous critics are coming.' Professor Ram shot his cuffs in an offhand way.

Now Shastri put down 'Jacques Derrida: Plenary Paper' on the brochure, where it listed the big noises who were coming to this conference, and then he put down 'Gayatri Spivak'. Then he discovered that a writer called Foucault was given good publicity by Always Already, and so he copied down 'Michel Foucault' from one of her course outlines. Then he put down some of the doyens of Indian aesthetics, recommended to him by Professors Ram and Nagarajan. It was only after Professor Ram had irretrievably sent out the printed version of the brochure that Dr Arul stopped by his office and asked what in blazes he meant by having Foucault on his list, when Foucault was sewing mailbags in purgatory, or proofreading *The Law of Tort in Sixteen Volumes*, or doing whatever scribblers did in the hereafter to expiate the many volumes of clotted prose they produced in this world. Then Professor Ram looked up this character, and was very put off when he discovered that Foucault had gone belly-up in the year 1984. This made Professor Ram either a gruesome necrophiliac or a liar when he stated in his brochure that such a deader-than-a-doornail theorist was coming to a conference in Chennai as a guest of the university. Every conference schedule, in consequence, had to have an *Erratum* slip which said that Foucault was actually unable to make it.

After a while it turned out that Derrida and Spivak ('To Be Confirmed') were not actually coming to Chennai this year either. Nor were the doyens of Indian aesthetics. They were presenting papers at the New Zealand Association of Commonwealth Studies conference, or the MLA, or some such, and had no time to stop at Professor Ram's little paperfest. What with one thing and another, it turned out that the only conferees from outside India were Chunky and Caroline. The only thing that redeemed the conference was that the V-C persuaded Dr Annie Kurien, very highly thought of in many universities across the world, to stay on and attend the conference after she came to Chennai to sit on the panel that interviewed Chunky and Jiva.

Well, Professor Ram had put his funds bucket under the University Grants Commission, the British Council, and the United States Information Service, and had milked all of them serially and energetically, and had even put the bite on some corporate houses, precisely on the strength of the world-famous theorists who had agreed to attend his conference. Now he smelt very embarrassing indeed, and his chances of being elected president of the ACS were ruined completely.

So, naturally, he made Shastri step forward and take all the blame.

So now the conference schedule had to have a much longer ERRATA page. This page, which was what Shastri was pasting over every schedule, as part of his expiation, listed all the people who were not actually able to make it to the conference.

As Shastri pasted and pressed, pasted and pressed, he slowly fell into a daydream. He imagined that he was tall and attractive like Sundar. In his dream, he was walking on the beach hand-in-hand with a woman. The woman was his wife. She was luscious, like an alphonso mango in midsummer. Like Always Already. I do not need to remind you that Shastri was not tall and attractive, but short and skinny like a runt. It was widely rumoured that the vice-president of Students for Democracy once lit a cigarette as he walked a few yards behind Shastri, and when he blew out his match, Shastri fell over.

If the campus community considered Shastri to be a joke and a byword, it was really his father's fault. It was no secret that Shastri's father refused to get Shastri married before Shastri found a job. This was not because Shastri's father had any shortages to speak of. Oh no. Shastri's father was an inspector with the Chennai police, and being a very accepting man— accepting both legit lolly and the sub rosa kind in sackfuls, from the best families—he could easily have supported a young couple. But he declared that it would embarrass him among his relations if they caught Shastri's putative wife stretching her hand out, palm up, every time she needed chink for soap and hair oil. Shastri's father also would not hear of Shastri's quitting his Ph.D before he finished, since he had already spent fourteen years on it. As Shastri's father said, that was as much as Sri Rama spent in the wilderness, or as Charles Sobhraj spent in jail. Thus was Shastri's father cutting off his nose to spite his face or, as his elderly aunt told him acidly, quarrelling with the lake and going off in a huff without washing his bum. This, anyway, was the reason behind Shastri's extreme emaciation, and the dreams he dreamt today, and the hair on his palms. As the elderly aunt said, if Shastri took himself in hand at this rate, he would have nothing left when it came time to produce an heir.

All this is neither here nor there. But these dreams saw Shastri through a great deal of tedious pasting and pressing, until 171 ERRATA papers were spliced with 171 schedules. There was somehow no schedule to attach the 172nd to. His task completed, Shastri sat down to put the finishing touches to that month's *Brahmassthra*, which, in case you've forgotten, was the organ of the TamBrahmAss and the clarion call that went out each month to all those who wore the sacred poonal thread like a percentage mark between the nipple and the navel.

First of all, Shastri read through a piece that Professor Nagarajan had contributed:

Atrocities on Brahmins

Before speaking of all the atrocities on Harijans, please think about the sufferings of upper caste Indians who have to trust a Harijan doctor with their God-given bodies. This Harijan doctor probably has got a medical seat through the Reservations system, in spite of having a low academic percentage. Consider the politicians who vote in favour of Reservations, especially people like Dr V.P. Singh during whose infamous Prime Ministership the Mandal Commission was constituted, for the express purpose of extending the Reservations policy. Where does Dr V.P. Singh go for his dialysis? Not to the Public Health Centre, but to the United Kingdom. The present writer is convinced that all such politicians who support Reservations should be forced to have themselves and their families treated by such substandard unsanitary semi-atheistic doctors and face the consequences.

The *Rig Veda* says: Let noble thoughts come to us from all sides. And so, my dear TamBrahmAss friends, I hope that even though we have to fight for our nation and for our dharma we will do so with no evil thoughts, but only the best interests of our beleaguered brethren at heart. *Lokah samasthah sukhino bhavanthu.*

Shastri corrected a few typos and turned his attention to his own piece. He felt that Professor Nagarajan's essay paled to a shadow beside his own Edit Page contribution. Instead of labouring over a prose editorial, Shastri had written a poem. The subject of this poem was Professor Ram. Shastri was immoderately pleased with the result. His arch-rival, Sundar, no matter what else he did to ingratiate himself with Professor Ram, had never written a poem. It was a tough act to follow:

Professor Ram

In Kaliyuga, the times are sad
Our future prospects are so bad.
America all our boys entises
Our motherland is in a genuine crises.

At this point dear **Professor Ram**
Is radiating satvik calm,
Champion of uptroden masses
A chance to help up he never passes.

When our mood is dull and depressed,
Because of the way we are oppressed,
He is giving zest to each proceeding,
Not taking rest and receeding.

On Professor Ram we are depending
His efforts are never ending
To save our precious Indian culture
From all who attack it like a vulture.

He will restore our Hindu glory
And reconstruct each Sanskrit story.
In sport, art and refluxology,
We'll hold our heads up without apology.

Shastri had barely finished gloating over this achievement when his arch-enemy came in with a pile of books and a pile of foolscap paper. He sat at a table across from Shastri,

unscrewed his pen and began to chew it. For Sundar had made
no progress with his paper.

'~~William McGonagall has the undeserved reputation
of being the worst poet in the world.~~'

Sundar remembered that it was this reputation that had
recommended him to Professor Ram. 'We will show the world,
Sundar,' Professor Ram had said, 'that anyone, even the worst
poet in the world, can be made enlightening when seen through
the perspective of Sanskrit poetics.'

'What,' Sundar blasted off again, 'do the Scots poet William
McGonagall and the famous Sanskrit critic and theorist
Abhinavagupta have in common?'

Sundar read the McGonagall oeuvre one more time, and
he diligently marked passages in Abhinavagupta, but he still
could not say what they had in common, except that they were
both shattering bores. He sighed, for his thoughts were
elsewhere. Without his realizing it, his hand began to doodle
on a sheet of foolscap. The doodle looked like this:

but Jiva does not love Sundar she is beautiful
when she sings it makes me get a hole in my
stomach I hope she gets the job maybe if she
does I will ask if I can give her a treat idiot she
has lots of friends why should she go with
you what shall I do shall I write to her

Sundar's tongue stuck out of his lips and he knit his brows as he continued:

dear Jiva you don't know me well but I want to spend my whole life with you please will you marry me or at least go to the canteen for a cup of tea with me tomorrow shit it is the lousiest love letter in the world I could copy something from a poem

He leafed through his *Norton Anthology*. To his disgust, there were no poems to dark beautiful girls in all its tissue-thin pages, only to lily-white ones.

dear Jiva you are like a black rush imbedded swan, darkening the daytime torchlike and your voice revives the leaden strings and if any beauty I did see which I desired and got 'twas but a dream of thee oh shit I've got to call off these wedding plans why does Uma want to marry that moron Chunky hey that bastard Shastri is looking at me go jump you wanker

Sundar was thinking so hard about Jiva with his eyes half shut that he began to imagine he could see her through the window, passing through the arcade outside. Her braid was swinging as she walked. She was carrying a sheaf of papers and a bottle of glue.

Now Sundar knew that beautiful maidens in visions carried all sorts of things, but he had never yet heard of one who was caught carrying a bottle of glue. He zoomed out of the common room and into the corridor so fast that he set up a small hurricane. All the papers on his desk and on Shastri's desk blew about, and Shastri's feelings on this matter can only be indicated by a skull-and-crossbones and several asterisks.

'May I help you?' Sundar said to Jiva in his usual strangled croak.

'I'm putting up these posters,' Jiva said, with a hesitant smile. 'Are you sure—? They are for the SFD. And your friend Shastri is sticking his nose through the common room window to watch us.'

'I'm sure,' said Sundar. 'And Shastri is *not* my friend. He can tell Professor Ram anything he likes—I don't care.' Sundar read the pamphlets as he pasted them. One of them was titled 'Why Ambedkar? Why not?' 'I like this one especially.'

'Thanks. I wrote that one,' Jiva said.

'Er—after you finish these posters, what are you doing?' Sundar said, nearly choking on his own daring.

'Going to the canteen for some coffee. You want to come?'

'Gggg,' Sundar said, and she took that to mean yes.

Professor Ram staggered into the university late Tuesday morning, looking more than a little haggard. Though he was dressed as nattily as ever, and though his hair was combed flat and his eyebrows were oiled, there were bleary bags under his eyes, and the different strata of his neck were tending to run into each other with exhaustion. He was feeling very nervous. He had, as we know, missed his full quota of beauty sleep, and his heart was brooding on the symbolism of his dream. Once Jiva gets that job, Ram, the dream seemed to say, all will be over with you. You will be finished, a has-been, obsolete—oh, keep her out, Ram, Lord of the English department, keep her out. Fail her in the viva voce and let the V-C know, and the job will be Chunky's. So sang the voice in Professor Ram's head, over and over, like a chant.

As he came up the stairs to his office he saw the V-C

himself, standing in front of the English department notice-board. The V-C's shoulders were shaking uncontrollably. Professor Ram had a fleeting impression that the V-C was laughing, but this was evidently a trick of the light. When the V-C turned around and saw him coming up, he was more sober than a judge who chugged nothing but gripe-water, on or off the rocks.

'Good morning, Professor,' said the V-C.

'My God!' said Professor Ram huskily, his eyes fixed on the notice-board beyond the V-C's head. 'Another one!'

Dwarfing the announcements about CONFLUENCE 2002 and the department football game was a sheet of paper. On the sheet of paper was a message in red marker like this:

SALE! SALE!! SALE!!!
Proffesor Ram's 2nd book!
Original maniscript! First edition!
As a result of all the publishers rejecting,
Proffesor (Wancker) Rambo is selling it at the
disstress price of only Rs. 1/-!
Buy one get one Laryngeez tablet free!
Goody goody gumdrops!! Ha Ha!

'This is what I have been telling you about, Dr Mohan!' said Professor Ram brokenly. His hand trembled as he touched the paper. '*This* is what I have to put up with!' The V-C could tell that he was completely mashed up by the message, for a Professor Ram in full possession of his faculties would never ever have used a preposition at the end of a sentence. In fact, it was just the kind of grammatical error he so disapproved of in Thamarai Selvi and Rufus.

'Terrible—cannot be tolerated,' said the V-C, and he got so emotional that he was obliged to turn away for a minute. 'P-pp-preposterous,' he snorted, taking his handkerchief out. 'A

great n-n-nuisance!' He wiped his face. 'F-f-fully as bad as
Internet pop-ups.' He blew his nose. 'I was actually looking at
this other notice here. It looks like it was done by one of the
organizations you—er—sponsor.'

Professor Ram looked.

Agasthiyar, not Ambedkar

Why the University is allowing caste-conflict to enter its
premices by giving space to an idol of Ambedkar? Even
though we respect all, please remember that Ambedkar is
only a man. He is not fit for being a university symbal.
Why not a statue of Devi Saraswathi or any other
goddess from our glorious ancient undying Hindu
tradition? Why not Agasthiyar?

Friends, be proud to be Hindu!

Do not give in to the evils of Reservations system!

Humanism, not protectionism!

Join us in a procession today evening (Tuesday) 6 P.M.
to condemn this imposition of unnecessary caste creed
and colour politics into our pure minded youth.

Starting place: English Department

Ending place: VC's residence

Committee for the Renewal, Acceptance and Promotion of
the Poonal and Society for Hindu Ideology and Thought

Professor Ram looked again, and he saw another poster
beside the first one.

Why Ambedkar? Why not?

We are grateful to our high-caste friends for reminding us
that a statue is not the best way to represent Dr
Ambedkar. We agree because

1. he himself was against hero-worship and dogma

('There can be no finality of thinking,' he wrote).

2. political organizations of every colour, including saffron, are putting up statues to him these days.

Even so, his statue can remind us

'that if the parties place creed above country, our independence will be put in jeopardy a second time and probably be lost forever.'

Is anyone reading the news about Gujarat?

Students for Democracy

'Looks like there is going to be plenty of traffic around my house today,' the V-C said dryly. 'Just when I was going to spend a long quiet evening without my wife, finishing my book.'

That word 'book' gave Professor Ram an attack of acidity. He hurried into his office. He was hoping to hear today from one of the two dozen publishers he had written to.

Unlike many publication-hounds of no pedigree whatsoever, who appeared with remorseless frequency in the MLA citation index, Professor Ram had only managed to publish one book so far, and that was *Daddy, What Is the Significance of the Poonal*. Even this book only reached the public because Mr Varadarajan of V.R.V. Publishers could not resist the rustling music that Professor Ram's crisp hundred-rupee notes made when he went personally to V.R.V.'s Kottivakkam office to hawk his manuscript. V.R.V. rolled out one thousand copies of *Daddy*, and cleaned up quite handsomely, especially when you consider that Mr Varadarajan never bothered to send out any review copies, though that may be because he did not wish the reviewers to make unkind remarks about the five or six printer's devils he put into each paragraph. When the book was reviewed in *The Bindhu* by Professor Ram's uncle Mr Swaminathan, on his own initiative, naturally Professor Ram had his servants clean up his driveway and put out the welcome mat for the fan club. But somehow, the public never did clamour for this immortal work, and the best part of the first edition lay bundled up in some sacks at the back of V.R.V.'s godown. The covers exhibited grey-green patterns that the designer never included; V.R.V. did not lay out any funds on dehumidifiers or silica gel or anything else to keep the damp out of its godowns.

Of course, a prophet is not recognized in his own country. Professor Ram felt that since his publication profile followed that of a prophet in most details, he had better chances of being recognized in somebody else's country. Accordingly, when he completed his second book, a year earlier, he mailed dozens of copies to publishers in the US and the UK and Canada and Australia. This book was a biographical-critical study of a little-known contemporary Canadian poet called William Poopnoodle, whom he had met on one of his visits to Canada, and it was called *Mute But Not Inglorious: William Poopnoodle's Life and Poetry*. But each publisher Professor Ram sent the manuscript to punted it back to him so expeditiously that Professor Ram wondered if there was an echo somewhere. Indeed, some experts calculated that if Professor Ram kept on receiving rejection slips at the present rate, the world's remaining rain forests were likely to disappear by the year 2009. It is a fact that Professor Ram made a tidy little income every month by selling these markers of his failure by the kilo to the wastepaper mart. Indeed, Professor Ram may be forgiven for thinking that there was an international conspiracy to avoid publishing his work.

But failure only made Professor Ram determined to achieve, one day, the *Ram Omnibus*, and the *Complete Works of Ram*. He bombarded at least ten publishers a week with e-mails urging them to consider the merits of the Poopnoodle book. He wrote to them again and again, even after they had sent him polite rejections. After the West Nile disease carried Mr Poopnoodle off in August 2000, Professor Ram also wrote frequently to Mrs Poopnoodle, relict of the late poet, because he wished to keep filling in the gaps in the information he had supplied to readers of the biography.

If you ever write the long-awaited biography of Professor Ram, you will study a large bundle of letters going back and forth from him to Mrs Poopnoodle, and among them you will see the following samples:

12/12/2000
Dear Mrs Poopnoodle,

I am so glad you agree with me that the late Mr Poopnoodle was a genius unrecognized in his own lifetime, and that we must consecrate to his memory our poor efforts to make him better known in the world. As I myself have found, a prophet is not heeded in his own country. But in this country, India, readers will doubtless be intrigued and fascinated both by Mr Poopnoodle's interest in the Transcendentalists and by his insights into the philosophies of the Orient, especially the *Upanishads*, on which sacred texts I have reason to believe, without danger of falling into undue immodesty, that I am something of an expert. The poem *Brahma Revisited* alone should place him among the immortals.

I hope you are recovering from your bout of 'flu, and I am glad it is not anything serious. I hesitate to say 'Happy Christmas' because I know what a difficult time this must be for you, but please accept my greetings for the festive season.

Sincerely,

Ram (Professor Pattabhiraman)

P.S. I am enclosing a little vade mecum of my own for your edification, called *Daddy, What is the Significance of the Poonal and One Hundred Other Questions about Hinduism*. It is just the kind of thing your husband would have appreciated, and a reviewer here has been pleased to call it 'a little gem of a book'.

21.3.2000

Dear Professor Ram,

Thank you for the book. It was very entertaining. My! India is so exotic! I didn't know you had all these pretty beliefs and quaint customs, though I must say I still find the gods rather strange and heathen. I was visiting with my daughters over Thanksgiving and Christmas, and did not have a very rough time. Do you still want me to send you copies of the letters between my husband and his agent Paul Straub?

Yours,
Lynn Poopnoodle

P.S. Do call me Lynn. I hate being formal.

30/8/2001

Dear Lynn,

The book is almost complete, and I have sent the prospectus for it to several publishers. I am afraid the response to date has been somewhat discouraging, but I am one of the never-say-die people, and I am making every effort to place the late Mr Poopnoodle's work before an admiring audience.

In one of the letters you sent me, written to Mr Paul Straub, Mr Poopnoodle praises the poetry of one Alyson McBride. I think she was a student of his during his stint as Visiting Lecturer on Poetry with the Ontario Poetry Circle. May I trouble you to seek among his papers for any letters to/from her or any examples of her work, or even her address?

Yours gratefully,
Professor Ram

P.S. I hope you will do me the honour to call me Ram.

18.12.2001
Dear Ram,

I am glad you're still interested in my late husband's work. I wish his colleagues had been as impressed as you are. I daresay poor Bill's last days would then have been happier. By the way, I am enclosing copies of the letters between my husband and Paul Straub. Apart from being Bill's agent, Paul was also a trusted friend. In fact he was Bill's best friend for many decades, and the funny thing was, he died just weeks after Bill passed on.   .

As for the letters you asked about, I don't think there is any record of a correspondence between my husband and an Alyson McBride. I think you are right. About her being his student, I mean. But I'll certainly look again, and let you know if I find any signs of letters.

I am sorry you are having trouble getting the publishers interested in this book. I wish you all the luck in the world. I can hardly believe it—it's a whole year since we started corresponding!

Merry Christmas and best wishes,

Lynn

12/3/2002
Dear Lynn,

I have just discovered, in one of the letters between your late husband and Mr Straub, a mention of a secret compartment in your husband's desk drawer. 'Paul, do me a favour,' Mr Poopnoodle writes. 'If I ever kick the bucket, pardon my French, without clearing out my desk, get the AM letters out of the desk—you're the only bugger that knows how to find the drawer—and burn the bloody lot.' I quote verbatim, of course, Lynn.

If you get an expert carpenter to examine this

article of furniture, I believe you may discover something that will be of interest to both of us. From your husband's veiled references, it seems to be clear that no amateur in the field of woodwork will be able to locate this compartment.

Yours in haste,
Ram

This is where the correspondence rested at the moment. At first, Mrs Poopnoodle wrote Professor Ram at his home address. After the fifth letter or so, Professor Ram noticed that Mrs Ram looked morose on the mornings when Mrs Poopnoodle's missives fell into the post-box, and served up his meals lukewarm in quite a marked manner. So he requested Mrs Poopnoodle to use his office address for her letters and parcels. This was why the latest letter from her was lying on his desk today. Professor Ram pounced on it with great eagerness. He was very excited by what might be discovered in the secret compartment. He hoped that he would be mentioned if it got into the papers. In fact, he already had a photograph of himself with Mr Poopnoodle touched up and ready in case the Press begged for it.

15.03.2002
Dear Professor Ram,

This may seem rather sudden, but I will no longer be corresponding with you. As a matter of fact, I took your advice about calling in an antiques expert to examine my husband's desk. She opened the secret drawer thingy that you wrote about. She discovered a bundle of letters written by Bill—I don't even like to write his name anymore—to Alyson McBride, and by her to him. They were wrapped in cling-wrap and tied with a pink satin ribbon. A more lurid, immoral, offensive and pornographic record of illicit meetings and hasty couplings in college WASHROOMS I can't remember ever having encountered. It looks like the last six years of our marriage were a complete travesty. I am afraid I can't be expected to help you any more to promote HIS literary work. In my humble opinion, anyone who used up so much energy on this kind of non-literary work shouldn't even have bothered to aim at literary success.

I'm sure you'll understand that I have no interest left *at all* in pursuing the matter of your book on my husband, although I will not presume to raise any objections to its publication. My doctor has recommended a change of scene and I am leaving for Cancun shortly. The most important thing is, I'm enclosing the bill the antiques expert sent me, with her astronomical charges (the cost of repairing the desk which was damaged during her investigations are included). I hope you will be gentleman enough to take care of the payment.

Yours truly for the last time,
Lynn Poopnoodle

Professor Ram's dewlaps suddenly felt strangulated by his collar. No longer corresponding! No longer interested! And a bill, he said to himself, a bill from Mrs Bill! With a grunt of pure pain he filed this letter among the other letters in his Mrs Poopnoodle file. Satin ribbon! he thought, taking out his calculator and trying to convert the dollar amount on the bill into rupees with nerveless fingers.

As he pushed the file away from him, his eye fell on the other letter that awaited his attention on his desk. It had a UK stamp on it. With the same listless fingers Professor Ram picked up the silver-filigree paper-knife that he had got from the Lions Club for being at the Cutting-Edge of the Arts, and disembowelled the second letter.

Dear Professor Pattabhiraman, (said the second letter)
Our Acquisitions Editor has read your manuscript with considerable interest. He has advised me to inform you that though he appreciates the point about the need to recognize the poetic achievement of the late Mr Poopnoodle—if only posthumously—he regrets that Dodder and Spouton's publishing programme does not accept scholarly volumes coming out of India. We will be glad to consider any fiction that you have written, something with peacocks and maharajahs in it, ideally, or fire-eaters or snake-charmers. As you know better than most people, a gritty documentary realism is all the rage at the moment.
Best wishes,

Jennifer Masterson

This was terribly disappointing. Though he did not show it, and though his upper lip was rigid at all times, he was all broken up inside, like a smashed coconut. 'Try, try,' he said to himself, holding back an ocean of tears, and thinking long and hard about King Bruce and the Spider. When he smoothed the letter out to file it, a sticky fell out of it. This sticky appeared to have accidentally adhered to the back of the letter at the Dodder and Spouton office. It said:

Jenny ducks, get this effing woggo
Pattycake or wtever his name is off my back,
will you, but be as nice as you can about it.

Professor Ram put his head down on the desk and wept.

In which Professor Ram goes forth, and his Thoughts are Red Thoughts

--- ～ ---

AS THE UNIVERSITY clock's hands climbed towards the noon hour that fateful Tuesday, many little accidents announced that it was going to be another stretch in the boiler for Chennai's citizens. On Mount Road, a sunbeam refracted by a little old lady's glasses set a policeman's moustaches on fire. Outside Pondy Bazaar, Bucket Maami let her shopping-bag's flap open, while she paused on the pavement to hitch up her sari; in an instant, all the cool-green ladies fingers on top turned into red-hot Andhra chillies. On the twentieth floor of Seshadri Towers the air-conditioner failed. It took half an hour to get a new one, and by then, as a result of vexation and fluid loss, Mr Seshadri weighed eleven pounds less than he did when he got out of bed that morning. All the moisture was absorbed by his three-piece suit, for Mr Seshadri believed in power-dressing under all weather conditions, and his flunkey, Mr Rami Reddy, had to send for a doctor to peel the suit off him.

Indeed, only one other April day had been as hot as this in Chennai's recent meteorological history. On that day, the vaulting mercury had clearly been driven by artificial circumstances. Three sprawling slums in different parts of Chennai had burned down simultaneously. That was in the year 1989—the year in which Mr Seshadri wiped away Chennai's bad memories of smoking thatch and displaced persons by immediately acquiring the lands on which the slums once stood, and beautifying them with Brownstone Gardens, Hi-rize Paradize and Connemara Colony. Today, the temperature seemed set to beat that record, for it was already in the mid-forties outside the university's windows, and it was only just coming up to midday.

Inside Professor Ram's inside, it was hotter than in the belly of a blast furnace, and three times as uncomfortable. That sticky from Dodder and Spouton's acquisitions editor alone had damaged Professor Ram's cranial thermostat so badly that the grey matter was seething gelatinously, for all the world like trotter-stew on a wood-fire in a low military dive. This cranial agitation made his scalp undulate quite some. And when Professor Ram's scalp undulated, his eyebrows waggled ferociously.

I have mentioned Professor Ram's eyebrows, haven't I, sharp-eyed reader? Don't you remember how these eyebrows were a black bushy streak right across his forehead? When Professor Ram waxed dreadfully wroth, he raised eyebrow A, which, because it was coupled to eyebrow B, looked like a caterpillar bunching up its back half to propel the front half forward. I have known people, when they saw this happening, willing to wager that the whole eyebrow would scoot off his face presently, like a caterpillar that had just spotted a fine cabbage in the distance.

Of course this was an oversimplification. Professor Ram's eyebrows merely danced in place, conveying a multitude of meanings. And Professor Ram's students had learnt to read his eyebrows like tea-leaves. Thus, at noon on Tuesday, when Professor Ram marched into his first year Romantic Poetry class and thumped his *Palgrave* down on the table, his students trembled in their PVC sneakers, for they saw at once that he was going to be a Stickler.

You've met Sticklers, learned reader. They tend to stickle

about particular things, such as how commas should be distributed, or how much salt they like in their sambhar. In Professor Ram, however, we have a rare example of an all-round stickler, a Renaissance stickler, a veritable Leonardo among sticklers, an Eight-Task-Adept among sticklers, a stickler who could stickle at the drop of a hat about anything you would care to name.

Today, Professor Ram decided he would stickle about diphthongs. (No, gentle reader, a diphthong has nothing to do with ladies' undergarments.) He loved stickling about diphthongs because there was a sense of grand futility about it, given the scrambled accents of the masses at Chennai University. Mind you, when he grew up in Pazhavinaiyur, and before he went to Porlock Polytechnic (Somerset), Professor Ram himself did not know the difference between a diphthong and a didgeridoo. Some time during his four years in the land of Southey, the BBC, and mad cow disease, however, he received a full-fledged diphthong epiphany, and his vowels became more elegant than Naomi Campbell and more curly than noodles. Indeed, not since the East India Company's governors settled in at Fort St George were the closing and opening English diphthongs furled and unfurled so sweetly on the shores of the Bay of Bengal, and it was for this achievement that All-India Radio had honoured Professor Ram with a bag of gold-plated wood-shavings. Naturally, as a custodian of the language at Chennai University, Professor Ram wished to spread the benison of diphthongs among the natives, and help them approach, as closely as they could, the way English people spoke Professor Ram's stepmother-tongue. Especially such English people as were named Nigel or Julian and would not be seen dead hobnobbing with off-white people like Professor Ram.

So Professor Ram opened his *Palgrave* and looked around the class for a suitable victim. His eye fell on Thamarai Selvi.

'Thamarai, will you read this poem aloud,' he said.

Thamarai licked her dry lips, took the book and read like this:

'I wan detlon lee-a syay cloud
Thatflo tsoneye worevale sanyill
Svennall atvans-eye sawyay crow
Da hostoff—'

'He-ust,' Professor Ram hissed, looking up from the book. 'A he-ust, of ge-ulden daffodils. Try to pronounce the diphthong.'

'Ah hostoff—' Thamarai began again, for she came from Palayankottai, where they celebrated this white man's burden even less than they did in Pazhavinaiyur.

'*He-ust*,' said Ram again, making vermicular mouths. The voluptuous ripple that went through his chins was a wonder to behold.

'Hawest?' pleaded Thamarai, with her ear cocked towards Professor Ram. She was trying to hear the difference.

'He-ust! E-u! E-u!' gobbled Professor Ram. 'Any goat or pigeon on your father's farm could do it!'

By now, other rustics from other backwater mofussil towns pitched in helpfully.

'Heewst!' they cried. 'Hawsutt!' 'Hoist!'

'Eu-dious, eu-dious, eu-dious Reservations people...!' Professor Ram muttered. 'Eu-ver-running the universities!'

'Another one-by-two?' Sundar asked. He was floating eu-tiosely on a fluffy pink cloud in heaven, though actually it was only a stone bench under a tree outside the library.

'Okay. But I will pay this time,' said Jiva. They dived into the solid wall of lunch-seekers at the canteen counter, and when they removed themselves from it, after getting another cup of coffee and an empty cup, there was a sort of sharp sucking sound, and the hole they made closed at once.

'Why aren't you presenting a paper for the ACS conference this Saturday?' Sundar asked, when they had settled down under the tree again.

'Didn't I tell you the other day? Professor Ram passed the Call for Papers to his other students, but he did not show it to me.'

'Yeah, I know. But couldn't you have asked him yourself?'

'Are you joking? A Reserved Category student *asking* if she can present a paper?'

'Look, Jiva, I can't write my paper at all,' Sundar said. 'I don't have a single idea in my head. Nothing. But you have a completed thesis, no? You could present a chapter from it. Shall I ask Professor Ram to switch our names? It won't be a problem at all—most of the people he had on the original list are not coming anyway.'

'Don't do that!' Jiva said sharply. 'I am already in trouble about the interview. Next week is my viva voce. He will definitely fail me if I start anything.'

'What trouble? About the interview, I mean?'

Jiva explained how Professor Ram had wished her to oblige with a no-show so that Chunky could have a clear shot at the Drama and Folklore job.

'But it's your field! And you're his student! And that Chunky is the world's biggest operator! So he has to have a walkover for a job in India, does he, on top of sitting on some four hundred fellowships in Canada, the *assho*—the *fat*ass! I hope you told Professor Ram that he is a *total*—'

'Sssh.'

Professor Nagarajan scuttled past, his ears flapping like a flock of flamingoes touching down at Pulicat for the winter.

'Good afternoon, sir,' Sundar mumbled.

'Good afternoon,' said Professor Nagarajan. 'Ah—Sundar, if you see Shastri, let him know that I want to add a paragraph to my article.'

Sundar's jaw dropped.

Professor Nagarajan went around the corner, spinning a gossamer thread between snout and spout.

'Oh shit!' Sundar gasped before he could stop himself. 'Oh holy shit!'

'What is it?'

'I left something on the table in the common room—when I ran out to see you—I have to go get it!'

'Is it something important?'

'Yes—it's private,' Sundar said. In his mind's eye he saw Shastri reading his letter to Jiva—taking it home, drooling over it, jerking off on it, passing it around. '*Shit!*'

He began to run towards the common room. Then he remembered that he did not know how to find Jiva if he wished to see her again. Jiva watched him run back with an old-fashioned look.

'Now what? Shall I come with you?' she said.

'No, no. But I want to see you again—I don't know how to get in touch with you—'

'For that, machaan, you have to get in touch with me,' drawled a familiar voice, and a hand gripped Sundar's shoulder.

Sundar jitterbugged. 'Akilan, machaan, did you see your picture in today's *Bindhu*? Too cool, man, you'll have to give me your autograph sometime. But I can't talk now, got to go somewhere, urgent.'

'Ey. Wait, man, stop jumping around like a grasshopper. Nothing is so urgent. You want to see Jiva again? Ask Akilan Maama. Because I am having a plan.'

'What plan?'

'Tomorrow, Jiva is presenting a play with her troupe in Paravai village, which is her native place. We have to go for about two-and-a-half hours by car or bus. I am taking Caroline in a car to see this play, for her research work, and there is extra space in the car. So she has sent me to ask Jiva if she wants to come. No charge. Still there are two seats left. One for you. Do you want to come with us? We have to stay there for one night.'

'*Yes*,' said Sundar. A whole evening with Jiva—he wriggled in his sandals with pure delight. 'Yes, yes, yesyesyesyesyes. Where shall we meet?'

'Give me your phone number, man, and I will tell you all the plans. Caroline says she wants another friend to come also, so we have to co-ordinate.'

Sundar gave Akilan his number. 'I'll see you soon!' he called to Jiva as he bounded towards the research scholars' common room like an electric rabbit.

Professor Ram's eyebrows continued to make figures-of-eight all through the Romantic Poetry class, and even after it, for his first-year students stood behind the fluted pillars in the long university corridors and shouted 'Howest! Heust! Hoost!' as he headed back to his office. He was very upset until he remembered how R.M. Guru, the man who changed his life with a book on reflexology (*Press Your Way to Prosperity*) had also written a book about getting rid of bad karma and evil vibrations by making water (*The Amazing Power of Positive Tinkling*). But Professor Ram's students were lurking in the toilet stalls too. They waited for him to unzip, and they shrieked, 'Haaaweest!' This distracted him so much that he chose the third urinal from the end, which no one used, because some years ago the pipe leading out of it had rusted and broken off completely, and so pissing in it was just the same as pissing on your foot.

And Professor Ram did not even register this faux pas for he noticed, above the piss-line discoloration that had been steady since the Empress's day, proving that they did not aim any better under the Raj than they do in free India, a familiar illiterate scrawl, in red marker:

Proffesor (Jerk-Of) Ram could not make V.R.V
Book Publishers to take his second book
becoz it was so bad. V.R.V is Very Roten
Vanity Book Publishers. They publish boks only
if you pay them, like Proffesor Ram's first
book. Do you want to know my name.

Professor Ram was so upset that he just shook mechanically
and zipped up, in a reverie. He did not even understand why
the comedians outside the toilets studied his ankles and chortled
themselves into convulsions until he got to his office and, with
a start, felt the wetness of his trouser-hems and the saturation
of his socks.

For Professor Ram's magnificent grey cells were beginning
to work on the Poison Pen Problem. The clues, he said to
himself, suggested an Inside Job. How would anyone outside
his circle know about the payment he made to V.R.V. Publishers
to bring out his first book, or about his bad luck, no doubt
momentary, with his second one? And how could she (for
Poison Pen messages are always a Woman's Crime) know
about a matter that was strictly a jugalbandhi or pas de deux
between his organ of generation and the pink side of his hand?
Who could possibly be privy to his most secret affairs in this
terrifying way and also hate him so much?

'Siva-Siva! After lunch I must really go and see the V-C
again and demand that the university take this matter more
seriously,' Professor Ram said to himself, shivering all over
with rage and mortification. He took off his socks fastidiously
with his silver filigree paper knife. What was he to do with
them? If they were hung out to dry conspicuously, and the
students saw them—Professor Ram's heart contracted at the
thought. He left the socks on the floor beside his desk for the
nonce. Then he took up pen, ruler and paper to make his list
of suspects:

Name	Motive	Opportunity
Laurentia Arul	Hates me, hates all my ideals, a low-caste person	Can come into my office any time she wishes, esp. during my classes. Capable of anything
Jiva	Hates me (?) Active member of miguided campus groups, motiveless malignity, a Harijan girl	Can come into my office when she is here to see me about her thesis. Would she dare check my papers?
Students for Democracy	Hate me. Misguided campus group, anti-Brahmin, low-caste or Harijan mentality	Can come into my office. Can also bribe the fools who work as department clerks and secretary.

Professor Ram paused for a moment and a wild thought darted through his head.

'*Sundar?*' he wrote, but immediately scored it out. That was too unthinkable, it was mere anarchy—and here Professor Ram's hand was arrested as the subject of his third book came to him in a flash. He scribbled down some notes on a different paper. Yes, Professor Ram thought, it shall be called *Mere Anarchy is Loosed Upon the World: Appeasing Caste Groups and Minorities*. It would be a study of how, with every passing year, the insubordination on campus got worse, and how civilization was being undermined in institutions like Chennai University.

Professor Ram began to feel better. His eyebrows gradually flatlined.

'I must not become unnecessarily upset,' thought Professor Ram. 'These messages are probably from one of these so-called progressive groups on campus. Oh, how I loathe and despise low-caste feminists who stir up such things! When will righteousness prevail?'

He heard a knock on the door. The socks!

He just had time to flip open the mahogany casket that he had got from the Chennai Cultural Club for being a Treasure-Chamber of Culture and to whip the socks into it before Professor Nagarajan walked in.

'Just thought I'd drop in for a moment, as it were,' Professor Nagarajan said, fingers flying from dong to luminous nose. This time his hand lingered at his nose. He sniffed his fingers suspiciously, and then he twitched his nose at the air all around him. 'I think you have a mouse in your office, Ram.'

Professor Ram looked up, startled. 'What—where?'

'I don't see it, but it was this same smell—like, erm, urine—evidently mice make water everywhere, as it were— that alerted the computer laboratory technicians to the fact that there was a mouse-nest behind the main server. Considerable quantities of wire chewed up. Watch out for it— the computer fellows have got a good trap, I hear. Did you see my article for *The Brahmasstra*?'

'Yes, my dear Nagarajan, I have passed it on to Shastri. Pertinent, crisp and singularly timely. I think those poor Brahmin boys, like my student Sundar, who are standing up for their principles and denouncing the Ambedkar statue, are very vulnerable right now. Mark my words, there are going to be more atrocities in the near future.'

'Hmm—I'd be careful about Sundar, if I were you, Ram. I saw him just now, on the most cordial terms imaginable with—erm—the girl I interviewed, your Harijan student, what is her name? Ah yes, Jiva.'

'Nonsense. He must be trying to get some information from her about what the other side is planning. You can be the first one to congratulate me, Nagarajan, and I am telling you this mainly to set your mind at rest about that boy, but he is about to become my son-in-law soon. You will receive the invitation by Friday.'

'What? Congratulations! Congratulations! What auspicious news! Ah—I think there is someone knocking at the door, Ram, so I'll take my leave.'

The door opened and Professor Ram's old servant-woman Thaayi wobbled in with his lunch, walking the peculiar indecisive walk which so irritated Professor Ram. She bumped into Professor Nagarajan who was on his way out. Thaayi had worked for Professor Ram's family since before he was born— Professor Ram inherited her from his father—and she did not seem to want to go away. Naturally, since Professor Ram was completely devoted to maintaining his family traditions, he paid her the same wages that his father paid her in the 1950s, which were the same wages his grandfather paid Thaayi's predecessor in the 1920s, for aught I know, and so on, back into the Middle Ages, when they did such a fine job of calibrating and fixing the wage-structure of India's labouring classes that subsequent generations of employers could not at all see the point of making any unnecessary modifications to it. This was a most satisfactory arrangement for all concerned, especially for Professor Ram. It even made up for the fact that Thaayi was not a Brahmin. As a matter of fact, it was impossible to get Brahmins to do the menial things which Thaayi had to do.

As Thaayi came in, she heard a subterranean rumble, like gas collecting in a sewer system and getting ready to explode. She hoped it was just hunger. But it was not. It was rage. It swelled up in Professor Ram's belly and made him quiver from the tips of his sidelocks to the soles of his sodden Bata shoes.

'How many times—how many *times* have I told you not to barge in when I am engaged with somebody?'

'But Ayya, the last time you were with someone, I waited, and you were so angry, because you said your lunch got cold,' said Thaayi.

'Backtalk!' Professor Ram bared his teeth. His eyebrows

began to spike and shimmy like a Kathakali dancer's. The insolence of servants these days! 'No backtalk from you! Just look at the way you are pouring sweat—like a filthy waterfall! It is unclean!'

'Yes, Ayya. It is very hot, Ayya. I had to walk from the bus stop. But I am holding your lunch basket far away from my body, and there is a cloth around the handle, Ayya, look.'

Thaayi placed Professor Ram's lunch-basket on the table and backed away.

The coverings that concealed Professor Ram's lunch from the world and kept it hot were peeled away, like the layers of an onion—though I daresay this simile would have killed his appetite. Professor Ram's steel tiffin-box was made up of four distinct tubs, each one nesting neatly into the last, the whole held together by a clamp. He unscrewed the lid of the top tub of the tiffin-box and stared at the contents. He lifted this container out and looked in the next one.

Then in the next.

And in the last one.

Professor Ram's eyebrows were sidewinding so fast it was a miracle they did not become airborne. His hands began to shake.

'*Thaayi!*' he bellowed. 'What is this?'

For twenty-four years, rain or shine, Professor Ram had reconstituted the corporeal man at lunchtime with three different kinds of rice, a vegetable, a pickle and a bottle of buttermilk. Today, in the place of sambhar-rice, rasam-rice and curd-rice, slippy-sloppy, just-so, and hot-hot, Professor Ram saw idlis. Nothing but idlis. Idlis indifferently coated with chilli-powder and oil. No sambhar. No chutney.

'*What is this?*'

'What, Ayya?' Thaayi twisted the end of her sari nervously in her hands.

'What have you done with my lunch?'

'Nothing, Ayya. I brought it here, the same as usual.'

'Liar! Thief! You ate it and filled up my lunchbox with idlis!'

'Ah, don't say that thief word, Ayya,' Thaayi quavered. 'I have never stolen anything in my life. I brought it to you just as Amma gave it to me.'

Professor Ram pulled the telephone towards him and stabbed out his home number with vicious fingers. He wanted answers. How had these interlopers gotten into his tiffin-box?

The telephone in Professor Ram's house rang once, twice.

Mrs Ram was at this moment listening to Sri Sri Sri Sastrigal in his office.

'You have inner beauty,' he was saying. 'The people you live with ought to appreciate your sacrifices more than they do.'

The telephone rang on, five, six times.

'You need to acquire a more flexible understanding of the whole duty of the Hindu wife,' Sri Sri Sri Sastrigal was saying, in the silkiest of voices.

There was no cook to answer the phone at the Ram residence today. The phone went on ringing, eight, ten, fourteen times. Professor Ram slammed the receiver down. He wiped his hands and fell to, for he was famished.

When Mr Iyer of Tambaram wrote to *The Bindhu* to say the Jagadambal idli tasted like therma-coal, his description had been strictly accurate as far as the immediate effects of rehydration were concerned. What he had not known, and therefore had not mentioned, was that any delay in the consumption of this idli made it harden rapidly. The specimens in Professor Ram's tiffin-carrier, being at least an hour-and-a-half old, had already acquired the consistency of solid concrete. So when Professor Ram tried to break a piece off the topmost idli, he found that it was very like trying to break a piece off prefabricated rural budget housing. He tried a second idli and met the same resistance. Indeed, this idli seemed to be leering at Professor Ram defiantly, and the red chilli-powder on it was the same colour as red marker, and all it needed was a hammer and sickle to be found somewhere in the corner of each idli for a complete symbolic declaration of class war. Professor Ram put the buttermilk bottle to his lips and took a long swig to soothe himself. Such was his rage that even that was like knocking back a Molotov cocktail.

Professor Ram looked up at his gods for guidance and he saw—he saw that the light in the plastic Ganesha's insides had gone out.

At about the same moment, Dr Laurentia Arul, on her way back from the library, glanced all around her and noted that the lobby was deserted. She felt that Akilan had put his heart and soul into the casting of the Ambedkar statue. She had longed to stop and admire it, but she did not wish the students to think that she was gloating over her own contribution. Now she could gaze without discomfort.

Sundar half tumbled down the stairs as Dr Arul wiped away a few specks of dust from Dr Ambedkar's book. She jumped back in embarrassment. But Sundar hardly seemed to notice her. He was looking all around him with the intent, searching look that people have when they have lost a contact lens.

'Good afternoon, Sundar,' Dr Arul said, clearing her throat.

''Daftnoon Dr Arul. Have you seen Shastri, ma'am?' Sundar asked breathlessly.

'No, Sundar,' said Dr Arul. 'He could have gone home.'

'His things are still in the research scholars' common room.'

'The canteen?'

'I just came from there. Maybe the library. Thank you, ma'am.'

As Sundar went out the main door, Dr Arul heard a noise

like a thunderclap, which was followed by a clattering. Professor Ram's servant-woman came hurtling around the landing as fast as her arthritic old legs would carry her. Professor Ram was hurling himself down the polished wooden stairs an arm's length behind, pausing only to take aim before he lobbed a cement-hard idli at her. From the way he lobbed it, you could tell he was wishing it was a home-made pineapple with the pin taken out.

As for Professor Ram's wrist action, any cricket-lover who observed it would have spat on the ground and said Professor Ram was a *chucker*, making the word sound a lot like *fucker*; a chucker, in a cricket-lover's opinion, being a remarkably scaly entity, superior only to match-fixers and commentators who spiced up their reportage with non-stop local proverbs and country wisdom. Professor Ram undoubtedly did n̥ owl that idli; he *chucked* it at Thaayi. How did Thaayi respond? Instead of turning and taking guard like a proper stalwart of the willow, she skittered about weightlessly like a ping-pong ball that had fallen off the table, and finally fetched up behind Dr Arul.

As he came off the last step, Professor Ram's momentum carried him right up to Dr Ambedkar. There he was pulled up short; for he saw Dr Arul doing acts of worship, and he also saw, just beyond her elbow, and beyond the cowering Thaayi, the 172nd conference schedule that Shastri would never unite with its ERRATA sheet. On this schedule, in that same red marker, was a message:

Proffesor Ram is a liar and also a pisser-king. He pissed all over the toilet floor. Just smell his sox, they are in his office. This is my identy: Yabba Dabba Doo.

When Professor Ram turned around, his eyes, more scarlet than supermarket tomatoes, were starting madly from their spheres. Dr Arul's face wobbled before him like a Doordarshan newscaster during a bad transmission. In fact she looked to Professor Ram like a newscaster who spread sedition in the name of newscasting.

Dr Arul backed away hastily from Professor Ram. She backed away so fast that she tripped over the fallen idli. She threw out her arms to regain her balance. Her handbag flew up into the air and burst open, disgorging a banana skin, *Persuasion*, three ballpoint pens, a book of stick-its, a handkerchief and two markers, a red one and a green.

A red marker.

When Professor Ram saw that red marker, he became inflamed, the way the sages in the old epics became inflamed. You know the ones I mean—the blokes who stood on one foot and underwent austerities for a squillion years and acquired enough yogic powers to start rearranging the universe and show the gods who was boss. He got good and mad the way some contemporary heroes got good and mad, the ones who grew several feet taller and turned green and burst out of their clothes. A magenta mist swam before his eyes. Every time a wisp of the mist broke off, it turned into a vicious message about Professor Ram's personal life.

'You—you—yoububbub! Blub! Markerblub! Youweretheoneblub!! How dare you! How dare you besmirch my good name by writing these appalling messages! Reportyou—thisinstant—lowcowardly, dastardlyact!' He lapsed into incoherence, frothing at the mouth.

'Pardon?' said Dr Arul, who, puzzled by the effect she had just created, was trying to marshal the contents of her handbag. 'What messages?'

'These scurrilous, false, damaging messages about—don't bother with that puzzled expression!' Professor Ram shrieked, pouncing on the red marker and waving it about like a vajra or thunderbolt (*vide* 'Daddy what is a vajra or thunderbolt?' *Daddy What is the Significance* p. 29). 'Do you think I haven't worked it out? I am going to report this whole disgraceful incident to the Proper Authorities! The Disciplinary Committee will meet this evening, or my name is not Pattabhiraman!'

Dr Arul shrugged, giving up the struggle to understand what this was about. 'Well, all right, report and be damned!' she retorted.

Professor Ram was generally accustomed to hearing many people saying around him, in many diphthongless but breathlessly-eager-to-please accents: Yes, Professor Ram; You are absolutely right, Professor Ram; and It is excessively good of you to say so, Professor Ram. Naturally, when Dr Arul spoke to him like this, he thought he had misheard her.

'What? Whatwhatwhatwhat?' he shouted. 'Whaddid you say?'

Dr Arul repeated her point. Directly, the praana, or breath, went out of Professor Ram with a giant whoosh.

'Backward-caste mongrel-dog!' Professor Ram hissed at her.

'Reactionary pinnaaku!' Dr Arul spat back, recovering an old skill. The old Anglo-Indian missionary at the Bethel Mount orphanage had tried to sow the seeds of Christianity in her, but they had not taken too well. On the other hand, she had graduated with the ability to swear quaintly and felicitously in two languages.

'Orphanage brat!'

'Bloodsucking Brahmin petty-bourgeois opportunist sorinaai!'

'Feminist critic!'

'Writer of third-rate mannaangatti crib notes for BA students!'

'Dirt-eating Ambedkarite seditionist!'

'Unreconstructed romanticist kammanaati!'

'Cabbage-faced upstart!'

'Third-rate pseudo avant-garde theatrical mayiraandi!'

At this Professor Ram's blood-pressure shot up so high it

punched several new holes in the ozone layer. His hippocampus major parted from its moorings. He took a long run-up and heaved an idli at Dr Arul, putting plenty of the old bodyline into it, but Dr Arul had not come unscathed through many years of orphanage scrimmages for nothing. She ducked expertly, and the missile whizzed over her head towards Dr Ambedkar standing in the niche just above her.

Whatever the cricket historians say, I think that Dr Ambedkar got some practice at the nets with his friend Palwankar Babu. He swept this idli to the square leg boundary. The next idli that Professor Ram sent, Dr Ambedkar played defensively, tapping it right back at Professor Ram. It dotted Professor Ram over the onion, and the concussion made him even more non compos than before. Dr Ambedkar was definitely settling in nicely at the crease, and might well have gone on to Slam Ton, as *The Bindhu* always expressed it, except that Professor Ram now found that he had run out of idlis. Now he tried to bludgeon Dr Arul with the only weapon he had left, which was his many-tiered tiffin-box. When Dr Arul wove as before, the tiffin-box sideswiped Dr Ambedkar.

Dr Ambedkar began to topple over. But Dr Arul remembered the time she had snaffled up the woodapples which her friend Kanagam shook out of Father Xavier Arulanandam's tree in the parish house behind the orphanage. She leapt backwards, applying the same technique, and though at least fifty-seven reflexology points in her hand felt the crunch when they met Dr Ambedkar's bronze edges, she hung on to him without flinching. Akilan had piece-cast Dr Ambedkar, and he was not excessively heavy, but a bronze statue is a bronze statue, not a roll of paper towel. Dr Arul's hands were fully occupied, and her sari was rucked up a bit. Finding his enemy at a disadvantage, and his enemy's gambs exposed, Professor Ram forgot himself completely, dropped down on all fours and sank his teeth into Dr Arul's left ankle.

Dr Arul certainly did not taste sweet and tender, like a

gulab jamun or a tin of condensed milk. She tasted bad and bitter, like an old radish. Even so, Professor Ram gnawed at her ankle as if he hoped to make up for a lifetime of vegetarianism and get his full supply of animal protein. Sundar, who had come back in through the main doors a few moments earlier, winced when he saw this. No doubt many a native beater in the heyday of the Raj winced like this when he saw one of the man-eaters of Kumaon crunch up a colleague like a digestive biscuit.

Sundar gripped Professor Ram's collar. 'Professor Ram!' he cried, 'Stop that! *Don't do that!*' and he tried to tear Professor Ram away from Dr Arul's ankle. He pulled mightily. But he had nothing to show for his pains except Professor Ram's Tantex vest, which came away completely in his hands.

Dr Arul took no notice of this development. With infinite tenderness she returned Dr Ambedkar to the pavilion. Then she picked up her handbag, which stood beside her, and, bringing to bear all the expertise of one who hoed the vegetable garden at Bethel Mount every day for many years to earn her keep, she clipped Professor Ram with it above the ears. Professor Ram only just remembered to holler cop and doctor before he lost interest in cannibalistic rites altogether. Professor Arul dusted her handbag off and hobbled up to her office, leaving a trail of gore. When Sundar offered to help her, she waved him away. The tiffin-box, meanwhile, trickled away from this scene of carnage until Thaayi snapped it up, just two feet short of the third leg boundary.

'Mmmph!' said Professor Ram in a weak voice.

He was lying on a sofa in the V-C's office, the centrepiece of a whirl of activity. In one corner, Shastri was on the phone, telling Mrs Ram what had happened to her husband. In another corner, Professor Ram's own family doctor was writing out a medical certificate. The V-C was sitting at his desk, drumming his fingers testily on the table and saying, 'I cannot believe that such a thing happened on campus. Dr Arul! I would never have thought it!' Beside Professor Ram's sickbed, Professors Nagarajan, Venkataraman, Subramaniam and Sambasivan were holding water to Professor Ram's lips, pressing ice cubes against the bump in Professor Ram's coconut, massaging balm into Professor Ram's temples, and holding Professor Ram's hand while they moaned that they always knew it would come to this, ever since the Reservations Policy tied their hands and made them accept into the university people who were not fit to—they caught the V-C's eye and refrained from saying what these people were not fit to do.

'Way-ish-Shoongar?' Professor Ram wished to know.

Something was clearly wrong with Professor Ram's mouth. Was it a stroke? Would they never hear the fruity baritone declaim immortal verse again?

Professor Ram himself seemed to become aware of this defect in his speech.

'Wy feef!' he gasped, feeling all around his mouth with his tongue. 'Wy feef!'

'Ah!' said the doctor, who came up to take a look. 'He seems to have lost his dental plates.'

'My God! She hit him so hard that his teeth fell out!' whined Professor Nagarajan.

'Shastri!' said the professors as one man, for even undying friendship did not make them eager to collect Professor Ram's post-prandial curd-rice chompers. 'Find Professor Ram's teeth, wash them well and bring them back!'

'Yes, sir,' said Shastri.

As soon as Professor Ram got his teeth back he said, 'We cannot let this despicable crime go unpunished, Dr Mohan. It may be a case for the police.'

'No, no, Professor Ram, it would look terrible if the university were to get into the news—professors knocking each other out—fisticuffs! It seems to me to be a misdemeanour that we should deal with among ourselves, what do you say?'

'I must insist on my right to redress, as a citizen, Dr Mohan—assault and battery, a grave issue, very grave. And behind it all there is diabolical cunning and conspiracy which will undermine this university. It is not for myself I plead, Dr Mohan,' Professor Ram's voice broke. 'It is for the Future of Education.'

'Yes, Dr Mohan!' chorused Professors Nagarajan, Venkataraman, Subramaniam and Sambasivan. 'Consider the Future of Education!'

'Nevertheless—that is—how about trying what the University Disciplinary Committee can do, Professor Ram? Eh? Before we resort to more extreme and public measures?'

'I will agree to this alternative only if the Committee can meet today. Right away.'

'Certainly, certainly.' The V-C was relieved. 'I'll see what I can do. Of course I must make sure Dr Arul is here to present her side of the case—I think she went home—I'll call her—'

'If there are going to be delays, for any reason whatsoever, Dr Mohan, I must let you know that I am going to file an FIR at the police station.'

'All right, all right, we'll have the meeting without her,' said Dr Mohan. He wished, more than anything else, for the university to stay clear of strange kinds of notoriety during his tenure as V-C. 'Perhaps you will be kind enough to give me, in writing, a full account of what happened. I will rustle up the members of the Disciplinary Committee. Well, we already have Professor Sambasivan here, and myself, of course, and I can easily get Dr Rangarajan on the phone—yes, I don't see why we can't have the meeting today.'

The V-C began to make phone calls. Professor Ram dictated the letter in a faint voice while Professor Nagarajan typed it.

To
The Disciplinary and Grievances Committee,
Chennai University.

Dear Sirs,

I beg to bring to your notice that an assault took place in these hallowed corridors of learning on the afternoon of 16 April, 2004. This unprovoked and horrifying assault was perpetrated upon me by Dr Laurentia Arul, whose recalcitrance regarding several matters such as course material, and whose tendency to lead students towards sedition, destabilization of the country and moral ruin, in the name of free thinking, are legendary. Dr Arul has become a byword for obstructing the proper conduct of the English Department's affairs. Her reputation will allow you to readily believe the details of the incident, which are as follows:

At exactly 1.15 p.m., as I emerged from my office and came down the stairs into the main lobby of Chennai University, I observed Dr Arul worshipping false gods, i.e., paying obeisance to the statue of the man she is pleased to call the Architect of our Constitution. On approaching closer, in order to discourage such primitive rites, unbecoming to say the least, in the groves of academe, I observed that there was writing on the base of the statue. On perusing this message, I at once became aware that I was the subject of the aforementioned calumny, whose substance (after deleting the unprintable content) was that I had suffered an episode of incontinence.

When I challenged Dr Arul to confess that she had perpetrated this and other recent atrocities too gross and numerous to mention here, she flatly refused, whereupon I attempted to remind her of the value placed on truthfulness and tolerance in our shastras.

At this moment, to my grief, horror, and excruciating physical pain, she brutally attacked my head with her handbag, *in a totally unprovoked manner*, and indeed delivered such savage blows to my head and body that I lost consciousness. My doctor informs me that I barely escaped severe cranial injuries, and indeed, my memory of the whole event is somewhat hazy, a typical sign of concussion (Medical Certificate enclosed).

I hope you will take appropriate action, though what action may be appropriate when a highly respected member of the University community behaves like a rabid pariah dog, I can scarcely venture to imagine. The severest possible penalties seem to me to be justified in this case, in expectation of which, I remain,

Yours truly,
Professor Pattabhiraman

'Siva-Siva!' said Professor Nagarajan, moved to tears by the sad tale he himself had typed. 'All this, as you pointed out, Ram, because of the statue! How prophetic!'

'Yes indeed, sibylline leaves,' said Professor Sambasivan, who was a Miltonist.

'Surely, Dr Mohan, you will not let the cause of this outrage—the final cause, as it were—stand in the lobby! It would be an insult to Professor Ram!' Professor Nagarajan looked grave.

'Come now, Professor, the statue itself is just a thing of metal and granite. It has been incorporated into the Campus Beautification scheme, and we've scarcely finished setting it up. Surely you do not expect me to give orders that it should be taken down!'

But it seemed this was just what the professors expected.

'Why did it have to be an Ambedkar statue? Why not a statue of the Unknown Soldier?' Professor Venkataraman, who taught the War Poets this term, fumed.

'Or of Sri Aurobindo?' added Professor Sambasivan, who taught the immensely tedious epic, *Savitri*.

'Or of—er—Goddess Saraswati?' said Professor Nagarajan, trying to keep up.

'Goddess Saraswati!' exclaimed Professor Ram, bouncing upright and quite forgetting to keep up the faint voice, now that he was all excited. 'I would personally take responsibility for putting up a statue of Goddess Saraswati, and pay for half of its cost! The other half can be met through prayer meetings!'

'In the sea!' shouted Professor Sambasivan. 'Like Golden Beach! Like Manhattan!'

'A colossus!' cried Professor Venkataraman, warming to the theme. 'The tallest free-standing statue in south India!'

'I don't know about the sea,' Dr Mohan rubbed his forehead tiredly. 'There are rules about that kind of thing, you know. But yes, I don't see why we shouldn't extend the Campus Beautification project to include the image you gentlemen desire. I'll have to get the syndicate to approve, however.'

'Let us look at the Yellow Pages!' cried Professor Nagarajan, thoroughly swept away. 'Find a sculptor—today!'

'No, Nagarajan,' said Professor Ram. 'I know just the person who can help us with this noble project. And this very evening,' Professor Ram got off the sofa weakly and staggered about while his friends hovered near him with touching officiousness, 'I will go and meet him and see what we can do to carry it forward. But now, if I can have your arm, my dear Nagarajan, I must use the lavatory, and see if I can spruce myself up for this appearance before the Disciplinary Committee.'

Professor Nagarajan solicitously helped Professor Ram to the bathroom.

'Man, how many fingers?' Akilan said, holding up his hand and giving Sundar the up-yours sign.

'It's *true*, machaan!' says Sundar. 'I'm not smashed! I know it's weird, but I saw it with my own eyes! He *bit* her, like an Alsatian dog, and she just clumped him on the head with her handbag. Like that: *thup!* Then she went up to her office. And she wouldn't let me help. Jiva, maybe if you go—'

'Paappaan fuckers are not biting non-Brahmins, machaan, it is very bad for their purity. If they bite like this, it is worse than eating a cow. For seven generations they must have baths only in Ganga-water. Jiva, this paappaan boy is having heatstroke, take him to the sea and throw him in, it will cool him down.'

'Shut up, Akilan,' Jiva said, half-laughing. 'I'll go up and see if Arul needs anything.'

Sundar and Akilan had a one-by-two coffee while they waited.

'Have you heard anything about the trip yet?' Sundar asked Akilan.

'No, machaan, I have not phoned Caroline. This evening I am meeting her. At 5.30.'

When Jiva came back she looked furious.

'Is she okay?' said Sundar.

'I don't know. I caught an auto for her and she has gone home. She promised to see a doctor, but I don't think she will. Do you know what is going on in the seminar room now? The Disciplinary Committee is meeting, to make a decision about this incident.'

'Oh deadly,' Sundar said. 'So Ram is in deep shit!'

'No. *Arul* is in trouble. The typist told me. *Ram* is giving his side of the story to the Committee and *she* has gone home. I am an idiot—I should have taken her to the doctor myself, and made sure she got a medical certificate to say she is hurt. Otherwise they will pretend that she attacked Ram.'

Indeed, this was what was happening in the English department seminar room. Professor Ram's letter and the sad state of his clothes carried the day with the Disciplinary Committee. Most of its members, including Professor

Sambasivan and Professor Rangarajan, had been Professor Ram's cronies since way back when they all shared slate-pencils in kindergarten and ate their strictly vegetarian tiffins together under the tamarind tree, and they would rather believe Professor Ram when he mentioned six impossible things before early morning pranayama than Dr Arul when she spoke the unvarnished truth.

'Oh, the sinners—may the gods rot their books with mildew! But we can get the students who have seen what-all happened to write a letter. They are the witnesses. Can't we take them to the Committee meeting now? Ey, Sundar, who else was there, man?' Akilan said.

'No one—only me—and that old servant lady who brings Professor Ram's lunch,' said Sundar.

'Then you have to tell them what happened,' Jiva said. 'Let's go.'

When Jiva and Sundar went to the seminar room, where the emergency meeting of the Disciplinary Committee was being held, the department secretary said she had no authority to let them in. The V-C's secretary would not hear them out long enough for them to explain why they wished to talk to the committee. As for Professor Ram's anxious friends, who had assembled outside the seminar room to offer moral support and pray that justice would prevail, they became very agitated.

'Out! Out!' said Professor Nagarajan. 'What are students doing here? This is a faculty issue. Get out at once!'

'This is a private meeting!' Professor Venkataraman said, shutting the door in Sundar and Jiva's faces. 'Next thing, you will be wanting to have a say in the administration of this university!'

Short of crashing through the glass door, they could do nothing for the moment.

'We should have written a letter,' said Jiva, making an angry fist. 'We may have been able to get a letter into the V-C's hands. He's generally quite fair. Let's go to the common room and write out a letter.'

'But it is too late to change their minds now!' groaned Sundar.

'Yes, but we can demand for them to reopen the inquiry tomorrow, or sometime after that,' said Jiva. 'If necessary, Students for Democracy can take a procession out, dharna the V-C, do—oh—*some*thing.'

So they collected Akilan at the canteen again and went to the research scholars' common room. Just around when the Disciplinary Committee concluded its deliberations and ruled that Dr Laurentia Arul should be suspended for sowing the seeds of discord in the groves of academe, Jiva and Sundar finished writing their account of the Ram-Arul encounter as Sundar had seen it. Jiva looked at her watch and exclaimed, 'I am late for my rehearsal!'

'You go ahead, Jiva, I'll type this out and have it all ready by tomorrow.'

All this time Akilan was lounging about the room and poking around among the books and papers which Shastri had left on one of the tables. Now, pocketing two Spearmint packets that Shastri had forgotten, and various little odds and ends that he felt would be useful to him, he said he would go with Jiva.

'What about you, Sundar? You are not going home?' said Jiva. Sundar glowed at her casual use of his name.

'I still have to finish something,' he said. 'My damned paper.'

After Jiva and Akilan had gone, Sundar sat down at the computer and typed out the letter they just had drafted, and saved it as 'Protest Letter'.

Then he decided to try a completely new approach to his paper.

'I will start with narrative,' he said to himself. 'Something gripping and full of facts. Then I will sneak the theory in.'

'The air,' he wrote, 'is buzzing with eggs at the Nethergate Circus. Soon the tomatoes are flying side by side with the eggs.

The circus performers and clowns creep away from the ring. The umbrellas behind which they are hiding have been torn to pieces by the onions and tomatoes and eggs; by the fish and bread and flour and bottle caps that the crowd is hurling into the ring. What is happening? The poet William McGonagall, who has unfortunately not had the forethought to bring an umbrella, is reciting a poem:

"Arabi's army were about 70,000 in all,
And virtually speaking, it was not very small."'

Sundar stopped to take thought, and a new idea occurred to him. While they were writing letters to the V-C about the things that Professor Ram did to Dr Arul, why not mention what he did to Jiva just before her interview? That way, it seemed to Sundar, the administration would be alert to any Machiavellian moves from that quarter when Jiva's viva voce came around. He opened 'Protest Letter' again and added what Jiva had told him about her exchange with Professor Ram just before her interview. Then he made a print-out of this letter and put it in his pocket. As he returned, groaning extravagantly, to McGonagall, the door swung open and Professor Ram blew in.

Sundar gaped at him. He was torn and dishevelled and bloody from head to foot. Sundar simply did not understand how he got this way, for when he had pulled him away from Dr Arul's Achilles' tendon and parked him on the floor of the lobby, he had looked quite as usual, except for the slab of Dr Arul's ankle that hung from his lips like an Edward G. Robinson cigar. Well, between you and me, this was how it happened. When Professor Nagarajan escorted Professor Ram to the toilet, he latched the door and whispered to him:

'Er—Ram, I do think we could lend an added touch of verisimilitude to the accusation if your appearance were—to be precise, if it were somewhat more—erm—battle-scarred, as it were.'

'That is very far-sighted of you, my dear Nagarajan,' said Professor Ram, his voice equally low. Like any veteran of the boards, Professor Ram knew that costuming played an important role in winning an audience over. He suffered Professor Nagarajan to rub some streaks of dirt into his shirt, and tear it here and there. If he looked a little doleful it was because the nice Ralph Lauren pastel shirt was ruined, and not because he had suffered a crick in his conscience. Professor Nagarajan also felt that the ink in the offending red marker (unaccountably in Professor Ram's pocket) should not be wasted. So he made Rorschach blots on Professor Ram's shirt and Professor Ram's neck. Thus Professor Ram looked considerably more pathetic while he presented his story to the Disciplinary Committee than he had done when he lay on the sofa in the V-C's office.

'Such an awful thing to happen, Sundar,' sniffed a voice behind Professor Ram. 'We came as soon as we heard.'

Then Sundar realized that Professor Ram had not come in alone, but en famille. Up popped Mrs Ram from behind him, sniffling decorously into a silk handkerchief. Jayanthi was also present. Mrs Ram was suffering agonies of remorse. Professor Ram had given her a shellacking about those idlis. He said he felt like a warrior, brought home half-dead, who, when he sat down to his supper and lifted the lid from the stew-pot, found nothing in it but a frog.

'I heard that you came to the seminar room to inquire after me, my boy,' said Professor Ram tremulously. Professor Ram was a believer in the Method School, and he had almost succeeded in convincing himself he was desperately wounded and only half a step away from extinction. 'I was presenting my story to the Disciplinary Committee, as you must have gathered. I am all right now, and in fact I am determined to put up a brave front. We have to do somehing decisive, Sundar. I am counting on you. What about this evening's procession to the V-C's residence? You do have clear plans, I hope? Good, good,' Professor Ram rubbed his hands together. 'Don't forget to mention this outrage on my person, and make sure that you present a strong case for the removal of the Ambedkar statue. Write a letter about it, a petition. Of course, we are going to put up our own statue, and I'll explain our plans to you soon. Now, Sundar, I had promised Jay that we would go to Elliot's Beach this evening, and I am going to have to disappoint her because I must go now to Seshadri Towers about our statue. Why don't you work together right here on the letter to the V-C?'

Jay opened her mouth, but before she could reply, Professor Ram said, 'That's settled. Good, good. I'll pick her up when I finish with Mr Seshadri, and that way I can give the procession my blessing. Six o'clock, wasn't it? Outside the English Department? Excellent. Now I have to stop at home for a moment to make myself presentable, so, Charu—shall we?'

'Normally I would stay with you, Jay,' Mrs Ram said mournfully, 'but today my place is with your father'. She reflected that when Professor Ram had been getting himself torn to pieces by some fury in the English department, she had been letting Sri Sri Sri Sastrigal hold her hand and whisper in her ear what practically amounted to an improper suggestion.

'But sir, I have to finish my paper—' Sundar said feebly. It was hard for him to think of intelligent things to say when people were strong-arming him, and he wished he had Jiva's clarity on these matters.

Before he got his wits together, the professor was already a rapidly receding speck in the corridor, and Jay was saying to him, 'Oh let's not sit here in this muggy room. Let's go out— to Elliot's Beach. Let's stop an auto, shall we?'

'Okay. But first I have to phone my family and tell them I will be late.'

'Oh boy, it's three years since I was there. It used to be a regular lovey-dovey place, especially at night. Is it still, like, a den of vice?'

'Yes,' said Sundar gloomily. 'It still is.'

In which there are Wheels within Wheels

———————— ～ ————————

AT 4.30 THE same evening, Sachu was astonished and alarmed
to see Professor Ram, followed by a younger man neither taller
nor thicker than a matchstick, bustling into the magnificent
air-conditioned lobby of Seshadri Towers.

'Is there anything wrong, Professor?' she asked, all a-
twitter, for she thought Sundar had misbehaved and Professor
Ram had come to tell her the weddings were off. 'Is it—
Sundar?'

'No, no, I have come—without an appointment, I'm afraid,
to see Mr Seshadri about a statue—a huge statue—that the
university wants to commission from your company.'

'Of course!' Sachu exclaimed. 'Totally spiritual! Always
doing good deeds! I will personally speak to the boss, Professor,
please take a seat.'

Sachu conferred with someone in a low voice over the
phone. A shiny personage in a glass cage motioned Professor
Ram and Shastri over and gave them ID tags to wear.

'Please return when you are leaving,' she said.

In a moment Professor Ram and Shastri found themselves
whizzing up in the gold-coloured lift so fast that their stomachs
were unable to keep up with the rest of them. When they
passed Seshadri-Cosmo Granites on the fifth floor they felt

their stomachs were still with Seshadri-PVC Flush Doors on the first, and when they soared above Seshadri Sanitaryware and Seshadri Soapstones on the seventeenth floor, they felt that they had deposited their innards in Seshadri Garden Statuary and Seshadri Furnishings on the eleventh. They stepped out of the lift like people on a cruise who had not found their sea-legs. The floor in the penthouse office, which was Mr Seshadri's own lair, had a disconcertingly springy feel to it. Mr Seshadri had got his architect to put in a goodish storage space between the false floor and the real floor, and in that space Mr Seshadri kept his small change. If it made you feel as if you were walking on a million dollars, it was because you were. Professor Ram, however, merely felt dizzy when he waded into this office. On top of the springy floor there was a carpet, pinker than a cat's yawn, its pile higher than Mr Seshadri's profit margin; and there were windows on three sides that looked out vertiginously on Mr Seshadri's demesne. Mr Seshadri was very fond of gazing out over Chennai and seeing all the buildings he had built poking up towards the heavens like ziggurats.

Mr Seshadri was swivelling gently from side to side in a splendid leather chair. He, too, was feeling like a million dollars. He was already five tots to the good, and burping extra special highland malt. He was looking forward to his evening at his watering hole, the Gymkhana Club. No wonder he was expansively pleased to see Professor Ram.

'Professor Ram! Welcome, welcome to my humble office, please sit, please feel free!' said Mr Seshadri, smiling up and down his oleaginous face. He flicked a button on his vast mahogany desk. 'Thirumalai, three coffees!'

'No, no coffee for me—!' said Professor Ram politely.

'I am going to partake, Professor sar, so please you also partake something, just for company sake! Cool drinks? Soda? Tea? Buttermilk?'

'Coffee,' said Professor Ram in a resigned tone.

'So, how is your good self?' said Mr Seshadri, shooting his cuffs, lacing his fingers together and placing them comfortably on his belly, thus covering with his palms a good proportion of the fat of the land, and almost half the Johnny Walker supply in Chennai.

'I am very well,' said Professor Ram. 'How is your family?'

'She is very fine, and Friday-Friday she is breaking a coconut in your name at Balaji temple. Because of you only my Ranganathan is able to get pass mark.'

Professor Ram did not have particularly fond memories of this Ranganathan. In fact, if he remembered right, Ranganathan was a Grade-A loafer and duffer in spite of being born Brahmin. He had even made spelling mistakes when he copied out his exam answers from the notes on the insides of his shirt-cuffs. Only the grace marks which Professor Ram gave him from time to time pushed him through his MA course.

'What I can do for you, anything?' Mr Seshadri wanted to know.

'Yes, Mr Seshadri. I am trying to find a good person to make a statue. Mrs Vaidyanathan kindly suggested that I consult you about it.'

Thirumalai scuttled in with the coffee, and handed it around.

'Oho, for what purrposs statue, sar?'

'A big statue, to be installed outside the university, maybe in the sea.'

'In the sea!' gasped Mr Seshadri, dazzled by the beauty of this plan. What vistas it opened up! The last bit of sea coast in all of Chennai that did not yet have apartments put up by Mr Seshadri! How he could see, five years from now, many more statues, dotted here and there around Marina Beach, all cast in concrete in his workshop! How he could see Mr Rami Reddy's hands going flicker-flicker under a government-issue table at the Secretariat, and hear the sweet rustle of big-denomination lollipops in some public servant's ears, and smell the sweet smell of graft in some other public servant's nose! How all these auspicious signs led up to a meeting with representatives of the university and the government, and how at the meeting the representatives said: Take the land, Mr Seshadri, and give us a theme park!—but aha! said Mr Seshadri to himself. By then would he not have contested the elections, and would he not himself be chief minister? Mr Seshadri was a very public-spirited gentleman, and not at all tight, except in his arteries, and he had long nursed a desire to construct such a theme park in the heart of Chennai, named after him, with giant-wheels, rollercoasters and slot-machines.

'You are having permission?' said Mr Seshadri, his eyes glistening sentimentally.

'Actually we don't, Mr Seshadri, and that is why I have approached you. I believe you have a magician among your employees—'

Mr Seshadri waved his hand to let Professor Ram know he need say no more.

'Very good idea, very good, it is an easy matter, no problem for Mr Rami Reddy. Now question is, what statue. At the moment we are having a sale of Dharma items. Deep discount items including Medicine Padmasambhava, Bodhisattvas, etc. cheap and best! Many neo-Buddhists are appreciating. Just like the big Buddha statue in Hussain Sagar lake in Hyderabad. Do you want any Buddhist items, Professor sar? Shall I take you to downstairs showroom?'

But Buddhist statues were the last thing on earth that Professor Ram wanted. Dr Ambedkar had embraced Buddhism and Professor Ram wished to stamp out Dr Ambedkar, not find common cause with him.

'No, I want to see what you can do for me by way of Hindu gods—or better still, goddesses.'

Mr Seshadri pressed that button again. 'Whatever is your wish and will, Professor sar. Thirumalai, bring the book catalogue for sar!'

Thirumalai scuttled in with the catalogue.

'Full pictures are there, sar. Online catalogue also is there.

You see, you select, you order. Page fourteen to sixteen, Knowledge Goddess, that is Saraswati Devi, three different type, with or without veena instrument; page eighteen to twenty-four, eight type of Cash Goddess, that is Ashtalakshmi Devi; page twenty-five to twenty-eight, Frightful Goddesses, Kali Devi—'

'You need not translate for me,' said Professor Ram with a good deal of asperity. 'I have actually—'

'No, no,' Mr Seshadri slapped his desk in remorse. 'Not for you! You are the highest respectful teacher sar. Why I must translate for you? For the many NRI people, yes, they are not even knowing proper names of the gods. Also, the tourists are coming from foreign and asking what god's names, symbal of what, which-which goddess means which-which things, etc. Not for you!'

'—I have actually written a book on Hinduism.'

'Yes! I am aware of this book, as my friend-guide-and-philosopher Sri Swaminathan, who is writing a *famous* book on Hinduism, he was writing a article about your book in *The Bindhu.*'

'Yes,' said Professor Ram, though he was not too chuffed at being known by refraction.

'A great man, very afraid of God. But one time,' Mr Seshadri leaned confidentially into Professor Ram to tell him this, and a hot gust of distillery-breath made the professor rock in his chair, 'one time, before his convushun, he is living with a porcupine'.

'I beg your pardon?' said Professor Ram.

'A downfallen lady. A dancing girl. Easy-virtue lady. A porcupine. A small house. He is never married, then also he is having one underground relationship. Day by day country is going to dogs.'

'Mr Swaminathan is my uncle,' said Professor Ram. 'My mother's own brother.'

'Oh.' Mr Seshadri felt the horror of his gaffe. He belched

apologetically. 'Very sorry, don't mistake me,' he said, washing his hands of the subject like a fastidious housefly. 'So, Professor sar, which of the goddess you are liking best?'

'I want to have an image of Saraswati, as she is the goddess of learning.'

'Very good! Brilliant choice! University also is for learning! Now let us see details, Professor sar. What kind of base you require? We are having different kinds of bases, Lotus, Cupcake, Cutlet, Corinthian. Also Up-to-date, which the NRIs are liking, to show that Hindu gods are today also relevant.'

'What are the Up-to-date bases?'

'Optical Mouse base, Xerox Machine base, Microwave Oven base, Nuclear Missile base—no that is something else—'

'I think I would like the Lotus base, it seems very appropriate in a university setting.'

'Aha! A very pure traditional mind! What cup size you are preferring?'

'Cup size?' said Professor Ram.

'Different-different people are preferring different-different cup size for chest of the goddess. Every day the fashion is changing, pages thirty to thirty-four, Twiggy, Dolly Parton, Madonna, Pamela Anderson models—foreign tourists are wanting one size bust, pages thirty-five to thirty-nine, Aishwarya, Madhuri, Sridevi, Kevlar Vest Devi models—Indians are wanting bigger. One size is not fitting all! If I am making the full statue, Professor sar, it is just money waste, time waste, no use. So I am making certain parts sep-rate, then I am getting it assembled, as per your requirements. Bust sizes 32 to 44, cup sizes A (Oomanly), B (Wonder-ful) and C (Magni-fishent). My sculpture R and D department is making the special screws so that we can fix the bust on the statue before installation. Customer is king.'

Professor Ram hesitated. The Size 32A model looked a lot like Mrs Ram to his eyes. So he chose 44C, which looked as if the goddess had hung a couple of zeppelins around her neck.

'Best choice! I have gone to Asstralia last year for business contact. Asstralia ladies!' Mr Seshadri rolled his eyes. 'Big!' He made the international sign of supersize knockers, and Professor Ram looked very austere.

'Good, when you are wanting the statue? Statue charge sep-rate, sar, transport charge sep-rate, and installation charge sep-rate. Plus tea-money for the government people and shut-up money for save-the-turtle fellows.'

'Can you have the statue ready by tomorrow?'

'I am already having one Saraswati Goddess in the showroom, Professor sar. Goddess items are fast-moving items. I don't think so there will be any problem of assembly. But we have to pay extra for master shilpi's overtime. This week only the master shilpi is busy—we have order for six twelve cen-chary antique pieces, and export antique bronze items are taking six weeks to make.'

'Send the invoices care of myself at the university, Mr Seshadri,' said Professor Ram.

'Anything for your Missis, Professor sar? Any soapstone items, small-small agarbatti stands, polyresin Roman gods for garden purpposs, corning-glass lucky Ganeshas, presentation items? No? Any time you are wanting, just phone, sar, we are doing all the needfuls.'

Mr Seshadri pressed the button.

'Thirumalai! Take sar downstairs to his car!'

Sachu joined the professor again when he got into the lift.

'I hope the invitations are going to be ready soon?' he said to her. 'I'd like to send them out to my side of the family before the weekend.'

'Yes, yes, they'll be in your hands tomorrow itself, Professor Ram. Today in my lunch-break I went to Nalli Silks and got one wedding sari for Jayanthi and the two reception saris, and also the saris for Mrs Ram and her sister.'

'Excellent,' said Professor Ram. 'I hope there is adequate gold thread in all of them.'

'If you stop in my office for one minute, I can show you,' said Sachu, punching in the number of her floor.

'Certainly. Shastri, wait outside.'

When I told you in the last chapter about Sachu's angina, dear reader, I hope I didn't give the impression that she was faking it. If I did, then expunge that half-truth from the records immediately. Sachu's palpitations during the Ram-Vaidyanathan summit early that morning were strictly on the up-and-up. What happened was—

Oh no, you are no doubt saying to yourself, not another sodding digression. And yet, if I do not give you the full picture, you may never know what courage and determination it takes to be the mother of a Brahmin bride, especially a Brahmin bride who is the colour of chocolate bon-bons, by no means a permitted colour among Brahmins.

Back, then, to what happened. Early that morning, on his way to work, Professor Ram had sat on the mangy sofa at No. 5, Varadan Street, once again, with Mrs Ram on one side and Chunky on the other. They sipped hot coffee from steel tumblers.

'In view of Uma's—er—complexion,' Professor Ram began. 'In view of Uma's complexion, we are willing to agree to this mutual alliance only with some conditions.'

'What conditions, Professor?' Sachu sat on the edge of her chair.

'A substantial part of the expenses for both weddings and both nuptial nights will be borne by your family,' Professor Ram explained. 'If you don't wish to agree, we can cancel these plans.'

'No, no, Professor.'

'We'll take care of putting up the guests on our side of the family, and of Uma's wedding sari. We don't really believe in the dowry system, of course.'

Sachu's ticker almost stopped working altogether when she added up the bills in her head. As follows:

Item, wedding saris.

Now everyone knows that if a well-born bride does not show up at her wedding like a million-kilowatt magnesium flare that can be seen at least two districts away, she is considered practically naked. Indeed, when our chief minister's foster-son got married, a great international dispute broke out among astronomers. Some claimed that they had seen an unseasonal aurora borealis display over south India, and others claimed that it was the Temple-Tuttle meteor showers; the chief minister's PR man had to issue a press notice to say that it was only the bride's wedding sari and ornaments scintillating all over the place, to stop the astronomers from beaning each other with telescopes. I myself have taken to going to weddings in welding-goggles, because after one look at the bride with unprotected eyes, I can't see anything but bright dancing spots and swirling patches of darkness for a long time. I find it very disconcerting when these spots and swirls suddenly resolve themselves into relatives, and such relatives as generally make me hanker for a bargepole just so that I can have the pleasure of not touching them with it. Anyhow, what I meant to tell you was that Sachu had to buy saris that set her back several thousand rupees, though Uma pointed out angrily that such saris were of no use whatsoever after you had been united in matrimony, since you could never wear them to anybody else's wedding, one aurora borealis being enough for any public occasion.

Item, gold jewellery, preferably set with diamonds.

Sachu's palpitations speeded up when Mrs Ram made a list of the twenty-four carat trinkets and sparklers and silver utensils she expected Uma to bring to her marriage so that she could live up to Chunky's condensed-milk complexion. Everyone agrees that brides in the best families need many many carats, for the more carats they get, the more vitamin A they absorb.

Thus they never run the risk of night-blindness; though the way some of the bridegrooms look under their wedding duds, you might not think night-blindness such a bad thing as all that. But gold and diamonds are especially efficacious in bringing up the complexion of dark-brown brides, more effective even than saffron-and-milk, and I am told that some girls in my family who were like tamarind-sauce to begin with, turned whiter than mothballs after they put on their wedding jewellery. This is why it is becoming a common practice nowadays for brides to be carried into the wedding pandal on stretchers, since they are so gold-plated that their pins cannot hold up their weight and they keep falling down. And of course, it is very undignified to enter a wedding pandal on all fours.

Item, video man.

Sachu had to pay for this personality to come and trip up the guests, and criss-cross the place up into a tangle of wires, and dazzle little old grandmothers with his psychedelic lights. I don't know if you have ever been invited to a wedding in one of the best families. If you have, no doubt you noticed that the most important person was the video man, and that the bride and groom were just a kind of side-show, not part of the main action. Sometimes brides and grooms have to get married again and again, from different angles, if the video man shouts 'Cut!' and 'Retake!' which he does if he does not get enough good footage. I hear that some families are thinking of getting rid of the bride and groom altogether and just having the video man. All the aunts and uncles like to see themselves immortalized on film as they nosh down their third helping of sambhar rice, especially the aunts and uncles who look like the back of a bus that abruptly met the front of another bus somewhere between Palayankottai and Dindigul.

Item, car.

Sachu was punch-drunk when Professor Ram informed her that she would have to pay for a new car for Chunky to drive in Canada. He added that it would have to be a new SUV;

it appeared Chunky would not drive anything except new SUVs.

Item, flight tickets.

Chunky also condescended to let Sachu take care of the flight tickets when it came time to return the two couples to Canada. At this, Sachu was out for the count, and had to be carried to bed. And there were expenses which she had not added up yet, such as the Brahmin priests—for ritual did not come cheap—and the wedding hall, which was nearly impossible to book at short notice, and miscellaneous, which included anything from rose-water and coconuts for all the guests to rooms in a five-star joint for the nuptial night.

Item, food.

Sachu did not feel poorly for too long, though. Propped up on pillows and sipping the coffee which Pati heated up for her, she was already thinking that if she got Jagadambal's catering department to supply the food, she could wangle a really big discount. The rest would have to be done through a loan against the house from Seshadri Chit Funds, though Sachu knew better than anyone that the Seshadri rates of interest were higher than a ganja-boy. Perhaps there would also have to be a visit or two to the Marwari gentleman, this gentleman being a great hand at dispensing loans at ruinous rates of interest against collateral such as gold bangles and other gewgaws.

Now where was I?

Ah yes. In her office, Sachu closed the door and took out the saris from their tissue covers.

'Not bad, not bad,' said Professor Ram, fingering the brocaded silk. 'Mrs Ram will probably want to make sure the jewellery is to her taste before the wedding. Do give us a tinkle when you've purchased it.'

'I will,' said Sachu. The bruised twitching of her upper lip was a smile. She was smiling that she might not weep. 'I certainly will.'

Not once did Sachu think of blaming the Rams for any of

her troubles. She accepted that this was what mothers had to do when their daughters chose to have the wrong complexion. If anything, she was grateful to the Rams for not demanding any dowry, and for charging her nothing more than a few lakhs here and there to take her daughter off her hands. She knew that if they did not do this, the girl would slowly get past her sell-by date, and a Brahmin bride sitting on the shelf long after her sell-by date was the most desiccated and unfashionable thing in the world.

When Sundar and Jay stepped out of the auto and headed for the water on Elliot's Beach, the sands were still deserted. It was only under cover of darkness that Chennai's lovers made for this beach in vast numbers, and sat shoulder to shoulder, jamming up the sands so prodigiously that it was considered quite excusable for Romeo A to fondle a lady who belonged to Romeo B. If Romeo B helped himself by accident to Romeo A's paper-cone of chick-pea sundal, the wronged party would send up a moderate beef. However, if Romeo A kissed Romeo B by mistake, at least five or six parties would end up broken in several places, including Romeos C and D, who were too jammed up against the parties of the first part to duck when things got hot. All of which makes me think that the Bard was visiting Chennai when he wrote those lines about the path of true love never running smooth.

The reason why the Romeos and their sweet potatoes jostled each other like this on Elliot's Beach is that it was the only place in Chennai where such turtle-doves had the licence to do some occasional billing and cooing and hand-holding. Chennai's upright citizens did not approve of parties falling in love, and thought of holding hands as a very revolting practice, which led to other even more degenerate practices such as mouth-to-mouth guzzling, and practical demonstrations from the *Kamasutra*, which they considered the end of civilization as we know it. True, some of the most vertical of these upright citizens regularly made the beast with two backs with ladies-of-the-night in the back rooms of the old flea-and-bedbug joints behind the Central Station. But when they put on their public faces, they did not think anything of breaking up love's young dream left, right, and centre.

'Shall we walk towards the Theosophical Society?' Jay said.

'OK,' Sundar said. 'But we'd better get down to the water.'

'Yeah. My sandals are lousy for walking in this hot sand.'

It was hotter than a burning oil rig out there at 4.30 in the afternoon. When they reached the tidemark, it seemed sensible to wallow among the breakers awhile. They lay, half in and half out, of the water. In no time at all Sundar and Jay were completely soaked. While this soaking did nothing spectacular for Sundar's looks, it made Jay look very appetizing. Sundar stole a look at her. Her thin cotton shirt and capris adhered to her shape most lovingly.

Sundar was beginning to feel rather drowsy when Jay turned to him and dropped her first bombshell.

'I know most men here wouldn't think so, but I believe women should have as much sexual experience as they can before marriage, don't you?'

'Er, yes,' said Sundar, hoping fervently that he was not expected to provide any of this experience. As far as the Omar Sharif stakes were concerned, he felt like a complete non-starter. He looked around desperately, hoping the policeman posted among these dunes to prevent any offhand hanky-panky—for the government aligned itself with the upright citizens as far as hanky-panky went—would come along and perform his duty with zeal. This worthy was not among those present. There was not a soul on the beach, except maybe the Over-Soul, and possibly the ectoplasm of some of the departed members of the Theosophical Society, for the society's grounds lay immediately beside them on the left.

'I mean,' Jay prattled on, 'a bit of pre-marital nooky is cool. Just imagine bonking no one all your life except your husband. Have you ever read that poem *Gather Ye Rosebuds While Ye May*?'

'Herrick?'

'Mm-hmm. I think I know what he was talking about there. Rosebuds are clearly a symbol for the male genitals. I don't think your husband's rosebud should be the first rosebud you ever see, don't you think? I mean, if you're a woman? I'd like to gather a whole bunch.'

Sundar blanched. In his family, the privates of both sexes were strictly off-limits as topics of conversation, and if they ever came up, they were referred to as 'there', without even the benefit of a qualifying 'down'. It took him years to say 'Fuck, machaan', with an authentic gangsta inflection. Naturally, he was startled to hear Jay talk like this. This was why the conversation moved in fits and starts. Everything that Jay said gave Sundar a fit, and as he did not provide any helpful responses, she had to start again on a fresh topic.

'I mean, I'd hate to find that I'd never experienced a twelve-inch hard-on in my life just because my husband's schlong was only, like, four inches from root to tip, right?'

'Oh—oh yeah.' Sundar felt panic rising within him. Where did she get a figure like twelve inches? He had never thought of placing his trouser-snake against a measuring tape. How big, how big was it when turgid?

'Have you read Masters and Johnson?' Jay said. 'I'd like to think that the person I marry will have as complete a knowledge of female anatomy as possible. Like, have you ever had that experience where you're done with foreplay and you're all ready for some real blazing genital-to-genital stuff and the dumb klutz you're with just kind of loses it?'

If the astral bodies of the theosophists were floating about, Sundar thought, Jay's conversation must be making them blush. Even such hardened cases as the one who interfered with minors.

'No, I can't say I have.'

'Am I shocking you?'

'What? Uh no, no, not at all.'

Jay rocked back with her hands clasping one knee. Conversation languished for a bit. Sundar could not think of anything to say. The situation took him back to the romantic jawing sessions he had on the blower with a female classmate at whose feet he had placed his heart in the Eighth Standard.

As follows:

He: 'So!'

She: 'So!'

He: 'So? Say something!'

She: 'You say something!'

Long pause.

He: 'So!'

She: 'So?'

And so on and so forth.

Silence on the beach. The crabs began to think they were part of the eco-system and started going walkabout on their legs.

'You know,' Jay said thoughtfully after about ten minutes, 'I'm beginning to think you're not really interested in me at all.'

Sundar's ideas about courtship behaviour were derived from the movies. This seemed the moment when the script called for action, not words. This was the moment the producer, conscious of the crores of rupees he was paying his celluloid lovers, would demand some succulent wooing on the screen. It was the moment for hip-swivelling, eye-rolling, and the rendering of love-lyrics. Only, Sundar did not feel up to any of these moves with Jay, except perhaps at gun-point. Though she was as easy on the eye as the Taj Mahal, he did not wish to woo her any more than he wished to woo the Taj Mahal. Besides, she reminded him of female cousins who did Bharata Natyam and sang geethams in platoons, and like many people, he found it embarrassing to wiggle his hips at his blood relations. On top of everything else, Sundar was a very sentimental young man. Even the thought of getting on any lovey-dovey or touchy-feely with Jay, when all the time he was in love with Jiva, made him feel like a heel and a philanderer.

The upshot was that he ignored the producer's demands and behaved like a strictly honourable Brahmin boy. He clenched his fists bitterly. For years and years he had yearned for an opportunity to get fresh, and when the opportunity finally came up, he felt about as fresh as mango-juice in a tetra-pak.

The silence dragged on. It was like the time Kicha insisted that his whole family try the fully rewindable murukku-on-a-spool that his research team had just patented. The new product had clamped people's upper jaws firmly to their lower jaws, and for a whole week not above three words had been spoken per head at No. 5 Varadan Street.

Sundar looked up at last to find Jay studying his face with frank curiosity.

'Tell me honestly. You're probably marrying me because you're being forced to—you know, for your sister's sake. You don't marry me—you ruin her life. That kind of blackmail. Right?'

'No,' said Sundar, without conviction. 'No.'

'I think Uma's really hot, by the way. I just can't figure it out—what do you think of Chunky?' she asked.

'Er—I don't know,' said Sundar.

'He's so cheap he steals plastic cutlery from other people's trays during international flights. I know, his ex-wife Lakshmi told me. He's always running after white pussy, but he's considered such a world-class turn-off that he's not managed to get laid since she left him.'

'Uh.'

'I'm not sure he got laid while she was still with him, come to that.'

Sundar could see that there was no love lost between Chunky and Jay. He was thrown by this. He himself thought very highly of Uma.

'You don't care for Chunky,' he said.

'You noticed. Jeez, Sundar. Chunky is a bad dream. The last girlfriend he had,' Jay traced lines in the sand, 'way back before he was married, in 1995, realized she was gay on the night of her very first date with Chunky. She says that when he groped her it really hit her that she couldn't stand men. This is kosher. You should tell your sister, you know.'

'Yeah.'

'And she might be interested to know that he has haemorrhoids.'

'Ah.'

'And man-boobs,' said Jay. She traced two circles in the sand.

'Huh?'

'And I think, on the whole, even if Uma does want to marry Chunky after you give her these bits of information, you can still wriggle out of marrying me if you don't find me attractive. I don't think my parents will fuss too much if there's only one wedding instead of two.'

'No,' said Sundar in a hollow voice, fixing the horizon with the yearning look of a man who wished he could dive in and keep up a strong crawl until he reached Tasmania. 'I think you're very attractive. It's just—'

'It's just what?' Jay bent forward.

'It's just that—holy shit!' said Sundar, looking at his watch. 'I should be at the protest march!'

While Sundar was dallying with Jay on the beach, things had hotted up at the TamBrahmAss end. When he got back to the university it was a few yards shy of six o'clock. As he ran up the stairs he noticed that the banisters were covered with large pieces of cardboard on which people were painting and stencilling messages.

Saraswati—goddess of wisdom!
Ambedkar—symbol of fashism!

We demand Professor Ram to be compensated by the government!!!

Prevent atrocities against Brahmins!
Demolish Ambedkar statue!

Long live the poonal! Down with minority rule!

The jacquerie had gathered on the second-floor landing and was spilling into the corridor outside the English department. There was a chair against the far wall. Shastri climbed on to it. He was aware that Professor Ram was in his office next door. Shastri was set to prove once and for all that he was one of the masters of the universe. He held up his hands to quell the wild cheering, though there was no cheering such as anyone would notice; the muttering actually came from members of the brotherhood who were affronted that they had such a homely-looking leader, and a leader, moreover, whom they could not see when he turned sideways. Shastri harangued them in a high thin voice.

'Friends, we must protest today against the sad decline of Brahmin culture in south India. Day by day we are getting pushed out of government jobs because of the Reservation Policy. Yesterday, a statue of the anti-Brahmin anti-Hindu Ambedkar was set up in this university. Also, today there was a dastardly casteist attack, by the non-Brahmin lecturer who financed this statue, on our own beloved Professor Ram. He is severely wounded! It is a conspiracy against Brahmins! We must condemn it! Friends, let us observe a one-minute silence for Professor Ram's injuries!'

'We demand the V-C to remove the Ambedkar statue!' a member of the mob shouted after about twenty seconds of twitching. 'Somebody should pay for this attack!'

'The V-C must remove Dr Arul!' suggested a branch organization. 'Down, down, Dr Arul! Long live Brahmin solidarity!'

'The governor must remove the V-C! We demand the V-C to resign! Down, down, Veeee Seeee!' howled a rather radical segment.

'Yes! Also the mayor of Chennai should resign!' cried a small splinter group which was famous for upping the ante in all the meetings of the TamBrahmAss. 'We demand a judicial enquiry—'

'Defend your sacred thread!' Shastri croaked, trying to get some focus. 'End this reverse discrimination!' But Shastri's slogans were by no means a hit. They lacked the simple rhythmic quality that marchers of limited intellect generally appreciated.

'Ah, Sundar!' Professor Ram called out above the din as Sundar fought his way to the head of the stairs with Jay. 'I am so glad you made it! Have you got the letter to the V-C written out?'

'Yes, sir,' said Sundar, patting his pocket, for a happy scheme had just occurred to him.

'Good,' said Professor Ram. He raised his voice. 'My dear friends from the TamBrahmAss and its sister organizations! It would not be right, of course, for me to encourage anti-university activities, but under the leadership of Sundar—' and here Professor Ram drew Sundar forth and displayed him to the disaffected, 'I hope you will uphold our high Brahmin ideals. Let us say a prayer together.'

Shastri, who had thought for a minute that his greatness was ripening, let his shoulders sag in the very act of handing out the banners, and was seen to make chopping movements with a knife hand as the procession wound down the stairs.

The V-C's residence was a considerable distance from the English department. That was the trouble. The marchers, all cranked up with rage at the moment, began to get soft, and any protestor worth his salt will tell you that when a procession goes soft, things are bound to become deplorably sloppy. When the mob clattered down the stairs, there was enough fervour to fuel six or seven all-India strikes. As it wound around the canteen there was a slight falling off, for some parties realized that they were feeling quite weak with hunger, and developed a great hankering to get outside some onion pakodas and tea. As the march moved across the quadrangle in front of the gents' hostel there was some more depletion, for some parties remembered there was an India vs Pakistan one-day international match on ESPN tonight. Many of the stragglers who peeled off quietly to encourage the Indian Eleven were the parties who had provided a sharp extremist edge to the proceedings and had insisted to their less bloodthirsty comrades that anything short of the impeachment of the President of India and the complete extermination of all Ambedkarites was practically snuggling up with the enemy.

In short, the stuffing went out of the protest march to a great extent, especially when Shastri tried to feed it slogans like 'Meritorious Brahmin candidates for competitive exams' (Response: Long live!). Nobody could get the timing right, and things in general were fairly creaky when the posse reached the V-C's front door. When Shastri rang the doorbell three times and got no answer, the marchers decided they might as well strike the set and go home to bed.

'He has gone out! I told you, friends, it is a conspiracy!' Shastri cried, trying to whip up some passion.

'There is a light in the house! He is hiding inside!'

'But his car is not here!'

'Maybe his wife has taken it!'

'Now what shall we do?' Sundar asked.

'Let us shout something,' said the sometime leader of the

TamBrahmAss. 'Let us shout a slogan, or everyone will go home.'

'What shall we shout?'

'Anything.'

'Hey, man!' someone shouted. 'Look at this! We have no water to wash our underpants in the hostel and the V-C has water to fill his lily-pond!'

There was an uproar.

'Down, down, lily-pond!' Sundar began. It was the first political slogan he thought of. From the way it injected new life into the proceedings, he could see that it was quite snappy. He seemed to have inherited a certain facility for rabble-rousing from his father.

'Down-down! Lily-pond!' the protesters hollered. They kept this up for a few minutes. They ate some bananas between slogans and threw the skins viciously at the V-C's windows. They even kicked some flower-pots over and threw the compost at a cat which was wandering about. But it became clear that the political will was weakening.

Sundar fiddled idly with the front door-knob. The door opened so suddenly that he nearly fell inside.

'Sundar opened the door!' Shastri shrieked. He had a nasty glint in his eye. 'As our leader, he should go into the house and challenge the V-C!'

'Ey Shastri, if someone calls the cops I'll get stuck in jail, man—'

'Go in, Sundar!' yelled Shastri.

'Go in, Sundar!' yelled the mob.

Several pairs of hands came out of the darkness and thrust Sundar into the open door. When he turned around to get out again he found that the mob had pulled the door to and was hanging on to the Godrej lock so that he could not turn it from the inside. Sundar wandered into the house, vaguely hoping to find some other exit, such as a window, which would allow him to leg it out of there. He wanted to get home before Akilan telephoned about the trip.

Sundar saw that he had stepped into a passage. The first room leading out of this passage seemed to be a sort of study, and even though it was as dark as a railway tunnel, he could see that this room had a bay window. It was the only window in the room that was big enough to let a man out, and Sundar thought it would do as an exit route. As he went towards the heavy jacquard drapes that hung before this bay window, Sundar noticed a pair of feet. He dismissed his first idea, which was that they belonged to the drapes. He bent over cautiously to study these feet, for he wished to know what kind of body was attached to them. As he examined these feet he became aware that a sofa on the other side of the room was sprouting a head, and he could not understand what the world was coming to, with body-parts apparating all over the place in an empty house.

'Who is this?' a voice hissed from behind the drapes.

It was the voice of the V-C.

'It's Sundar, Dr Mohan,' said Sundar. 'Research scholar, English department.'

'I know you.'

'I can explain,' said Sundar.

'You had better,' growled the V-C. 'Have you ever heard the word rustication?'

Sundar was about to ask if it had anything to do with the 75 per cent of India's population that lived in the villages when the Godrej lock on the front door chirruped a bit. The front door opened and someone came into the same passage Sundar had come through. From the sound of it, the person was accompanied by an importunate cat and about forty shopping bags.

The next step was a bit of a blur to Sundar. The head behind the sofa was evidently attached to a body capable of lightning responses. It dived past Sundar, clapped the study door shut and shot the bolt.

Sundar saw by the sliver of brightness under the now-closed door that a light had snapped on in the passage beyond it. Now that his eyes were getting used to the dark, Sundar could see that the person who had locked the study door was Always Already. If he were less inclined to be shy, he would have eyeballed her with great interest, and entertained impure thoughts, for the suit she stood up in was her birthday suit. When he turned his head away courteously, on the other hand, Sundar could not help seeing the V-C struggling into his pants. Since he had never seen such a sight as a man in a truss before, he studied the picture with scholarly interest.

'Sundar,' Always Already whispered. 'Don't turn around. I've got to get into my clothes.'

The study door began to rattle. The party who had just come in, who turned out to be Mrs Mohan, indicated that she wanted a piece of the action.

'Why is this door locked?' she cried, hammering. 'Who are all these people outside? What is going on? Mohan? Are you in here?'

With great presence of mind, the V-C stepped across to a massive ceramic sculpture of Sri Rama seated beside his divine consort. He knocked it over with a sharp backhanded blow that smashed it to smithereens. Then he put his shirt over his mouth and shrieked like this:

'Dontph cphome hereph! He's got me! He's phmmbroken the lovely statue which was our wedding anniversary present from the Rams and he's holding a glass pphiece against me and says he'llphmm injure me if anybody comes in!'

'Who is it? Is it a burglar? Is it one of the students? Who is it?' shouted Mrs Mohan from the other side of the locked door. 'Let me at him!'

'I can't!'

'I'm going to call the police!'

'Nopphhh! Nopphh—he's getting angry—no phpholicemm!'

'How could you forget to lock the door?' whispered Always Already, now in her underwear.

'I did lock it when you came in—it was the cat, I forgot to lock it after I put out the cat!' Dr Mohan hissed like an aerosol spray.

From this exchange it was clear that Mrs Mohan had not given her permission to Always Already to be standing in her living room in nothing but a lurid push-up bra and a pair of very suggestive ivory knickers.

'How am I going to get out?' Always Already whispered as she shrugged herself into her salwar suit.

'I don't know! Damn! She said she would be out all evening!'

Sundar could see that the study had only one door: the door into the passage, outside which Mrs Mohan was poised.

'You could go through the bay window behind you, ma'am,' Sundar said.

'Are you crazy?' hissed Always Already. 'In my bright white salwar suit, with about two dozen of your gossip-mongering Tambrahm bastards swarming all over the lawn?'

This was not language that Sundar was accustomed to hearing from lecturers. Still, it helped him see her point.

'Good point, ma'am. What about—if I create a distraction?' he asked. 'If I get everyone out to the other side of the house, you can slip out.'

'Yes,' said Always Already, with a prayerful look. 'I could. Go ahead. Go on!'

'Sir,' Sundar whispered, very respectfully to the V-C, 'sir, if you want me to, I can get these students out of the way and also support your story with Mrs Mohan. But you have to read this letter which I have written to you, and act on it. Otherwise—'

Sundar did not mention otherwise what, but he held out his printout of the Protest Letter file, in which he had included the full facts of the Ram-bites-Arul story and all the details of Jiva's meeting with Professor Ram before her job interview.

'I will read your letter. Give it to me—I'm putting it in my pocket. See? I will do anything you want. Now, for God's sake, go!'

'Mohan?' Mrs Mohan shrieked from the passage outside. 'Don't worry! A boy here—Shastri—is carrying a cellphone! We are getting help!'

'Noophnmm!' mumbled the V-C. 'He says that if you get help he wiphnmnm not be responsible for the consequencephnphnm!'

'Okay, Dr Mohan,' Sundar said, taking a deep breath. 'Please don't forget, sir. Ma'am?'

'Yes?'

'Come out when you hear, like, a big yell.'

Sundar opened the glass of the bay window just a crack and took a peek at the mob. Most of the protesters were concentrated around the front door. It was a moment's work for Sundar to step out and saunter over to mingle with the back-benchers. One or two saw him pop out of that window, but they had forgotten who he was. Then he galloped around the lily pond and shouted:

'He's here! A man! He came out of the back door—I saw him!'

'Where? Who is it?' they cried and surged towards Sundar. Shastri pushed all the others out of the way and placed himself at the head of this group, while Mrs Mohan brought up the rear.

'Here! In the bushes!'

When Sundar saw that all the protesters were thrashing about among the shrubs that skirted the lily pond, he placed a firm palm between Shastri's shoulderblades and leaned in. Always Already, who was standing poised by the study window, jumped straight in the air when she heard a splash followed by the mating cry of the Nilgiri langur. That was only Shastri screeching that he could not swim.

～

When Sundar came home after all the events of this exhausting day, he found Vaithy leaning weakly against the gate with his helmet on his head and two cigarettes going at the same time. Sachu charged out as she heard the gate, and buttonholed Sundar.

'Ma, did I get a phone call this evening?' Sundar said.

'I cannot understand her at all!' Sachu moaned. 'Is it considered the modern thing to do, to leave your would-be in the living room and take some total stranger up to your bedroom? She says she's showing him some books!' She flapped her hands. 'Sundar, do something! Appa, I appeal to you! Don't stand here smoking cigarettes!'

Vaithy tossed both cigarettes down, ground them into the earth with great ferocity, and immediately lit another couple.

'Who is in whose bedroom?' asked Sundar. He had not been given enough context to help him understand this situation.

'Your sister and some big black fellow who just walked in—your friend, he called himself—I have seen him somewhere before—I don't know where—oh, what will he think?'

'The big black fellow?' said Sundar.

'No! Sankaranarayanan!'

'Chunky? He's here too?'

'Again!' Vaithy groaned hollowly. 'That anus is here again, can you believe it? He says he heard you took his sister out, and he wanted to see his fiancée today too. Couldn't you have left the bugger's sister alone? What did you want to take her out for?'

While these exchanges were going on outside the house, Chunky was not left to his own devices. Kicha had kindly undertaken to entertain him. Kicha rooted about in the passages of what he used instead of a mind, and presently he surfaced with his tail wagging, like a dog that had found a dead bandicoot behind the lantana bush. Between his teeth was a joke from page 112 of *One Hundred Party Jokes*.

'Ha ha!' said Kicha, 'Sankaranarayanan—ha ha ha!—have you got a match?'

'What? No—I don't smoke.' Chunky brooded.

'I have, my face and your ass. No, that is not correct—*your* face—match—*my* ass—ha ho *ho!*'

'Hggh hggh,' Chunky assented through gritted teeth. 'Would you mind asking your sister to come downstairs?'

Chunky hoped to collect Uma quickly and be gone. When Mr Seshadri built No. 5, Varadan Street, wire screens were one of his little economies, and the mosquitoes were making Chunky feel faint with anaemia.

'That reminds me of another joke.' Kicha was as happy as the day was long, for he had never before remembered two jokes together on the same evening. 'I will tell you another one. You must buy this book, Sankaranarayanan, it is called *Fifty Latest Jokes* and it has fantastic jokes. Listen. A man goes to a Chinese doctor, and he says, "Doctor, can you help me please, as no woman is falling for me, in spite of all my efforts."'

Chunky scratched his arms irritably.

'Itchy?' Vaithy said, coming in. 'The mosquitoes are getting you? Where is your poonal, ey? Sundar, show Sankaranarayanan how to scratch his back with the poonal! You don't have yours? Tch tch! How can you get married if you are not wearing your poonal?'

'Hi, Chunky,' said Sundar in a deadpan voice. 'I'll see if Uma's coming down.'

'She seems to be upstairs,' Chunky said poutily, 'with Akilan'.

'The Chinese doctor examines him for a long time, and takes his pulse, and checks his blood pressure, and finally says, "Walk towards me!" and the man walks towards the doctor. Then the doctor says—'

'Yes!' Sachu gasped. 'They are looking at some books.'

'It's Akilan?' Sundar brightened up at once. 'Great! Hey, Akilan!' he yelled as he bounced towards the stairs.

'Then the doctor says, "Walk away from me!" and the patient walks away from the doctor. Then the doctor says, "Walk towards me on your hands and knees!" and—'

Before Sundar's foot hit the bottom stair he heard Uma coming down.

'I don't know *how* you can think P.D. James is better than Ruth Rendell,' she was saying. 'You're buying that stupid poetry-writing sensitive cop rubbish.'

'No,' said Akilan, bumping into the walls as he came down behind Uma, his steering hampered by a pile of paperbacks. They represented Uma's entire collection of Agatha Christie. 'I'm talking of the Cordelia Gray stories. She's really good, Uma, specially the first three, no?'

'—and the patient walks towards him, and he says again, "Walk away from me on your hands and knees!" and the patient does what he is told. And then the doctor says, "You have Ed Zachary disease." Then the patient asks—'

'Hey, Akilan, man, I thought you'd forgotten about the trip,' Sundar said.

'What trip?' Sachu said sharply.

'Oh, just a car trip, to a village, near here.'

'With whom?'

'Some students who are at the university, Ma,' says Sundar.

'When?'

'Tomorrow.'

'Tomorrow? With you having to be measured for your wedding suit?'

'—the patient asks, "Oh how terrible, what is it, doctor?"'

'Oh Ma, that can wait for one day. So—is Caroline's friend coming, machaan?'

'Yah,' Akilan replied. 'It is a girl called Jayanthi.'

'What?' said Sundar. 'But—'

'That would be my sister, Akilan,' Chunky cut in smoothly. 'And Sundar's fiancée. And if Sundar and Jay are going on this trip, I think Uma and I should go too. Right, Uma?'

'Yes!' Vaithy cried. 'Of course she should go with her fiancé! You can hold hands! Right, Uma?'

'When are you going?' Chunky asked.

Akilan studied this situation narrowly. It was the first time he realized there was a connection between Chunky and Uma.

'—then the doctor says, "Yes, it is terrible!"'

'Tomorrow,' said Sundar.

'Are *you* going?' Uma asked Akilan.

'Yah. Jiva, Caroline, me—there won't be space in the car, man,' Akilan said firmly to Chunky.

'The patient says, "What kind of disease is it, doctor?"'

Chunky stroked his tussocks thoughtfully. 'I'll get Caroline to hire a van instead of a car. She won't have to pay very much more. That way, we can all travel quite comfortably.'

To Sundar's dismay, both Akilan and Uma agreed. As soon as Chunky wished to go, Sachu found that she never actually had anything against such a trip, after all.

'Good!' snorted Vaithy. 'How you will all enjoy yourselves!'

Kicha whacked his hand down firmly on Chunky's thigh, for he felt the punchline coming.

'And the doctor says, "It is Ed Zachary disease! Your face *Ed Zachary* like your ass!"'

In which Paravai village acquires
a new Local Myth

ON WEDNESDAY MORNING, the Sri Satya Sai Baba Tourist Car Rental sent an ancient pea-green Matador van to No. 5 Varadan Street as requested. It was mercifully cool and dark at 5 a.m. The sun got its act together only at about six. Sundar and Uma let themselves quietly out of the house, for it was not a water-lorry day, and people were catching up on their sleep.

It became clear to the passengers in the first five minutes that the vehicle they had hired was a very dilapidated old milk-can. It evidently hated being woken up at this ungodly hour and kept up a deafening blasphemy of protest. The driver was a trifle absent-minded, and what he was absent-minded about was which pedal was the accelerator and which one the brake, and his way of sorting out this little problem was to use one or the other at random, until he was satisfied with the effect. So Sundar and Uma found themselves proceeding through the deserted streets of Chennai in leaps and bounds. The van had practically no springs or shock-absorbers. By the time they stopped outside the university hostel at 5.25 a.m., Sundar noticed that his spine was sticking out through the top of his head to the extent of the top three vertebrae, and he had to push it back down into place. Uma felt around carefully all over the seat to locate her hairpins, shaken loose by the ride. I will say this for the driver: he was a great hand at controlling the vehicle when he was blowing his nose into his palm, and he only actually ran into lamp-posts and policemen when he put his hand out the window to wipe the product on the scratched paintwork of his door.

Sundar and Uma were mighty pleased to be alive to welcome Jiva into this old tea-kettle at the university hostel. When Jiva switched on the light briefly to put her things in the dickey, Sundar stared at her in mute adoration. She wore a lemon-yellow salwar suit that set off her dark skin, and the glow of the rosy-fingered along the sea lit her up like an old Chola bronze princess that Sundar had once seen in a museum. Sundar had never before seen any sight that was so beautiful.

'You know, you are staring at her,' Uma whispered in his ear.

The driver set off again, and the orange streetlamps flashed past. Jiva's face, now in the light, and now in shadow, became thoughtful as she observed the driver's technique.

'I thought we were supposed to go in a car,' she said.

'Chunky made Caroline ask for a van, because he wanted to come too, and we needed extra space,' Sundar said. 'The driver—Arumugam—says this was the only van left at the last minute. All the other vans were booked long ago.'

The old saucepan ate up the miles between the university and Cathedral Road, and stopped in the large portico of the Chola Sheraton. Caroline parked her luggage in the dickey and climbed in with her laptop. Now the van looped back towards Mandaveli, with Jiva telling the driver to turn right and turn left, until they fetched up at a dead-end at the bottom of a dingy little alley. The driver started to do the tic-tac-toe to decide which pedal was the brake when Jiva yelled 'Stop here!' But he got it wrong. They juddered to a halt with the front fender crumpled cosily against the walls of a tenement, and it was such a ramshackle tenement that they dislodged a lot of plaster.

There was no one waiting there, and no one came down when the driver honked a merry tune on his horn.

'Are you sure this is the house?' Sundar looked doubtfully at Jiva.

'Of course I'm sure!' Jiva said, peering into the dark. 'I have come here so many times. He's probably still asleep. We'll have to go up and wake him.'

'I'll go,' said Sundar.

'Thank you. It is the flat on the top floor,' Jiva said, pointing to the terrace.

Sundar ran up dark, dilapidated stairs that many generations of tenants had decorated with betel-juice stains. The landings were heaped with old pots and pans, broken chairs and plastic milk-packets. The stairs stank, as the toilets for some of the flats were under them. When Sundar reached the top floor and came out on the terrace, he saw that Akilan, though he had only one poky-looking room at one corner of the terrace, was the sole master of a toilet at the opposite corner. There was no sign that anyone was stirring in this flat. Sundar banged on the door.

Akilan heaved himself up from a mat in the corner of his room.

'Ada paavi!' he groaned as he opened the door and blinked at Sundar. 'You sinner! What are you doing here, man? It's the middle of the night!'

'Uh-huh. It's almost six o'clock. We're supposed to be gone from Chennai in half an hour, unless we want to bake in the sun.'

'Ai-ai-ai. I overslept.' Akilan swept a dozen empty Old Monk bottles from the only chair in the room. 'Sit, machaan, I'll be ready in five minutes.'

While Akilan shuffled across to the toilet, Sundar sat at his desk and studied the contents. Akilan's ashtrays and candlestands and penholders rang the changes on the bottle motif. In fact, when Sundar looked more carefully around the room, he realized that there was not a thing that did not seem to be related, at least by marriage, to wines and spirits. The table beside the mat was nothing but a tray propped up by four sand-filled McDowell half-bottles. On the desk, at Sundar's elbow, stuck under a paperweight which had once held a quarter of Hercules Triple X, was a letter that began:

> 'Dear Sir
>   I am a poor orfan boy who is Def and Dum, but in spite of my problems I am inventing a special fuel that can be used for motor cars, which is a Top Secret formula made of herbal substance. But I am not having any capital to devlop this mooligai petrol. It is a great bisness oppertunity. I therefor apeal to you—'

In trying to get at the rest of the letter, Sundar dislodged a curious object suspended from a black string, and this object rolled off the table onto the books below.

'Sorry.' Sundar picked it up. 'What's this, machaan?'

Akilan paused in the act of stuffing a few necessities, such as a half of Triple X and a quarter of McDowell's, into a cloth satchel.

'It is a magic made of goat's balls. It can get you a girl,' he said.

Sundar whooped in amusement, fingering the amulet. 'Does it work?'

'Don't laugh, man, it always works,' Akilan said. He slapped himself on the belly. 'You see this belly? I am getting it when I was sixteen, and my mother says I will never get a girl. But always I am getting any girl I want.'

Sundar gazed at the belly with reverence, for it was indeed substantial. It looked like a camel's hump that had slipped around to the front and was hanging there. Sundar studied Akilan all over. It was clear that he was not in the running for Mr Universe, and if Akilan got all the girls he needed, Sundar thought, the amulet had to be very effective indeed.

'Where did you get this, machaan?'

'I am working as a part-time maama for two months last year, man, and my boss has given it to me.'

'Maama?' In Sundar's world, a maama was an uncle, just as a maami was an aunt.

'What? Oh. A pimp, paappaan-boy. Imagine, you don't know even that. Lousy job.'

'Oh I see. Akilan... can I wear this for today?'

'No problem, man.'

As Sundar put the amulet around his neck he remembered Jiva saying she came to Akilan's flat all the time. An acute cramp seized him just under the heart, and he knew it was jealousy.

'Akilan,' he said, choosing his words carefully. 'Would you say Jiva was your type?'

Akilan's belly jiggled all over with mirth.

'My *type*? As if I am looking at young or old or fat or thin or black or white. Give me anything between sixteen and sixty-nine. My boss is telling, "Akilan, first affection, then mutton injection." But machaan, there is one thing that you can't avoid in life. Some girls are saying to you, I want to be like your sister. If they say that, you have to leave them alone. Okay, man, let's go.'

'So Jiva said she wants to be your sister?' Sundar persisted as Akilan locked his door.

Akilan's eyes slid sideways and his mouth twitched. 'Yah, paappan-boy. Why you want to know?'

Sundar made no reply. The cramp receded. They hurried down to the waiting van. At 6.15 a.m. they arrived at First Main Street, Mylapore.

The lotus! Pure symbol of Hinduism! It evidently played the same role in Professor Ram's design scheme as the bottle played in Akilan's. I would not advise you to look at Professor Ram's residence suddenly on an empty stomach. The compound wall was encrusted with plaster lotuses. The driveway was lined with grey cement elephants, gaily decked out in pink and purple and yellow cement tassels, holding cement lotuses in their trunks. On the gate-posts were fibreglass lotuses containing light bulbs that could be switched on in the evenings.

The soundtrack that accompanied this mutant flower attack, curiously, was a whumpity-slap, whumpity-slap coming around the side of the house, and a voice that gasped like this:

'(Whumpity-slap!) ninety-seven (whoosh!), (whumpity-slap!) ninety-eight (whoosh!), (whumpity-slap!) ninety-nine (whoosh!), (whumpity-slap!) one hundred!'

This was a great mystery to the people in the van, until the scion of the House of Ram hove into view, trailing a skipping-rope. Jay came out of the front door with her bag at the same time, and settled herself in the bone-shaker that Sri Satya Sai Baba had provided.

'Ey! Put my bags in the van!' Chunky shouted to someone inside the house. He dropped the rope. 'Take in my rope!'

Thaayi hobbled out of the house with Chunky's bags, and Sundar helped her put them in the dickey.

'You're late!' Chunky grumbled in the general direction of the van as he mopped his face.

'Don't pay any attention to him,' said Jay softly. 'He only got ready about two minutes ago. One whole hour in the loo.'

'Waxing his underarms? Curling his hair?' Sundar wondered.

'Nah. Straining on the pot,' Jay said.

'Like my brother Kicha,' Uma remarked. 'The Toilet King.'

'Naturally, it takes a long time,' Akilan said. 'They are both paappaans, no? See, the shit has to come all the way from their heads!'

Mrs Ram came out with a huge wicker basket. She smiled at all the people in the van, though it is true that when she took in Jiva and Akilan her smile got thinner than a supermodel.

'Your father is still very unhappy that you are going on this trip, Chunky,' she said. 'I assured him that you would not pollute yourself with unclean food. You know how *particular* he is. So I have packed everything you will need for today and tomorrow, you and Jay and also Uma and Sundar. Also steel tumblers and separate plates. Don't forget to open all the small containers, there's plenty of chutney and chilli-powder in them, and the big container has the curd rice.'

Akilan opened his mouth and then closed it again when Jiva gave him a warning look. Professor Ram toddled out with something under his arm, looking very sulky and not acknowledging anyone except Caroline.

'Here you are, Caroline,' he said. 'This is the book I told you about when we met on the night of the play. It will give you deeper insights into Indian culture than any other publication of its scope.' He pressed *Daddy, What is the Significance of the Poonal* into her hands.

At last, all the bags were piled up in the dickey. Professor Ram chanted a prayer for their well-being and purity. The young Rams said twenty times each, 'I will go and come.' Chunky tore himself away from his mother's arms and opened the side-door of the van.

'Sorry, Chunky,' Akilan said lazily. 'It's full here. You should get into the front seat.'

Chunky pouted mutinously as he climbed in beside the driver. How did he happen to miss sitting next to Uma? He turned to see how the others had arranged themselves.

In the last row, facing the front of the van, were Caroline, Akilan and Jiva.

In the second row, facing the back of the van, were Jay, Sundar and Uma.

'Care to trade places with me, Akilan?' Chunky asked, in an offhand way.

'Sorry. I have to help Caroline with her notes,' Akilan replied, without looking up from Caroline's laptop screen, where FlashMan was destroying unspecified evil forces.

'Sundar?'

From where Sundar sat, he could see Jiva etched in profile against the dawn, one devastating, perfectly muscled arm crooked over the window. Sundar was not likely to swap with Chunky.

'Uh, why don't we start?' Sundar said vaguely, over his shoulder.

The driver fiddled with the ignition and the van jolted forward again with terrible shrieks and groans. Professor Ram and Mrs Ram stood in the lotus-ridden porch, aghast. The murky morning light was giving way to brightness. They noticed, for the first time, the long gash along the left flank of the van, the back fender—smashed in three places—and the right flank— a sea of dinges and dents. The van looked more like cigarette-foil that had been crushed and straightened out than like proper metal. It is a good thing they didn't see the front fender. My guess is that they'd have run after the van all the way to Paravai, just to pull their children out.

Ten kilometres later, Akilan shook his head and leaned past Sundar's shoulder towards the driver. 'This brother is not understanding the brake and the accelerator. Thambi—' this to the driver—'what is your name?'

'Arumugam, sar.'

'Arumugam, brother, these people are from foreign. Indian driving is really terrifying for these foreign-returned types.'

Chunky laughed contemptuously.

'It's pretty obvious you've never been to the States, Akilan,' he said. 'Hitting the Interstate at 200 kmph—now that's what I call real driving. The speeds are really something. And don't forget I've lived in India for twenty years—man, I've seen it all, highways, city roads, village tracks, wooden bridges, ghat sections, you name it—*Aaaaarrh*!'

All this time Arumugam had hidden his light under a

bushel. As they hit the highway, he spat on his hands and really got down to it, and the fibreglass Venkateswara dangle-dolly spun three times around the rearview mirror and pasted Chunky a juicy one over the left eye. He stopped talking and rested one palm over his eye, which was watering freely.

'What's that stuff lying on the sides of the road, Ack-eelan?' Caroline said hesitantly. She was not sure if driving like this was a native custom or not, and she was torn between documenting it as a quaint death wish and forbidding it. 'Looks pretty—like heaps of sugar candy. Is it an offering of some kind?'

Chunky's arm lay along the back of the driver's seat. His face appeared over this arm. The left eye was an interesting colour, and there was quite a marked sneer around the lips. 'Sugar candy!' Chunky scoffed. 'That's glass—the debris of highway accidents, probably fatal. This is India, Caroline, not the West,' he said. 'Jeez, you haven't seen anything yet. Some of the trips I've made—overtaking trucks while hugging the edge of a cliff, beating a train acoss a railway crossing by a split second—*ack! Ack ack ack*!!'

A buffalo crossed the road without looking to the right, to the left and to the right again. Arumugam spun the wheel and accelerated at the same moment. The van flew off the road and hit a banyan tree root. The Tidbit Chunky was sucking, to get that zingy minty-fresh breath confidence that would allow him to swing into action later with Uma, went up the wrong tube, and Chunky broke off his peroration to choke.

'The *buffalo*!' Caroline shrieked, forgetting all about accepting the Otherness of native cultures. And a little later she shrieked, 'The *pig*! Oh my gawd, the *goat*!'

The home life of the chickens, goats, pigs and other livestock all along the road to Paravai was profoundly unsatisfactory, judging by the way they came out one by one and tried to throw themselves under the wheels of the van. And though Arumugam was a beardless youth who had a thoroughly gentle face, he was evidently a tough personality when it came to livestock. He seemed to think that a pig was nothing but pork vindaloo on the trotter, and that the best way past a goat was straight through it, and that since all flesh was as biriyani anyway, the sooner it got slaughtered and cooked up, the better for all concerned.

'Stop this van and let me out this minute!' Chunky screamed, taking his hands away from his face.

'Power steering!' Arumugam explained calmly.

'If you don't slow down, you maniac, I'll see that you lose your licence!'

Arumugam turned to Chunky with a pure, saintly smile.

'I thought of that,' he murmured. 'That is why—' here he paused while he puréed a chicken, '—that is why I never got a licence!'

Chunky insisted that he stop the van. It turned out he had some business behind a bush. The spot was very scenic, with toddy-palms stretching into the sky on both sides of the tarmac as far as the eye could see. The others acquiesced, secretly pleased at the chance to let out their breath, which they had all started holding around forty kilometres earlier.

'Ackeelan, can you run through the names of my informants at the village?' Caroline sat down under a palmyra tree and opened her laptop up again. She felt up to entering some notes, now that she no longer was in danger of immediate annihilation.

Chunky came around the bush. Jay and Uma sat next to each other, and on Uma's other side was a palmyra tree.

'Move up, Jay,' Chunky said. He dropped down next to Uma. Uma shifted towards the tree.

'So, Caroline, how're the interviews going?' Chunky said. 'Anything solid?'

'Oh, lots of interesting stuff,' Caroline said absently.

'You know,' Chunky said, 'women are at a real disadvantage where ethnography is concerned'.

'What's that supposed to mean?' Caroline's head snapped up.

'Don't go off the deep end. It's just one of the facts of life, you know. Real ethnography is done when the guys get together and hit the bottle.'

'You're an Eng. Lit. guy, Chunky—what do you know about ethnography?'

Chunky wrote his papers the way they made bhel-puri in the railway stations. He put in a little bit of this and a little bit of that, tossed all the ingredients together and wrapped it up in an old scrap of newsprint. Ethnography was one of the things he put in. He was actually interested in doing some research on his own account during this trip, though he did not want to put this on a formal basis. He was tired of the paper that he had already presented at thirteen conferences; but he disliked the idea of a drain on his purse.

'I always put in some thick description in my papers, Caroline. Goes down well with the postcolonial crowd. I've done a couple of ethnographic projects I'm quite proud of. Like two years ago, I wandered around south India, living it up with the locals and collecting material on street art. We must have killed six or seven full bottles of strong stuff each day. It is my experience that the solid information comes out when the booze starts flowing.' He swept his arms around the scene. 'If we had the time I'd have suggested that we indulge in a spot of lubrication. Nothing like a little toddy to get the interviews rolling.'

'Ah, but we have a lot of time,' Akilan said silkily. 'Our driver is very fast. So why not we get some toddy? I can see they are still tapping.'

The dark bodies of the tappers were silhouetted against the sky as they hitched themselves up the palmyra trunks by their fibrous harnesses.

'Let's get some!' Uma leapt up, excited. 'I have never drunk toddy before!'

Chunky caught her hand and pulled her down again. 'Don't be stupid, Uma. You don't want to start drinking toddy—you have no idea—'

'Anything for a beautiful woman,' Akilan cut in, scrambling to his feet and calling the toddy-tappers.

'I'd like some too,' said Jay, looking at Sundar.

'Is it—like, hygienic?' said Caroline.

'Straight off the tree,' Sundar said, collecting a clay pot for Jay. Of course he did not mention that sometimes the bees and flies fell through the strainers and then the tappers picked them out of the toddy with their fingers. 'Jiva? Will you have a pot?'

'I should not drink today—I have to be fresh for this evening. It will be a waste getting a whole pot for me.'

'What's it taste like?' said Caroline, sniffing at Jay's pot.

'Sweetish early in the morning, but a bit sour now,' Sundar said. 'By this time it's pretty fermented. It packs a hell of a punch.'

The tappers came up and passed more pots around. The driver took one.

'So how many pots for you, Chunky-boy? Three? Four?' Akilan asked. 'I myself will have three.'

'Oh, just one.' Chunky's mouth turned down as Uma took gleeful sips. 'I'm not in the mood today.'

'Okay. Sit down here only, Chunky.' Akilan patted the grass. He unscrewed a bottle from his satchel and poured its contents into his own pot. 'We don't want you to go off here and there and give your toddy to the plants.'

Sundar lowered himself onto a grassy patch next to Jiva. 'Take a few sips, Jiva?' he said, offering his pot.

Jiva did not take the pot. There was a curious look on her face.

'You are not worried about the uh—pollution?' she asked, finally.

'What?' Sundar said. His arm ached from holding the pot out.

'You don't think you will be polluted if we drink from the same pot?'

'Me? Of course not—no! I never—why should anyone think something—so weird?' He thrust the pot towards her.

'My father,' Jiva said, sipping from Sundar's pot as if she didn't quite believe him, 'had to leave Paravai, which was his village, because he would not stop drinking from the teacups meant for the caste people. In the tea shop. The Padayachi landlord sent a bunch of goons with sickles to our house.'

Sundar frowned. He had read somewhere that there were villages in which Dalits were still segregated, but until this minute he had never given it any thought.

'Maybe that's true in the villages—I read in the papers that the farming castes like the Naickers have clashes with the Dalits. But educated people—I mean people in Chennai—are not that stupid—'

'No—not in the same way,' Jiva said. 'They usually don't beat us up, I grant that. But I went to—to a professor's house the other day because I had to bring him something. He gave me a glass of water. Afterwards I heard him telling his wife that she must not mix that glass up with the other glasses.'

Jay looked up. 'Would that be my dad?'

'Yes,' Jiva said.

'Figures. He's an old asshole.'

'*Jay!*' Chunky spluttered. The toddy from his pot splashed down his shirt front. He wiped himself irritably. 'Damn. Now I'm going to be sticky all over.'

'This—this discrimination—it goes on among educated people?' Sundar asked, ignoring Chunky. 'Man, I had no idea!'

'There, you see,' Akilan said. 'He had no idea!' He mimicked Sundar's voice, wobbling his head in comic disbelief. 'That is a typical paappan-boy for you! Only world-class oppressor like the paappaan will say he can never see any Dalit fellows with his own two eyes, even though he is having his own right foot in the Hush Puppies shoe on one Dalit fellow's neck, and his left foot in the Adidas on another Dalit fellow's back!'

That third pot of toddy fitted comfortably under Akilan's belt. He had barely wet his whistle, but the tappers informed him that the party was over, as they had run out of toddy. He extracted a half of Old Monk out of his satchel and sucked on it.

'I think I've had about enough of this, you—you wannabe!' Chunky shouted. He was still nursing his first pot, but his snout was beginning to look pulpy and porous and incarnadined, like a used tampon. 'If you had any decency, you'd stop badmouthing Brahmins when there are so many of them around you. Especially genuine radicals like us! It's just disgusting, the way you guys go on whining and complaining about the caste system—why, since I came to India this trip I've hardly seen any sign that it still exists! And if it exists, I think it's you—*you guys who keep bringing it up*—who keep it alive!'

'Okay, Chunky-boy,' Akilan said, putting away the Old Monk and clapping a hand to his thigh. 'Stand up and defend the Brahmin honour. Show me your fists, Chunky-boyoo!'

Chunky stared gloomily into his pot. Uma watched the two of them, her mouth slightly open.

'Paappaan no good in fighting. Bruppie dickheads! All thinking that caste system is wiped out,' Akilan said derisively. 'They don't feel it, so they are thinking it is gone.'

'What's bruppie?' Caroline asked.

'A Brahmin yuppie. Haven't you heard this word? Caroline,' he said solemnly, holding up a warning finger, 'never trust a paappaan. A paappaan means a Brahmin fellow. Bastard is having curds in his veins instead of blood, and he will eat you up. Bastard is hungry because every day he is eating only curd rice and spinach, nothing else.'

'I will not listen to any more insults!' Chunky screeched. He stood up and dusted off the seat of his pants. 'I'm going to the van!'

'Oho! And who is going to pay for the toddy?' said Akilan. Chunky fished out a wallet and groped in its recesses.

'Not enough cash—bank strike—total bandh—Sundar?' Sundar squared the toddy-tappers. Jay slid up to him.

'See what I told you?' she whispered. 'You heard of Scrooge?'

'As in Donald Duck?' Sundar asked.

'I was thinking of Dickens, but Donald Duck will do as well. Well, Scrooge could take Chunky's Thrift 101 course and change his life. You warn your sister, Sundar. Chunky's the original guy who buys gently-used condoms at the charity bazaar.'

'It was worth it. God bless fermentation,' said Sundar as they climbed back into the deathtrap. He was feeling on top of the world at this minute. The toddy was giving him a warm buzz; Chunky had come within an inch of being thumped; and the seating arrangements had been unaccountably altered. Sundar was now sitting between Jiva and Jay. Jay's feet, stretched out, were resting casually against Caroline's feet. Uma was wedged up quite tight against Akilan and they were reading a Faye Kellerman together.

'And also God bless the matter I put in this toddy for the kick,' Akilan added, turning the page.

'What? What matter?' Chunky cried, twisting his head around.

'Chunky-boy. Tch tch tch. You are the liquor expert, no? Then why you have not noticed that country arrack taste in your toddy? Don't worry, I put only four packets. Only in yours and mine. Nothing in the girls' pots.'

Sitting right next to Jiva had the disadvantage that Sundar could not stare at her any more. However, there were compensations. Jiva's hair was bursting out of its rubber band like a black fountain, and whenever the wind blew it against Sundar's arms, his own hair stood up with static. His whole left side, which was in contact with the fabric of Jiva's chiffon scarf, was burning with localized lust. Sometimes, when the van zigged madly to avoid some oncoming mofussil bus or zagged frantically to pass a truck full of logs, Jiva's flesh actually touched Sundar's, and then a million filaments in his skin sizzled and crackled and sparked with concupiscence. He was amazed that Jiva did not seem to be aware of this.

About twenty kilometres short of Paravai, the passengers noticed that not a single chicken had perished in the last ten kilometres. These were splendid statistics indeed. The bullock carts were racing past them at the speed of light. It became clear that Arumugam had finally taken Chunky's criticism to heart. In fact, he seemed to have developed a great affection for Chunky, for he was driving with his head on Chunky's shoulder in a chummy kind of way. When Chunky saw ancient donkeys passing them at a gay pace and dawdling children overtaking the van on their way to school, he got a little impatient and asked the driver why he did not get a move on. But still the van creaked along like a snail taking an after-dinner stroll. Just before they turned off the highway into Paravai, it stopped altogether. In the silence that ensued, the passengers figured out that the sound they had begun to hear half an hour earlier, which they thought was engine trouble, was actually Arumugam snoring. He had evidently driven while fast asleep for the last thirty kilometres at least. No matter how loudly they called his name, and how much they shook him, Arumugam would not wake up, and so the passengers had to collect their bags and take it on the hoof up the last kilometre or so, accompanied by several friendly dogs.

'The Brahmin streets are on your right,' Jiva said to Sundar, as they trudged through the village. 'The Vishnu temple belongs to the Brahmins. Fifty years ago, Dalits were not allowed to even step into this street. You see that tamarind tree? They had to stop there and shout for their landlords to come and take the harvested grain.' They went past the Vishnu temple's courtyard and the vegetable shop, past a street with a Pillayar temple and the two-storeyed houses of the Kallar and Naicker farmers who owned most of the land around Paravai, past a tea-shop and the Nattar's grocery shop and past the Paravai Unlimited Meals Hotel. As they crossed the coconut grove and the Kali temple, they heard the sound of many children singing out their sums.

'This is the Dalit part of the village,' Jiva said. 'I used to go to that school when I was very young.'

As they passed the windows, the children craned their necks to see them, but went on with their lessons. Akilan had worked with the citizens of Paravai for other ethnographic projects before this, and he had drilled them in the behaviour that Ford Foundation expected of informants. The children had stopped asking the researchers for pens, and the adults were quite blasé about scantily-clad scholars of both sexes. On his first assignment at Paravai, Akilan had learnt about the pitfalls in the life of a native informant. He had taken an ethnographer from Columbia University to Paravai to record the subversive boat-songs that the citizens used when they went fishing on the lake.

Now, it happened that Paravai had enjoyed a brief season of prosperity in the 1980s, after these boat-songs were first reported in the Western world, and one of the results of this prosperity was that the villagers installed Kirloskar engines on their country boats. These citizens gradually forgot the boat-songs because they no longer needed to keep the rhythm of rowing. When Akilan discovered this, and explained the problem to him, the ethnographer flew into a rage and wished to have his money back. Akilan had already laid out this capital on certain investments. It was all very awkward until the Oldest Inhabitant, a remarkably creative and resourceful personality, especially when stimulated by the McDowell's Premium that Akilan had brought, suddenly remembered enough boat-songs to sink an ice-breaker, even though these boat-songs had never been heard in Paravai before, or anywhere else, if it came to that.

There was a great spreading banyan tree at the near end of

the street, and under it there were some cement slabs which functioned as benches. One of these benches was occupied by some old-timers who did not go out to work in the fields. These old-timers, the Oldest Inhabitant among them, acted as the reception committee to the group that had arrived in Paravai. Under the tree was a little tinbox shop that provided beedis to this committee when it wished to smoke, and areca nuts and betel leaves when it wished to chew, and bananas when it wished to eat. To this shop the Oldest Inhabitant sent Akilan, with instructions like this:

'Bring some Colour for the guests.'

Sundar noted that Akilan came back with seven bottles of Pepsi. He offered to pay, for Pepsi was expensive, but the old-timer waved his money away.

'Ey, mapillai—son-in-law,' the Oldest Inhabitant said affectionately to Akilan, 'have you not got yourself a wife yet? I told you not to show your face in Paravai again without a wife, didn't I?'

'I am getting married soon, Thatha,' Akilan replied placidly. 'And you? Have you got the patta-document to show you own your land yet?'

'What shall I say, mapillai. We have paid all the money. The panchayat council just has to give us the documents, but they will not. They are angry because we have a candidate for the panchayat council—one of our boys. They say they will not give back our money, or give us the pattas, if this boy stands for the election. They also say they will not take our milk anymore for the milk co-operative. I don't know what will become of us. I suppose we should be happy that they have not yet burnt any houses in our street. This lady—can she speak to the government?' He indicated Caroline.

'I don't think she can, Thatha, but I will ask someone else I know in Chennai.'

'Ai-ai, look at me, talking about our problems, and you all coming from so far away. You must be tired. The ladies are making food in your mother's house,' he said, turning to Jiva. 'They have current there—we have borrowed a fan from our friend in the next village. How do you like the stage?'

He pointed at a makeshift theatre that two men were hammering up on the other side of the banyan tree.

'Very nice, Thatha,' Jiva said.

The visitors took their leave and set off for Jiva's home, which was at the other end of the street. The houses in this part of Paravai were very simple. Some of them had brick walls and a little stoop in front, with a thatched awning on wooden pillars. But most of them just had walls made of palmyra and coconut matting, and were also thatched with the same material, which was convenient for the landlords who owned the two-storey houses on the other side of the village, for they were inordinately fond of burning these houses.

At the door of the last of these houses, a brick one this time, a lady was waiting for the party, and they guessed at once who it was. Jiva's mother was a grey-haired version of her daughter. She wore a big smile when she welcomed the travellers. The house was dark and cool, with polished utensils glowing in the fitful light of the fire. On the woodstove in the corner something was boiling that made Sundar's stomach rumble quite a bit.

'The paappaans have their own food, no?' Akilan said, inhaling deeply.

Sundar looked at the fresh-caught fish that floated in the tamarind gravy, cheek-by-jowl with big pieces of raw mango, the whole smelling of woodsmoke; and he looked at the heaps of hot rice in a pot.

'Jiva,' he said, 'if your mother says it's all right, I want to eat what she has cooked.'

In the end, Chunky was the only one who unwrapped the food Mrs Ram had packed in the wicker basket. He had never eaten in a Dalit household before, though he had travelled so extensively, and he had no wish to experiment with low and dangerous foods. Caroline found that whatever she put in her mouth threatened to take off two layers of her palate, so she declined everything after a few attempts and ate some sandwiches the Chola Sheraton had packed for her. The rest of them fell on the rice and fish ravenously. For one thing, they had not had any breakfast, and for another, those close encounters with the Grim Reaper had whipped up a rare appetite in them.

After a while, when the sharp edge of their hunger had worn off, various parties began to talk of this and that. Jiva's mother asked Caroline if she was married. Caroline explained her marital status in Tamil. Though she had learnt Tamil for two terms at Ontario, no one understood what she was saying, and Akilan had to earn his rupees by translating.

'She likes to talk to the women,' Akilan explained to Sundar in a low voice. 'She says these days Americans and Canadians don't like to be on talking about poverty and female infanticide in the Third World, so it seems we have to think of some new things, like gender subversion, for them to talk about.'

At some point Sundar felt he had packed away more than his share of the food, and he stopped eating. Caroline began her interviews. Akilan got busy translating. Uma vanished. Jiva went to the kitchen and came back with a pitcher of water and tumblers for all of them. She said to Sundar, 'I am going to wake that Arumugam up and bring him home to eat. Are you coming with me?'

Through the corner of his eye Sundar saw Chunky sidling up towards him, his mug drawn into grumpy lines.

'Quick,' Sundar said, 'let's go!'

'Sundar,' Chunky said, 'have you seen Um—?'

But Sundar had gone.

∼

At six o'clock that evening Sundar sat outside the tinbox shop with the old-timers, looking wistfully towards the makeshift shed behind the stage. Jiva and her fellow performers had shut themselves up in it an hour earlier to put on their make-up. Jay and Uma wandered down to the lake and traded stories with the women who were thumping their washing on the rocks to get the dirt out. Caroline typed busily on her laptop while Akilan and Chunky explained the phenomenon of the koothu to her.

'In the Tamil month of Chittirai, which is April, the villagers in Paravai and all round are taking a collection,' Akilan said, 'for financing a koothu performance'.

'That is standard practice for villages in the slack agricultural season.' Chunky said in an *Encyclopaedia Britannica* accent.

'Yah, but this is special, because most of the audience is Dalits. Today, this troupe is doing the story of Draupadi,' Akilan said.

'The Draupadi cycle is part of the standard repertoire of most troupes,' Chunky explained. He turned to Sundar. 'By the way, Sundar, have you seen Um—?'

'No!' Sundar said.

'But this is a special koothu troupe,' Akilan went on. 'It is completely women, except the teacher and two musicians. The women are putting on the men's parts. Traditional koothu troupe is completely men, and the men are putting on the women's parts.'

'Doesn't the teacher mind, like, deviating from the tradition?' Caroline asked.

'No, he is agreeing to teach this all-women troupe when Jiva asked him,' Akilan said. 'The government is paying for their classes.'

'Is it?' Chunky raised his eyebrows. 'Hmm. I'd think the government had higher forms of art to worry about.'

'Chunky, some people think it's important for folk theatre to survive,' Caroline snapped.

As the sun turned into an orange sphere on the horizon, and the cows came home under a coppery sky, and the bee-eaters and blue-jays and orioles curled up in their beds in the branches, the citizens who lived in the hamlets round about gathered together under the banyan tree to watch the Paravai Koothu Manram tackle the story of Thiraupathi or Draupadi. Sundar slid closer to the stage, feeling suddenly breathless with expectation. Uma and Jay sat near him. They had somehow contrived to put a few bodies between themselves and Chunky. The oil-lamps on the stage-frame were lit, and the drummers and the harmonium-player and the flautist began playing. In the dusk, it sounded very uncanny and beautiful. The chiming of the cymbals called even to the little children who clambered up and down the cement slabs and hung upside down from the branches of the banyan tree. They settled down by their mothers and grandfathers and uncles and aunts, hushed and awe-struck.

'Wow, cool!' Caroline breathed softly. 'They've begun!'

Two women came out, holding up a long sea-blue satin screen with designs all over it. Meanwhile, the singers invoked the gods and blessed the stage.

'Who's that?' Caroline said, as a character swaggered out in striped trousers and a parti-coloured shirt.

'That is the narrator guy,' Akilan said. 'He'll tell us the whole story and also make jokes about the village. Now he is saying if you give him a beedi, he will tell you all about the government doctor in the Public Health Centre. The doctor is never coming to this village except on the first day of the month. That day he is coming to sign for his salary and for smoking a beedi.'

'The narrator, as you may see by his costume, has a sort of jester's licence to speak the truth,' Chunky added.

Chunky put in his two-paisa worth of commentary right through the first half of the play. He began to fade somewhat by the second half, though Caroline barely noticed. The arrack with which Akilan had spiked his toddy was rotgut country moonshine, guaranteed to set fire even to cast-iron digestions. On Chunky's delicate insides it had a most disquieting effect, especially because it had been thoroughly joggled up by the ride.

'Who's coming on now?' Caroline demanded, as a new character appeared behind the screen.

'That is Tharmarajan, the fellow who is gambling away his wife Draupadi in the dice game,' Akilan said. 'He is a king, but a big gambler character, so he is wearing pink make-up.'

Each new character was introduced by the narrator and danced for a while behind the screen—'That is Sakuni'—'That is Archunan, he's a good fellow, so he is having green make-up'—before he or she came out. Finally, a most exciting character burst out into the lamplight and stood on the bench, sword raised in the air, and the audience roared with disapproval because it could see at once that he was an unmitigated villain.

'That is Thurchaasanan, the bad prince who is going to insult Draupadi,' Akilan said. 'He is a cousin of Tharmarajan. He is a villain, so his face is red and black.'

The voice of this Thurchaasanan made Sundar catch his breath. He recognized Jiva's dark haunting timbre, though Jiva's shape was practically invisible behind the heavy robes and massive epaulettes and splendid crown this character wore. He was quite startled to find that his love was enhanced by the sight of his beloved twirling a wicked pair of moustaches. Strange are the ways of the libido-god.

Chunky's milk-white mug was shiny with sweat. The fizz was fairly coming out of his ears, and if anyone wished to witness a practical demonstration of the Big Bang Theory, they would only have to find Chunky's plunger and depress it.

Chunky turned to the nearest local informant and tapped his arm to get his attention.

'Toilet!' he said hoarsely.

'Huh?'

'Toilet! Bathroom!'

The local informant waved his hand in the general direction of the village and turned away. Thurchaasanan was in a great frenzy and he expressed this by whirling in wild circles all over the stage. The informant felt vast admiration for the athleticism of these pirouettes.

Both on the stage and off it, the pressure was building up to breaking point.

'Akilan!' Chunky leaned across Caroline. 'I need to use a washroom!'

'Over there, Chunky-boy!' Akilan gestured into the night.

Chunky got up and edged towards the trees Akilan had pointed to. When he got there, he was already feeling runnier than a soft-boiled egg, but there was not a likely structure in sigh⁺

On the stage, Draupadi was being dragged by her hair and disrobed. Lord Krishna was offsetting her losses with an endless supply of textiles, and Thurchaasanan was getting very tired of hauling at all that fabric. Off the stage, Chunky caught the Oldest Inhabitant by the shoulder and juddered him about.

'A washroom!' Chunky cried in his green-card accent. 'Bathroom! *Lat*rine! *Toi*let! Ka*ckoos*!' he bellowed in this peaceable old man's ear, pummelling his shoulder with every synonym he uttered. Well might Chunky have sounded like Roget's *Thesaurus*, for he was feeling like a man who had swallowed a cactus. The Oldest Inhabitant peered into Chunky's face for a long time. He was known far and wide for his wise handling of many crises and he had not been attacked like this by anyone since the showdown with the high-caste police in 1985.

'Mapillai,' the venerable native subject said to Chunky, 'there is a story behind our latrines. Sit down quietly now, the koothu is very moving. After the koothu I will tell you about it. It is a long story.'

'I have to go!' Chunky wept, getting more and more incoherent. 'Where? Where?'

Some mothers, whose babies were sleeping in their laps, hissed with irritation. Chunky was ruining the great drama of Draupadi's ecstasy and Thurchaasanan's desperate efforts to humiliate her. He was making their babies whimper.

'*I want to fucking use the fucking washroom fucking now!*'

The old-timer decided that nothing but the story of the latrines would calm Chunky down. He began to explain in a low voice how a rich builder called Seshadri from the big city had landed the prefabricated rural hygiene project and how he had got government funds to put up latrines in Paravai, and how the latrines had fallen down in the first monsoon. In fact, though the Oldest Inhabitant did not know this, this project had been Mr Seshadri's first big triumph. His profit margin had been phenomenal, and when he next advertised a public issue, many subscribers were killed in the stampede.

'So, mapillai, *these* are the latrines,' the Oldest Inhabitant concluded, slapping the slabs they sat on. 'Only these slabs left. We are sitting on Paravai's latrines, mapillai. Ah, look at Thiraupathi Amman now! She has shown those fellows how to behave!'

'No TIME!' Chunky roared. '*Now! Ippo! Inge!*'

The koothu-players began to sing the *Mankalam*, the last sòng in the play, because they could see there was no point going on with their entertainment when there was such a major side-show going on. They stepped down from the platform and surged around Chunky. By the time he finally realized that there were no latrines and started hobbling towards the fields, a good-sized procession of men, women, children, dogs, goats and chickens was following him, and at its tail were Caroline, Akilan and Sundar.

In the middle of the street, in the middle of the village, the demon gripe bit Chunky in the bowels and he could walk no further.

'Right here,' he said with finality and relief. 'I cannot walk a step further.'

The venerable elder seemed to understand what was coming. 'Poyya!' he shouted to the crowd, making shooing movements. 'Pongomma! Poda thambi!'

Nobody moved. The elder grumbled to himself.

'What's he saying, Ack-eelan?' Caroline asked eagerly, fingers poised over her keyboard.

'He is asking them to go, get lost, but he says that the women do not listen to anything he says ever since they start the women's self-help micro-credit organization.'

'Ah-some. Why aren't they going?'

Akilan gave her a pitying look.

'Caroline,' he said, 'this is the first time this village has an upper-caste street entertainer for entertaining them. They never had so much fun for years and years.'

'What is he going to do, Amma?' the little children tugged impatiently at their mothers' sari-ends.

'Sssshhh!'

The audience waited to see what vision was to be vouchsafed them next. Chunky made it clear that his next step was to unbuckle his belt and drop his pants. The Oldest Inhabitant thought quickly when he saw Chunky's incomparable bottom emerging from cover.

'The screens!' he called out. 'Bring the screens! Malaichami! Lourdu! Muthu! Hide the man!'

The women who had held up the screens for the characters in the koothu brought down these props. Some young bloods of the village took position, holding them aloft and blocking the womenfolk from the sight of Chunky. The audience was amazed and cheated, because it could not understand the point of concealing the show like this. So it packed itself around the two or three citizens who could still see the action, and these citizens passed the news to the citizens behind them, and so on, until the citizens in the last row were brought up to date.

'He has taken off his pants!' '...has taken off his pants!' '...taken off his pants!'

'He is squatting!' '...is squatting!' 'Squatting, did you say?'

The Oldest Inhabitant lit two beedis and inhaled their smoke while Chunky made a series of gurgling and spluttering noises such as you might be familiar with if you live, as I do, in an old house with faulty plumbing.

'Paappaan-boy no good at drinking fire-water!' Akilan chortled to Caroline.

'The squits!' the telegraph announced. 'Terrible!'

'Periyavare, give us a beedi too, the mayiru smells something awful,' one of the screen-caryatids begged.

'Machaan, he is spray-painting the koothu props,' Akilan said to Sundar, with a look of great distaste. It was true. Chunky was spattering archipelagos across the sea-blue screens.

'Paper!' the cry went out after a while. 'Now he is asking for paper!'

'Paper!'

'Where will we get paper from?'

'Does any of the children have paper?'

'Why does he want paper?'

'I don't know! These are city people, who knows what they want?'

'Does the white girl have any paper?'

'Caroline, do you have any paper?' Akilan translated.

'No—I'm using my laptop for all my notes—except—Oh wait a minute!' she said. 'I've got this—' and she passed *Daddy What is the Significance* via the village telegraph.

'I don't care for the ways of the city people,' said the Oldest Inhabitant, switching his beedis from one side of his mouth to the other. 'They have no respect for book-learning. Now they have combuter-machines, and they use books only for this kind of purpose.'

Finally, the screens were moved aside and the lone entertainer staggered out and collapsed on the nearest slab. The villagers gathered around him.

'Where is Uma?' he asked in a choky voice.

Uma was not to be found anywhere.

The Oldest Inhabitant called out for a bottle of Pepsi to be bought for Chunky. He sat down beside him and said:

'Mapillai, don't mistake me, but didn't anybody tell you that it is unhygienic to empty your bowels like this in the middle of the street? Many years ago Gandhi-Thatha told us this, and we carry a spade to bury our excrement even when we go in the fields. Every year, the government sends an educated man like you to tell us that it is not right to just empty our bowels anywhere. Ask any of my grandchildren—they will tell you all about the diseases that spread because of this, and also the correct way to dispose of your excrement. But here, in the middle of the road—ey, what will we tell these children who will ask, in years to come, why the clever man from the big city far away dirtied up our only path through the village? And the screens—mapillai, I think I have to ask you to clean up. The ladies will give you soap, and there are rocks by the lake to do the washing.' He sighed and held out his hands in wonder. 'Such an educated man, and he can't do a simple thing like go to the fields. Mapillai,' he said very forbearingly, 'could you not have asked us when you wanted to go?'

Less than an hour after Sundar went to sleep on a mat in Jiva's house, he woke up with a terrible thirst. He was afraid of disturbing the other sleepers if he blundered about in the dark looking for the water-pitcher. He remembered seeing several brass pitchers full of water by the well in the backyard. He went out, lowering his head carefully to pass through the low door-post.

A nightjar far away sang tik tik tiktiktiktiktik, like a marble falling on the floor, bouncing high and then lower and lower to the ground. The half-moon silvered up the palm trees in the distance. Sundar could see the lake through the gaps between the houses, and the moon's glittery track along its centre. A brass pot sat on the rim of the well with a rope around its neck.

Sundar sent this pot down in search of water, but he did this
with such a clumsy motion that the pot crashed against the
sides of the well as it went down, and generally made enough
noise to rouse the dead. The pulley squeaked as he brought the
pot back up.

'Who is that?' Jiva's voice called. She was drying her hair in
the doorway of the tiny enclosure at the end of the yard, where
the women bathed. She twisted her hair into the towel, wound
the whole into a knot. Her skin, still glazed with water, reflected
the moon; there were very few electric lights in Paravai. Sundar
thought she looked like a nymph carved in mahogany, and the
sight of her caused considerable tumult in various parts of his
anatomy. He gnawed his lip in confusion. On the one hand he
worshipped the ground she trod on, and on the other he
wished to whisk away the petticoat she had wrapped around
herself like a sarong and do unspeakable things to her bare
flesh. While he tried to resolve this, the bugs took up residence
in his mouth and made him cough.

'Who is it?'

'It's me, Sundar. I needed a drink of water.'

'Did you get it?'

'Yeah, I got it out of the well. I'm wondering how to drink
it.'

Jiva came over, picked up the pot and poured out the
water for him. He cupped his hands and drank a gallon or two
without stopping. He could have gone on drinking until he
burst, just for the pleasure of being this close to Jiva.

'Thank you.'

'That's okay.'

As Sundar straightened up, Jiva's hair tumbled out of its
knot and covered his face. He felt about two hundred and forty
volts coursing through his frame. Maybe it was the toddy, or
maybe it was the smell of her skin—bark and collyrium and
mango-flowers and jasmine and molasses and he could not tell
what all else—but his head began to buzz.

'Jiva.'

'Mmm?'

'Er—' He remembered Chunky's line. 'I think your performance today was fantastic.'

'Thank you.'

'Really villainous.'

'Mmm.'

'I think you are the most beautiful woman I've ever seen.'

Jiva rested the pot on her hip and tipped her head sideways.

'Why are you telling me this?'

'Because I—'

'Say it, Sundar!' the toddy whispered, laying hold of his left ear. 'Go on, say it!'

'Don't say it! Don't say anything!' shouted the spectres of his mother and Mrs Ram and Bucket Maami, who were having hysterics in the region of his right ear.

'Go on, Sundar, you miserable poltroon! Say it!' said the moonlight, joining the toddy at his left ear.

'No, no, never!' screeched the ghosts of Professor Ram and Chunky, garrotting him with their poonals, ramming *The Complete Works of Manu* and several pages of *Daddy, What is the Significance* down his throat, and dotting him on the back of the head with pink concrete lotuses. 'Discretion is the better part of valour!' said Professors Nagarajan, Venkataraman and Sambasivan. 'Remember, oh Brahmin son! There is an etymological connection between caste (from the Portuguese *casta*, from the Latin *castus*) and chastity!'

'Think of love!' cried the little god with the sugarcane bow.

'Think of Manu! Think of "Tidbits of Vedic Wisdom"! Think of the Whole Duty of the Hindu Husband!' said the astral bodies of Mr Swaminathan and Sri Sri Sri Sastrigal and the editor of *The Bindhu*.

'Go on, you can do it!' said the amulet Akilan gave him, from where it lay against his thumping heart.

'Because—' Sundar gasped, holding onto this amulet for strength, 'I love you!'

'Oh.' Jiva said. She put down the water-pot and stared at him.

Sundar silently cursed the moon and the toddy and the amulet. 'Me and my big mouth. I guess,' he croaked, 'I guess now you'll just slap me, or tell me to get lost or—'

'Why should I?' Jiva asked softly. 'Why shouldn't I—like you too?'

All around them the mango flowers were falling. The air was thick with summer. There was nobody about except the birds and the bees, and even the bees were asleep. It is not clear which of them made the first move, but they ended up taking each other in WWE holds, and nuzzling noses, and smooshing lips, and doing all the other things that people do when they fall in love. But I am afraid I can give you no details, as their passion steamed up my contact lenses, and I saw very little except two brain-fever birds clashing their bills together on a palmyra tree in the background, and two mangoes rubbing against each other in a grossly improper manner in the foreground, and right at my feet, a lady cricket stridulating a love lyric in a voice so much like Lata Mangeshkar's that you could not tell the difference, and a gentleman cricket listening to the same.

Sundar and Jiva wound up in the shadows by the mango-thope without any clear recollection of how they got there. It is possible that the mosquitoes carried them over, because when they came up for air from time to time, they could hear the skeeter-party going on all around them. When the mists of passion lifted a little, they realized that they had donated a good deal of blood to this party, and that the skeeters in their immediate vicinity were looking very well fed indeed, while they themselves were coming out in lumps all over. So it came about that they both needed some scratching of inaccessible places on their backs, and this was when each one knew that the other was the One, for even if all the rest amounted to nothing more than mere infatuation, accuracy in the matter of back-scratching is a never-failing test of compatibility.

'You *really* like me?' Sundar asked.

'Yes. Now stop asking, because I'm not going to keep telling you.'

'Okay. Will you marry me? A little higher,' Sundar said. 'A little more to the left. Aaah, perfect!'

'What will your family say?' Jiva asked. 'There's a spot on my right shoulder—I don't want to hear that you have been locked up and your whole family has to go to Kashi to clean itself in the Ganga river.'

'My father will be on my side, I think. He is a trade union guy. I don't care what my mother thinks. Oh, my sister will be delighted.'

'Trade unionism is not a guarantee of broad-mindedness, Sundar. Paappaans are paappaans. They will talk about freedom and equality till they are half-dead, but if a Brahmin tries to marry a Dalit, they will remember all the customs of their village—how Dalits should not walk in front of them with slippers, or ride cycles, or come to the front door for anything, or eat fresh food from their kitchen. Don't tell me anything about paappaans.'

Sundar sighed, for he could not dispute this.

'But tell me if you will marry me,' he said. 'I don't care what other people say.'

Jiva was willing to put her consent on a maybe-maybe-not basis. Sundar had to be content with this, for before they could discuss it any further, the night was shattered by a noise:

'Aaaooouuaaargh!'

'What on earth—is it an animal?'

'AAAAOOOOUAAARGH!!!'

'No,' said Jiva, listening attentively. 'It is your friend Chunky. I think he is—'

'Yes,' said Sundar, '—vomiting.'

They sighed with contentment and sat in the moonlight, holding hands and one thing and another, and Sundar never noticed that the goat's testicle amulet had been ripped off the black string around his neck and lay on the grass beside him, soaking up dew.

In which Chunky tries to launch Hyperloco-Globality at the ACS conference

―――――――――― ∼ ――――――――――

THE VERY FIRST thing that happened to Sundar on Saturday morning, when he came downstairs in search of a free bathroom, was that his mother asked him if he had a poor and deserving friend called Anantharama Iyer, because three letters addressed to that individual seemed to have found their way into the No. 5 Varadan Street mailbox.

Sundar sat down at the big dining table and examined the missives with some puzzlement. He had never, as far as he could remember, had any Brahmin friends, or at any rate not deserving ones, unless they deserved to be covered with red spots and black spots and ridden out of town backwards on a donkey.

The doorbell sang *Happy Birthday to You*. Vaithy, who had just come in to collect the paper, flinched like anything, because he was afraid it might be Chunky again. But when he opened the door he cheered up a good bit, because it was not Chunky at all. It was the big burly character with a face like a murderer's who had showed up on Monday, he remembered, and had given Sachu a headache that had not really cleared up till last night.

'You!' said Vaithy cordially, collaring the paper. 'Come in, come in! Excuse me!' He marched upstairs, calling 'Ey, Kicha! If you don't get out of that toilet, I'll tell the Jagadambal authorities that you are going to picket the office with me next week!'

'Hey, Akilan!' Sundar said. 'What's going on, man?'

'Ah—I came to see if you are having some letters that belong to me,' said Akilan. 'Good morning, Auntie,' he said to Sachu, giving her his most alluring smile, but she just ran out of the room, making gagging motions as she went.

'I think your mother is not liking me much, man,' Akilan grimaced. He snatched up the mystery letters. 'Ada paavi, here are my letters.' He began to tear them open carefully, as if he thought they contained something important.

'Hmmm,' said Sundar, who was beginning to have an inkling of the nature of Akilan's little side business. 'I see. You are a poor and deserving Brahmin boy?'

'Yah,' Akilan nodded matter of factly. 'Small investments are yielding big returns. Last week I am a chariot-puller and week before I am an electronic spiritual man who is willing to telephone God through my cellphone to ask for personal favours. Machaan, you have no idea what people send money for. See?' he held up a cheque. 'One hundred and one rupees. From our own Professor Ram's Poor and Deserving Brahmin Boys Vedic Education Project.'

'Machaan—' Sundar was about to say that all these activities seemed to him somewhat underhand and not likely to get the blessing of the law, but he thought of Professor Ram, and of Professor Nagarajan, and of the various TamBrahm organizations, and he suddenly felt a great affection for Akilan.

'What?'

'Nothing, machaan—just be careful.'

'I am very careful, man. Look, fifty chips from Professor Sambasivan. It is enough!'

'Enough for what?'

'For—Mysore Sandal Soap. Don't worry, Sundar, I am not forgetting the forty I have taken from you. Tomorrow only I will return it.'

'No problem, man.'

'Um—Sundar.'

'Yes?'

'Your sister is already leaving for work?'

'No man. Shall I call her?'

'Yah.'

Sundar ran upstairs to Uma's room. On the stairs he came upon Sachu who cupped her face in her hands and moaned in a broken voice that she could not understand what that fellow *wanted*. For a second Sundar entertained a hope that Uma fancied Akilan and would call off the double wedding that was ticking like a bomb at the back of every thought Sundar had thought in the last few days. But Uma received the news of Akilan's presence with such indifference that he had to put this hope in the shredder.

'Oh?' she said. 'OK, tell him I'm coming.'

Sundar went downstairs again.

'It's just terrible,' Sundar said, 'I can't see Jiva all day today, because I will be stuck in this filthy ACS conference and she can't come.'

'I remember, Caroline told me about this conference,' Akilan said. 'She is presenting a paper.'

'Don't talk to me about presenting papers, man, it gives me a stomach-ache. I still don't have a paper for my session tomorrow, and I've run out of excuses to give Professor Ram.'

'Tell him you have a dangerous fever.'

'You know, man, I read a David Lodge novel in which one character is saved at the last minute from reading his paper, which is not written—'

'Just like yours—'

'—just like mine, because all the people think that there is a person with a contagious disease at the conference and they run away. But who cares about contagious diseases in India?'

Uma floated down the stairs, looking pretty as a picture-postcard, except for the slightly bored expression on her face.

∽

At a quarter past nine in the morning, as Sundar dragged himself up another flight of stairs, towards the English department, he saw, on the first-floor landing, a big white placard that announced:

Association of Commonwealth Studies

CONFLUENCE 2002

Saturday Session

Centenary Hall

This placard was decorated with arrows and advice to the conferees about where to find the Centenary Hall and where to find the sanitary facilities. Sundar paused for a moment, partly because the thought of seeing Professor Ram was causing him intolerable agony, and partly to add arrow-heads to the butt-ends of the arrows on the placard, thus introducing the fourth or fifth type of ambiguity into its composition. Before he finished this job, he saw a vision walking down the stairs towards him in the light of the big rose-shaped skylight, and it was a vision that made the blood sing sa-re-ga-ma up and down the scale in his arteries and his spirits soar like a dozen helium balloons in an updraught. You have already guessed, dear reader, that this vision, reading from left to right, was Jiva. She was wearing something blue and summery, her eyes were bright, and her braid was lying over her shoulder. She was smiling. She was trailing one hand along the banisters, and naturally Sundar had to put his own hand on the banisters too, and naturally the hands got somewhat tangled up, though anyone can tell you that the authorities did not approve of tangled-up hands at Chennai University any more than they approved of students indulging, outside the Dean's office, in the sixty-four sexual postures explored by the author of the *Kamasutra*.

For a spell, Sundar just drank Jiva in with a slack, witless grin that pushed against his earlobes on both sides. His head was buzzing like a chain-saw and his heart was thumping like an irrigation pump.

'Listen, Sundar!' Jiva said, her voice slightly tremulous with excitement. 'Our letter to the V-C worked! The Disciplinary Committee has withdrawn all the charges of assault against Professor Arul!'

'Fantastic!' Sundar said. 'That's the best news I've heard all day!'

'No one knows this at the moment except Dr Arul,' Jiva said, 'The V-C himself phoned her to let her know.'

'How is she?'

'Her leg has become infected. Her doctor says there seems to be some strange poison in the injury that is making it septic, so she must rest. But she will come in for a while in the afternoon, because today is the day they are voting for the new president of the ACS.'

'Oh yeah, I forgot. She's one of the candidates, right?'

'Yes. The other candidate is Ram.'

'I hope she wins,' Sundar said fervently. 'You know, Jiva, I wasn't expecting to see you today. I thought you weren't coming to the conference because of the registration fee!'

'I'm here to represent the Students for Democracy. We decided we should make some kind of statement about the registration fee. We are going to walk into the hall without paying,' Jiva said. 'Paper ready yet?'

Sundar sighed. 'Uh-uh. It's hopeless. I've been scratching like a monkey for the last two weeks but I haven't found a single louse. McGonagall is bad enough by himself, but combining his crap with Abhinavagupta's is mental torture. Ai!' All his troubles closed in on him again. 'What am I going to tell Rambo now?'

They stopped in the corridor outside Professor Ram's office, knocked backwards by the agarbatti-incense that was pouring out of the chinks in Professor Ram's door. The smell was particularly strong this morning, because Professor Ram had set his heart on becoming the president of the Association of Commonwealth Studies, and he was making sure that his smoke-signals reached all the way up to heaven, where he hoped that Ganesha and Sri Rama and the Knowledge Goddess were rigging the votes in his favour this very moment.

Sundar put a hand on the doorknob.

'Jiva,' he said, 'I cannot do this. Let's get a cup of coffee first.'

'Okay, let's go,' said Jiva. 'We still have more than half an hour before the conference starts.'

They did an about-turn, giggling and becoming intertwined in a most unbecoming fashion. But as they reached the stairs, they heard a sound like a lorry's tire blowing out, and a prolonged malevolent hiss like all the air escaping. They turned around reluctantly. Professor Ram was standing at the door of his office, wreathed in a purple agarbatti-haze.

'*Sundar!*'

Under the overhang of his waggling eyebrows, Professor Ram's eyes were glittering horribly.

Sundar's hand dropped lifelessly away from Jiva's. He knew how freely Professor Ram interpreted the slogan that the personal was the political, and he saw how this scene between Jiva and him appeared from Professor Ram's perspective.

'Sundar,' Professor Ram said, huffing stertorously in his rage, 'I was just about to distribute your *wedding invitations* to all my friends at the conference.' He looked Jiva up and down as if she was something scaly that had popped out of a sewer. 'I don't know if you are aware of this, Jiva, but there is the small matter of Sundar's upcoming marriage to my daughter. I know your cas—*type*—has no morals, but I am sure even you understand how inadvisable it is to attempt to seduce my future son-in-law one week before your viva voce examination.'

'Is this true, Sundar?' Jiva asked in a soft papery voice.

Sundar stood like a freeze in one of Professor Ram's plays, neither confirming nor denying this statement, and Professor Ram opened up one of the invitations that V.V.R. Publishers had just rolled out, and held it in front of Jiva's nose. He was careful not to give it to her.

'I see,' Jiva said, swallowing. 'Con—congratulations, Sundar. Thank you for telling me, Pro—Professor Ram.' She turned around and went down the stairs without another word.

Sundar came back to life in a second, and turned around to follow Jiva as Professor Ram's voice continued:

'As for you, Sundar, if you defy me now, I will make sure that your scholarship gets cut off. I'll ensure that you never get a university job in your life. In fact I'll make sure you never get any job.'

'Jiva,' Sundar called out, leaping down the steps. 'Wait! Listen to me!'

Professor Ram trotted after Sundar. He was getting good at chasing people down these stairs like the Hound of Heaven.

'If you jeopardize your marriage to Jay, Sundar, you will be sealing your sister's fate. Not only will I call off her wedding to Chunky, but I will also personally make sure that not a single groom will step forward to marry her, either here or among the NRIs. It is not as if your sister is so fair and beautiful that you can be fooling around with an immoral trollop. You will have ruined Uma's happiness, Sundar!'

'Jiva. Listen to me for one minute,' Sundar said.

'And Jiva will never get her degree, you can take that from me!'

Sundar stopped. He had a strong sense of déjà vu as he saw Jiva's back whip around the last flight of stairs and move beyond the frame of his vision.

～

In the spacious new lobby of the university's Centenary Hall, the preparations for the opening session of the ACS conference were in full swing. Sundar was palely and listlessly loitering just outside the door, wondering if this was a good time to take up smoking, and showing an uncharacteristic lack of interest in the five-star catering people who were carrying the hot breakfast from their van to the tables that were set up in one of the adjoining rooms. Right next to one of the doors leading into the hall, Shastri was sitting at the registration table, collecting last-minute moolah from the conferees, and dispensing passes which they wore like badges of honour on their chests. In a central location, on the wall between the two doors, Chunky was mounting some kind of display. The reason Sundar knew this to be Chunky, even though he was bent over, was that his bottom was clearly visible. It was the scene of another great battle between cellulite and trouser seam. Chunky, it was clear, could never know the pain of the wedgie, for a wedgie requires a superfluity of fabric, and the underwear had not yet been invented that covered Chunky's wondrous nates and left any fabric over.

Sundar could see through the glass panes of the door that the display consisted of two large collages. One of them had what seemed to be a large dried cow-pat in the middle surrounded by pictures of famous buildings from all over the world—cathedrals and ziggurats and places of commerce. If Sundar had been closer, he would have seen that this picture was called *Diasporic Melancholy II*. The other collage, which bore the title *Anguish: Peripheries*—not that Sundar could see this—seemed to be mainly a copy of a famous picture that Sundar remembered was called the *Mona Lisa*, except that it had a large cowdung-pancake over the lady's left breast, in the region of her heart.

As Chunky stepped back to study the total effect of the display, Professor Ram came galumphing out of the conference hall with a face like thunder.

'How could you let in these—these *seditionists*?' he bellowed at Shastri, spit flying from his lips.

'I didn't let them in, Professor!' Shastri whined. His eyes were as big as saucers. Sweat dripped down his face and saturated his shirt. The veins on his forehead bulged and throbbed. His hands were convulsively mashing registration forms. 'They came in themselves when I left my seat to print out the draft of my thesis!'

'Your *thesis*!' Professor Ram screamed. 'I don't want to hear about or see that worthless piece of—of *garbage*!' He flung out a hand, for words failed him.

Sundar skipped breakfast to see what this row was about. He coughed up his registration fee, pinned on his badge and wandered into the conference hall. There he saw a row of chairs occupied by a group of students who sat in an orderly fashion with placards pinned to their chests. Read together, the letters on these placards made a suggestion:

Free discussion, not fee collection

Sundar understood that this outrage had been organized by the Students for Democracy. Its members could by no means afford the half-grand that Professor Ram was charging up front for entry into this conference. Amandeep and Rufus, who were leading this unlettered horde of registration-dodgers, looked as if they had recently been in the wars. They had, in a manner of speaking. Many students had, since the night of the play, taken pleasure in addressing them as Mr Fairy Amandeep and Roofy Poofy respectively, and they had found it necessary to retaliate. Their appearance certainly brought down the tone of the conference. Naturally, Professor Ram ground his teeth. How would Theseus and the Athenian aristocracy have felt if Philostrate had scalped cut-price two-drachma tickets without permission from anyone, and all the slaves and the women had got into the royal enclosure to watch *Pyramus and Thisbe*?

Professor Ram was about to take strong measures to get rid

of the protestors when the British Council representative appeared in the lobby. He was followed closely by the United States Information Service representative, who came in practically arm-in-arm with the University Grants Commission representative. As Professor Ram was up to the nose-hairs in obligation to these gentlemen, who had put up the capital for this conference stunt, he cancelled his plan to stamp out the insubordination and began to fly from each of these parties to the next, sucking up to them most oleaginously. Professor Ram's academic PR manner was so oil-rich that many men of science who ran across him in other such lobbies during coffee breaks, all over the world, thought that he and his kind might actually be the alternative to OPEC, and the answer to the prayers of those who drove SUVs during this fuel crisis.

It was networking time. Professor Ram was buzzing around, busy, busy, busy, here and there and in sundry places, laying up goodwill against the voting for the president's post this evening. He regretted only that he could not cut himself up ten ways, like the ten avatars of Lord Vishnu, for if he could schmooze in ten different spots in the lobby with ten different academic pashas, he would have a walkover. His eye fell on Chunky, and his heart swelled with emotion. 'What a blessing,' he thought to himself, 'that I have Chunky, my second self, the only one who can carry forward my projects with complete sincerity. That Sundar—' Professor Ram thought bitterly, 'oh, how I have been deceived in that young serpent!'

Professor Nagarajan's bleat roused him from his ruminations.

'The photographer is here! Bring up some chairs!'

Professor Nagarajan was eager to be in all the photographs. The best ones were printed in the university's annual, and they would help explain to after-comers what an important person Professor Nagarajan was. This photo session is a rare opportunity for us too, eagle-eyed reader. Maybe we will now finally be able to see who these academics are, because under normal circumstances, they are all travelling to some place or returning from it, and to you and me they are usually a rapidly moving blur. Most of the top-notch academics hear the call of the road all the time. Being far-sighted, they can even see, on clear days, the greenbacks goddess with the ledger and the cornetto giving them transpontine come-hither looks, and they are unable to resist these seductions.

Who are these people in the photograph? All the really significant parties, such as Professors Ram and Nagarajan and Sambasivan, and also the British Council rep and the United States Information Service rep and the University Grants Commission rep are on chairs, and so is Caroline, by virtue of being Caucasian. All the semi-significant people are standing up in the back row. The juniormost but still upwardly mobile ones are sitting on the ground right up in front, at the feet of their masters. Some of these academics are astonishingly red in tooth and claw, for they have just come away from some other conference where they cut some fellow-academic's throat to corner the chairpersonship of some professional body or the other, or tore open some other fellow academic's belly and drank up her blood to get a promotion. In the top right corner you can just about see the tip of a dark finger—a wisp of grey hair. The head to which it belongs, which is the head of Dr Thangadurai from a small college in Palayankottai, has been cut off by the photographer, who is astute enough to know that junior lecturers from mofussil colleges do not really count for anything, since most of them never go abroad, and some of them are even Dalits. An even more fleeting blur in the distance is actually one of the catering staff crossing the camera's frame in the distance, but he is in the picture purely by mistake.

So, dear reader, now we know.

All over the hall the conversations were going on.

'Oh, *well met*, Professor Venkataraman!' Dr Agnihotri exclaimed. 'How was the seminar in Frankfurt?'

'Yes, Frankfurt, marvellous place. Say what you will about Japanese goods, nothing like Germany for electronic goods is what I always say,' Dr Venkataraman replied.

'They miscalculated my increment again this year,' Dr Susheela complained to Dr Khurana. They had compared notes about their increments since their first conference together, forty years ago.

'Stingy fellows. The administration of your college is full of uncultured tradesmen,' Dr Khurana said. 'They will take seriously every move the students make to increase their fellowships. But will they hand out the right increments? Ha! No, a thousand times.'

'Did you hear that Mukherjee has wangled another sabbatical? Within two years of his last one!' said Dr Chaturvedi, who was of the crème-de-la-crème, and as such had not been caught standing still in one place long enough for his students to know him by sight. He had long, romantically windswept snow-white hair and midnight-black eyebrows, and was known to break a new female scholar in at every conference.

'Really? Where is he going this time?' Dr Tripathi was less-travelled and eager to move.

'Urbana Champaign, I believe. I really must find out from him what his method is. I've applied to my university for funding to go to the Australian Literature Society Conference in August, by the way. Admin is bound to cough up this time; they turned me down for the Canadian Postcolonial Conference up in Montreal. Have another puri, old comrade.'

'Thanks. Excellent food, you can count on Ram for that,' said Dr Tripathi, chewing.

'Tell us more about this Australian conference, Dr Chaturvedi,' Dr Sharma begged. Dr Sharma was a greenhorn, with no personal experience of jet-lag as of now. He gamely hung around jet-set luminaries like Dr Chaturvedi, ready to snap up the secret mantra the second they dropped it.

'Oh that—it sounds marvellously pleasant,' Dr Chaturvedi

said in a languid voice, his glims on a young woman with a very exciting shape who had swum into his ken just beyond Dr Sharma's clunky shoulder. 'Bondi Beach. Good hotel, sun and sand, blonde beachcombers, no doubt, quite a jamboree. My dear!'

'Me?' Dr Sharma jerked his head in alarm. He didn't realize that he had just been retired from the conversation.

'My dear young lady,' Dr Chaturvedi burbled to the nymph. 'Why don't you join us? If crabbed age doesn't offend a maiden of such winsome looks?'

'Thank you, Dr Chaturvedi, I'd love to,' the shapely young scholar said, adoring Dr Chaturvedi with lustrous eyes.

'So what are you working on, my dear?'

'A comparison between Dalit writing and Australian aboriginal writing. They seem kind of related,' the beauteous one said, blushing all over her peachy face.

'Now, my *dear*, that is a really *brilliant* observation,' said Dr Chaturvedi, slipping an avuncular hand under her arm and steering her clean away from the other two conferees. 'Now I think your paper would be perfect for the Australian conference I was just talking about. Why don't we discuss it over some coffee?'

'Dalit studies are getting quite a lot of recognition these days,' Dr Sharma said to Dr Tripathi in a very flat voice.

'Yes, yes, a good choice. I recommend Dalit studies to all my Ph.D. students. Mark my words, Sharma, it is the meal ticket of the future. Everyone is into subalterns these days. Why, Gayatri Spivak—the famous postcolonial scholar—herself is supporting subalterns. She even showed up at the Subaltern Studies conference at Hyderabad a few years ago! Hello, Ram! Good show so far!'

Professor Ram was slithering from one knot of academics to another, spreading the old butter.

'Aren't you joining us, Dr Ram?' Dr Kurien asked, pointing to the hot puris the caterers were dishing up.

'No, thank you very much, Dr Kurien, but right now I am involved in reading the section of the *Ramaayanam* known as the *Sundarakaandam*, and I have to maintain the strictest standards of purity imaginable. My servant-woman will be coming in after the plenary session, and she will bring me my home-cooked lunch. But help yourself, help yourself,' Professor Ram said very suavely and graciously. 'If the guests have eaten, the host is satisfied.

Professor Sambasivan drifted up. 'So, my dear Ram, has your new cook settled down?'

'No, my friend, she has been absent all week,' Professor Ram said mournfully. 'In fact, I don't think she is coming back to work for me. Keep your eye open for a lady cook—strictly Brahmin, you understand. By the way, I hope you have been active on my behalf in the matter of this evening's election...' They moved towards the coffee table.

'Oh, here is Sankaranarayanan!'

Chunky was eating puris with the caution of a man who had undergone a complete colonic irrigation. He had been bleached and dehydrated, purged and purified. Ever since he had returned from Paravai, he had not once engaged the adversary constipation. His bowels had been expressing themselves frequently and prodigiously.

'Are you all right? You look a little peaky. Your eye—an accident? Tch tch. Your fingers—they have just recovered from an injury, I understand,' Professor Venkataraman oozed sympathy.

'Yes, erm—I noticed they were bandaged at the interview, but I did not want to ask you about it,' said Professor Nagarajan. 'Was it an accident too?'

'No, it is a problem called Digital Overuse Syndrome,' Chunky replied. 'I attended so many international conferences recently, just before I flew down here, that I actually developed a form of rheumatism from it.'

Chunky did not elaborate, but I believe an eminent

orthopaedic specialist has described his condition in *The Lancet* as Rheumatoid Quotitis, this being a major professional hazard for academics, especially academics who attend international conferences. It afflicts academics because a clear third of the words in the English language, such as Art and Nature and Man and Woman and Nation and Literature and so on, are of strictly questionable provenance nowadays, and not to be mentioned in public without the scare-quote arabesque on either side of them. As any academic will tell you, this arabesque is very tough on the finger-joints.

At last the clock struck ten, and the academics filed into the hall. They looked more enthusiastic than conferees usually look on these occasions, because they were under the impression that they were going to get an eyeful of the sadist who cooked up Deconstruction. India's finest minds were postponing bolting from the conference to after the plenary session, because they had a bone to pick with this character. They had barely gotten used to the New Criticism when this even newer criticism had popped up out of left field. Because many people had not studied their ERRATA sheets closely—in fact it was a long time since they had read anything closely—they did not realize that Derrida had been replaced by Chunky. But they were careful people, and they packed themselves away near the doors.

That is how it came about that when the speakers in the plenary session climbed up onstage, the chairs near the three exits were just encrusted with academics, sometimes three or four thick, while all the chairs in the middle of the hall were empty except for the one row that was occupied by the registration-dodgers. The academics twisted about in their seats to see where Derrida was sitting on the stage, but they only saw Professor Ram, who was clearing his throat to make the opening remarks, and Professor Nagarajan, and Mr

Swaminathan of *The Bindhu*, and an obese academic who was certainly not an elegant Algerian-French deconstructionist.

'Don't be backward,' said Professor Ram, making his famous elegant passes over the podium, 'to come forward'. His diphthongs were as curly as a pi-dog's tail and seemed to declare that the last Englishmen were in India.

'I welcome all the conferees to the first session of the ACS conference. Mr Swaminathan, who is a very well-known writer on Hinduism, has kindly consented to be our guest of honour,' said Professor Ram. 'Five years ago, Mr Swaminathan put his fingertips on the pulse of Indian culture, and he found it growing very weak, owing to a shocking lack of knowledge about our ancient traditions. He took responsibility for its resuscitation. My own modest contribution to the intellectual corpus (*Daddy, What is the Significance of the Poonal*) was inspired by his shining example. Of course, I must confess to a closer connection: Mr Swaminathan is my own uncle.'

Professor Ram waited for the polite applause to subside. Then he turned and threw out an arm towards Chunky, who was tearing at his hangnails with his teeth.

'The plenary speaker this morning,' here Professor Ram assumed an intoning stage voice, 'is my son, mine own Telemachus, Sankaranarayanan, who is in the process of completing his Ph.D. at the University of Western Ontario. In his plenary paper called "Cast(e) in Cowdung: Arvind Sridhar and Diasporic Cultural Radicalism", Sankaranarayanan brings together aesthetics and politics. He focuses on the work of a relatively unknown south Indian artist domiciled in Toronto, Canada. It is a great privilege and pleasure to also be the practical means of bringing the work of this artist to this country. Those of you who were fortunate enough to partake of the excellent breakfast this morning would have seen two of Mr Sridhar's irony-laden canvases. These were kindly lent to us by the artist himself, who is unable to be present in the flesh on this occasion, though he is here in spirit. After the morning's plenary paper, coffee will be served. My book may be seen on display in the lobby, with a special price for the conferees of Rs 15.50 only,' Professor Ram concluded. 'Those who wish to have their travel expenses refunded may meet Mr Shastri in the hall after coffee.'

Chunky took over the podium. Somewhat nervous, he began talking in a high electronic chirrup, mopping his brow, which was lavishly bedewed with sweat, and kicking the podium rhythmically.

'Two years ago,' Chunky began, 'I was walking down Yonge Street, which is one of the main thoroughfares in Toronto, when I walked into a little art gallery in the heart of the metropolis. I wish to use the word "metropolis" in two...'

There was a great clattering of chairs and scattering of conferees that swallowed up the next few sentences in Chunky's paper. All the academics who were thinking on their feet realized that Derrida was not going to show up. They shot out of the doors like pellets from a BB gun.

'... tracking the ways in which Sridhar's cowdung "art"'—here, and in sundry other places in his paper, Chunky daringly put up his newly recovered fingers and waggled them on either side of his words—'simultaneously valorizes "subalternity" by a play on alterity and abjection and also radically interrogates Eurocentric "aesthetics" by turning the commercial/ metropolitan space of art display into a site of resistance, where the metropolis is provincialized through the studied rejection of its historical media, and the infiltration of its sensory field by the quotidian sights and smells of the Indian rural landscape.'

Amandeep leaned over to tell Rufus that he never realized that this conference was to be held in foreign tongues. Rufus replied that they should at least have had translators. What with one thing and another, they both missed several paragraphs of Chunky's paper before they realized that he was merely using the selfsame double-dutch that was now the currency of academic confluences all over the world. After a while many people were able to follow Chunky's paper in snatches, and some of the Students for Democracy made notes, and some of the junior lecturers from the mofussil colleges followed suit because they thought that when Chunky said 'provinces' he meant Dindigul and Palayankottai, whereas he did not mean this at all.

These bumpkins did not seem to be aware that note-taking at seminars and conferences is very bad form, because it implies that what the seminars and conferences are about is exchange of ideas. Of course, all the seasoned academics knew quite well that this was not the case. The seasoned academics ignored all this scratching of pencils on notepads the way high society ignores oafs who chug down the finger-bowl water in a classy five-star joint.

'Mixed with straw, as we all know, and dried on the sides of rough rural walls, dung is an important fuel resource. The formal and material signatures of Sridhar's cowdung texts replicate the inconclusive multiplication and contestation of the significations of the terms "centre" and "periphery" that are achieved by the choice of medium. For Sridhar's circular cowdung patties, sometimes positioned in the centre of his canvases and surrounded by iconic representations of the "master"-pieces of Euro-American "art", and sometimes placed in more marginal positions on the canvas, metonymically evoke, by their association with the cowdung cakes that female rural subjects in India construct as "fuel", both the "global energy crisis" caused by the acceleration of Western fuel consumption, and the more-communal, more-environmentally aware, less-phallocentric sphere of peasant production. More importantly, they gesture towards the image of the *wall*, the loam and rough-cast(e) space on which these patties dry in the local context, with all the overdetermined significations of what we may term *murality*, which concept encompasses both *liminality* and *division*. Indeed, the collages invite us to transfer our gaze from the patties and from the materially *present* space of the physical wall in which they are cast(e), to the wall as the *gap* itself, or, in other words, to *differance*.'

∼

Professor Ram was making copious notes on his notepad. Though it looked as if he was keeping track of Chunky's paper, the fact was, Chunky lost his Daddy when he started in to explain the intricacies of cowdung politics. Professor Ram was drawing up an inventory of who was actually attending the conference and who had gone shopping, and a special list of the guests who were well disposed towards him. These last he would contact during the coffee break to hint that their duty lay in casting their votes for him that evening. He was pleased that Dr Arul was not around to make a case for herself. Perhaps, if he passed the word around about her terrible assault on him, it would get so scorchingly hot for her in Chennai that she would seek the shade of some mofussil university. He brooded on the identity of the graffiti writer. Could it have been Sundar after all, and not Laurentia? He had been deeply shocked by the scene outside his office between Sundar and Jiva. Siva-Siva.

'Indeed,' Chunky droned on, 'the most significant theoretical point that arises from such a reading of Sridhar's polysemic texts is the radical destabilization of the polarized signifiers "global" and "local", and the foregrounding of the complex ligatures that bind these terms together, challenging us to reconfigure not only the geopolitical contexts that we term "transnational" or "local", but also the entire discursive economy of "post"-coloniality in terms that take into account the polyhegemonic rather than panoptic operations of identity and authority in these spaces. Thus we not only have what I will term the *demarginalization* of the "province" taking place through the *peripheralization* of the "centre", but a radical reconfiguration of the very *ground* of both marginality and centrality by the evocation of what I will term the *paradoxical hyperloco-globality* of the cultural production of the postcolonial "artist" exhibiting his/her work in the metropolis.'

In the audience, there were many yawns and yearning looks at the doors. Many people had done themselves too well on the puri-masala and they were regretting this, for they were not only bilious but also sleepy. As I said before, it is a great misconception to think that academics attend conferences in order to share their ideas. They do not wish to do this any more than the French aristocracy wished to join the festivities at the guillotine. Indeed, the only people who were truly joyful this morning were those who had had their air-fare paid both ways, both by Professor Ram and by their universities, and had never made it to the Centenary Hall at all.

In general, academics come to such gatherings with two purposes in view. The first purpose is to renew their desiccated erotic lives, as Dr Chaturvedi, who had wisely guided his butter-biscuit to a dark corner of the hall, was doing at this very moment. His hand was definitely caressing the beauteous one's right buttock, though his eyes were fixed on Chunky, and he had already found out that the beauteous one was interested in coming to Bondi Beach, and that she had no husband, and that she was free this evening after nine o'clock. The second purpose is to renew their wardrobes and to generally consume things and experiences. Everyone knows it is not the grail but the shopping bag that is the prize in the conference quest; it is the silver lining and the gold border of every boring session the academics attend. Some academics pursued this second goal right through Chunky's paper, quietly discussing what sales were on, and where good bargains could be had. Instead of making notes, they wistfully made their Diwali gift lists and Christmas plans. Many of them felt that if they wished hard enough, the day's business would just disappear, leaving them free to lay out their travel allowances and daily allowances on rustling silk saris with temple borders, or fine gold jewellery wrought by hand, or exquisite handicrafts, or glossy leather handbags, which is why they had come to Chennai in the first place. Some of them even slid sideways noiselessly, glazed eyes fixed faraway on Nalli Silks, Vummidi Chetty Jewellers and Victoria Technical Institute's leather exhibition.

'Thus,' Chunky ground away, 'the shifting, elusive subject-position that Sridhar represents in his cowdung collages emerges under the sign of *travel*. Clearly, postcolonial diasporic concerns and selves may be identified, though not in any simplistic way, with Dalit concerns and selves, as both the diasporic artist, inevitably perceived and represented as the racialized, homogenized and underrated Other in the context of globalized metropolitan cultural production, *and* the female Dalit worker in the hyper-local space of the incompletely decolonized south Indian rural community are in a real sense *cast(e)-offs*, or abject, and *cast(e)aways*, or drifting signifiers.'

Professor Ram glanced at the audience to see if he had left out any important persons when he did his schmoozing this morning. In a depressed kind of way he noted that there were many feminists in the audience, all bunched together, which was a most repulsive sight to Professor Ram. In the last few years, Professor Ram's conference experiences had become exercises in masochism, for no matter what he said, he was soundly whipped by the lash of political scorn. 'It was only the feminists at first,' he thought, feeling bile rising into his mouth. 'But these days the feminists have joined forces with the Reserved Category hordes.' He felt like a man who had a toothache on top of lumbago, and he was very sorry for himself indeed.

Professor Ram was all for living and letting live, even where feminists were concerned. He himself did not mind going along on the basis that if a radical academic would scratch his Leavisite back, he would scratch her postcolonial or feminist one. 'But the feminists do not respect these little courtesies!' Professor Ram thought. 'They have killed my greatest pleasures!' He remembered sorrowfully the kick he got out of taking apart some of the less experienced female academics who had the daring to come to major conferences. To the same extent that Professor Ram saw it as his duty to spread the balm of flattery over the most powerful academics, the chiefest *pleasure* of conferences, for him, was to superintend or personally effect the complete public undoing of a fellow academic who was low down on the scale. Ever since the feminists had joined forces with the Reserved Category people, he had been forced to discontinue this pleasure. He sighed for the good old days. 'In fact,' he thought, 'if this massing of forces continues, I don't see any point in attending any more conferences. Look at them, sitting there like pretty maids all in a row—these stormtroopers who attack traditional Hindu values, Annie Kurien and Kalpana Kamath and Caroline and next to her, with her face almost obscured by her hand, Lak—'

Professor Ram gave a strangled cry, blenched, and clawed at Professor Nagarajan, waking that gentleman out of a pleasant dream in which he was sitting down to a large dish of cabbage. Professor Nagarajan instinctively checked that the connection between his snoot and his root had not been not severed.

'What?' said Professor Nagarajan. 'Why, what is the matter, Ram?'

'She's here!'

'My dear chap, you are shaking, as it were! Do control yourself, Ram, we are in full view! Who is here?'

'*Lakshmi* is here!' Professor Ram wheezed.

'Who? *Who* is Lakshmi?' Professor Nagarajan whispered.

'My—my son's ex-wife!'

'*Ex*-wife? This is very extraordinary! I was unaware, as it may appear, that your son was divorced, my dear Ram!' Professor Nagarajan exclaimed, edging away from his bosom friend.

'In short,' Chunky ploughed on, 'I have argued that we

may read Sridhar's artistic production as at once ironically imbricated in Europe's knowledge-production concerning Hindu culture, invoking as it does the stereotypical representation of the Hindu as worshipping the cow, and a recuperation of traditional Hindu values as they pervade the rural imaginary, and as they offer themselves for mobilization in a critique of Western conspicuous consumption and phallicization of the sphere of production. It is more productive to read Sridhar's politics of dung as a radical intervention that not only both constructs and resists identification with the subject position of the gendered subaltern subject, but also, through this same unstable identification, functions as a marker of the arrival of *hyperloco-globality*.'

Chunky stepped back from the podium with the look of a hen that had just laid a magnificent egg, and the audience understood that the paper was finished. Chunky yearned to plant his neologism in the rich manure of international post-structuralist theory, and as he concluded his paper, adding helpful emphasis to create brand recognition, he dreamt of the citations that would flow from this moment (*'hyperloco-globality*, to use Sankaranarayanan's economical term for this phenomenon'). Generally, a neologism can be launched if some big shots in the audience notice it and take it up for discussion. But Chunky appeared to have shot this arrow in vain, for in the silence that followed his paper, Dr Kurien was heard to say quite clearly that while personally she would not give four annas for *hyperloco-globality*, she wished to propose the term *phallogorrhea*, if someone had not already proposed it, to describe male academics congregating at conferences and suffering from verbal incontinence in spades.

'Any questions?' Professor Ram snapped rapidly in the voice he used when he wished to shrivel Thamarai Selvi in her rubber slippers, or to make Rufus turn into a block of stone. It was a voice meant to discourage inquiry. He wanted to close up this session quickly, for he needed as much time as possible to sort out the Lakshmi problem, and to hustle support for his candidature.

A hand went up among the registration-dodgers. Professor Ram affected not to notice it, for he could see from the corner of his eye that it belonged to Jiva.

'No? In that case, ladies and gentlemen, let us adjourn to the lunch-room, on your left as you go out, to do justice to the traditional vegetarian gastronomic delights that await us,' said Professor Ram unctuously.

Immediately, three more hands shot up. Attached to the third hand, unignorably and squarely in the middle of Professor Ram's field of vision, was the angular arm and sinewy shoulder of Dr Kurien.

'Uh-oh, Daddy has mucked up,' said Chunky to himself, bracing his arms against the podium and kicking it as if it was Dr Kurien's shin. 'It is always a bad sign when the Chair shows too much eagerness to close up a session.'

Professor Ram looked like a cornered rat. 'Yes, Dr Kurien? Your question?'

'I think the young lady in the third row had her hand up before I had mine,' said Dr Kurien, implacably.

'Ah yes, arr-hrrm, your question, Jiva?'

'I was wondering,' Jiva said, 'if Mr Sankaranarayanan is arguing that this radical intervention by the artist—Mr Sridhar—benefits Dalits.'

'Because of the great complexity of class/caste relationships in postcolonial India,' Chunky said, 'we must not be in haste to draw conclusions. Nor is it productive to ask simplistic questions or make knee-jerk responses to a situation of—of great er—*complexity*. While we may admit that these relationships are by definition *problematic*, and er—*complex*, we need to think these questions through very, very carefully.'

'I understand all this,' said Jiva, 'I just meant, when he sells his paintings, who gets the money?'

'Uh,' said Chunky, 'is it not somewhat simplistic to assume that an individual artist of the diaspora can change the material situation of millions of people overnight? The radical quality of the paintings lies chiefly in their alteration of the *imaginary*, and their effect cannot be taken in such a literal-minded fashion. Your question, Dr Kurien?'

'I think,' said Dr Kurien, 'that the young man in the last row had his hand up before mine.'

'I was just wondering,' said Sundar, before he could catch himself, 'in relation to what you said about the fuel crisis, what your own views about excessive fuel consumption were. For instance, I thought there was a hidden invocation of the SUV.'

'Er—ah, that is a very *interesting* question, though I do not really think this is the forum for it. Of course, it goes without saying that I am totally in favour of a more environmentally-conscious mode of travel. Your question, er—' Chunky saw Lakshmi for the first time and his face turned a maggoty shade. He coughed, swallowed and began again. 'Your—your question, L-Lakshmi?'

'I just wanted to suggest that your facile conflation of Hinduism and Dalit identity is questionable, since a number of Dalits have pointed out that they are not exactly Hindus.'

'And I wanted to suggest,' said Dr Kurien, 'that the celebration of Hindu tradition as a space where feminist initiatives are encouraged seems somewhat premature'.

Chunky took out a large handkerchief and swished it over his mug. His silk jibba was completely transparent with perspiration, and clearly visible just behind the ethnic chic was a T-shirt that said B.U.M. Equipment. Chunky had run out of comebacks.

Professor Ram decided to throw his body between his first-born and the wolves.

'I have pointed out in *Daddy, What is the Significance of the Poonal*, under the heading "Daddy, What is the Role of Women in Hindu Tradition?" that in the Vedic Golden Age, our own country's most illustrious women included—'

'Dr Ram, if you are going to trot out Ghosha and Gargi and Maitreyi again, please don't bother,' Dr Kurien said.

Professor Ram shuddered with rage, because these were exactly the names he had been about to hurl at Dr Kurien like Lord Vishnu's discus of righteousness. Was this not what he had feared when the V-C asked Dr Kurien to stay behind? Was not Dr Kurien Professor Ram's nemesis and number-two enemy, and did she not frequently haunt his dreams in the form of a giant Doberman Pinscher? Was it not rumoured that at conferences she showed a great partiality for a certain kind of unclean meat, which was pork, and not any old pork but pork carved from the sensitive shanks and sides of male chauvinist pigs?

'Ladies, ladies!' Professor Ram chirped archly. 'We are running out of time for the coffee break, and it would be most disrespectful to our next speaker, the revered Mr Swaminathan himself, to push this discussion any further. Let us continue this amicable argument over the hot, crisp samosas and the fragrant coffee!'

Dr Kurien shrugged, smiled and rose from her chair.

'Professor Ram,' Shastri whispered as the academics elbowed each other aside in their race for the doors and for more food. 'The V-C wants you on the phone.'

'Professor Ram,' the V-C said on the phone in a grim voice, 'I believe we've had the university prankster at work again.'

Something icy clutched at Professor Ram's testicles, and for a moment he was quite unable to breathe. At once he began to press his reflexology point for mental stability.

'Are you there, Professor?' the V-C said impatiently. 'Well, apparently the graffiti artist's latest statement involves some collages that you have hung in the lobby outside the Centenary Hall. He plastered these reproductions of beautiful works of art with bullshit. Thank God, a Campus Beautification Committee member saw it in time. I didn't want to interrupt the morning session of your conference by asking you for advice in this matter, so I took matters into my own hands and got the maintenance staff to scrape off the offending substances and clean up the canvases at once. But we still have a problem, Professor. The er—marker is indelible.'

The telephone dropped from Professor Ram's nerveless grasp, and he dashed out to see what had happened to the great examples of the higher indigenism. In front of *Diasporic Melancholy II* and *Anguish: Periphery* there was quite a crowd, in the middle of which Chunky was standing, eating samosas in a way that signified deep misery. The dung-doilies had gone, but someone had written in red marker on the *Mona Lisa* canvas:

Proffesor (Dickface) Ram invites a dead theorist called Foucaut to his conference. He just takes all the conference money to get his daughter married. He should be throne in the sea, and we should get a new Head for the English Department. Smell his sox. Na na na naaana!

Pinned on either side of this notice was a familiar-looking, nasty-smelling sock.

While Professor Ram was busy on the blower, Sundar managed to waylay Jiva as her group straggled out of the hall.

'Jiva, can I talk to you for a minute?'

'What for? Are you going to invite me to the wedding?'

'No, let me explain,' he said. 'It isn't what you are thinking.'

'What I am thinking, Sundar, is that this is another typical case of how a paappan treats a Dalit. I don't want to hear your excuses. There's only one thing I want, and that is to never speak to you again, as long as I live.'

∼

Many of the academics who shopped at Nalli Silks and Vummidi Chetty Jewellers that afternoon noticed two women who were making very substantial purchases.

'Take this one,' the fatter of the two women, who was none other than Bucket Maami, said to her companion. 'It has more sovereigns. NRI people are appreciating maximum sovereigns.'

'But Uma will not wear such heavy things, Maami,' Sachu said. This shopping was a bittersweet pleasure. Sweet because it was very nice always to try on and buy trinkets, even though she herself would never wear them, and bitter because she had put No. 5, Varadan Street up the spout to get the bankroll that was paying for them.

By the end of the day, Sachu was more tuckered out than a channel-swimmer, but as the auto took her and Bucket Maami and the purchases down Taramani Road, she remembered she had another errand to run.

'Maami, the Post Office only empties the Varadan Street postbox once in three days, and I need these wedding invitations to go off at once. Will you stay in the auto with the bags while I jump out and post them?'

As Sachu stuffed dozens of invitations into the pillar box, she imagined she was releasing these white symbols the way the chief guest at a sports meet releases a bagful of doves. The envelopes bore messages to the 335, and they were a sign of the covenant with Professor Ram, and a sign of her freedom from further obligations to her offspring, and also a sign, above all, that she would fly frequently on missions that would take her across the ocean. She swung her arms jauntily as she walked back to the auto, in a happy dream.

At Varadan Street, as Sachu and Bucket Maami unloaded the auto and carried all the bags in, Pati mentioned that Uma was not back from work yet.

'What on earth can be wrong with that girl?' Sachu said crossly, paying the auto fare. The auto left. She turned on Sundar. 'And what is wrong with *you* today, looking like a monkey that bit the ginger? Just look at you! Not a word of thanks to their mother for all this, Maami. I fully expect Uma to come back and shout that the bangles are too thick for her taste. At least Sundar may like the bangles I have bought for Jayanthi. Give me the jewellery bag, Maami, let me show him the bangles.'

'But *you* brought in the jewellery bag, Sachu,' Bucket Maami said.

'No, Maami, I don't remember—Muruga! The jewellery bag!' Sachu's fair face seemed to crack apart.

'Where did you put the bags? On the sofa? Take up the cushions! Maybe it has slipped behind the sofa!'

Bucket Maami energetically turned all the cushions over.

'Oh look!'

'What is it? Did you find—'

'*Cook and See*! So this is where you lost my book! This is a good omen, Sachu!'

They turned the living room upside down in a matter of five minutes. It became clear that there was no jewellery bag.

'Let us search outside!' Bucket Maami said.

'Oh! What is the use, Maami? It must have been left behind in the auto! I never even saw the auto man's face! It is gone forever!'

'Come now, Sachu, no inauspicious thoughts at an auspicious time like this!'

'I am an ill-starred woman! Nothing but reverses and losses all the way!'

'What losses and reverses?' said Uma, coming in. Her eye was strangely bright, and she looked flushed and secretly pleased about something.

Sachu was so flattened by her loss that she forgot to put Uma on the mat for coming home so late.

'All the jewellery for your wedding and Sundar's,' Sachu said in a quiet moan. 'All gone. All three lakhs' worth.'

'Oh Ma!' Uma said. 'There's only one thing to do. We have to telephone the police.'

In which Mysteries are Solved and Loose Ends tied Up

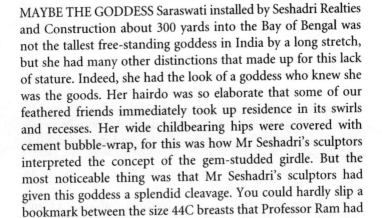

MAYBE THE GODDESS Saraswati installed by Seshadri Realties and Construction about 300 yards into the Bay of Bengal was not the tallest free-standing goddess in India by a long stretch, but she had many other distinctions that made up for this lack of stature. Indeed, she had the look of a goddess who knew she was the goods. Her hairdo was so elaborate that some of our feathered friends immediately took up residence in its swirls and recesses. Her wide childbearing hips were covered with cement bubble-wrap, for this was how Mr Seshadri's sculptors interpreted the concept of the gem-studded girdle. But the most noticeable thing was that Mr Seshadri's sculptors had given this goddess a splendid cleavage. You could hardly slip a bookmark between the size 44C breasts that Professor Ram had ordered. It was as if Mr Seshadri's sculptors were trying to account for Lord Brahma's five heads, which he got because he was trying to keep his divine consort in view at all times.

It was the second day of the conference. The multitudes had gathered to witness the public dedication of the statue. Professor Ram himself was there, gazing up at this concrete evidence of his tenacity and dedication to Culture. He stood, in the hour just before his glory, on the temporary wooden causeway, stretching from the beach to the lotus-base of the

statue, which had been built to allow Sri Sri Sri Panchapakesa
Sastrigal to reach the scene of operations. Sri Sri Sri Sastrigal
was to consecrate the statue. From where he stood, Professor
Ram could see, on the beach, a gay, multicoloured pandal
raised up on poles to give his guests cover from the April heat.
Under this canopy, everyone who was anyone in Chennai, like
Mr Swaminathan, mingled with the university authorities and
the conference guests. People were guzzling Pepsi out of bottles
as they waited for the festivities to begin. The V-C had been so
resistant to the idea of a semi-religious affair that Professor
Ram thought he would skip the event, but there he was. Mr
Seshadri had phoned to say he would arrive late. All the
professors who were with Professor Ram when the statue idea
was mooted—was it only four days ago?—were present.
Professor Ram's gaze took in the feminists—Laurentia! What
was *she* doing here?—and grim thoughts of sabotage went
through his head. To make himself feel better, he searched for
his family and friends. Ah. There they were, a little off to one
side: Mrs Ram and Chunky. Jay was chatting with Caroline.
Rufus, Thamarai Selvi, Amandeep, Murugesh and Jiva appeared
to be finding the goddess very amusing: gales of laughter issued
from that corner of the pandal. Professor Ram's blood fairly
boiled at the thought of these riff-raff mixing irreverently with
the select invitees. He noted with relief that Sundar was not
with them. He was with his family, which was represented by
Sachu, Vaithy, Uma and Kicha.

Rope boundaries had been placed all around the area to
make an enclosure for the special guests, with staff members
milling around to keep the hoi polloi at bay. But the unemployed
fisherpeople and the passersby had collected in large numbers
to gaze up worshipfully at the goddess or to offer art-criticism.
Some of them did not respect the ropes but slipped under
them or over them, and as if this was not bad enough, some
vendors saw this event as a business opportunity and wove
about among the proletariat, hawking chick-pea sundal and

popcorn and even—Siva-Siva!—fried fish. This sight gave Professor Ram that awful stinging-nettle sensation, and he hastily unscrewed his Avil bottle and swallowed a couple of antihistamines.

There was a cough behind him.

'Finished, sar,' the technician said to Professor Ram, coming down the ramp. He had set up a microphone at the base of the statue, for Sri Sri Sri Sastrigal to use when he chanted the goddess into sanctity.

There was another microphone on the platform that had been constructed within the pandal, on the beach. In a moment, Professor Ram trotted across the causeway and climbed onto this platform. Assembled on it were a number of notables, including Mr Swaminathan and the V-C and Sri Sri Sri Sastrigal. Professsor Ram went up to the mike and tested it, and said:

'We are honoured to have the great Sri Sri Sri Panchapakesa Sastrigal with us today. From the moment I conceived the idea of having such a symbol of India's noble heritage on the beach, Sri Sri Sri Sastrigal has shown great interest, and he has advised me about auspicious times to inaugurate it, and has himself offered to consecrate it according to traditional rituals.'

Have you seen Sri Sri Sri Sastrigal in the flesh, gentle reader? He was in full regalia on this occasion, and I must say that I cannot at all blame Mrs Ram for laying down her mid-life crisis at his feet. For many years Sri Sri Sri Sastrigal was not less homely-looking than Shastri, and had the same emaciated appearance. Then the NRI population began to follow the general economic trend pioneered by the US corporations: outsourcing. It began to outsource spirituality and ancient heritage and prayers and pujais and bits and pieces of the old motherland. It began to outsource brides and grooms from India, and astrologers and caterers and pandals and gold jewellery and all the other jing-bang paraphernalia of weddings. Sri Sri Sri Sastrigal was one of the captains of the completely outsourced wedding industry, and he grew so sleek on the proceeds, and draped his shoulders with such magnificent brocade shawls that many many ladies like Mrs Ram wished him to hold their hands during their menopausal years, and some even long before they reached them. And all these faithful lady disciples were simply horrified by what happened next.

What happened next: as Professor Ram lassoed Sri Sri Sri Sastrigal with a sandal-paste pellet garland, Shastri jumped up onto the platform, where he by no means belonged. He grabbed Sri Sri Sri Sastrigal by his garland and gave him the bum's rush with such terrible force that the sandalwood pellets were sprayed halfway to Lakshadweep, and Sri Sri Sri Sastrigal's august topknot came undone. Then Shastri stood right up against Professor Ram, and in a Dirty Harry voice said just one word:
'*Freeze!*'

Quite understandably, Professor Ram thought this was a mighty absurd request on a day like this, when the mercury was bursting out of the thermometers, and the sand was practically setting his shoes ablaze.

'Don't be silly, Shastri,' he said. 'And stop poking me with that—'

The very next second Professor Ram realized that it was possible to freeze after all, even under such difficult conditions. For Professor Ram, like every literate citizen, knew what an *encounter* was. Now an encounter is nothing but the police bumping off a party by plugging him in the back—especially if the party is unarmed and running away—and informing the papers the next morning that they were forced to take him out in self-defence. Anyhow, what I mean to tell you is this: what Shastri was poking into a sensitive place exactly midway between Professor Ram's sixth and seventh ribs on the left side was one of these light firearms that the gendarmerie were very fond of using when they had these encounters. While Professor Ram did not know much about fire-arms, he knew the difference, same as myself, between a deadly weapon and a water-pistol, and he did not expect Mickey Mouse to jump up out of the little baby that Shastri was carrying and play *Fur Elise or You are My Sunshine.*

'What on earth—' said the V-C, unaware that Professor Ram was realizing for the first time how sweet life was. He tapped Shastri on the shoulder. 'Young man—'

'No-o-o!' quavered Professor Ram, into the mike. 'He has a gun!'

The audience could hear a sound like castanets, which was Professor Ram's dentures chattering with terror. Many women in the audience screamed and ran out of the pandal as if their lives were at stake. Shastri stepped up to the microphone.

'I won't harm anyone,' he said in a high, hysterical voice. I once saw a movie in which a gopher turned feral and ate half the citizens of New York before Bruce Willis, or Arnie, or whoever was the only man who could stop it, stopped it. Shastri was the spitting image of that gopher at this moment. 'I want Professor Ram to come out to the statue with me. If I see anybody calling the police, I will kill him and *his mother and his father and* HIS AUNTIES AND UNCLES! As well as Professor Ram!'

A gap opened up in the crowd and Shastri led Professor Ram through it, never ceasing to press the gun against Professor Ram's hide. The V-C followed them at a distance, a worried frown on his face.

'Is it a real gun?' bleated Professor Nagarajan, as Professor Ram went past him. He knew how hard it was to get a gun in India, having tried to in his youth, before he got into English teaching, when he wished to bump himself off after failing the Civil Service exam for the sixteenth time.

'Yes,' Professor Ram croaked, 'I think it definitely is.'

'Where would the boy get a real gun, Dr Mohan? It must be a fake—a prop!'

'Professor Nagarajan,' said the V-C between clenched teeth.

'The boy's father is a Crime Branch Inspector in the Tamil Nadu Police Service.'

'Maybe the gun is not loaded!' Professor Sambasivan suggested.

But Professor Ram did not show any more spirit of inquiry in this matter than Rufus did in the matter of Daffodils in Romantic Poetry, especially when Shastri giggled and offered to blow one of Professor Ram's ears off just to show that he had bullets. Shastri marched Professor Ram down the causeway to the lotus-base of the statue and pushed him onto it. Then, climbing onto the base himself, he took a red marker out of his pocket and gave it to Professor Ram.

'I want you to write what I dictate on the statue's base,' he said.

'My God!' Professsor Ram gaped incredulously. 'You! All those scurrilous messages...*you*?'

Shastri laughed a dreadful laugh, like the sound the cat makes when it sits down on the harmonium keys to scratch its ears, hacking and dissonant.

'Yes, me. You never thought it could be me, did you? Now write: "Professor Ram"—No! Bigger! *Much* bigger! I want everyone to see it from the beach. Aha! So this is how you spell "Professor?"'

The people on the beach watched anxiously as Professor Ram inscribed on the lotus base, big enough to be visible at the other end of Chennai, the following legend:

Professor (Wanker) Ram is an asshole.

Shastri is a genius.

'Hmm,' said Shastri. Then he tapped the microphone intended for Sri Sri Sri Sastrigal, said 'Hello-hello' a couple of times and called out like this:

'Now I want the large brown suitcase that you will see near the north-west corner pole of the pandal.'

At once all those people who, thinking that the danger was past, had come back into the pandal, thought this was a bomb and started to shriek and run helter-skelter again, and some of the larger men did their best to trample the women and children down as they tried to leave the pandal. Vaithy, who was standing right next to this suitcase, was heard to say, 'It will be very interesting to see what happens to the different parts when the Cosmic fellow disintegrates,' but he strapped on his helmet and, ignoring Sachu's pleas and flapping hands, rolled the suitcase down the causeway to the statue.

'Go back,' Shastri screamed when Vaithy hesitated for a moment by the statue after delivering the suitcase. Vaithy shrugged and retreated.

Mrs Ram now believed Shastri was going to blow her husband up. She twisted her hands together and looked to Chunky for support, but clearly Chunky was overcome by tension at his father's plight, for, apart from asking her once or twice, 'Mummy, does Daddy have his life insurance all paid up and up-to-date?' he never said a word. So Mrs Ram went over and tried to faint into Sri Sri Sri Sastrigal's arms, after dusting him off a bit, because he had taken on sand all over him when he hit the ground earlier. This was very nice for a while, except that Sri Sri Sri Sastrigal began to look around at all the other middle-aged wives who were yearning for spiritual fulfilment, and naturally he wished to begin the snake-oil ayurvedic massage on them immediately, and of course it was quite impossible to give snake-oil ayurvedic massages to one menopausal lady disciple if you were toting another menopausal lady disciple in your arms. So the living saint lowered Mrs Ram ruthlessly to the ground and she was forced to recover rapidly, as the ground was too hot to lie on.

'Shastri,' said the V-C on the pandal mike, 'drop that gun, please.'

The audience snorted collectively to make it clear that this was a very feeble move. Dr Sambasivan, who had taught

Spenser that year, remarked scornfully that it was like a knight-at-arms sidling up to the curmudgeonly old dragon as it clamped the maiden in its jaws, and saying to it, 'Drop it, Rover! Drop it now!'

～

There was no bomb in the suitcase. That much was clear. Shastri had made Professor Ram unzip it, and Professor Ram had not gone ker-splat yet. He was lifting several quires of paper out of the suitcase and stacking them in three neat piles on the lotus-base. Shastri pulled the mike to himself with a rock star's insolence.

'Professor Ram,' he said in a grating voice that set the audience's teeth on edge, 'the first draft of my thesis was 187 pages. The second draft was 231 pages, the third, 197, the fourth, 193, the fifth, 204, the sixth, 214, the seventh, 216, and the eighth, 220 exactly. Yes, Professor Ram, I have written eight drafts of my thesis titled "Hedgerows, Hardly Hedgerows: Dwarf Plants and Crotons in Wordsworth's Poetry". This is amounting to a total of 1,662 pages. All the drafts are in this suitcase. What you are going to do, Professor Ram, is eat the drafts.'

The audience emitted a collective gasp.

'Eat—*eat* them?' Professor Ram asked in a very feeble voice. 'Did you say—*eat*?'

'Yes, Professor Rambo, you *fucking* wanker! EAT THEM!' Shastri screamed suddenly and poked the gun so hard into Professor Ram's ribs that it pushed out his spine at the back, and Professor Ram could already see his own obituary notice in *The Bindhu*. 'Chennai Mourns Favourite Son,' it said. 'Doyen of Culture Passes Away.' The thought brought tears to Professor Ram's eyes.

'IF YOU DON'T EAT THEM I WILL KILL YOU!' Shastri hollered.

So Professor Ram fell to, and for the next few tense minutes there was nothing but the sound of rumination. On and off, Shastri came on over the mike, reading some of Professor Ram's marginal comments off a page before he gave it to him to eat.

'"How many times must I tell you not to end a sentence with a preposition?" Ha!'

The audience could see that Professor Ram was finding Shastri's thesis very indigestible. From time to time he made gagging motions. Anyone will admit that it is very hard to eat 1,662 pages of typescript, even if they are double-spaced, and within the first five minutes, Professor Ram was wishing with all his heart that Shastri had finished his thesis ten years earlier and left the university, right hand or no right hand. Now and then, Professor Ram peeked at the piles of paper to see how he was making out, but this was depressing, for it seemed that no matter how many pages he wolfed down, he never disposed of more than the top inch or so.

'"Your ideas in this chapter are vague, half-baked and incoherent,"' Shastri quoted. 'I hope they give you stomach ache!'

The audience got quite involved in these doings. One segment of the lumpen proletariat was willing to wager the shirt off its back that Professor Ram would never finish all the paper. Another section pointed out how his appetite picked up wonderfully every time Shastri screeched a bit and rammed his gun home, making it pretty obvious that it was quite all right with *him* if it became Exhibit A in a homicide inquiry. A more soft-hearted segment deplored the fact that Shastri had not supplied any sambhar or mango-pickle to make the pages go down more easily. And while one segment of the crowd was convinced that Shastri was insane, the other pointed out how he provided carefully against the Black Cat Commandos sneaking up on them from behind the statue in hydrofoils or launches or some such, by making Professor Ram circumnavigate the statue. Some people felt that Professor Ram was collecting plenty of good karma by doing this, but others disapproved of the way he was frisking around the lotus-base like a Nilgiri mountain goat on Viagra.

At this point there was a distraction. The audience looked up and noted that Mr Seshadri had arrived at last, puffing like a kettle and smelling like a drop too much. He was groaning violently. He staggered up to the V-C and groaned:

'Oh-oh-oh, V-C sar! Just now my master shilpi—that is the man who makes this goddess—is revealing that he is using a very hazardous material for this statue base! I have told him sea-grade and he is thinking C-grade, bleddy idiot! Oh-oh-oh! Bleddy donkey fool! This is a calamity, V-C sar! As soon as I have heard I am coming to tell you!'

'Are you saying that the statue's base is not safe?'

'Yes, Mr V-C, even by itself only it is not safe, on top of that two people and one tonne paper, oh-oh-oh very life-threatening, sar!'

'What could possibly happen to it?'

'The sea-waves are breaking it up, and then the whole statue—O Lord of the Seven Hills!—is tumbling down like Humpitty Dumpitty.'

'What can we do now, Mr Seshadri?' the V-C asked.

'Nothing! Oh! Oh! Same mistake I am making with Ocean Crest!'

'Shastri, are you listening to me?' the V-C called out into the microphone on the pandal stage. 'Shastri! The statue's base is not safe! It may break apart! You must give up this foolish charade now, and release Professor Ram. Are you listening to me?'

'"Rewrite this draft with more focus on the imagery,"' Shastri hissed into the mike. He was making Professor Ram take another spin around the statue. '"*Rewrite! Rewrite! Rewrite*"!'

'Shastri, did you hear—'

'I don't care!'

Professor Ram heard the V-C clearly enough. He looked up and he remembered that the statue's bust was only screwed on. He wished he had ordered a size 32A, which would give him a sporting chance of living with a mere broken spine if any disembodied mammaries came down unannounced. Now he was going to be squashed flat, like a cockroach.

By and by, Mr Seshadri got to thinking about what would happen if the lotus base did break up, and it occurred to him that it might be necessary to square the law, which was nearly as tricky as squaring the circle. So he reached for his cellphone to call Mr Rami Reddy. There was no bigger whiz at this job than Mr Seshadri's all-purpose factotum, who was famous for wheedling warrants away from the constabulary, and sending them away, before they knew what happened, with two dozen gilt-edged securities in any one of Mr Seshadri's firms. Then Mr Seshadri remembered that Mr Rami Reddy was at Davos at this very moment, not on vacation, for he never went on vacation, but representing Mr Seshadri's interests at the World Economic Forum jamboree. Mr Seshadri thought of the scandal that would result if Professor Ram got mashed up by the statue, and the bad name it would bring to Seshadri Realties and Construction, and the cessation of all further plans to build the Seshadri Theme Park on the last strip of empty beach in all of Chennai. His face crumpled up, and he began to hiccup in quite a heartbreaking way.

'Will you stop doing that, Mr Seshadri? I'm trying to concentrate,' the V-C snapped. 'Shastri!' he tried again. 'That statue is a deathtrap!'

'Ha ha!' Shastri replied.

At this, Mr Seshadri was so overcome that he tried several times to drown himself in two feet of water. But each time he was about to go under, the wave receded and left Mr Seshadri lying on the sand in his seersucker suit like a beached whale, and he soon had to send for his personal medicine man to peel the suit off him. He was weeping buckets, and what with this, and the length of time he spent marinating in the waves, we can believe the tales of fishermen as far afield as the Andaman and Nicobar Islands, who reported that they found the mermaids unable to steer their dolphins properly, and fish, both large and small, who were by no means able to say British Constitution.

Now there was another commotion among the many-headed. A burly citizen came pelting over the sands. Indeed, as he rounded the Triumph of Labour statue, he looked as if he was flying. The watching parties could not make out whether he was zipping along because he had lost a slipper and the sand was biting his instep, or because there were a couple of uniforms coming on at his heels, also at a spanking pace. Some university people recognized the fugitive as Akilan, but whether they recognized him or not, the assembly could see that if he kept up this pace he would become the second personality ever to walk on water, in spite of the strong headwind. One of the uniforms that followed him was clearly in better shape than Akilan, and for a while appeared to be gaining on him. Then this uniform's moustaches unravelled and started to get under his feet, and any athlete will tell you that it is mighty hard to figure-skate properly on your own moustaches. The second uniform, who was a considerable way behind, was clearly a very senior officer, for he was clean-shaven, and carried a gut as big as a fat, midsummer pumpkin.

The V-C recognized the senior gendarme, for he called out:

'Inspector Shastri! We are so glad you are here! You are the only one who can solve this problem for us! Your son—er Shastri—has taken a hostage! He has a gun!'

The watching parties looked at this gendarme more closely and they saw that his face was nothing but a gopher-face, same as Shastri's, only it belonged to a gopher that had eaten not wisely but too well.

Inspector Shastri put his hands on his hips and studied the scene for a spell.

'"This is an unsupported assertion; find more evidence of Wordsworth's partiality for the lesser celandine,"' Shastri read, still oblivious.

'SHA-A-*STRI!*' Inspector Shastri thundered, and though he used no mike at all, Shastri took off vertically as if he was shot full of rocket fuel.

'Daddy!' Shastri said hoarsely into the mike.

'YOU MISBEGOTTEN SON OF A WHORE! COME OVER HERE AT ONCE!' Inspector Shastri said, slapping his thigh. The way he said this was a whole world away from the way the V-C had said something similar a moment ago, and the populace realized that Inspector Shastri would never need any assertiveness training, and that when he ordered a balking mule to jump through a tennisquoit, the mule would jump. A great cheer went up.

'I'm coming, Daddy,' Shastri whispered into the mike.

'Bring the gun with you!' shouted Inspector Shastri. 'If you lose the gun, I will personally drown you! Guns don't grow on trees!'

'Yes, Daddy.'

'And don't let it get wet either!' he shouted a couple of ticks later.

Suddenly, at the very moment Professor Ram stepped down from the lotus base onto the causeway, there was a mighty crack, like a glacier parting from its parent mountain. This was followed by several staccato sounds like musket-shots, and everyone thought Professor Ram was meeting his maker after all. But it turned out that this was only the statue breaking up. As the base cracked open, the upper half of the statue split into two halves and the 44C bazooms came down smash-badoom on the wooden causeway and pulverized it. Some members of the hoi polloi speculated, as they began to come down, that if these cement missiles were dropped on the Legislative Assembly, they would flatten at least two dozen corrupt politicians, though many listeners took exception to this statement on the grounds that 'corrupt politicians' was a tautology, like 'stinky halitosis' or—

These citizens never got to finish their sentence because a loud screech cut through their ideas like this:

'Oooooh! My *hubby*!'

It was the voice of Mrs Ram, and most people judged that she was justified in this, as the causeway had turned into a mass of splinters, and Professor Ram and Shastri had been pitched headfirst into the mulligatawny. Unless someone rescued them, it seemed as if they would both prematurely attain positions at the lotus feet of Lord Venkateswara of the Seven Hills, or maybe, which was more likely, of Davy Jones. For the sea looked rougher than emery board today, and there was a strong tide going out seawards, which was, needless to say, very, very bad for the health of parties who could not swim.

Well, before you could say swimsuit, and even before the statue completely disappeared, Rufus and Thamarai Selvi had already hit the water and were heading with sure strokes towards the spot where Professor Ram and Shastri were burbling glub-glub for the third time. These two were the best equipped of all those present to undertake the rescue. Thamarai had spent her infancy in Rameswaram, on the coast, and one evening when her parents forgot to watch her, she had swum halfway to Sri Lanka before some fishermen found her and hauled her back home; and as for Rufus, he had won the state-level freestyle two years running and had also anchored the Chennai University relay team. These rescuers were coached every inch of the way by the proletariat, which shouted out many helpful snippets of advice like 'More to the left!' and

'Don't let him lose the gun!' and 'Hold his head above the water!'

Thamarai had a relatively easy time with Shastri, because he weighed less than she did, and because he was so concerned about losing the gun that he was a most co-operative subject. The public could see the gun at all times poking up out of the water like a periscope. On the other hand, there was quite some nail-biting onshore as Rufus connected with Professor Ram, for people knew all about Professor Ram's great allergy to Reserved Category students, and they wished to know if this allergy still held in a life-and-death situation such as this one. But oh joy! Professor Ram generously allowed himself to be rescued by a backward-caste party. All four of them washed up on the beach at about the same time, shivering with cold, for there suddenly was a big cloud-bank building up, as black as the money Mr Seshadri did not like to share with the government.

Mr Seshadri's personal doctor had lingered on the scene after he had extracted Mr Seshadri from his suit, and he offered to examine Professor Ram. It did not take him long to pronounce that there was nothing wrong with him that a dry set of duds would not cure. Some parties in the crowd grew quite resentful at this, and thought of asking for their money back. As a rule, they disapproved of endings in which not a single character came to a sticky end. The general consensus was that Professor Ram ought at least to be decent enough to have a heart attack at this point and die after shakily uniting the hands of the principal lovers in the plot, though the parties who proposed this were somewhat confused when challenged to name the principal lovers. Here was a strange drama, indeed, that had no lovers at all!

The crowd set that problem aside for a moment while it carried Rufus and Thamarai on its shoulders. The photographers who had come to cover the grand consecration were jostling each other to make sure of their pictures, and the scribes were trying to get a good scoop, or even an interview with the heroes of the day. Nobody noticed Shastri for the time being. In a moment, however, his daddy, who was planning the sixteen ways in which he would take Shastri's ear in his hand and detach Shastri completely from it, noticed that both the ear and its owner were missing. This was when everyone realized that instead of giving himself up to the irate Shastri Senior and taking his medicine like a man, Shastri Junior had ungratefully taken off in the general direction of Kanyakumari, which is the southernmost tip of the Indian peninsula. Moreover, he was still clutching the gun.

'Get him!' Inspector Shastri roared to his gendarmes, being too winded after his recent marathon to join the chase himself. 'And now,' he said, turning to where he had left Akilan, 'I have to take you into custody.'

The crowd evidently thought that Akilan was a hero too. It had covered him with sandal-paste pellet garlands and was making much of him, and in order to make his arrest, Inspector Shastri had to peel away the press and the admirers and the autograph-hunters and the dignitaries who were shaking Akilan's hand and commending his forethought in bringing Inspector Shastri to the scene. Naturally, as it was quite a novel experience for Akilan to be a hero, he did not think of announcing that he never meant to introduce any gendarmes into the script. In truth, the law was following Akilan because it did not approve of the little schemes by which he raised a few cowrie shells to keep the wolf from the door. The law wished to have a word with Akilan about these activities and possibly to book him under Section 420 of the Indian Penal Code. So, notwithstanding Akilan's admirers, Inspector Shastri put him in an armlock, and never let go until a quiet, dark, tubby individual standing just behind Akilan diagnosed the problem as a catatonia that would not be cured until large-denomination lettuce changed hands. Some of this lettuce, which is really quite a panacea when you come to think of it, came to nestle comfortingly in Inspector Shastri's pocket, and his grip on Akilan's arm loosened automatically. A seraphic smile lit up his face, though it wobbled a little when a dark husky lady came up to him and asked him if he had no shame, putting his hairy paws on a fine boy like her Segar, instead of arresting the boy who caused all this trouble for the professor.

This husky lady also took Akilan in a wrestling hold, and kept calling him Segar. At this, Uma burst out of the throng and tried to club her with a Pepsi bottle the way Modesty Blaise clubbed gigantic two-headed international assassins with her kongo. She did this because she was under the impression that the husky lady was trying to smother Akilan. But Akilan caught hold of Uma's wrist and explained that the husky lady had a right to squeeze him like this, as she was no one but his own adoring mother, from whom he had run away almost two years ago because she had pestered him day in and day out to give up sculpture, which he loved, and take up the family business, which he loathed with a powerful loathing.

'Segar!' the large woman sobbed, wrapping Akilan in her arms, 'I was wrong! Come back and make all the sculptures you want! It was sculpture that helped us find you! Yesterday we saw your picture in *The Bindhu*, and today we have come!'

The crowd surged around in an ecstasy, heads swinging from one party to the next, for there was nothing more dear to its heart than such family dramas.

'I know you now!' said Sachu, coming up from behind, for the penny had dropped at last. 'Mother Serious! Sculpture OK! All is Forgiven! Tirunelveli!'

'It is very good that you know me,' Akilan smiled at Sachu, 'because you are going to be like a second mother to me.'

Sachu sniffed disdainfully. 'I certainly hope not!' she said.

'You see,' Akilan continued, 'yesterday evening, Uma and I have brought our Peter Wimsey and Dr Thorndyke collections together by getting married in the registrar's office. Of course, we decided to sell our Charlie Chan collection to the waste-paper man, because it misrepresents Oriental people.'

'Married—Segar! This is your *wife*?' Akilan's mother exclaimed. She did not seem to mind wrapping her arms around Uma too, and she was smiling from anywhere to anywhere, in ways that defied anatomy, and showing a truly remarkable number of discoloured teeth.

'Wait a minute,' Akilan said, drawing forth the quiet, tubby individual whom we recently met as he crossed the law's palm with silver. 'This is my father.'

Since Sachu had fainted completely away, without even looking for any arms to faint into, Vaithy came forward. He seemed to get quite a kick out of shaking Akilan's father's hand, and bowing to Akilan's mother.

'Excuse me,' Vaithy said. 'Matter of factual accuracy. Is your name Segar or Akilan?'

Akilan explained how his real name was Kulasegaran, and how he had taken on the name of his favourite radical novelist to preserve his anonymity.

'Kulasegaran!' Kicha cut in rudely, spluttering and fuming. 'This is a disgrace to the family! It is not a Brahmin name! Uma, how do you think all this will be received at Jagadambal Pappadum and Condiments? If Jagadambal employees are seen as even *mixing* with people from the lower castes, let alone *intermarrying* with them all over the place, they run the risk of being fired! Do you realize what you have done?'

'This is a very strange assertion,' Akilan's father said. 'I am Loganathan, and I have been the owner of Jagadambal Pappadum for the last twenty-seven years. I never heard anyone say this before in all the years I have run the company!'

It came out that the family business Akilan ran away from, which Akilan's father owned, from electric murukku-machine to pincushion, was indeed Jagadambal Pappadum and Condiments International.

Professor Ram and Mrs Ram and Chunky overheard these developments. I need hardly tell you how much consternation there was in the Ram camp.

'What is going on?' Chunky yelled, jumping up and down in his rage and tugging at the tussocks on his chin. 'How can Uma already be married? She is supposed to be married to *me* next week!'

'Hew-hew-hew-hew!' Mrs Ram shrieked hysterically. Since the Rams had drawn up a mutual arrangement with the Vaidyanathans, the cancellation of the Uma-Chunky fixture meant that the Jay-Sundar match might also be off. Now what was she going to do with her devil of a pregnant daughter?

'I take this as a deliberate personal insult!' Professor Ram cried. 'Chunky's bride already married, and that, too, to a low-caste, brinjal-coloured non-entity! I am going to make a hundred per cent sure that we cancel Sundar's wedding with Jay, and furthermore, that he never gets married! I will let the whole Brahmin community know! Vaidyanathan, you will be ostracized! You will be despised! You will never dare to call yourself a Brahmin again!'

As Professor Ram was fulminating like this, Jay came up and put a hand on his arm.

'Daddy, calm down,' she said, 'It really isn't so terrible!'

'Terrible? Of course it is terrible!' said Professor Ram. 'It is an outrage! A sacrilege!'

'Where is the sanctity of Hindu marriage?' said Mrs Ram tearfully.

'I meant, not terrible from *my* point of view anyway,' said Jay. 'I was going to tell Sundar—later today—that I couldn't marry him, Daddy. I didn't get to it earlier because I didn't want to ruin my holiday completely. Uh—I have actually been living with a partner for over a year and a half, and I am madly in love. I couldn't marry anyone else in the world.'

'Ada-da-da-da!' sighed the crowd, vindicated in its faith that there were always lovers in every tale. '*Love* story!'

'You are lying!' Mrs Ram screamed. 'Don't say anything! You can still marry Sundar next week!'

'Who were you living with?' Chunky demanded hotly. 'I was watching you—making sure no one—'

'Jeez, Chunky,' Jay said heavily. 'You'd be just the type to assume that there is only one kind of sexual relationship and that is the heterosexual kind. I've been living—right under your nose, I may add—with Caroline.'

'What?' roared Chunky. 'You rug-chewing *bitch*!' he screamed, shattering the windows of a passing 27A bus. 'How did she corrupt you? My God! My own sister, a—a rug-eater!'

'Then,' Mrs Ram said, trembling, 'you're—you're not pregnant?'

'Of course not. Did you think I was?'

Caroline was watching these proceedings from where she stood under the marquee like a maypole above the wood-shavings. Now she pushed her way through the crowd and put her arm protectively around Jay. The citizens were rubbernecking as if they didn't care if their heads came unscrewed, trying to work out the meaning of this new development.

'Muruga!' Sachu covered her mouth with her hand, awestruck. 'A Lebanese!'

'I know this is a bit of a shock to you, Daddy,' Jay continued, 'but you'll just have to get used to it. Caroline and I are planning to get married.'

This was shattering news to Professor Ram and Mrs Ram and Chunky.

'Aaoooooh!' said the citizens, mesmerized. Some people thought this was a joke, for they had never heard of two women getting married before. Sundar, who had come over to investigate the situation, goggled with the best of them.

'It isn't possible!' Professor Ram cried.

'You see, Dr Ram,' said Caroline, 'right now, they're debating a Bill in Canada that will make gay marriages legal, and we're planning to get married as soon as that Bill is passed. Please don't take it so badly, Dr Ram. We were going to tell you anyway, at the end of our vacation. I'm just kind of sorry it had to come out like this.'

Have you ever had the experience, dear reader, of an antibiotic capsule bursting open in your mouth and shooting some unspeakably bitter and disgusting yellow powder right up against your taste-buds? This was how Professor Ram felt. He had not suspected that so much polymorphous perversity existed in the world at large, and he was quite sickened by the thought that his own family sounded like six chapters of *Psychopathia Sexualis*. No respectable family would have any truck with him after this.

He rounded on Sundar.

'You've brought this upon yourself!' he shouted. His face was as white as bird-droppings.

Kicha, meanwhile, had stopped worrying about his family honour, for he had remembered a lesbian joke which he thought would be of interest to Chunky and Professor Ram. He pottered over to share it with them.

'Ha ha!' Kicha said. 'How many lesbians does it take to screw in a lightbulb?'

Professor Ram gave him the look he often gave Murugesh, which had the same effect on Murugesh's gonads as cryosurgery.

'Come, Charu, Chunky,' he said in a thick, clotted undertone. 'Let us leave.'

Now that everyone's love life seemed to be accounted for, and the main characters seemed to be departing from the pandal, some parties stated that the action was all over, and that it was time to catch some lunch and a siesta. Other, more prescient individuals, who recalled that Shastri had not been captured yet, suspected that there was at least one more instalment to come. Their suspicion was justified. Just as Professor Ram emerged from under the pandal, on his way home, Shastri was dragged in by the constabulary. The gun was still in his hand, since the gendarmes felt that disarming him was a task best left to a loving daddy.

Shastri was quivering all over like a soap bubble in a high wind, and this was not because of the dunking. It was because of the thought of connecting up with his Daddy's fist. The quivering got stronger as he drew closer to Inspector Shastri, and when he was three paces away, it got so severe that the gun went off bang-bang in his hand. Professor Ram immediately dropped down like a turtle that had been flipped on its back, and stretched his length upon the hot sand.

When the echo of the blast died a plangent voice was heard crying, 'My nephew! Ayyoyyoyo! My nephew! You died in the prime of your life! Gone away! Oh you are gone!'

The crowd looked around in astonishment. The person who was sending up this lament was Thaayi, of all people. Professor Ram's bosom friends clicked their tongues at the familiar way she called Professor Ram her nephew, and Professor Nagarajan pasted her a couple of times under the pretext of curing her hysteria. Even Shastri stopped waving his gun around and listened with renewed interest.

'Don't knock her down!' said Mr Swaminathan of 'Tidbits of Vedic Wisdom' fame, in a very shaky voice. 'She is merely telling the truth. *Ram is her nephew. He is also—my son!*' Mr Swaminathan opened his arms wide in tragic surrender. 'Alas! I wish I had told him before!'

The audience pressed up to catch this information, as it was considered the juiciest thing heard in Chennai since the M.R. Radha murder case.

'Tch-tch-tch-tch!' it said as a body, sighing and mourning the passing of Chennai's favourite son. 'Ada-da-da!'

'It is all my karma!' said Mr Swaminathan, dashing the tears from his eyes. 'It is all my fault for keeping an establishment with a low-caste dancing girl for many years. You see,' he told the audience, 'she—er—accidentally conceived twins. She died in childbirth, though the children survived. When my childless sister saw Ram, who was a fair, chubby boy-baby, she immediately offered to bring him up.'

'Ayyo!' Thaayi groaned, rocking to and fro. 'My only living flesh and blood! Gone where your mother went before you! Never will you shout at me again for letting your lunch grow cold!' She fell on Professor Ram's body and was broken up by sobs.

Mr Swaminathan was broken up with sobs too.

'Oh! All these—sob—wasted years!' he cried.

Mrs Ram sat down abruptly on the sand, because she was not sure if it was appropriate to be broken up with sobs when her husband was just revealed as fifty per cent low-caste.

'Mr Swaminathan!' Shastri said, voicing the thought of the many-headed. 'What about the *other* baby?'

Inspector Shastri thought enough was enough, and he took possession of one of his son's ears.

'Not yet, daddy!' begged Shastri as his daddy tried to lead him away. 'Just let me hear this story to the end!'

'It was a girl,' Mr Swaminathan said, taking out a pocket handkerchief and wiping his face. 'An ugly little girl. Dark-skinned. Naturally, my sister didn't want this child. I left her in a pressure-cooker on the doorstep of a Christian orphanage.' He gazed out at the darkening sea. 'I once asked about her on her sixteenth birthday and I learnt that she had survived infancy and girlhood, and was being educated at the mission's expense.' Mr Swaminathan sighed. 'In fact she was considered rather brilliant.'

Dr Arul, who was at the outermost margin of the action, felt around her feebly, found a chair, and sat down on it.

'Which orphanage?' she demanded in a strange, haunted voice.

'The Bethel Mount orphanage in Palayankottai. The missionaries told me the girl was named Laurentia Arul, for Father Arulanandam, who was the supervisor at the time.'

At this the late lamented sat up as if someone had carelessly lit an onion firebomb under his tail. The fact was, Shastri's bullets, when he had accidentally fired the gun, never came remotely near hitting him. They hit the ropes that held up the pandal a few yards away, bringing it down—not that anyone noticed this in all the excitement—and covering Sri Sri Sri Sastrigal and four of his female devotees for several minutes. Some people say that God blessed three of these devotees with babies ten months later. But I myself shut my ears to these rumours, because I know that scandal-mongering is perniciously rife in this city.

As for Professor Ram, he had merely assumed he was getting his quietus.

'How—' said Professor Ram. 'Howhowhowhow?'

'Yes,' said Shastri impatiently, for his ear was semi-detached and he was finding it very painful. 'Yes, how is *she*—' and here he pointed a skinny finger at Thaayi, '—his *aunt*? Surely she's not your sister?'

'No, no,' said Mr Swaminathan, shuddering, 'Thaayi is Ram's *mother's* sister. She undertook to stay with Ram's adoptive parents—my sister and brother-in-law, that is—and look after the boy for her sister's sake.'

'Professor Ram!' Shastri cackled as his daddy finally hauled him away. 'You have to resign from the TamBrahmAss!'

Professor Ram felt routed. Yes, hanged, drawn, quartered, pulverized, ploughed into the soil, the resultant crops pulled up, burnt, and the ashes scattered to the four winds, was how he felt. In fact he was so horror-stricken by the revelation of his origins that he tried to hold his hands away from his body, like a scarecrow, so that he would not have to touch himself. It is terrible when you become allergic to yourself. He shrank even as the audience watched; his chins became impacted, his eyebrows turned white on the spot, and a strange, pale-pink, lotus-shaped ectoplasm left his body. Some say this last was his Brahminness, and some say it was Culture, and some say it was just bunkum, but the truth is, Professor Ram was never the same again.

And Mrs Ram? Her eyebrows would never again come

down in this life. Still, she stoically went over to be by her husband in his hour of need, especially as she could see from the corner of her eye that Sri Sri Sri Sastrigal was getting on like a house on fire with a buxom lady in a green kota sari.

~

Now that it looked as if the Ram saga was really finished, the hoi polloi drifted away. Dr Kapoor, who was the last term's president of the ACS, went to the mike to wrap things up:

'Ladies and gentlemen, we have all suffered with Professor Ram today as he underwent this harrowing ordeal, and I think this has changed our moods to such a degree that we no longer can settle down to the papers scheduled for the morning session. We know that the paper presenters must be deeply disappointed—especially—' and here he consulted his schedule, '—V. Kalyanasundaram ("William McGonagall and Abhinavagupta: An Intertextual Exploration") and Dr Lakshmi Raghavan ("Writing the Spouse: Women and the Divorce Novel"). We will publish these papers with the other seminar proceedings, nevertheless. We must express our gratitude to our heroic and quick-thinking friends Rufus and Thamarai Selvi, who risked their lives to save the lives of their professor and fellow-student.

'A few announcements before we head back to the Centenary Hall annexe for lunch. The results from last night's voting are in, and it appears that I will be handing over office to Dr Laurentia Wesley Arul, lecturer in the English department of Chennai University. Congratulations, Dr Arul, and we wish you a happy three years as the president of the ACS. Let us give her a big hand, ladies and gentlemen! Dr Arul, would you like to say a few words?'

'Thank you, Dr Kapoor,' said Dr Arul. 'I just want to thank all of you for your support. I read it as a sign that university culture can be genuinely egalitarian. It seems an appropriate moment to announce that for the first time in the history of the English department of Chennai University, a Dalit candidate has been chosen to fill an Open Category post. Congratulations, Jiva.'

All the academics cheered and clapped. Then they gathered up their things and hurried towards the university, because a freak midsummer storm was coming on. As the V-C went past, he twinkled merrily at Sundar, and said, 'All's well that ends well, young fellow!' Sundar was not at all sure that he did not wink.

Sundar congratulated Jay and Caroline, who seemed to have been disowned by the Rams. When he went to give Uma a hug and welcome Akilan into the family, he found that Sachu was putting up a major beef.

'If you children were not that keen on getting married in the first place,' she was crying, 'why didn't you just say so before I ran up all these debts for your sake, and mortgaged the house and put myself in hock upto the back teeth?'

'But Ma,' Uma said, 'Akilan and I can take care of each other! We don't want any of those saris or jewellery or—or anything. You know something? Our wedding would have cost just twenty rupees, if we had waited a month. We wanted to marry without publishing the banns, so we spent a little more to bribe the Registry clerk.'

'You see, Sachu?' Vaithy said. 'Haven't I always told you that these things can be done in this sensible way? Why don't you just return everything to the stores—the saris—of course the jewellery is lost—the silver pots and pans?'

'You have no sense of obligation at all! Uma is settled—but what about Sundar? Soon I will have to look out for another bride for him—Muruga, what a task that will be! What about *his* wedding expenses?'

'Hmm,' Vaithy said. 'Uma, what did you say a marriage licence cost at the Registry? Twenty rupees? Let me see.'

He slapped his pockets one after the other. From the shirt

pocket he hooked out a soiled ten-rupee note and thrust it into Sundar's hand. From a trouser pocket he extracted a five rupee coin, bright and shiny. He patted his other pockets, but they did not yield any coin of the realm. 'I'll have to pay you the rest in cigarettes,' he said, and counted out five Charms Minis. 'There, that's done,' he said. 'And Sundar, you can have my blessing if you want it.'

'Thanks,' Sundar said dully.

'Now,' Vaithy said, 'let's find a couple of autos and get back home. Akilan, I think your parents should come back with us.'

'Thanks?' Sachu cried as they trudged towards the road. 'Do I get any thanks for anything I have done? All these years, slaving away so that my children could have decent, proper weddings, somehow scraping—'

'But Ma, I don't *want* a proper—'

'—scraping the money together for the jewellery, the saris, the caterers—'

'Caterers!' Kicha said wonderingly, for a thought had come to him. It had come to him that he had completely neglected to write a new cheque for the caterers after the old cheque got soggy because some idiot poured water in his pocket. 'Ma,' he said portentously. 'I have saved you a little money. I decided to wait and see how the marriage preparations were going before paying the cheque to the caterers.'

'Oh, what a relief! Now we will only lose the money we paid for the wedding hall, because everyone knows they will never repay that,' Sachu said. 'I can always return the saris—'

'Ah,' said Kicha, putting out his hand to stop an auto. 'I never booked the hall either! Pallavakkam!' he said to the auto-driver, who seemed to be peering at Sachu with an odd expression.

'What, madam,' the auto-driver said, 'did you lose anything in an auto recently?'

'Yes!' Sachu cried, looking at him suspiciously. 'How do *you* know?'

'I thought it was you. Was it this packet?'

When Sachu saw the jewellery bag she just tore it out of the driver's hand and began to check if the contents were intact.

'I saw that it was jewellery,' the auto-driver said. 'And I took it back to your Pallavakkam place just before this. An old lady in your house said that you were all here on the beach. Jewellery is nothing but a big headache,' he said. 'That is why my daughter got married in the same cotton sari she wears to work everyday. Not a scrap of gold on her.'

When Sachu found everything in pristine condition, she felt like a swallowed seaman who had just been sneezed out by the whale.

'Hurry up and get in, Sundar,' Vaithy said as he thrust his long legs into the auto. 'It's going to start raining any minute.'

'I'm not coming home now,' Sundar said. 'I have to go back to the conference.'

'All right, then the rest of us can go.' Vaithy waited until the auto started rolling. 'I really like your ideas about jewellery,' he said to the auto-driver.

'Rich people spend too much money on weddings. Poor people copy them. Me, I am starting a new party,' the auto-driver said. 'It will be a party for poor people.'

'Then you will find the reward really useful,' Vaithy said.

'What reward?' Sachu cried.

'The reward for returning the bag,' Vaithy said implacably. 'Even if we had gone to the police, we would have paid it.'

'This is good news,' the auto-driver said. 'I will come to your house and collect it. Watch out for me one of these days,' he said. 'My name is Thiru.'

While Sundar was delighted that Uma had escaped Chunky, whom he considered nothing but a fate worse than death, and also that he was now no longer engaged to Jay, he still had the worst attack of lovesickness since Devdas. In fact, when he heard a great crack, he looked into his shirt front to see if his heart was broken, but it turned out it was only thunder. Naturally, like all miserable lovers everywhere, he needed a spot of solitude to wallow in his misery. So, instead of returning to the conference, he walked to the frilly edge of the sea, and sat down with his trouser-cuffs in the froth.

Our old friend, the sea-breeze, magnified into a gusty wind, gleefully tore up the remains of Professor Ram's pandal and stirred up the waves over Mr Seshadri's statue. It ruffled Sundar's hair, which began to stick out in all directions, like a sparrow in the rain. Sundar watched a distant sailboat rocking on the swell. Over the Bay of Bengal, the sky was completely overcast, in a way that Sundar found very agreeable, for it reflected his mood exactly.

By and by, Sundar felt some disembodied fingers combing his hair down and when he looked up, whom should he see but Jiva.

'Um, I came to give you this,' she said. She was kneeling on the sand behind him. Her arm was stretched out, and on one finger she was dangling the love-charm he had lost in Paravai. 'You dropped it in the mango-thope.'

Sundar had to hold down his heart with both hands, because it threatened to jump right out of his chest.

'I thought—' he croaked, 'I thought—'

'I know. Remember how Akilan was messing around with Shastri's papers in the common room on Monday, when we were writing that letter to the V-C?' Jiva sat down beside him and the sea-froth lapped at her feet.

'Yes?'

'Remember how he took something from the table?

'Two packs of Spearmint?'

'And a letter which he felt that Shastri had no business to have on his desk. This letter.'

The letter was only on foolscap and it began with a big heart, and inside the heart it said 'Sundar loves Jiva'. Sundar began to see the light.

'Akilan found it on Shastri's desk?'

'Mmm-hmm.'

'And?'

'He gave it to me. Just now.'

'You—you read it?'

'Mm-hmm. It was very thoughtful of him to give it to me, though he says he only did it because Uma made him. Otherwise, he was planning to frame it and hang it over his desk, so that whenever he wanted to laugh, all he had to do was look at it.'

Sundar winced. No author enjoys having his compositions put through the grinder by critics like Akilan.

'And?'

'And I think your marriage to Jayanthi is not going to take place. No?'

'No, thank God.' Sundar put his hand around Jiva's waist and drew her to him. 'Our relationship is very, very problematic,' he said. 'We must think *very, very* carefully through the *complex* issues before we make any simplistic knee-jerk formulations.'

'We must *map* the always-already impossible, liberal-democratic discourse of romantic love before we *situate* ourselves in its aporetic embrace,' Jiva said, as she put her head on his shoulder.

'Oi!' said the gendarme that the government posted in these parts to prevent offhand hanky-panky. 'Shenanigans on the beach! Do your parents know what you are up to? Move along, move along! Get on home with you! Making the world impossible for decent people!'

And then the rain came down solidly over the whole world, like a curtain.

Epilogue

SO, DEAR READER, that is the end of my story. The Hindu International Association tried to prove that the disintegration of the statue was actually a terrorist act, but they were unable to find proof that it was anything but the wrong-doings of Seshadri Realties and Construction. Mr Seshadri paid a lot of compensation to the people concerned, and this cleaned him out completely, or anyway, he seems to be down to his last billion or so, and maybe this was why he did so badly when he stood against Thiru's Podhumakkal Katchi or Common People's Party in the next by-election.

Bucket Maami ostracized Sachu completely for two months, but forgave her just before she came in to say goodbye. Her daughter is pregnant in California, and Bucket Maami is crossing an ocean to help bring a new little Brahmin baby into the world. Kicha and his research team are going great guns, I hear, and the latest thing on the market is the prune and fleaseed husk de-constipating instant ragimalt, which is flying off the shelves in all the areas, such as Mylapore, where the sacred thread is honoured and the bowels are stopped. Thatha and Pati cheerfully look after little Raja while Chitra attends university courses to finish her MA. Though Uma and Sundar no longer live with her, Pati is not dejected, because they come to Varadan Street with their spouses every weekend, and she is able to feed them up.

Sundar changed his Ph.D. topic and his supervisor, but when I asked him what the new topic was, the last time I met him, he gave me a very vague response. 'Isn't Jiva just deadly?' he said. He was absorbed in watching his wife playing the role of Kannagi in a new koothu. When I asked him whether he had finished writing his new Ph.D. proposal yet, he said, 'Isn't Jiva fabulous?' and I judge that he has an incurable case of mooncalfitis.

Akilan and Uma fight happily all the time, particularly when Akilan tries to promote any johnny-come-lately thrillers over the cosies. Between belts at Inspector Maigret and Poirot, Akilan makes statues and stirs things up with the government. The Dalit citizens of Paravai have now got a telephone, and pattas for their land, and a new sewage system. In fact, Akilan stirred things up so much that it is getting a little hot for him around Chennai and the last I heard of him, he was writing to ask Caroline if she could send him admission forms for the University of Western Ontario.

Professor Ram has developed tractatophobia, which is a hysterical and virtually tetanic locking of the jaws whenever he is near any piles of paper, especially if the paper is part of a dissertation. For the remainder of his career, he will stress to his students the advisability of abridgement. 'Condense,' he implores, a hint of a sob in his voice, 'only condense'. His personal life is all shot to pieces, as Mrs Ram frequently reminds him that she has married beneath her, and I hear that on the days when she does not feel like cooking, which is almost everyday, Professor Ram has to cook, and wash the silver tumblers he drinks out of, and make the beds, and iron his shirts, all by himself. He has become quite a hand at eating brinji-kurma at the canteen, especially on the days Mrs Ram finds it necessary to visit Sri Sri Sri Panchapakesa Sastrigal to get herself purified up, which is almost everyday.

The way Professors Nagarajan et al never accompany Professor Ram to the canteen or anywhere else, you would never think they had all shared their pure vegetarian idlis under the tamarind tree back in the First Standard. Indeed, Professor Nagarajan is very busy being the head of the English department these days, and he does not have any time for Professor Ram, since he has enough headaches holding the English department fort against its enemies, which include the new junior lecturer, P. Jiva, and Always Already, and Dr Arul. Dr Arul took Thaayi away from the Rams and made her a part of her own household, showing a degree of spite unbecoming in a full professor.

Oh, Shastri was spliced by his Daddy to a suitable Brahmin lady and has started an alternative career as a manicurist.

Chunky has settled down to a meaningful relationship with Dolly. Dolly is a fully-inflatable lady of somewhat passive disposition and rubbery aspect who offers endless pneumatic pleasure after she is connected to a football pump. Jay and Caroline are very happy, because soon after the events I have just described, Canada passed a law saying gay couples could be legally married. They honeymooned at Niagara Falls, and Caroline wrote a very good paper on the scopic politics of Brahmin abjection in the Dalit village which got accepted for the CACLALS conference at Winnipeg. In fact, when I met her at this conference she gave me a warm bear-hug and said:

'You know Lakshmi, you should write about it.'

'I will,' I said.

And I did write, and here is the result, as you can see. Some people who read it, like the editors of sundry publishing houses who tossed it back to me, said, 'Not a bad plot, but your characters are quite unbelievable, especially Chunky. I mean— that butt!'

I can only plead that I know every one of the characters I wrote about, and studied them for many years; as a matter of fact I even lived with Chunky and personally watched his haunches wax prodigious between 1996, when I married him, and 1998, when, dear reader, I divorced him.